A Dark Imbalance is the conclusion to the *Evergence* trilogy, following *The Prodigal Sun* and *The Dying Light*, from Australian science fiction writers Sean Williams and Shane Dix. Their first collaboration, *Unknown Soldier*, published in Australia, was hailed as "fast paced and thoughtful space opera" by *The Leading Edge*.

SEAN WILLIAMS has been writing full time since 1990, with approximately 50 published short stories. He has won a prize in the 20th Writers of the Future Contest, been recommended by *Year's Best Horror & Fantasy* and *Year's Best Science Fiction* anthologies, and won Australia's two most prestigious SF awards. His first solo novel, *Metal Fatigue*, won the Aurealis Award for Best SF Novel (and also reached the top 15 in the Internet Speculative Fiction Database's Top Books of 1996). His second, *Resurrected Man*, received the Ditmar Award for Best Novel of 1998.

> "An unusually fine story-teller . . . phenomenally prolific . . . one of Australia's hottest new science fiction authors . . . shows every sign of becoming the next successful writer to break out from Down Under."
> —DAVE WOLVERTON

SHANE DIX has been writing fiction since he was 15. His story "Through the Water That Binds" won the 1991 Canberra SF Society's short story competition. The story was also featured in the Australian landmark science fiction anthology *Alien Shores*. In addition to science fiction, he has had published mainstream stories, poetry, and articles about the state of SF in film and television.

D0191503

EVERGENCE

A Dark Imbalance

SEAN WILLIAMS & SHANE DIX

ACE BOOKS, NEW YORK

EVERGENCE: A DARK IMBALANCE

An Ace Book / published by arrangement with
the authors

PRINTING HISTORY
Ace edition / March 2001

The Penguin Putnam Inc. World Wide Web site address is
http://www.penguinputnam.com

Check out the ACE Science Fiction & Fantasy newsletter
and much more on the Internet at Club PPI!

ISBN: 0-441-00811-9

ACE®
Ace Books are published by The Berkley Publishing Group,
a division of Penguin Putnam Inc.,
375 Hudson Street, New York, New York 10014.
ACE and the "A" design
are trademarks belonging to Penguin Putnam Inc.

PRINTED IN THE UNITED STATES OF AMERICA

10 9 8 7 6 5 4 3 2 1

For
Richard Curtis and Ginjer Buchanan,
without whom this project would have remained
forever incomplete.

"One knows what a war is about
only when it is over."

H. N. Brailsford

"Unser Leben geht hin mit Verwandlung."
(Our life passes in transformation.)

Rainer Maria Rilke

PART ONE:

SOL SYSTEM

PROLOGUE

The former COE Intelligence Head of Strategy didn't need to study her stolen fighter's instruments to know that something strange was going on in Sol System. Something strange and very unsettling.

Page De Bruyn swung her fighter down into the plane of the ecliptic, braving a navigational nightmare as she went. The reopening of the Sol anchor point behind her had allowed—and continued to allow—a flood of vessels into the system. In the first few minutes, she catalogued fifty vessels whose design matched none in her records, and logged markings of fifteen new nations. None of them was the one she sought—and she had barely touched the surface. According to the fighter's instruments, the total number of ships, stations, and launchers present in the system might well be on the order of several hundred thousand. Given that she hadn't properly surveyed the innermost and outermost extremes, she wouldn't be surprised if that figure doubled by the end of the day.

Possibly a million ships, then, representing maybe tens of thousands of nations, near and far. She had heard of larger gatherings, but never in a solar gravity well. Even the combined fleet that had assembled in this very place to destroy the Sol Apotheosis Movement two thousand years earlier had, according to records, numbered barely ten thousand ships. Whether or not that record was accurate, she was now unsure, but the point remained: nothing like this had occurred in or near the Commonwealth of Empires before. And it would make finding her quarry that much more difficult.

As she skimmed the morass, she was scanned and hailed twice but not challenged. There didn't seem to be a central authority operating anywhere. The system was a mess. But the longer she looked at it, the more she realized that this might not be a bad thing after all. It might even work to her advantage. She could travel freely through it, confident that no one would notice a single fighter among the other ships. That was indeed a good thing, for the journey to Sol System had been long and exhausting, and she was going to need rest to prepare for the days ahead.

She had to work out what was going on, and how it related to an unaspiring orphan whom she appeared to have completely underestimated. And to do that, she needed to be closer to those who had spurned her.

She instructed the fighter to hunt for COE signals among the babble of transmissions filling the spectra around her. It wasn't a sophisticated craft, but it would do that for her. Once registered as TBC-14, she had renamed it *Kindling* upon stealing it from Intelligence HQ. Although she was, theoretically, a fugitive from justice, in reality she had enough friends remaining in high places to divert attention from her, provided she didn't ruffle anyone's feathers too soon.

The time would eventually come, though, when she wouldn't care whom she offended or how she offended them. The question of why she had been so abruptly dismissed from her post in COE Intelligence was proving a vexing one, and one that became increasingly far-reaching the more she probed. She refused to let it go unasked.

Obtaining an answer was all that mattered to her, now. That, and revenge . . .

Six hours after she had arrived in Sol System, *Kindling* detected signals from a vanguard of the COE Advance Fleet. De Bruyn ordered the fighter to approach, carefully. She didn't know quite what to expect—although, given the COE's proximity to Sol System, it was only natural to suppose that it would have a role to play in the emerging power base in the system, however small. That there would be such a power base before long she didn't doubt, for it was the nature of Humans to coalesce into groups. Maybe not one single group, but something larger than isolated clusters. Looking for such an emerging group in the obvious Pristine camp was something she was sure others would be doing also.

Whether this focus of attention on the Advance Fleet would work to its advantage or detriment was difficult to tell. De Bruyn wasn't convinced the COE Armada commanders had the ability to exploit such a situation properly. It needed someone with a flair for intrigue, someone prepared to be ruthless, someone who knew an opportunity when she saw it.

She smirked in the dim light of *Kindling*'s cockpit. It would be the COE's loss, disposing of her the way they had. She would show them that she wasn't someone to be trifled with, to be used up and tossed away. She would pursue the mystery of her dismissal no matter where it led. And if it brought down the Eupatrid himself, then so be it. She would allow nothing and no one to come between herself and the answer . . .

And Roche.

The thought of that name made her fists clench, as it always did. *Damn* that woman! Roche had disobeyed her superior officers, jeopardized her mission as an Intelligence Field Agent, even caused a diplomatic incident over the theft of the *Ana Vereine*— and yet she had been allowed to walk away—*free*. And the sole person who seemed to care about righting this wrong was penalized for being "unduly enthusiastic."

De Bruyn would give Burne Absenger—chief liaison officer with the COE Armada—*unduly enthusiastic*. That she promised herself. She would expose the truth: a truth so large even *he* would choke on it; a truth she sensed hiding deep in the data, deep in the mystery that was Morgan Roche.

All she needed was information. All she wanted was *proof*. No matter how long it took, she was dedicated to finding it.

She sent a coded message to a drone on the edge of the Advance Fleet. It relayed her message to a nexus deeper within the COE camp. There, her message triggered a coded response from a communications AI, which sent another message higher still in the command structure. From there, it was out of her hands— but she was sure one of her contacts would see the message and work out what it meant. It was just a matter of tracing her message to its source. To her.

In the middle of the second largest fleet ever assembled by Humanity, she settled back to wait.

And when, finally, *Kindling* told her that it had recognized the distinctive camouflage signature of the *Ana Vereine* as it entered the system, she clasped her hands together with something approaching eagerness. This was precisely what she had been hoping for. If Roche thought she could just walk in and throw everything into a spin to suit her own ends, whatever they were, she was about to be disappointed.

De Bruyn sent a brief, coded message to a Dato warship she had found lurking nearby, notifying it that the stolen property of its Ethnarch had arrived in the system.

Then she settled back to see what happened next.

1

COEA *Lucence-2*
955.1.29
1860

The feet of Morgan Roche's suit came away sticky as she stepped across the bridge of the *Lucence-2* toward the commander's chair. She stopped a meter from it, staring with a mix of apprehension and disgust at the fist-sized object lying on the brown-spattered cushion. She didn't need to touch it to know that it was organic.

<It's a heart,> said the Box through her implants.

She nodded mutely as her gaze panned around the bridge, the light from her suit's helmet cutting through the dark to reveal the carnage: here, a dismembered body, there, walls splashed with swaths of blood. She couldn't smell the blood through the triple-thickness armor of her powered Dato suit, but she could imagine its stench.

"Commander Roche?" The voice of the Basigo first officer crackled loudly in her ears, his accent as thick as that of a Hurn peasant, and not dissimilar.

She didn't respond for almost thirty seconds; it took that long for her to find her voice—and even then all she could manage was a grunt of acknowledgment.

"Commander?" the first officer repeated.

"Forget the 'Commander,' " she said. "I'd prefer that you just call me by my name."

"Whatever," the voice shot back impatiently. "Have you found what you were looking for?"

Her helmet light once again caught the organ in the commander's chair, and she winced. "Yes and no," she said, turning from the disturbing sight. "You say you intercepted this vessel on your last orbit?"

"We were in close to the primary when it intersected our orbit. We hailed it, but it didn't respond. We thought it was a derelict, so we boarded it."

Looking for bounty, she didn't doubt.

"That's when we saw your name."

She nodded. She had seen it too, painted in blood on the wall in front of the main airlock, where no one could miss it. The fact that it was painted in letters six feet high made certain of that.

"And its orbit was highly elliptical?" she said.

"Aye, that it was," he said. "Would've swung past us and headed way out-system if we hadn't slowed it down a touch during docking."

Headed right for us, she concluded, privately. The Box had superimposed trajectories before she had come aboard. Barely had they arrived at Sol System's anchor point when the ship they were chasing had been hurled at the *Ana Vereine* like an insult, filled with the blood of its crew.

But even if the Basigo scout hadn't intercepted it, Kajic would have seen the ship approaching long before it became a serious threat, and avoided it with ease. Such a crude tactic would never have worked. Roche knew that it was never intended to.

"Repeating herself," Ameidio Haid had said upon the discovery. Jelena Heidik, the clone warrior who had hijacked the *Lucence-2*, had committed the same atrocity in Palasian System within days of her first awakening, that time to the crew of the *Daybreak*. "Honing her skills," he added somberly.

Heidik had gone on to single-handedly kill more than five hundred thousand people in Palasian System before escaping. Roche shuddered to imagine what she could accomplish here, in Sol System.

"It might be a trap," said Uri Kajic from the *Ana Vereine*, on a channel the Basigo weren't listening to.

<I sense no life.> Maii's words came from the same source but by utterly different means. The reave's voice sounded like a whisper in Roche's skull, as though the very cells of her brain were listening. It came with an image of a bone picked clean by the elements. <But that means little. Cane is closed to me now—even his senses—and Heidik could be doing the same. If she were standing next to you, I might not know.>

Roche nodded, waiting to see if Cane himself would say anything, but he didn't. The clone warrior she had once been happy to call *ally*—who was at least distantly related to the woman Jelena Heidik—had been reticent since his awakening from the coma in which he'd been imprisoned by Linegar Rufo. Under the circumstances, she wasn't sure she blamed him. Nevertheless, it still made her uneasy. . . .

"We've lost her, haven't we?" said Haid from elsewhere in the ship.

Roche glanced at the pools of blood around the bridge. "I think so," she said, unsure whether to feel relieved or piqued. The clone warrior presumably had more important things to worry about now that she was in Sol System. And Roche would have no chance of finding her unless Heidik chose to attack—a notion she didn't particularly care to entertain.

Switching back to the Basigo channel, Roche came to a decision. "We're going to disable all the drives except for attitude adjustment and program a warning beacon. It shouldn't be disturbed any more than it already has been. Do you agree to that?"

"It's not my place to decide," said the first officer with some relief. "They're your bodies, not mine."

"*My* . . . ?" Roche started, a sick feeling rising in her stomach.

"Hey, they were addressed to you," he said. "And that's good enough for me."

By the time Roche and Haid returned to the *Ana Vereine*, the Basigo ship had already gone, powering in-system on a torch of blue energy as though its crew was keen to put as much distance between it and the death-ship as possible. Roche could at least empathize with this. Behind her, the *Lucence-2* had been scuttled with cold efficiency, its navigation AIs wiped. Its only remaining sign of life was the beacon, warning people away.

"Heidik knew we were following her," Roche said aloud as she stepped out of the back of her suit and down onto the rubberized floor of the changing room. The moment the suit was empty, it walked itself to an empty niche in the wall for recharging.

Haid watched her from a bench in one corner, his dark skin and biomesh glistening with sweat. "It couldn't just be a lucky guess?"

"She wrote my name in six-foot letters on the bridge of that ship, Ameidio, using the blood of the people she'd murdered." Roche ran a hand across her stubbled scalp. "Trust me, she knew we were coming after her, and exactly when we would arrive, too."

"She could have destroyed us if she'd really wanted to," Haid mused.

"But she didn't," said Roche. "My name was written there for someone to find, and that wouldn't have happened if the ship had been destroyed." She slipped a loose top over her head. "No, the *Lucence-2* was only intended as a parting shot—a spit in the eye."

"That's one hell of a spit," said Haid humorlessly.

She shrugged wearily, as though settling a burden on her back. "Our options now are limited. We keep looking for her—although just how we're going to do that, I don't know. Or we warn whoever's in charge to keep an eye out."

"You really think someone is in charge, here?"

"Not yet. But that won't stop someone trying."

Haid paused before saying: "There's something I still don't understand, though, Morgan." He didn't wait for her to respond before continuing: "How *did* we know where she was going?"

Roche avoided meeting his eye. "I told you, the Box talked about the gathering here before we left Palasian System. Before it was destroyed."

"Yeah, but how did *it* know?" said Haid. "We could have been heading into a trap."

Roche snorted. "Didn't we just do that?"

"You know what I mean," said Haid. "The Box could have been sending us—"

Kajic's voice over the intercom interrupted him: "Morgan, you're receiving another hail."

"Me specifically?"

"Yes."

"I don't suppose the Basigo simply forgot something?"

"No," said Kajic. "It's a representative of the Eckandar Trade

Axis in what looks like a Commerce Artel ship. They're radiating an impartial sigil, anyway."

"What do they want?"

"They haven't said. I can open a line if you like."

"Give me a minute to get to the bridge." Roche indicated for Haid to come with her. He tossed the towel aside and followed her from the changing room, along a stretch of corridor and to an internal transit tube. Two harnesses awaited them there, ready to whisk them across the ship.

Not that their physical presence was actually required on the bridge. The *Ana Vereine* was as advanced as anything the Dato Bloc could build; in some areas it was even slightly ahead of the Commonwealth of Empires. Roche could run the ship in every respect from any point within it—or beyond its hull, if necessary. But being at the heart of the ship helped her concentrate, she had found, and it was as good a place as any for everyone to gather.

Maii was there when they arrived. So was Cane. The dark-skinned clone warrior watched impassively from where he stood off-center in the large room, facing the main screen. On it was an image of a ship: flat, petal-shaped, with a sheen to it like that of polished bone. There were no visible markings, although on ultraviolet a repeating pattern of symbols raced around the undulating rim. Artel sigils, as Kajic had already noted.

There was no obvious means of propulsion to the ship, but it advanced steadily toward them.

Thinking of Heidik, Roche said: "Be careful, Uri. It could be a trap."

"I am battle-ready," said Kajic.

"I would not attack like this," said Cane, facing Roche. "They are foolishly exposed. Until it is clear who are your enemies and who are your allies, it would be best to wait."

"Then what is it they want?" asked Haid.

"Let's find out." Roche indicated for Kajic to open a line to the Artel ship. "This is Morgan Roche of the vessel *Ana Vereine*. What is—?"

"Ah, Roche." The long, gray face of an Eckandi in middle age appeared on the screen. "My name is Alwen Ustinik. I am sorry to trouble you, but, having been advised of your arrival, I thought it prudent to contact you as soon as possible."

"Advised? By whom?"

"An associate. I do not speak for myself, of course. I am merely the representative of a number of interested parties. The Commerce Artel has many such representatives scattered throughout this system, as I'm sure you would expect. Even at a time such as this, the possibilities of trade are enormous. So many new contacts to make and avenues to explore . . ."

She's trying to distract me, Roche realized. "Get on with it, Ustinik."

There was a pause, then a smile. "Naturally," Ustinik said. "The people I represent have an interest in seeing justice served, as I'm sure you do too, Roche. When people are hurt, they desire recompense—or, at the very least, a sense that some attempt at retribution has been made. How one dispenses punishment depends on one's society, of course, but there tends to be more overlap than dissent, I have found. The majority decides, and, where the justice system fails, it is often up to the Artel to facilitate corrective dialogue."

Roche sighed. "Can we get to the point here? I have no idea what it is you're talking about."

"I am talking about war, Roche," the Eckandi said evenly. "The ultimate destabilization an economy can experience. Yes, it may have its short-term benefits, but in the long term it leads to nothing but hardship. The legacy of death and heartbreak is enduring; everyone pays in the end."

Roche thought of the clone warriors, spreading dissent throughout the galaxy, and guessed that Ustinik had been sent to get her hands on Cane. Why? For a show-trial, perhaps, to suggest that her "associates" knew what they were doing. Or in a last-minute, desperate attempt to obtain information . . .

"I'm not turning him over," she said, despite her own misgivings about having him around.

"Please reconsider. I speak on behalf of those who have had the misfortune in the past to be on the receiving end of his business dealings. He is a mercenary and a terrorist who has not fully atoned for his crimes—"

"Wait a second." Roche gestured the other woman to silence. "Are you talking about *Haid*?"

The Eckandi frowned. "Yes, of course."

Roche frowned also. "But what the hell would you want with him?"

"I am here to ensure his return to a corrective institution," said Ustinik, "where the remainder of his sentence can be carried out."

Roche was momentarily taken aback. "His sentence was repealed by the High Equity Court—"

"Not formally—and under some duress, if the information I have at my disposal is correct. I am told that, quite apart from the crimes committed before his capture, he was also the leader of a resistance movement on Sciacca's World, and that this movement overthrew the legally appointed warden of the planet."

"The warden was corrupt, and colluding with the Dato Bloc—"

"The Artel doesn't get involved in regional disputes, Roche." Ustinik's tone was calm but commanding; not once did her pitch rise, nor her face display any annoyance or anger. "There is still such a thing as due process. My clients are dissatisfied with a pardon extracted at gunpoint. If they do not make an example of his flagrant disregard for the law, where will it end?"

"It wasn't like that. If you'll let me explain—"

"No explanations are necessary," Ustinik cut in again. "Or desired. To resist would only implicate yourself further, Roche."

"Are you threatening me?"

"My clients' words, not mine." The woman's smile was economical and short-lived. "I am a mediator, nothing more."

Roche's fists clenched. "And I have more important things to worry about."

"Regardless, the facts remain: you helped Ameidio Haid evade justice, and you continue to shield him from those who wish to see that justice served in full. I doubt they will smile on your venture, no matter how important you think it is. Turn him over to my custody, and you will have nothing further to worry about."

Anger flared, but Roche kept it in tight check. "Give me ten minutes to think about it."

"You have five." Ustinik killed the line without any change in facial expression.

"You should've asked her who she was representing," said Haid after a few moments.

"I was hoping you might be able to answer that one," said Roche.

"Well, there are a number of people it could be." The ex-mercenary shrugged. "Maybe all of them. I was busy for a long time, Morgan."

"Great." Roche sighed. A representative of the Commerce Artel would be easy to ignore if the woman was on her own; but if some of her clients showed up to back her claim . . .

<She represents several factions from the M'taio and Reshima Systems,> said Maii, <plus a venge-seeker from Imi.>

"You can read her?" Roche asked.

<Her shield is strong, but not leakproof.> The blind Surin smiled from her place in one corner of the bridge, black lips pulling back to crease her ginger-haired cheeks. <It's nice to be useful again.>

Roche smiled also; she had missed Maii's input in Palasian System, where the reave's abilities had been dampened. "How serious does she think her clients are? Are they prepared to use force if we don't give them what they want?"

<She believes so. She has been authorized to threaten us with it.>

Haid hissed between his teeth. "I should have known that i-Hurn thing was going to cost me one day."

"We're not handing you over," Roche said. "It's not even an option. There must be some way to convince her to see reason."

"Will her side of the conversation be monitored?" asked Cane.

"Probably," said Roche. "Uri, can you detect any signals leaving her ship?"

"None," said Kajic. "But given the strong possibility that she would use a tightbeam, and the large amount of noise in this system, I doubt that I could detect anything at all."

"Then we'll have to assume that she's being monitored," Roche concluded. "Which means we can't just blow her out of the sky."

"You'd really do that?" asked Haid.

Roche shrugged, and grinned. "No, but it *is* tempting."

They discussed a number of more or less fanciful options for several minutes, until Kajic interrupted with the news that he was receiving another hail.

"Our friend Ustinik again, I presume, telling us that time is up?"

"No, Morgan. It's coming from elsewhere."

"What?"

"From a Surin *imaret* closing in on our position, to be exact."

"I don't believe this," said Roche. "We've been in-system just over half a day and we've already had one attempt made on our lives, one threat, and now . . ." She shook her head. "Put them through."

"Morgan Roche." The face of a large male Surin adult appeared on the main screen. "I am Fighter-For-Peace Jancin Xumai. You have one of our citizens aboard your ship, and we request that she be returned to us."

Roche was confused. "Returned? Why?"

"So that she may be reunited with her mother."

<No!>

Roche called out in pain as a bolt of anger and fear slammed into her mind. Clutching her head, her vision swimming with intense secondhand anxiety, she turned to face Maii. Through the discomfort she saw Cane move over quickly to the girl's side and take her shoulders in his large hands. A second later, as he eased her back into her seat, the debilitating emotions ebbed and died.

<I'm sorry, Morgan. I—I just . . .> The mental equivalent of tears soaked the girl's words, diluting her emotions.

"It's okay, Maii. I understand. It's all right. We're not going to let them take you. Did you hear that, Jancin?"

"I advise against that course of action." The Surin's unnerved expression belied the threat in his words. Roche supposed that he had felt a backlash of the girl's epsense projection. "The Surin Caste has a strong military presence in Sol System. Should you not comply with the wishes of the ruling Agora, I am instructed to call for backup."

"Then you'd better do just that," said Roche bluntly. "Because we won't be surrendering her to you—certainly not against her wishes."

"Her wishes are irrelevant," said Jancin. It is the mother's wishes, and that of the Agora, which are important here."

<I have no mother,> said Maii. Her words were edged with bitterness, and Roche could feel the anger inside the Surin girl wanting to break free. *<She sold me for medical experiments! These people are more family to me than she or the Agora could ever be!>*

Ignoring the girl's outburst, Jancin addressed Roche once more: "I urge you to consider the implications of going against the Agora. They only want the girl; they do not wish you or your crew any harm."

"No," said Roche. "No one ever does, yet everyone keeps threatening us."

She killed the line before Jancin could speak again, then turned to Cane.

"Thanks," she said to him. The clone warrior nodded a brief acknowledgment.

"We can't take on the Surin as well," said Kajic, his hologram appearing on the bridge.

"And we can't give them what they want, either." Roche tapped the arm of her chair. "Maybe this is what it's all about. Uri, have any other ships changed course to intercept us?"

"It's hard to say, Morgan." Kajic called up a display of the portion of the system surrounding the *Ana Vereine*. Even in that small bubble of space, there were over fifty ships following a wide variety of vectors and ranging in size from small, anonymous fighters to bulky cruisers. The display was awash with energy and particulate wakes. As Roche watched, a new cluster of six medium-sized attack craft appeared, following a high-energy elliptical orbit around the system's sun; who they were, Roche didn't know, nor did she care. All that mattered was that they weren't homing in on her ship.

Kajic ringed three craft. "There is a Dato pursuit vehicle that seemed to react to our appearance an hour ago, but so far has not displayed any hostile intentions. This ship, here, which I have not been able to identify, is almost certainly following us. And this one"—the third ship was a stationary speck in the center of the swirl of orbits—"has done nothing at all."

"Trying to remain inconspicuous?" suggested Haid.

"Trying a little *too* hard," said Cane.

"Exactly my feeling." Roche turned to the young epsense adept. "Maii? Anything?"

<This Jancin Xumai wants me because the Agora has heard about the experiments that gave me full epsense ability.> The girl's voice still had a thick edge to it. <They want to know how it worked.>

"Is that what you're reading from him?"

The girl hesitated. <No. I'm assuming, and nothing he's giving me contradicts it.>

Roche could understand her suspicions, but wanted hard facts, not suppositions. "What *is* he giving you?"

<He knows that we've been in Sol System for three hours, and he knew which region of the system to stake out. His or-

ders came from his superiors, though, so he doesn't know where that information came from originally.>

Roche nodded. "What else?"

<There's a lot of overlap in this system; it's hard to isolate individual thoughts without knowing precisely who to focus on. . . .> Roche appreciated the girl's difficulties, reaching out across space, clutching at any thought that seemed important out of the millions flung her way. <But I do sense a growing awareness of you, Morgan. Word is spreading.>

"What do you mean?"

"Don't be modest, Morgan," Haid put in lightly. "You've made a lot of enemies in the last few weeks. It's only natural they're going to be talking about you."

<Wait . . . There's something else . . .> Maii frowned and fell silent.

And into the silence came a new voice, a voice that resounded through their minds with discomforting familiarity:

<You have given my people everything we needed.> The speaker was a strong but faceless epsense presence. <For that, we will permit your existence.>

On the main screen, the stationary dot suddenly moved to a new course, away from them.

"*Now* what?" asked Roche, increasingly bewildered.

Maii's voice was hushed. <Grayboot.>

Haid stiffened over the weapons board. "*Olmahoi*? Here?"

<He's leaving us now.> The girl's relief was touched with an underlying fear. <He read me without me even knowing! He knows what happened in Palasian System; he knows about the *irikeii*. . . .>

"Great," said Roche dryly, rubbing at her forehead. The *irikeii*—linchpin of the epsense-dependent Olmahoi Caste—had been killed by a representative of the Kesh. If the grayboot had suspected that they were involved—and why else would he have tracked them down so quickly?—they were lucky to have escaped some sort of automatic reprisal. The Olmahoi retribution squads weren't known for their patience.

Still, Roche thought, having her brain instantly fried might just solve her problems right now. . . .

"Ustinik is hailing us again," said Kajic. "As is the Surin."

"Okay." Roche sat forward. "Uri, take us somewhere else—somewhere a *long* way from here, and as fast as possible."

"In-system?"

"Yes, but make it hard for someone to follow, without being too obvious about it. Use camouflage if you think it will help. Ustinik might be bluffing, and so might the Surin. Either way, I don't like being an open target."

Roche felt a gentle thrum through her fingertips and thighs as the ship broke orbit.

She waited a moment, then checked the main screen. Kajic's words only confirmed what she saw.

"Ustinik is changing course, at a discreet distance, and continuing to hail us. The Surin *imaret* has broken off communications and is heading away. That Dato ship I mentioned is still keeping quiet, but looks like it's going to follow too. There is another ship . . ." Kajic ringed a newcomer to the screen. "It's a COE fighter we passed before. Might be tagging along for the ride as well."

Roche used her controls to expand the view and scan the regions ahead of them. There were ships everywhere—all moving in wildly varying directions with dangerously different velocities, all orbiting the yellow star at the heart of the system. She was glad it was Kajic, and not her, piloting the ship.

"No sign of the Kesh?" she asked.

"None yet."

"Good." That was one less thing to worry about. If the Olma-hoi were annoyed at the Kesh for killing the *irikeii*, she was sure the Kesh would be just as annoyed with her for having destroyed one of their prized ships.

<Box? Any thoughts?>

<I think you correctly summarized the situation a moment ago, Morgan.> The voice of the AI whispered solely through her implants. Now that she was becoming used to the idea that it was actually part of her, living in her cells, she found its voice less discomfiting. It was almost like hearing another part of herself think.

<Someone is attempting to draw attention to you,> it said. <Any hopes you might have had of slipping unnoticed into Sol System and quietly going about your investigation have been effectively dashed. You are exposed, compromised, threatened. If, somehow, you were to—>

"Another hail," Kajic interrupted the voice only Roche could hear. "Another new one, I mean."

She shook her head. "Who now?"

"Assistant Vice Primate Rey Nemeth of the Second Ju Mandate, according to his ID."

"I don't recognize the name." She glanced about the bridge; no one volunteered anything. "I suppose he's following us, too?"

"No. He's coming in on a relay."

"Ignore him, then. Now—" She stopped herself in time and subvocalized: <Now, Box, what were you saying?>

<Nothing of any great importance. For now I suggest you simply continue your avoidance tactics. We will talk later.>

She took that as a sign that, at least in the Box's eyes, she wasn't doing anything outrageously wrong. That made a nice change.

"Uri, ignore further hails, unless you think it's something particularly important. We've got better things to do than listen to other peoples' grievances."

Haid grinned wryly. "You figure we have so many enemies already that making a few more won't make much difference?"

"That, and I'm loath to believe *anyone* at the moment. If, as we think, the clone warriors are interested in infiltrating and stirring up dissent, then they could be anywhere. Who's to say which complaint is legitimate and which a trap? I'd prefer not to take the risk either way. And anyway, it'll be easier for us to keep dodging than it will be for someone to catch us, no matter how many of them there are."

Cane nodded. "True."

Roche turned to face him. "And while Uri, Maii, and Ameidio see to that, maybe you and I should take the opportunity to have a private talk."

Cane shrugged. "Whatever you say, Morgan."

"Good." Roche stood. "I like the sound of that."

In the small room at the rear of the bridge, Roche sat in a chair opposite the large hologram emplacement where Uri Kajic had once projected his image. On a display she studied a detailed image of Sol System composited from old map records and incoming data. She had lost count of the number of ships they'd passed since leaving the anchor point, but the Box estimated that around seven hundred Castes were represented in various forms— from the fringe-lovers out where a comet cloud might once have once been to the hot-bloods in close. The sun had seen better days; there was evidence of large-scale waste-dumping in its outer atmosphere—unsurprising, she thought; it had to go *somewhere*—but thankfully no one had tried any tricks such as the Kesh had in Palasian System. One system utterly destroyed in a month was more than enough for the region.

Not that there was much to lose. Discounting the ships, the system was mostly empty. There was a faint but well-defined ring around the sun, approximately half a million kilometers in width and less than a thousand thick, just straddling the regions that might have been mundane-habitable had there been a planet to live on. Apart from the ring and the ships, the system contained nothing but vacuum. Anything larger than a pebble had been stripped back to molecules long ago, leaving behind only a wisp of smoke around the system's star.

If the system *had* ever been inhabited—let alone the birthplace of Humanity, as a few scholars had once suggested—nothing remained to show it.

Roche watched the endlessly chaotic dance of ships for a long moment, wondering who was in them and what they wanted. Then she turned to Cane.

He sat opposite her, his expression unreadable. The overhead light reflecting off his scalp made it look as if he had a third eye.

Appropriate, she thought.

"You wanted to talk to me," he prompted.

She paused, wondering, then asked: "Are you reading my mind?"

"Why do you ask that?"

"Just answer me, Cane."

"No," he said. "I'm not reading your mind."

"Could you, if you wanted to?"

He frowned. "Morgan, why are you asking me these questions?"

She held his gaze for a moment, then let it wander back to the screen. "On the way here, I talked to Maii. She told me in detail everything she'd picked up from the *irikeii* before he died. She says . . ." Roche sought the words, not sure she herself understood everything the young reave had told her. "She says that the *irikeii* was like a pit, sucking in thoughts. For him, minds were lights, or suns, and he was the black hole dragging them in. He experienced the universe through the minds around him, like a reave but with less selectivity; he experienced everything at once, all at once—which was why the Kesh and Linegar Rufo had him kidnapped. Once Palasian System had been enclosed he was able to search it thoroughly. And nothing could hide from him."

"Not even a clone warrior," said Cane.

Roche nodded. "In theory."

"It makes sense," Cane went on. "Had it worked, the advantage might have outweighed the inevitable backlash."

"It *did* work. To the *irikeii*, Jelena Heidik and you stood out like supernovae, by far the brightest things he had ever seen. He called you 'The Shining Ones.' "

"We radiate thought," mused Cane. "Is that what he meant?"

She studied him closely; he was still frowning, although now apparently at the puzzle posed by the *irikeii*, not at her. "Possibly," she said. "But we have no evidence to back it up."

"So . . . ?"

"So there's more to it than that." Roche leaned forward slightly in her seat. "Maii says that one of the *irikeii*'s last impressions was of your mind while under the influence of Xarodine. He was aware of a dark space behind the glare—a dark space similar to the one inside his own mind. He thought you and he might have had a lot in common."

"I don't see how that follows."

"Obviously the metaphor is strained." She couldn't tell if Cane was prevaricating. "As far as I can understand it, he thought that you too could absorb thoughts from the people around you. You're a sponge, soaking everything up. And the glare he described—"

"Was just a form of camouflage?" Cane finished. "Something to hide our epsense ability?"

Roche nodded slowly. "Something like that, yes."

"I am unaware of any such ability, Morgan," Cane said evenly.

"But how can I be sure you're telling the *truth*? How do I know you're not reading my mind right now?"

"Because I give you my personal assurance, Morgan."

She studied him for a few moments. He was perfectly still, hands folded in his lap, eyes not leaving hers for an instant. Even at rest, the air of strength remained with him. She had seen how fast he could move; she knew what he was capable of. And having witnessed what his siblings could do if they turned against the people around them, she was reluctant to trust him without reservation. She needed reassurance.

"That's all well and good," she said, "but I still can't help wondering. Heidik knew we were coming here; she even knew when. I can't believe it was just a good guess—so who told her? The COE squadron we left behind at Palasian System might have sent word to expect us, but how would she have got hold of that information? We were less than a day behind her. That's not long enough to infiltrate the COE presence here. We haven't even *found* them yet.

"And I keep thinking of that dark speck—and Maii. She's proof that epsense ability can be bioengineered. If you *were* made to blend in and to fight, what better way could there be to gather intelligence than to act as an *irikeii*—passively absorbing data from the minds of the people around you? Even if you couldn't actually read minds, you could at least see and hear through them—and maybe even communicate with others like yourself. If these black specks linked up somehow, you could share information, talk, plan, whatever you needed without anyone knowing."

"Yes—*if*," said Cane. "But ask yourself this, Morgan: if I *was* in touch with Heidik or any of the other clone warriors, why would I be here? My siblings were clearly made for a purpose; they have spread across the galaxy seeding dissent and destruction wherever they go. But I have not. So *why* would I bother with you if I shared their goals? Why would I not be with *them*?"

"Evidence of absence is not absence of evidence."

"Guilty until proven innocent?" Cane smiled slightly. "I'm surprised at you, Morgan."

"There's too much at stake to take chances, Cane."

"The only way to be sure is to take no chances at all." His smile disappeared and he relaxed back into his seat. "Space me, or imprison me—get me out of the way entirely. Better to do that than to be perpetually in doubt. The chance that I might betray you will never leave your mind until I am gone."

She nodded. That had occurred to her. For all the times he had saved her on Sciacca's World, the casual cruelty and treachery of Jelena Heidik had tainted him in her eyes. She would never be free of it.

And if he ever *did* betray her, she stood to lose everything.

Not just her life, but the lives of her companions and every other Pristine in the galaxy.

She wasn't sure she had the right to take that chance.

<What do you think, Box?>

<I know that if he could read minds, he would know that I continue to exist,> said the AI smoothly.

<What about using the command language Rufo was using? Could we force the truth out of him?>

<If we knew how to speak the language properly, we might—assuming, of course, that he isn't already telling the truth. But the exact use of the command language eludes even me; it seems a fairly crude device. I suspect it may relate to the capsules in which the clone warriors were born rather than the finished product. The best we could hope for is to nudge him to do our will.>

Roche fought a twinge of annoyance. Why did things have to be so uncertain all the time? She would welcome a single, uncomplicated fact with open arms.

<Besides,> added the Box, <if we use the command language, correctly or not, he will suspect that I gave you the knowledge to use it.>

"Morgan?"

She looked over at Cane to see him watching her suspiciously.

"Are you all right?" he said.

She brushed his suspicions aside by ignoring the question altogether: "If you *were* reading my mind, you'd know that spacing you isn't an option. And as there's no way you can prove conclusively that you're not in communication with the other clones, then all I can do is follow my gut instincts."

Cane nodded. "But again, I assure you that I am telling you the truth, Morgan."

She remembered the words he had tapped in code shortly after he wakened from his coma: *I'm as Human as you are.* That was patently untrue in the details—after all, she was not a genetically engineered combat soldier designed to blend in with the Pristine Humans and kill them—but in essence it might not be far from the truth.

"Okay." She exhaled slowly. "I'll believe you. Commander Gent must have sent word to his superiors after we left Palasian System. It's possible that Heidik already had a contact in the COE Armada, through which she found out when we were due to arrive. That's the only alternative I can think of."

"It is certainly a less speculative hypothesis." There was a glint of humor in Cane's eyes. "But if the rest of my siblings *do* communicate by epsense, I would be keen to find out why I have been excluded from the conversations."

That was a point Roche had not missed. "Maybe something went wrong with you: your capsule was damaged, or corrupted. There might even be others out there like you—others who could help us. . . ."

Before Roche could pursue the thought, Kajic's image appeared in the empty corner of the suite.

"My apologies again, Morgan."

She swiveled to face him. "Problems?"

His broad, pleasant face was concerned. "I have been ignoring hails as you instructed, although their numbers are increasing—as is the number of ships following us. There are eight currently matching our course, and I have detected emissions from another five suggesting that they might also attempt to do so. No one has actually made a move against us; although it is difficult to project the precise makeup of the regions ahead of us, I am doing my best to keep us out of any regions where forces are massing. But we can't keep this up indefinitely; sooner or later, we *will* miscalculate."

Roche could see what Kajic was saying: they ran the risk of running headlong into a trap. "So you suggest we stop running?"

"No, Morgan. There's something else." Kajic changed the view in the screen to a recent telemetry display. The eight ships tailing them were marked clearly in red; a handful in yellow were the ones he suspected were about to join the convoy. As Roche watched, one green dot darted into view from off-screen, angling down and toward her to match velocities with the white *Ana Vereine* at the center.

"Is that real-time?" she asked.

"Yes. This happened only a minute ago. I should point out that I am currently accelerating at seventy percent of my design tolerance."

The green dot braked effortlessly to a relative halt a hundred kilometers away. "What the hell is it?" Roche asked.

"A large drone or singleship. I'm not familiar with the design or its markings. But we clearly can't outrun it."

"Has it tried to contact us?"

"Not yet."

"Are we camouflaged?"

"Mildly, only in order to give the appearance of trying. Our position has been well-known since we arrived and we are currently too well-observed to successfully drop out of sight."

She nodded. "Drop the pretense, then. Hail that drone, or whatever it is. I want to talk to it."

Kajic's hologram abruptly dissolved.

Roche stood, and Cane followed her out of the small office. "As you said, Morgan: absence of evidence is not evidence of absence. Just because they haven't threatened you yet doesn't mean that they won't."

"At the moment, that's good enough for me." She assumed her usual station at the first officer's post. "Maii? Anything?"

<The craft is either unoccupied or its occupants are extremely well-shielded,> said the reave.

"I have a lock on it," said Haid. "Its E-shields and hyper-shields are down."

"I doubt it's defenseless," Roche said, watching a close-up of the craft on the main screen. It resembled a mushroom in shape: flat, circular cap with a trailing stem five meters long and two meters wide. There were no visible drive outlets or weapons ports. "Whoever it belongs to, they're more advanced than us."

"I have a reply," said Kajic. "The drone is a relay."

"Open a direct line. Let its source talk to me."

Seconds later, a voice issued from the bridge's speakers:

"Welcome to Sol System, Morgan Roche." The female voice was precise and clipped, and unfamiliar. "The Interim Executive Pristine Council has been expecting you."

"You're not the only ones, it seems."

"Your arrival has created something of a disturbance. As the news spreads, we expect the situation to worsen."

"Meaning?" Roche wished for an image to give her something to focus on.

"In case you failed to notice, the atmosphere in this system is somewhat tense. There have been many skirmishes in the last few days—even several attempts at outright war. As we speak, Olmahoi forces are preparing to engage the Kesh—acting on information you brought with you. You are a catalyst, Roche, a destabilizing influence. The council would ask you to restrict your activities before you cause more damage."

"Is that a request or an instruction?"

The woman's voice sounded amused. "It is an appeal," she said, "to your better judgment."

Roche was silent for a moment. "Perhaps you should tell me who you are and what exactly the council is."

"It might be easier to demonstrate," she returned. "Turn your instruments to the following coordinates . . ."

Kajic swung the view on the main screen accordingly, but only starlight dusted the empty space.

"There's nothing there," said Roche irritably.

"Give the light a chance to reach you," said the woman.

Even as she spoke, something appeared on the screen. It looked like a ship, but the perspective was all wrong. Where a dot might represent other craft, there glowed a tiny arrowhead.

"Whatever it is," said Kajic, magnifying the view, "it's millions of kilometers away."

The display was suddenly taken up with a huge vessel, and Roche found herself gasping at its immensity. It was shaped like a long cone flattened on one side, hollow at tip and base and bristling with instruments and weapons emplacements—some as large as the *Ana Vereine* itself. It had to be at least a thousand kilometers long and as much as one hundred and fifty wide; it made COE Intelligence HQ look like a drone.

"You're seeing the *Phlegethon*," said the woman. "It's a consistory vessel of the Skehan Heterodox. You have been invited to approach."

Roche stared at the screen a moment longer. The name meant nothing to her. "Why?" she said eventually.

"To discuss the situation," the woman replied. "For the duration of those discussions, at least, we can offer you our protection."

"Again: why?"

The woman hesitated slightly, as though Roche's suspicion annoyed her. "The IEPC exists to assess the threat presented by the clone warriors you seek. To do that, we must gather as much information as possible. Contacting you is an important part of that process. Understand, Roche, we are not asking you to join forces; we are not asking you to surrender control to us. We ask merely to exchange information, in return for which we will get your pursuers off your back."

Roche hesitated, thinking of the Surin backup Jancin Xumai

had threatened her with, and the Kesh, and the Commerce Artel, and Jelena Heidik. . . .

<Morgan,> said the Box, <I urge you to comply.>

<I thought you might.>

<They are exactly what we need: a significant presence in this system with the resources to investigate it properly. You will note that she is communicating with the drone by faster-than-light methods. Access to such technology will make our quest that much easier.>

<And what exactly *is* our quest, Box? I'm still a little uncertain about that.>

<All will become clear soon enough, Morgan. I suggest you take the opportunity given to us and see what happens.>

The AI was making sense. Any group with a ship that big would be a fair contender for the role of central authority in the system—and she had to take on allies sooner or later. She couldn't do it on her own.

"Roche? Are you still there?" The woman's voice sounded more amused than concerned.

"I was just considering your offer." Roche glanced at Haid, who shrugged: *Your decision* . . . "Very well. We agree to talk, at least."

"Good. I will instruct the Heresiarch to give you an approach vector to match orbits. We will contact you again when everything is in order."

Before Roche could reply, the woman had cut the line. A moment later, the drone accelerated impossibly fast, outward, away from the sun and away from them. Within seconds, it was gone.

2

Something stirred inside Roche as they approached the *Phlegethon*.

For the most part, the uneven surface of the giant ship's hull was bleak and lifeless, with only the occasional beacon sporadically flaring in the darkness. But as they moved along the length of the *Phlegethon*'s vast exterior, a patch of quivering energy some fifty kilometers wide followed, lighting up the ship's black, moist-looking skin. There were no windows of any description to be seen, yet Roche couldn't help but feel she was being watched. Not by the ship's instruments perhaps, but by the ship itself. It seemed . . . *alive* to her. And the *Phlegethon*'s only identifying mark, a mural of a giant, half-lidded eye on the flattened underbelly of the beast, only enhanced that feeling.

She suppressed a shudder as the bulk of it passed between her and the distant, yellow sun. This close to the monster craft, she felt intimidated, ineffectual. Worse, she felt vulnerable.

"The ships following us have broken off," said Kajic via the scutter's intercom. "Whatever the IEPC said to them, it's had the desired effect."

She could tell by the tone of his voice that he wasn't saying what was foremost on his mind. "You think I'm doing the wrong thing, don't you?"

He didn't reply immediately. When he did, he sounded almost relieved. "Yes, Morgan."

He didn't need to say anything more than that. Roche could see his reasoning: after Linegar Rufo had captured half her crew by luring them into his station in Palasian System, Kajic had every right to point out that she might be making the same mistake twice—and for similar reasons, too. But those reasons were sound, and they outweighed any risks to her personally.

She needed information, first and foremost, and she had information others might find useful. She had to take the chance that this Interim Executive Pristine Council—whatever *that* was—was in the system to help, not hinder.

And she had Maii with her, as well as the Box, hidden away in her flesh. Haid hadn't liked being left behind, but he could see that Roche needed the sort of help only a reave might be able to provide. If it was a trap, then she was never going to be able to fight her way out of the *Phlegethon* by force alone.

"Trim," said the traffic controller, guiding her in a perfunctory, almost disinterested manner.

She concentrated on flying the scutter. It had drifted slightly off course. She corrected easily, following the trajectory she had been given to three decimal places.

"We don't have a better option at the moment," she told Kajic.

"I know," he replied. "That's the main reason I've kept silent."

The scutter arced gracefully toward an open dock two thirds from the hollow tip of the *Phlegethon* to its base. A line of docks encircled the ship, one every fifty meters. Roche performed the arithmetic in her head: assuming the ring went right around the ship, that made almost a thousand docks in that band alone, and she could see several more bands in either direction along the hull. She could only wonder why they needed so many. Fighter launchers, perhaps?

There was no denying the sophistication of the vessel. How far it had come was still unknown, but she had no doubt it belonged to an empire of similarly spectacular proportions.

"You getting anything from the crew, Maii?" Roche turned unnecessarily to the girl. "Any clues as to where they're from?"

<Not much,> said the girl. She sat next to Roche in the co-pilot's station, wearing an undersized hazard suit that brought her

up to Roche's height and twice her thickness. Inside she would be safe from Xarodine or any other physical anti-epsense attacks. Roche wore a simple environment suit in Dato colors with a bare minimum of ceramic armor and an energy pistol at her side. <What I am getting suggests that the ship *is* their home. If there was a place prior to this, it didn't leave much of an impression on them. Most are simply focused on their jobs or their daily lives.> She paused for a few seconds. <And there's a lot of prayer going on, too—perhaps unsurprising given there are several million people on board.>

"Prayers? To whom?"

<No one I've ever heard of,> said Maii. <Whoever it is, they don't seem to be answering.>

Roche smiled. "What about the Interim Executive Pristine Council? Anything there?"

<There are a number of chambers warded by high-grade reaves toward the top of the cone. I haven't been able to worm my way in yet. My bet is the council work is done there, where it's most secure.>

"Well, keep trying," said Roche. "And let me know if you learn anything important."

<I will, Morgan.>

Roche eased the scutter into the large dock, bringing it to a halt in exactly the spot indicated. There followed a series of clangs and small bumps; then the traffic controller spoke again.

"You're docked," he said. "Praise Weryn, and welcome aboard the *Phlegethon*."

"Thanks." Roche unclipped her harness and stepped from the couch.

"Air outside is normal," said Kajic. "And so far our transmissions aren't being interfered with." He still sounded concerned.

"Good. I think we're going to be okay, Uri."

"You'd better hope so, Morgan," Haid put in over the open line. "Because if something *does* go wrong, I don't fancy our chances of getting you out of there."

"Personally, I don't give you any chance at all. Not against this thing." Roche forced herself to sound casual. "But let's hope it doesn't come to that."

<You could say a prayer,> said Maii. <That's what most people here would do.>

<Mine would just be another voice among the millions, then,>

said Roche. <A sigh in a storm.> She let the hint of a smile carry with her reply. <But you feel free to try, Maii, if you think it will make a difference. . . .>

A tall woman with a solid build met them outside the airlock bay. She was dressed in a sky-blue uniform that seemed part robe, part jumpsuit. It was hard to tell where the folds of fabric stopped or started. Her face was long and strong-boned, her chin curved and slightly protruding.

"My name is Hue Vischilglin," she said, taking both of Roche's hands in hers and pressing them to her forehead. She repeated the ritual with Maii, when Roche introduced her. The young reave, made awkward by the hazard suit, bowed slightly in return. "Be welcome here."

"Thank you," said Roche distractedly, glancing along the empty, curving corridor that connected all the various docks on the inside of the ship. It was so long that the air blurred the details in the distance, and so wide that, with gravity pointing down away from the center of the ship, it almost appeared flat. She shook her head. "I never expected . . . *this*!"

"Few do." Vischilglin smiled warmly and gestured for them to follow her across the plain toward a distant pillar. There was no one else in sight. "The Heterodoxies have come from the Far Reaches on the other side of the galaxy. They've known about the problem longer than most, and have possibly suffered its worst effects. This ship is all that's left of one of their fleets. Its Heresiarch—its 'captain'—rebelled when he was ordered to destroy a civilian outpost inhabited by several billion people. It would seem his superiors had been infiltrated by the enemy. He managed to escape reprisal and kept on running. Eventually he was contacted by others in similar situations and directed here.

"Like some of the other outermost Castes, their greater lead-in time has given him more chance to prepare for being here. On the other hand, his crew is exhausted from having come so far. That's probably why they're being so open-minded about the council running the show." She smiled widely. "Although I suspect they were as glad to get their hands on our ftl relays and advanced camouflage as much as we were glad to get our hands on such a figurehead. What a beast, eh? And to think this was just one ship from one of the Heterodox fleets!"

"So you're not one of them?"

"Oh, no," she said, surprised by Roche's misunderstanding. "I'm from the Rond-Spellor Outlook, myself." Catching Roche's reaction, she went on with even more surprise: "You've heard of us! That makes us practically family around here."

They reached the pillar, which turned out to be much thicker than Roche had first imagined; the lack of perspective was playing tricks on her eyes. Vischilglin waved a hand across a black panel and it slid silently open, revealing an elevator cab.

Roche hesitated outside. "Where are you taking us?"

"For debriefing," said Vischilglin. "Don't worry; you won't come to any harm."

"Sentiments I have had expressed to me in the past," said Roche cynically, then added: "No offense."

"None taken, I assure you," said Vischilglin.

"I just want my crew to know, that's all."

Vischilglin nodded. "We're aware that you're in contact with them; we wouldn't have it any other way." Vischilglin stood on the threshold. "Is there anything we can do to put your mind at ease?"

Roche shook her head slowly. "I'm just habitually nervous these days, that's all."

"As you should be. I'm taking you to the secure areas on level 391. Your reave would have noted them already, I'm sure. We keep them shielded as best we can to keep word getting out. Maybe it's effective; maybe it's not. Either way, we have to try. But we're not keeping secrets from our allies. That would be counterproductive. We're just trying to maintain security against our common foe."

"And do you know who *they* are?"

Vischilglin grimaced. "If you mean do we know their origins or the identities of the individuals, then no, I'm afraid not. But we are hoping you might be able to help us." She indicated the interior of the elevator. "Won't you?" she said. "They're waiting."

Roche forced herself to ignore the nagging uncertainty and stepped into the cab. Besides, what choice did she really have? If they wanted to spring a trap, then her position was already so compromised that she wouldn't be able to do anything about it, anyway.

Maii followed her in. As the doors closed, Vischilglin turned to the girl with an amused expression.

"You know, you're free to remove that suit any time you like," she said. When Maii didn't respond she added: "I hate those things. Too confining, constricting—and they *chafe*. We have more suitable clothing if you're uncomfortable."

<Are there any of my people where we're going?> Maii asked.

Vischilglin looked uneasy for a moment, and Roche suspected the girl had known the answer before she'd asked.

"There is one, yes," Vischilglin replied.

<Then I am quite comfortable as I am, thank you.>

Roche felt the slight tickle in her mind that meant the Box wanted to talk to her. <What is it?>

<I thought you might like to know that the Rond-Spellor Outlook has been in a state of civil war for some weeks, now.>

<You think they've been infected by the clone warriors?>

<Most likely. Or at the very least, *af*fected.>

<Could she be one of them?>

<I have no reason to believe so. Neither her name nor her appearance match any in my database, and one must assume that any organization devoted to the investigation of the clone warriors would take precautions against such an infiltration. Nevertheless . . .>

The Box left the sentence unfinished, but the sentiment was clear.

<Consider me warned,> she said.

<I have every confidence in your abilities, Morgan.>

<Let's hope I can live up to your expectations,> she said. <For both our sakes.>

The elevator didn't seem to have moved, but when the doors opened a second or two later, an entirely different vista was spread out before them. Water from gentle waterfalls washed down numerous curved walls into undulating ground between them, collecting in valley floors to form small, slow-moving streams which curled and divided in unpredictable directions, some emptying into numerous ponds scattered about the area. The air was moist and sweet—scented, Roche suspected, by the various plants growing in the waters.

The banks of the waterways, however, were gray and sterile—a striking contrast to the exotic flowers and reeds. And high above it all hung featureless white clouds. The vista gave Roche the impression of an attempt at terraforming by a clerical AI.

She moved out of the elevator. "Is this the right level?" she asked.

"Incredible, isn't it?" Vischilglin stepped up beside Roche. "The waterways erode giant, mazelike circuits around the ship. Given enough time, the Heterodoxies believe they will one day spell out the name of God. Or something like that." Vischilglin shrugged helplessly. "It all sounds like nonsense to me. Yet I can't help admiring it whenever I see it."

She led them through the strange landscape, across modest but elegant bridges and along the narrow valleys. As they climbed over each rise, Roche could clearly discern the curve of the floor beneath them; they were obviously higher along the cone than they had been before.

She realized then that nowhere on their journey had they seen another person.

<Are we blocked here, Maii?>

The head of Maii's suit rose when she spoke via epsense, uncannily as though she were looking at Roche. The visor was black, however, and the girl had no eyes to see with behind the white bandage she wore across her face; she was using Roche's eyes to guide herself.

<We have passed through several barriers,> she said, <and are now . . . Well, the best analogy I can think of is that we have reached the eye of a storm. I am not being interfered with, although I am finding it difficult to reach the outside world.>

<Can you pick up anyone else near here?>

<There is a large group up ahead,> Maii said. <They seem to be waiting for us.>

<Is it the council she was telling us about?>

<I think so. Look . . .> Roche received a mental impression of many minds congregated in one place, focusing intently on one thing. She couldn't make out any individuals in that crowd, but she sensed their combined will. <I suspect this might be an illusion,> the girl went on. <A powerful one. I can't break through it.>

<Interesting that they've made the effort,> said Roche.

They reached a flight of stone steps that twisted and turned around a sharp rise in the landscape like a thread around a screw.

"The place we're going is known as the *fane*," Vischilglin said, pausing at the base of the steps. "You and I would probably call it the ship's bridge, but that doesn't do it justice." She hesitated for a moment, then went on: "The Heterodox are great believers in ritual. There is some protocol you'll need to observe.

When you reach the nave, in the center of the fane, bow to the Heresiarch—you'll see me do it ahead of you, so you'll know who he is. When you're asked to speak, always address at least part of your reply to him. He may not speak directly to you, but if he does, look him right in the eye. Should you hear bells at any point, be prepared for everything to stop. That means the ship requires his attention."

Roche nodded her understanding, and Vischilglin began their ascent up the broad and shallow steps. After a while, cloud obscured not only their destination above, but also the area around them. It was composed of thick and surprisingly dry mist that smelled of ozone and left no residue as they passed through it.

Roche followed Maii, allowing the girl to use her eyes to navigate her way up the stairs. With each step the girl took, the suit struck sparks from the stones, but she expressed no discomfort to Roche.

"Not far now," said Vischilglin.

<Kajic, are you tracking us?> Roche asked via her implants.

<Yes,> he replied, <and monitoring via Maii's suit.>

<No problems at your end?>

<We're still holding in the position they gave us. There have been no other attempts to approach us. I suspect we are being camouflaged; we've fired a couple of base-line probes away from our position, but so far none have reported back. They seem to keep losing our location.>

<At least you're safe,> said Roche.

<If a little frustrated,> he replied. <I envy Ameidio: he can sleep at times like these.>

Roche smiled. <Years of practice, I guess.>

<It wouldn't be so bad if Cane was better company.>

Her smile slipped a notch. <Listen, make sure—>

<I know, Morgan,> he cut in. < I'm keeping an eye on him for you. He hasn't done anything suspicious, and if he did, I would notify you immediately. But I don't think he will. He knows he's being watched.>

<He also knows you're going to have to sleep *some* time. You're not the Box.>

<Don't worry about me, Morgan. Just take care of yourself, okay?>

Her smile returned. Under the concern in his voice she heard a genuine warmth. If they had become friends in the weeks since she'd taken control of his ship, then that was all to the better. It took some of the edge off the uncertainty she felt about her situation.

Roche's first feeling as she emerged from the cloud a few minutes later and looked out over the vast bridge—the *fane*, she reminded herself—was relief that it had been the Dato Bloc she'd fought on Sciacca's World and not the Skehan Heterodox.

She was standing in the middle of a wide, concave space carved out of what looked like dark gray stone. This space was one of many—like the petals of a flower—abutting a central bowl almost two hundred meters across. The bowl was stepped in the fashion of an ancient amphitheatre, but with no sharp edges; everything was rounded, molded—smooth, perhaps, from the generations of people that had sat on those seats and worn them down. A few were occupied now, as were spaces in the petals, where people stood rather than sat and observed what was happening in the bowl. At the bowl's center was a rough-hewn font filled with water.

Roche looked up. If symmetry was anything to go by, local gravity had taken a turn through ninety degrees in the clouds. Far above, hanging from the central point of a convex roof was a slender spike, pointing downward like a stiletto poised to strike. Its tip burned white, with enough light to cast a shadow from everything it illuminated below. Roche guessed that the spike and the font at the center of the bowl delineated the long axis of the ship.

Vischilglin led her along a short walkway through the petal, and down, toward the central bowl. When they stepped across its lip, the woman stopped and turned to face a man dressed in gold, who stood on the far side.

She bowed. Assuming this man to be the Heresiarch they'd been told to watch for, Roche bowed also. Beside her, Maii did the same.

"Morgan Roche wishes an audience with the Heresiarch." Vischilglin, speaking in a voice only slightly louder than normal, gestured toward Roche.

"Bring her down."

Roche couldn't tell who had spoken, yet the voice was as clear as if it came from someone standing directly beside her. The Heresiarch didn't appear to have moved.

They descended step by step into the heart of the central

bowl—the nave, Vischilglin had called it. When they reached the lowest circle, they stopped and waited. Even at the edge of the nave, the font was still some distance away.

Only when they came to a halt did the voice speak again: "Do you know who we are?" Roche was still uncertain as to who had spoken, but she knew it was directed at her.

She looked around. Apart from the Heresiarch in his gold attire, nobody else stood out. Most wore white robes or shipsuits; only a few, like Vischilglin, wore blue. All were watching Roche, waiting on her reply. She didn't dare presume that the Heresiarch was the one who had spoken, so when she did reply it was to the space in general: "No."

It was a few moments before the speaker continued, and when he did, the words still seemed to issue from everywhere at once: "Five hundred thousand years ago, more or less, Humanity diversified to the point where its origins were forgotten." The man spoke slowly and with a crisp, nasal tone. "Only the dimensions and attributes of the Pristine form remained known. In order to ensure that the cause of the Pristine would never be lost among those of the other mundane Castes, the framework for a council was established—a council that would surface from obscurity *only* when it was needed. All Pristine governors of all Pristine governances know how to summon the council into being, and all know that to do so improperly would have its . . . consequences." The word was chosen carefully. "Only the gravest of circumstances can justify such a summoning—as, for example, when the genetic code of our distant ancestors becomes threatened."

"But this is not such an occasion, is it?" said Roche. The silence which followed was filled with unspoken disapproval for her interruption.

"This council," continued the voice shortly, "was called forty-six months ago, and is now in full session."

"Forty-six *months*?" Roche exclaimed, not caring whose sensibilities she offended. She wanted answers, not speeches.

Movement to her right caught her eye as a figure in blue took a step toward her. She interpreted it as a warning against further interruptions, and ground her teeth together.

"We have been aware of this threat for that long. Only recently, however, did we learn about Sol System. Our data showed an apparent convergence upon this region, although not enough on its own to fix the location precisely. An attack on a nearby system helped us triangulate traffic among the civilizations we've been keeping an eye on, suspecting them to be corrupted. We were among the first to arrive here, barely a week ago."

The figure to Roche's right shifted once again.

"The speed with which word has spread is phenomenal," the speaker continued. "Ships continue to arrive at the rate of over one hundred every hour. We have reopened several secondary anchor points on the fringes of the system, to act as exits should congestion worsen. If that is not enough, we might have to close the main anchor point altogether. That way, only the most determined will be able to come here."

The figure in blue took several more steps forward, close enough now so that Roche could make out the face of a man, the blue-white light from the spike above casting deep shadows in the lines of his aging features. He was the one talking, not the Heresiarch.

"The situation here is approaching a watershed," he said. "The council senses a change coming, but does not know what form it will take, or to what purpose it comes. Some of us suspect that you might lie at the heart of it, Morgan Roche, and believe that you can help us with an answer to this question. Will you do so?"

"Of course," she said without hesitation. Looking at the Heresiarch, she added: "After all, That's why I'm here."

She saw Vischilglin nod approvingly as she turned back to the speaker.

"I am Esko Murnane," he continued. "My superiors in Pompili sent me as their plenipotent envoy to the council, and the council in turn has declared me chairperson for this hearing. You have already met Hue Vischilglin, co-adjutant to the leaders of the Rond-Spellor Outlook. Although a minimum of thirty Pristine nations are required to allow the full and proper council to sit, at present we number four hundred and seven. All have representatives here today, although few, if any, will be known to you. We will, therefore, forgo introductions for the time being. Should you be asked to join our cause, the identities of your questioners will become known to you then."

Again, Roche nodded. "I understand."

"Good. You stand before the council as a witness to the aftermath of the atrocity that recently occurred in Palasian System, and as someone who appears to have a deeper association with the enemy than most of us here." The slow steadiness of his speech combined with what he was saying lent Murnane an air of deep, long-standing authority. "All of us have been touched by the enemy, in one way or another, to our detriment and lasting regret. So we are keen now to hear all that you have learned."

He paused and looked around the enormous chamber, his eyes eventually finding their way back to Roche. When he spoke, they remained upon her, but his words were directed to everyone present.

"Who will begin?" he said.

"I will." The voice came from the far side of the chamber. Another male, but younger, and fair complexioned. "Each of the many nations in the council was drawn here under a different pretext, none seemingly more convincing than any other. We hope to find one that predominates, for that one might contain a shred of truth. By what name do you refer to the enemy, Morgan Roche?"

"At first," she said, speaking slowly and clearly, addressing her reply equally between her questioner, Murnane, and the Heresiarch, "we thought they were Wunderkind created by the Sol Apotheosis Movement. They had a base in this system, a couple of thousand years ago—"

"We are familiar with their history," the speaker interrupted. "So, have you ascertained another name for them now?"

"No," said Roche. "I'm afraid not."

"We are told that you have one of the enemy aboard your ship."

"Yes, we do."

"And what does he have to say on the matter?"

Roche shook her head. "Nothing."

Another voice spoke, this time a woman to Roche's left: "But he *does* have a name?"

"Yes," said Roche. "His name is Adoni Cane."

"A name of your choosing?" said the woman.

"No, it's what he called himself when we first met. I've never had cause to doubt him. Later it produced a match in Dato Bloc's historical records, confirming a link to the Sol Apotheosis Movement."

"Which later turned out to be spurious?"

Roche nodded.

"How do you account for that?"

<Answer that question carefully,> the Box cautioned.

She frowned, fighting her automatic urge to answer with the truth. The AI had faked the historical data in order to mislead the COE and other neighboring governments—and also to throw any of the "enemy" off the trail. If the enemy knew how close the High Humans behind the Crescend and the Box were getting—even if it wasn't very close at all—it might work to their advantage.

The fact that it still might, in the midst of the Interim Emergency Pristine Council, gave her cause to reconsider.

"Would you like the question repeated?" said Murnane.

"No, that's okay," she said. "I guess I can't account for the discrepancy. Maybe the data was deliberately corrupted by the enemy in order to throw us off the trail."

<Well done, Morgan,> enthused the Box.

"That is certainly a possibility," said Murnane, coming forward. "There is a risk of infiltration and perversion at every level. I fear we have not yet seen the full extent of the enemy's abilities or motivations. Until we do, we must assume the worst—even of ourselves."

"Has Adoni Cane ever revealed any detail regarding his origins?" The speaker, another woman, was very close and directly behind Roche.

She turned toward the voice, but was unsure which of the many faces looking back at her had asked the question. "He seems to have no knowledge of his origins," she said, addressing them all. "He doesn't know where he came from or why he's here."

"You're saying he has no memory?" This time Roche saw who had spoken: a young girl, tall and thin, with flaxen hair brushing the shoulders of her blue robe.

"Everything since his awakening is clear," said Roche. "But nothing before then."

"And you are convinced he is telling the truth?"

She hesitated, remembering her most recent conversation with Cane. "I trust him as much as I can," she said. "Under the circumstances."

"Because he claims to be one of the enemy?"

"Yes. That is, he talks about them as if they are his siblings; he shares certain characteristics with them."

"What characteristics, precisely?"

"Well, his genetic profile is profoundly abnormal," she said.

"And his body is patently modified in order to make him a good soldier. I haven't seen hard data on others like him, but I do know that if he set his mind to it, he'd be more than capable of the same destructive force that they have displayed. And when in Palasian System he did respond to a command language understood by the other clone warriors—"

Murnane held up a hand. "We will return to Palasian System in a moment," he said. "First we'd like to hear how you met up with this Adoni Cane, and what you have observed about his behavior to date."

She took a moment to organize her thoughts, then began to talk—describing succinctly how she and Cane had met on the *Midnight*, how they had escaped and crash-landed on the surface of Sciacca's World, and their pursuit and eventual escape from the penal colony.

"He helped you escape?" The question was from another council member whose thick accent was unfamiliar to Roche; she had to concentrate to understand what he was saying. "From prison wardens corrupted by a rival government? Do you know *why* he did this?"

"No," she said, with a shake of her head. "And I have to admit that it's puzzled me."

"Can you explain why his behavior is so different from the others?"

She shrugged lightly. "The best explanation I can come up with is that he's a freak," she said. "A mistake."

"You mentioned genetic data, earlier," said one of the previous speakers, the man with the fair complexion. "Will you give us access to this data?"

"Gladly," she said. "If I may contact my ship . . ."

"Your lines of communication are not being interfered with in any way," said Murnane.

<Uri?> she said, checking to see if this was true.

<We're still receiving you loud and clear,> Kajic replied. <I have all the info the Box compiled before it was destroyed. Do you want me to send it?>

<Yes, but I don't know where, though.>

<They've allocated me a buffer,> he said. <Leave it to me, Morgan.>

She was about to turn back to Murnane when she remembered

Maii's suit standing immobile beside her. <You okay, Maii?> she asked via epsense.

<I'm fine,> came the reply. <I'm having fun poking at shields. Did you know that there are five high-grade reaves within the nave alone? They're the hooded ones around the edge. I've never heard of so many being in one place at the same time before!>

<What are they doing? Probing me without my knowledge?>

<I wouldn't let them do that, Morgan,> the girl reassured her. <I think they're just trying to make sure *I* don't get up to anything.>

Murnane cleared his throat. "Thank you," he said. "We have received the data and will examine it later." He folded his arms and took a couple of thoughtful paces around the font. "But I am curious. At the time Cane was examined on the *Midnight*, news had not yet reached your corner of the galaxy that there even was a problem he might be part of, otherwise his capsule would have been instantly identified. And on Sciacca's World, your rebel friends had access to even more limited information about the outside world. Yet our sources in the Commonwealth of Empires reveal that in a very short space of time you determined precisely what was going on—bearing in mind the Sol Apotheosis Movement fallacy—and confronted your superiors with that knowledge. When was it that you managed to piece it all together?"

Roche opened her mouth to speak—then shut it again. If they had sources in the COE, chances were they already knew the answers to every question they had asked so far. So why go through the motions?

Then she reminded herself: trust no one. They could no more believe their sources than they could believe her—even if one corroborated the other.

She didn't envy them their position.

"It wasn't me so much who put it all together." She half expected a nagging voice in her ear telling her to be careful what she said. "It was the Box."

"What is this 'Box'?" It was asked in the same thick, unfamiliar accent as before, except that this time the questioner was female. "I take it you are referring to some sort of intelligence-gathering device?"

"An AI, yes." Roche nodded. "I was carrying it to Intelligence

HQ when I was intercepted by the Dato Bloc. That's how I ended up on Sciacca's World in the first place."

"This device reasoned that Adoni Cane was one of the enemy?"

"Yes," she said. "And everything afterward seemed to confirm it."

"How was this device able to do something you yourself were unable to do?"

"The Box was no ordinary device," Roche said, remembering to use the past tense. "It was a truly remarkable piece of engineering. It suspected from the very start who Cane was. It even faked the distress call that led to the capsule's discovery."

"So it had access to information which you did not?"

"Yes, like the command language. But it wasn't just that. It actually thought better than I did."

"Impossible. No AI has yet surpassed a Human intelligence."

Roche shrugged. "I told you it was remarkable."

"And who built this amazing device?"

"It was manufactured on Trinity," said Roche. "They specialize in AIs there."

There was a muted whisper. Then Murnane spoke. "We have no record of such a place."

"No?" She looked around and out of the corner of her eye caught the gold robes of the Heresiarch. She had forgotten he was there. "Go ask your sources," she said. "They'll confirm it exists."

Murnane stirred. "What say you, Trezise?"

Startled first by the familiar name, Roche almost jumped as a familiar voice followed: "We know the place. It's administered by a High Human we have had some dealings with—an entity calling himself the Crescend." The man's voice was flat, emotionless, almost dead. "The AI Roche refers to did indeed come from this place, but as to its other abilities . . ."

Salton Tresize, Roche remembered—senior aide to Auberon Chase, head of COE Intelligence. She should've guessed someone like him would be here.

"You are not aware of any facility capable of making Human-superior AIs in COE jurisdiction?" Murnane pressed.

Trezise's tone didn't change as he said: "I'd sooner believe in aliens."

Murnane turned back to Roche. "You will understand if we hesitate to accept this aspect of your story without any hard evidence to back it up," he said. "Unless you could produce this AI for us to examine, perhaps?"

She didn't need the tiny prod the Box gave her. "I'm afraid it was destroyed along with Palasian System."

"I see." A sigh carried his words. "Well, the exact manner of your discovery of the enemy is not the issue here. What is important is the fact that you learned of their existence and went seeking more data. What can you tell us about Adoni Cane that we have not already covered?"

"The Box thought we should check the introns of Cane's genetic code," she said. "But I don't know what for."

Murnane nodded as though the suggestion was trivial. "And your young charge here." He pointed to Maii. "Does she have nothing to contribute to this discussion?"

<Maii?>

<Ask him how I'm supposed to talk with everyone's minds walled up,> the girl shot back.

Murnane raised a hand before Roche could pass the message on. "Simply speak to me," he said, "as you would to Roche, and a relay will announce the message for all to hear."

<Oh. Only—>

"—words?"

Roche heard the girl's voice directly through her own senses and a split second later through the relay, aloud. The relay stood on the far side of Roche; it was disconcerting to hear the girl's voice coming from two directions almost simultaneously.

"And appropriate images, where necessary." Murnane inclined his head in welcome. "Please feel free to share with us any impressions you received regarding the mind of Adoni Cane and any other member of the enemy's number you have encountered."

Maii did so, conveying as best she could a number of conflicting visions. Cane possessed a mental shield that was difficult to penetrate, but did allow him to communicate with her by epsense and occasionally offered strange glimpses of what lay beyond. Sometimes, Cane's mind seemed to spin like a top; at other times it was as still and clear as a lake, or a mirror. The *irikeii* had imagined him as a glowing light-source with a speck of black at its heart, and also as a snake coiling and uncoiling around itself.

"What sense do you make of these impressions?" she was asked.

"None of them are necessarily true representations of his mind," she said. "They're like the different reflections you get off the facets of a diamond, or the different meanings one collection of sounds has in different languages. I'm not seeing the underlying reality, just the secondary effects."

She shrugged, and the heavy shoulders of the suit magnified the gesture. She sent an image, via the relay, of a crystal turned inside out: smooth and spherical outside, facets crossing and tangling inside.

"It's hard to find words for this," she said.

"Evidently," said Murnane. "But if you had to choose just *one* word to describe him . . . ?"

"I'm not sure. 'Complex' isn't enough. 'Incipient,' perhaps? 'Numinous' has too many spiritual overtones, and I don't believe 'unknowable' applies to anything. There's a great potential within him. I don't know what for, but it's there."

Murnane waited a moment, to see if she would add anything else—or perhaps to confer mentally with the reaves surrounding them. After a moment he said: "And what of the *irikeii*? What did he think of you?"

Maii was silent so long, Roche thought she wouldn't answer. Finally, she said: "He disapproved of me."

"We thought as much," said Murnane, nodding. "The Olmahoi Caste petitioned strongly for your capture prior to your arrival—as did your own government. Somehow the word of your existence has spread, although exactly *how* has yet to be determined. We decided not to become involved, for very good reasons; there are enough inter-Caste tensions as it is without the council seeming to take sides—and what happens in non-Pristine Castes is, ultimately, none of our concern." Murnane stopped and took a deep breath. "Still, it is clear that the events that occurred within Palasian System have had far-reaching repercussions—many, perhaps, still to be felt. Morgan Roche, would you care to explain to us what happened there?"

Roche did so, outlining the exploration of the system after it had been ransacked by the clone warrior, her disastrous attempts to cooperate with Linegar Rufo, and her clash with the Kesh. Later, she hoped, she would be able to discuss things in more detail, but for the time being she contented herself with an overview.

"You say that the name of the enemy in this case was Jelena

Heidik?" someone asked when she reached the aftermath of the destruction of Palasian System.

"Yes. It's one of a list of names we . . . found in an old archive. The others included Vani Wehr, Sadoc Lleshi, Ralf Dreher—"

"Do you know who they refer to?" Murnane interrupted. "Was there any other information in that archive, apart from the names?"

<Box?>

<No. But I can give you a full list of names, if you require it.>

"No," she said. She would give them the rest of the names later.

"And where is this Jelena Heidik now?"

"I don't know," Roche admitted. "We came here looking for her, but she's managed to get away."

"But you do think she's still somewhere in Sol System?"

"Yes."

"Why do you believe that?"

"Well, this seems to be where it's all coming to a head. She would hardly leave so soon."

Murnane leaned forward, his hands on each side of the font supporting him. "But *why* Sol System? Are we here following the enemy, or has the enemy followed us? We see patterns of movement across the galaxy, leading here, but we still cannot be one hundred percent certain that we are not fulfilling our own prophecy." He shrugged. "That is always a risk, I suppose, in any war of espionage; words and hints and suppositions carry little weight compared to maps and soldiers and bullets. So little is certain."

"We heard that Sol System was the location of an ancient battle," said Roche.

"It is the location of many things, if you believe the records; few stand up to strict examination. Which battle do you refer to?"

"I'm not sure," she said. "We've begun to suspect that the clone warriors—Cane and Heidik and the others—are seeking revenge for a war lost a long time ago. A war won by the Pristines."

"Do you know when?"

She shrugged. "As far back as we can remember. Half a million years or more. Back when there were only Pristines; the other Castes didn't exist yet."

"Do you have records to support this?"

"Nothing concrete—but surely that indirectly supports this theory? If there *were* records, someone would have found them by now. The fact that we haven't implies that they no longer exist—that the events we're looking for lie back in the earliest times."

"Perhaps." Murnane's expression remained impassive. "Remember, though, that many millions of civilizations have risen and fallen since then. That is an awful lot of data to sift through; if the records indeed are lost, not hidden, then we might never know. And without knowing when this battle you refer to took place—and who it was that lost—we have little to go on."

Roche conceded the point. "That's partly why we came here," she said. "We were following Heidik, yes, but we were also interested in seeing what happened. *If* the clone warriors attacked, then who they attacked first—and last—could reveal who their allies are, or who is related to their creators."

"Tell me, Roche," Murnane said. "Did you have any idea how complex the situation here would be before you came?"

"The Box had mentioned a gathering of sorts, and the COE commander I spoke to confirmed it, but that's all. I expected nothing like this."

"Did this Box of yours also happen to say anything about the composition of this system?" asked another voice. "There are several anomalies we have not yet fathomed, and I fear they may become hazards to navigation. More of these we do not need."

It took Roche a second to realize that it was the Heresiarch himself speaking. When she replied, she made certain she followed Vischilglin's advice and looked him directly in the eye—or at least in the direction of where he stood.

"I'm sorry, I don't know anything about that."

"The behavior of the solar wind is quite peculiar, and its effect on the gaseous volatiles of the planetary ring even more anomalous. If your AI had *anything* to say about that, I would've been grateful."

"Like I said," Roche replied evenly, keeping her attention fixed firmly on the Heresiarch. "It never mentioned a thing. I'm sorry."

She thought she saw him shrug, but he was too far away to tell for certain.

"There is no need for apology if one speaks the truth," he said, with wry humor to his tone.

"We have asked the High Humans for this information, too," said Murnane into the silence that followed. "They haven't told us anything that might conceivably help, on that or any other subject. I for one find their silence unnerving. Do you know why this might be the case?"

"No," said Roche.

"Given that your Box came from this Trinity, which had connections to this High Human called the Crescend, do you think its destruction would be of some concern to him? Would he respond to a call for more information, perhaps?"

"I really don't know." Roche hoped he would not respond; if the Crescend revealed to the council that she had lied about the Box's destruction, that certainly wouldn't count in her favor.

"The Crescend never contacted you while the Box was in your presence?"

"No, never."

"Do you expect him to?"

She resisted the urge to ask where this line of questioning was going. "Look, I went to Trinity to collect the Box, but met no one while I was there. I was rendered unconscious in orbit, and when I woke up the Box was . . . in my possession. That's all. You're obviously hoping that I can act as some sort of link between yourselves and the High Humans, but I don't see that as being an option. I've never communicated with them, and I doubt I ever will. Why should they bother with me? I'm just someone who happens to be caught in the middle of all this."

<I hope you know what you're doing, Box,> she whispered via her implants to the AI in her body.

<Trust me,> it said.

"We are *all* caught in this," Murnane said. "But outside of the enemy, few individuals have had such a catalytic effect as yourself." He paused. "Is there anything else you would like to tell us, while this council is in session?"

<Box?>

<No.>

"No," she repeated.

"Will you submit to a probe by one of our reaves to verify the answers you have given us?"

The question surprised her. "Why do you need that? The hard data speaks for itself, and I've no reason to deceive you."

"Nevertheless—will you?"

If she said yes, they would know that she was lying about the Box. Although she knew it would look suspicious, she had no choice but to say: "No. I'm sorry."

"Will you allow us, then, to examine you and, if necessary, take a genetic sample?"

She squirmed. <Box, could they find you that way?>

<The Dato missed me when you were captured,> the Box replied, <but that was partly because I had infiltrated their systems. I cannot rule out the possibility that the council will see something the Dato missed, and that I will be unable to suppress the information once it emerges.>

<Haven't you got into their systems?>

<Of course I have. But the Skehan Heterodox places great faith in the role of people in or alongside all its systems. At least one Human doctor would be present during your examination, and I see no easy way to suppress any knowledge that might emerge at that time.>

Again, she had no choice. "I'd prefer not to," she said. "I'm sorry."

Murnane studied her for a long moment. "As are we," he said. "But we cannot force you to submit to either examination—nor would we wish to." He gestured helplessly. "This meeting is now concluded. We would ask you to return to your ship, Roche, and—"

"What!" Roche snapped. "Aren't you even going to discuss what I've told you?"

"There is no need," he said. "We've been conferring by epsense the entire time."

"But you can't just dismiss me!"

"Can't we?" He took a step toward her. "Roche, we had hoped that you would provide us with information that is both new and verifiable. We had hoped that this might show us a way to combat the enemy we fear has infiltrated every group we deal with and perverts everything we attempt to do to stop them. Now it seems certain that you yourself have fallen into the same trap—either willingly or by accident."

Roche felt herself straighten, her tired back and stomach muscles tensing as though ready for attack. "Meaning?"

"You have told us *nothing*, Roche. You claim that Adoni Cane is one of the enemy, yet you can offer no explanation for this surety nor a reason for his atypical behavior. Of what value is his genetic data under those circumstances? You offer us names that you assure us are relevant, but do not give us a context in which to place them or access to the records you say they came from. On what grounds can we possibly use them as means to uncover the enemy among us? You cannot tell us why Sol System has become the focus of so much concern—you can't even tell us why *you* came here without resorting to vague explanations involving this mysterious AI of yours! And as to *that*, well, I hardly need to state how the council feels. *If* it existed at all, its tenuous connections to the High Humans might have been exploitable, but as it stands—"

"I'm telling you the *truth*," she broke in angrily.

"Are you?" Murnane moved closer again, his own anger evident in his face. "There is much to suggest that what you are doing is far from innocent. Ameidio Haid is a convicted criminal who, as the Commerce Artel points out, has not served his full term; who is to say you don't have criminal intent in mind as well? Add to that the fact that both your young friend here and the pilot of your vessel are the subjects of biological experiments; if Adoni Cane's genetic data and physiognomy turn out to be peculiar, could he not also be an experimental subject, and not the enemy you claim he is?

"Then there are the credibility gaps in your story. How did you come to the conclusion that Adoni Cane was one of the enemy? How did you survive Palasian System when even the Kesh destroyer sent to monitor the situation did not? Why did you come here? And why has your arrival caused such a furor among all those who have known you: the COE, the Dato Bloc, the Commerce Artel, the Surin, the Kesh, the Olmahoi . . . ?

"Even if what you are telling us is the truth, and Adoni Cane *is* one of the enemy, then how can we trust someone who openly admits to having one aboard her ship—as part of her *crew*?"

Murnane shook his head. "It may seem like we pre-judged you, but we have done nothing of the sort. We simply considered all possible conclusions prior to your arrival and allowed you to show us the one that best fitted the circumstances. Because you seem not to be dealing honestly with us, we are forced to conclude that Adoni Cane is a fake, or a misdiagnosis, or an enemy plant. We are unsure of *your* motives, but we are sure that we will no longer allow our precious time to be wasted examining your spurious claims and false offers. We have work to do, Roche, and a distraction such as this, even if not maliciously intended, does the enemy's work for them."

Tight-lipped, Roche forced herself to speak calmly. "If I could just say—"

"There is nothing more to be said," Murnane cut in. "Hue Vischilglin will escort you and your companion to your vessel. Once you're on board, the protection offered by the *Phlegethon* will be withdrawn."

Vischilglin appeared, expressionless, at Roche's side as Murnane turned his back and moved away without another word. The Heresiarch made no move at all. Roche let herself be taken by the arm and led away, furious but impotent, as a growing murmur filled the fane.

3

<*That* went well,> Roche muttered to the Box as Vischilglin directed her through the council and back into the petal from which they had first emerged. <'Talk to them,' you said. 'Exactly what we need,' you said. Whatever happened to getting access to their resources and getting on with the job?>

<You seem upset, Morgan,> the Box responded smoothly.

<Of course I'm upset! The questions you wouldn't let me answer were the ones that convinced them to send us away!>

<Be patient, Morgan. Time will tell if this trip has been wasted or not.>

<Yeah, right.> Feeling humiliated and frustrated, Roche avoided the eyes of everyone around her as she walked by. They thought she was a fool—or, worse, some sort of collaborator. <Sometimes I wonder why I don't just shut you up like De Bruyn did back in HQ.>

<The 'Silence between thoughts' override phrase would allow you to do it any time you wished,> the Box intoned casually. <I wasn't faking that period of disconnection.>

<I never thought that—> She stopped midsentence as its admission sank in. <Why *did* the Crescend give you an override

phrase that actually worked? It doesn't make sense—especially in the light of recent knowledge.>

<Given the degree of invasion that I am upon your person, it seemed reasonable that you be provided with a means to turn me off, should I become too much of an inconvenience.>

<In other words, the Crescend gave me an out.>

<Exactly.>

<Without *telling* me about it?>

<You learned in your own time.>

<Only by accident—the same way I found out that you're inside me!>

<I can only assure you that, had you learned the latter before the former, you would have been given the override.>

<Oh, naturally.> She couldn't help the sarcasm. The modified ulnar nerve along her arm was throbbing with remembered sensation. Data had burned along that path to the valise she had once believed the Box to inhabit. She wondered which pathways it used, now that it was completely inside of her. . . .

"Well, that could have gone better."

Roche recognized the man's voice as one from the interrogation. She looked up to see a fair-haired, diminutive figure waiting for them at the top of the stairs, an almost condescending smile beaming from his small, triangular face.

Vischilglin didn't give Roche a chance to reply.

"Stand aside, Junior Primate Nemeth," she said, pushing past the man and heading back down into the thick cloud they had climbed through to get to the council.

"That's *Assistant Vice* Primate to you, Co-adjutant Vischilglin," he objected, following them down the steps.

Only then did Roche realize something odd about the council—or rather the people who comprised the council. They were all plenipotentiary envoys, co-adjutants, assistant vice primates, senior aides—underlings with fancy titles. None of them were the real operators. Perhaps, she thought, the situation in Sol System was too risky for the superiors to come, so their assistants had been sent instead.

Then she realized another thing: she had heard the name of Assistant Vice Primate Nemeth somewhere before. She stopped and turned to the man. He stopped also, a couple of meters away, behind Maii. Mist from the cloud created a slight haze between them, but not enough to obscure the man's crooked grin.

"It was you who hailed us before we came here," she said. "Before that drone intercepted us."

Nemeth executed a slight bow of the head. "I'm flattered you remembered me."

"What do you want?" Roche was in no mood for small talk.

He gesticulated expansively. "Perhaps it would be more appropriate to ask what it is *you* want—from *me*?"

She studied him for a moment, then turned and continued after Vischilglin down the steps. "I haven't got time for these games," she muttered irritably.

<Can you read him, Maii?>

<Yes,> replied the girl, maintaining a steady plodding pace behind her. <He is devious, but not impenetrable.>

<So what's he after?>

<To strike some sort of deal with you,> said the girl. <Although I don't know exactly what kind of deal.>

<What do we know for sure about him?> said Roche. <What is most prominent in his mind?>

<It seems the government he represents has been proven to be compromised—therefore his influence within the council is on the wane. He spoke first during the session in an attempt to remind people that he was still there.> She paused for a few seconds before adding: <And he doesn't seem to like Esko Murnane.>

<That's the best thing you've said about him so far.> Roche could hear the footsteps of the man following her down. Vischilglin strode ahead of her, a tall broad shape plowing through the mist. Far from the chatty, affable guide she'd been when they first met, she had hardly said a word since the hearing.

<What's on *her* mind?> Roche asked Maii.

<She's embarrassed. She thought you would be more help to the council—to the people she represents. She feels . . . betrayed, perhaps.>

<By me?>

<No. By the people who encouraged her to think that you might offer a solution.>

<And who are they?>

<Some members of the council and various lower-echelon officials.>

Roche sighed. <I only came here looking for answers. I mean, what were they expecting to find in me? A savior or something?>

<To some, that's exactly what you are,> said Maii. <To others you are the heart of the enemy itself. But most people are just curious. They're listening to the rumors, but they're waiting to see what happens.>

<But how can so many rumors about me be started in such a short period of time?>

<Chen chen, fe,> said Maii.

Roche frowned. <What . . . ?>

<Something Veden once said to me,> the girl replied. <Words attract words. 'Morgan Roche' are two words that have been uttered many times in the last few weeks. It is inevitable that other words would attach themselves to them.>

Roche smiled now. <Well, whatever the rumors are, I think there are going to be a lot of disappointed people,> she said. <Because without the help of this council, I'm not going to be doing much.>

They stepped out of the clouds and back into the landscape of rolling valleys and trickling waters. Roche groaned inwardly when she remembered the distance they'd come to get this far. Her legs and back were sore from standing for so long.

As though someone had read her mind, an air-car resembling a large silver spoon hummed into view. There were seats for four people in the bowl, all empty.

"I thought you might be weary," said Nemeth from behind them. "As attractive as the scenery is, there's no need to view it on foot twice."

Roche glanced at Vischilglin, who was frowning. "You arranged this?" Roche asked, suspecting an ulterior motive.

"It is not the council's will," said Vischilglin, scowling.

Nemeth shrugged expansively. "Since when did the council start dictating courtesy? I'm offering you all a lift—including yourself, Co-adjutant Vischilglin." He smiled. "Well, are you coming or not?"

The air-car sped quietly across the uneven terrain, leaving the steps they had just descended far behind. Although they didn't move alarmingly fast, there were a couple of moments when the car slued to avoid a jutting ridge, making Roche feel a little uneasy.

Nemeth didn't appear to be troubled by the craft's sudden movements. He sat beside her, looking out at the rolling land-

scape sweeping beneath them, his face split by a seemingly per-
petual smile.

As if sensing her staring at him, Nemeth turned to face Roche,
and his smile widened.

"Now isn't this so much easier?" he said. "Perhaps we could
even take a more interesting route back to the docks." Over his
shoulder to where Maii and Vischilglin sat, he said: "Do you
think the council would approve, Vischilglin?"

The woman grunted an affirmation. She really had little choice
now, Roche thought. Nemeth laughed and turned back to look at
the scenery.

"Tell me," said Roche. "What exactly *is* it you think I want
from you, Nemeth?"

"Ah, now, that's the question, isn't it?" he said. "Make no
mistake: I can do any number of things for you, Roche." He
glanced over at her. "If I were so inclined, of course." When she
didn't react, he went on: "You come at a peculiar time, Roche—
when the council is desperate for answers that none of us have.
It feels constrained by the very precepts that allowed it to come
into being so quickly. It is . . . *limited* by its nature."

"You mean it's for Pristines only," said Roche.

He nodded. "But some of us fear that 'Pristines only' may
not be enough to combat this threat." He watched the view silently
for a few moments; when he spoke again, the smile had faded.
"I lost my family back home, you know," he said. "They were
caught in an insurrection while I was serving in a completely different system. A local terrorist branch whipped up enough anti-
government action—in the form of riots and infrastructure
sabotage—to warrant calling in the army. Thousands of innocent
people died in the ensuing repression, including my family, and
it achieved nothing for either side. It turned out that the enemy
was responsible for the whole thing. The terrorists were just a
tool—the means to an end. And that end was to cause as much
destruction and misery as possible."

Nemeth looked at Roche, who sat watching him carefully. He
remained outwardly relaxed, except for his hands: his knuckles
were white where they gripped the armrest. When he realized
this, he quickly loosened his grip and his smile returned.

"So, do you have any family, Roche?" Nemeth asked.

Roche felt a stab of pain. Never knowing her parents had been
a constant regret throughout her childhood. As an adult, she had

aspired to COE Intelligence in order to track them down. Upon reaching that goal, however, she had forgotten about her parents entirely, too busy with her own life to worry about the one she might have had.

"No," she said. Another part of her was glad that she could forestall his obvious gambit. While she could feel compassion for his loss, he would have to engage her intellect, not her emotions, in order to get what he wanted. Whatever that was.

If he was disappointed by her reply, he made no sign. He simply nodded and changed the subject.

"In a second we'll be entering one of the main longitudinal ducts that run down the hull from minaret to crypt," he said.

Vischilglin leaned forward in the cab. "That's fore to aft to us," she said.

"Even at the speeds we will be going," Nemeth continued, "it will take us ten minutes or so. But please don't be concerned by that," he added in response to a look of alarm in Roche's eyes: to travel any significant length along the giant ship so quickly would demand speeds greater than one or two thousand kilometers per hour. "We'll be perfectly safe."

They raced toward what at first appeared to be nothing more than a wall, but as they flew closer, Roche saw it for what it actually was: a giant tube lying on its side across their path, suspended by invisible forces ten meters or more above the rolling hills. It was so thick that its top was obscured by the cloud cover, and for a moment Roche wondered how they were going to get past it—or into it, if this was in fact one of the ducts Nemeth had mentioned.

A moment later the craft swept beneath the massive cylinder and into its shadow. Their speed eased slightly as the air-car rose toward an enormous portal on the underbelly of the tube, easily thirty meters across and hanging open like a slack and lipless mouth. From it issued a cold breeze; not strong, but enough to make Roche shiver.

"An air duct?" she said, hearing a faint susurrus coming from within. "Seems a bit primitive on a ship like this."

"Believe me," said Nemeth, "it's purely for aesthetics."

Then they were inside—and caught by a tremendous, rushing wind. The air-car lurched violently as it began to accelerate along the tube. Roche gripped her armrests as she was pressed back into her seat and knocked from side to side with every buffeting motion. Beside her, Nemeth laughed at her obvious alarm.

Another air-car—this one a single-passenger model shaped more like an egg with two limp, trailing spines—swept past them, barely missing by a meter. Startled, Roche looked around properly for the first time. Inside, the tube was easily wide enough to hold a hundred air-cars. Lines of lights trickled along the walls; every now and again, larger, brighter patches would rush by, too quick to take in. Other air-cars continued to pass theirs, less quickly than before, but thankfully none came as close as the first one.

"Aesthetics, huh?" she said to Nemeth over the sound of the wind; some sort of field-effect was keeping the worst of the turbulence at bay; otherwise he would never have been able to hear her.

He laughed out loud again. But this time it was with an almost childlike delight: he was enjoying the ride.

"You would've loved Palasian System," she said. <Are you okay back there, Maii?>

<Yes, Morgan. The view is spectacular. If you know when to look, you can see out the duct entrances and glimpse the levels as we go past.>

Roche looked around her, concentrating for the first time on the bright patches as they went past. Indeed, now that she looked, she could make out brief impressions of the levels as they flashed by: here, deep purple and icy; there, soft pastels. One of the portals was much larger than the others, and through it she glimpsed angular structures in the distance, across flat, metallic plains; levels devoted to the ship's working, she supposed.

Clearly Maii had lifted this method of looking at the levels from the way Nemeth moved his eyes.

<What is our guide thinking, Maii?>

<He's getting a huge thrill,> said the girl. <I can't read much beyond that. I suspect he's taken us this way because it gives him a natural shield to hide behind.>

Roche turned back to Nemeth. "Scenery is all very well," she said, "but when are we going to *talk*?"

"We can talk now, if you like." He swiveled in his seat to look at Vischilglin, who regarded him stonily. "Do you think the council would object to us having a little privacy?"

Before the woman could answer, the field-effect protecting the passengers from turbulence clove in two, leaving Roche and Nemeth in a bubble of their own. Absolute silence suddenly pressed against her ears.

The air-car had settled itself into a gentle, rocking motion, and swept along the tube with the other air-cars as though on any conventional road. If Nemeth had brought her along the duct in order to unnerve her, Roche refused to let it.

"I want to talk to you in a frank and open manner," said Nemeth after a few seconds.

"You've displayed little intention of that so far," said Roche.

"Games. I know." He dismissed her accusation with the wave of a hand. "The council is a bureaucracy; whether one is working within it or despite it, one is necessarily limited in one's options by this very fact."

Roche sighed. "Open and frank, remember?" she said, making no attempt to conceal her annoyance. "Can we just get to the point?"

He sighed, too, and looked away for a moment. Behind him, a white landscape flashed by. "Things are not going well for us here in Sol System," he said. "In that much, at least, Murnane and I agree. The enemy were here before we even arrived, and have made their presence felt in a thousand ways—sometimes subtle, other times not so subtle. Although there has been something of a lull in the last few days, every hour dozens more ships arrive, and with each ship the chances are high that more of the enemy are coming too. And we are not finding *any* of them."

He looked at her, then. "I am being completely and utterly frank about this, Morgan. I hope you realize that. Not even Vischilglin knows the depths of our failure. For all the council's collective experience and wisdom, for all the technology of groups like the Skehan Heterodox, for all that we have been studying the enemy for four and a half years, we are not even close to solving the problem here. Can you understand how galling that is?"

She didn't have to think hard about that. She had been banging her head against the problem for less than three months.

"So why not take a chance on me?" she asked. "If you're so desperate, what have you got to lose?"

"That's an interesting question, isn't it?"

"Do you have an answer?"

"A kind of answer," he said. "But it starts with a question."

He paused. "There are more than just Pristines in this system. Do you know what the Exotics are doing here, along with us?"

"Following the flow, I guess," she said. "Maybe coming to settle old scores. Naturally they'd be swept up in any regional conflict that might have started among the Pristines. I can see how they would be dragged here along with everyone else."

He nodded. "It's certainly a valid assumption. According to your theory, the enemy comes from a time in which the Exotic strands of Humanity did not exist, or at least may not have been so prevalent. Indeed, maybe they are a weapon created by an ancient alliance of *all* Exotics, in response to the age-old grudge that Pristines have it better than the others simply and unjustly because they are more like the original—although why this alliance would wait so long to wreak its vengeance is somewhat of a mystery. And why would a weapon created by Exotics allow the descendants of its masters to be dragged into such a dispute?"

"There may be only one way to find out," she said.

"Precisely. Here we come to your plan to wait until the fighting starts and see who doesn't end up dead at the end of it all, apart from the enemy. If anyone *is* left standing, they must be guilty. Simple." He raised a hand as Roche started to protest. "I'm sorry for seeming disrespectful. Your plan is ruthless and, perhaps because of that, likely to be more effective than most of the others bandied about. I simply fear that we will find out the truth only when it's too late."

"So what do *you* suggest?"

He shrugged, palms raised—and for the first time Roche noticed that the little finger on each of his hands was missing. "I told you: your plan is better than any of the others I've heard—including my own." He grimaced. "It's a hard thing to admit. If ever you doubt my sincerity, please recall this conversation—although I'd be happier if you kept it to yourself, otherwise."

She allowed herself a half-smile. "I don't know," she said. "Blackmail has a certain appeal."

"A kindred spirit." His own smile was wide and natural. "Perhaps we can come to terms, after all."

An air-car going the opposite way rushed past them; Roche gripped her seat until the rocking of their own car settled. When it had, Nemeth went on.

"We thought the lull recently might have something to do with you," he said. "Your ex-superiors in COE Intelligence have kept us up to date with your movements. Ever since we heard about Cane's existence, we've been quite curious to see what would happen next. Many of us expected the COE to start falling apart as a result. In fact many of us felt that the Commonwealth's proximity to Sol System, the very focus of everything, would put it under much more pressure than other nations farther out. But apart from that brief fracas with the Dato Bloc, nothing much seems to have happened. It's almost disappointing." He flashed his grin at her again before adding: "For some, that is."

"What does all this have to do with *me*?" she said, conscious that the ride would be coming to an end soon and wanting some answers before it did.

"You're an anomaly, Roche. An outlier. You claim to have survived two verifiable encounters with two self-declared clone warriors. For that alone you're worth observing. And—" He hesitated slightly. "And worth having on our side."

Roche shook her head. "Why? Because you think I'm *lucky* or something?" She was desperately trying to make some sense of what he was saying.

"No," he said. "Nothing to do with luck." Again the smile, but this time forced and uneasy. "But there is something about you. Something that doesn't quite add up. And, unlike Murnane, I don't think it's wise to turn you away without knowing what that thing is."

"But Murnane *has* turned me away," she said bitterly. "The council has already made its decision."

"It made *a* decision," Nemeth corrected her. "It wasn't necessarily the right one, and it certainly wasn't unanimous. It needn't necessarily be the *only* one it makes. I happen to know that there is enough support to back up the offer I'm about to make you—if only because in hindsight it may prove wise for the council to be seen as having made the other decision it couldn't officially make, where everyone could see it. By that I mean that the council has to cover every base it sees open, even though here and now it can't acknowledge even to itself what it is doing. For posterity's sake—for the sake of the future itself—every chance must be taken."

Roche was just managing to keep up. "You're talking about some covert group within the council?"

"One with its own agenda," he said, nodding. "Does it surprise you that such a thing might exist?"

Roche shrugged heavily. "Every bureaucracy supports such groups," she said. "I guess I just didn't expect one here, that's all. I mean, we all have the one common enemy, right? We have the same *aim*."

"True," he said. "But we all work differently to achieve those aims. The council has become concerned with method, whereas the Ulterior concentrates on intention."

Roche laughed at this. The *Ulterior* . . . "And every such group has to have a catchy name, right?"

Nemeth ignored the gibe. "We have no firmly entrenched protocol," he said. "If we see an opportunity, or even the potential for an opportunity, we will take it. We are less . . . scrupulous, perhaps, than many of our colleagues. And for that reason, we must remain as our name suggests: behind the scenes."

Roche regarded him steadily. "And you and your friends in this 'Ulterior' regard me as some sort of 'opportunity'? Is that what you're trying to tell me?"

"Isn't that what you wanted the council to believe?" he said.

"Yes," she said. "I guess it was."

"Working for us, you would obtain that goal, Roche. Indirectly. If you fail, of course, the council has no knowledge of you, having turned you away from the one and only official hearing it was obliged to give you."

"Of course," said Roche dryly.

"But if it looks as if you might succeed, then you will have the full support of the Ulterior—and ultimately the council itself."

"And why should I believe anything you're saying?" she asked him. "How do I know you're telling me the truth?"

He dismissed the objection with a shrug. "You don't," he said. "But you don't have many other options right now. And we need each other."

Roche sighed and, despite the apprehension she was feeling, said: "So what exactly are you offering?"

"A deal," he answered quickly, and with sudden enthusiasm. "We can't give you any formal protection or recognition, obviously, but we can give you information. This information has to flow both ways—unconditionally. If you learn anything new, we want to know about it. And if you find anything you think might work, we want to know about that most of all."

She didn't need the Box to tell her that she should take the deal. If she couldn't get the full approval of the council, this might be the next best thing. But she still had her doubts . . .

"It can't be that simple," she said.

"Well, there is something else we would like you to do for us," he admitted. "But I can't see how it doesn't fit in with your plans, anyway."

Here we go, she thought. "Meaning what exactly?"

"That you're probably going to want to go buzzing around the system, looking for the enemy, right? Poking your nose in here, seeing what turns up there; waiting for the fight to start so you can see who kills who. Well, that's exactly what we want you to do, too. Specifically, we want you to see what the Exotics are up to. That's the one area this damned Pristine council of ours can't see into properly—and any blind spots in situations like this are dangerous."

She nodded: that much at least was true.

"Do you have any other agents working in this area?" she asked.

"A few," he told her. "But nowhere near enough. Right now there are seven hundred and fifty-eight known Castes in Sol System, Morgan, not counting Pristine. Some are wildly Exotic; some are down the other end of the scale from the Skehan Heterodox—almost Low Castes."

"And High Humans?" she said.

He shook his head briefly. "None that we are aware of," he said. "But if you find anything that suggests there are, we'd be keen to hear about them too."

She was keen on the Box's behalf to avoid that subject. "So basically," she said, "if I find something, you take the credit. If I don't, or if I get into trouble, you disown me, right?"

"Obviously we will do everything in our power to help you," Nemeth said, "but our power is not unlimited. Unless you give us a reason to come forward, I'm afraid the Ulterior must remain just that."

She nodded slowly. "And will I have to pledge allegiance to the Ulterior? Swear a secret oath? Sign my name in blood, perhaps?"

He grinned. "Your word will be fine," he said.

<Is he telling the truth, Maii?>

<He thinks he is, for what that's worth. He has the mind of a man who could convince himself of anything, though.>

<That doesn't surprise me.>

"Okay," Roche said after a deep breath. "For lack of a better option at this time, we have a deal."

"Good," he said, smiling and extending a hand. She just looked at it. "If you're still worried about that genetic sample," he said, "you should know that I'm more likely to get a decent one from the armrest you've been leaning on than from shaking your hand."

She relented and took his hand.

"And not a moment too soon," he said.

The air-car had begun to decelerate and drift toward the wall. The bright patches passed more slowly than before, and Roche caught glimpses of endless docks like the one through which she'd arrived: row after row of airlock inner doors, ramps, and floating cargo-lifters. All empty. For all the traffic she had seen, the ship might have been completely sealed.

And maybe it was, Roche thought. That might have been the only option open to the Heresiarch and the council in order to prevent contagion.

"Oh," said Nemeth as they approached an opening and braked still farther, "there is one more thing."

"There always is," she said.

"We'd like you to take one of us with you."

"What? *You*? Forget it."

He managed to affect a hurt expression. "No," he said. "Not me. And not on board your ship, either. He'll have his own. But we'd like him there as backup, an observer—or a bodyguard, if you like."

They slid smoothly out of the duct and into the docks.

"As insurance?" she said.

"The only true necessity in all the universe," he said. "Or so I've been led to believe."

Before she could say anything, the air-car reached a safe travel speed and the partition between the front and back seats evaporated along with the rest of the cushioning bubble. They decelerated still further, heading for the dock where the scutter was waiting.

Unable to talk in privacy, Roche could only stare in alarm at the atypically enormous Surin warrior standing in full battle-dress at the inner door of their dock.

"You can't be serious," she said.

<He is,> said Maii, her mental voice sharp with dismay.

"It was the only way to get the Surin off our backs," Nemeth said. "Officially they want to make sure your young ward here is treated well; unofficially, they want in on the action." His eyes were hard. "You should be glad it's not an Olmahoi grayboot as well."

"Someone with a little more subtlety would've been better."

"I think you'll find our friend here quite suited to your task."

She grunted dubiously. "Any other surprises I should know about?"

"No," Nemeth said as the air-car slid to a halt. "At least, none that *I'm* aware of . . ."

4

Finding the sort of people she wanted was almost ridiculously easy. Finding the right *person*, however, was proving to be a little more difficult.

"I don't give a damn what you think, De Bruyn," said the obese Exotic on the far side of the partition, his voice a deep and guttural drawl. He had a tic on the left side of his body that seemed to move of its own accord: first his eyelid would twitch, then one finger, then a muscle in his neck, then something under the table would thump as his foot kicked out at nothing.

"You don't, huh?" She leaned forward and slid the partition aside, not caring anymore about his Caste's preference to avoid close personal contact.

"No, I don't," he repeated, backing away uneasily. His entire left side twitched—eye, finger, neck muscle, et al.—simultaneously. "What do we need someone like you for, anyway?"

"I told you," she said. "I have contacts; I can make things *easier* for you."

He snorted. "I don't see how getting dragged into this personal grudge of yours will make life easier," he said. "Grudges are bad for business. They can get messy."

She feigned indignation. "Now, who said anything about a grudge, Ken'an?"

"It's in your eyes," he said. "It's in the way you bargain. You're after something real bad—so bad you're practically drooling. People don't salivate for money, in my experience. The stomach rumbles for betrayal, revenge, hatred, jealousy . . ."

She retreated slightly. Maybe he wasn't so stupid after all. Still, she'd hoped for better. "So much for mercenaries," she said dismissively.

"If it's mercenaries you want, talk to Uyeno Lenz. He'll do anything for a quick credit."

"Yeah, including knife me the moment my back is turned."

"A distinct possibility," he said. "But I can't help you, De Bruyn. Like I said, getting involved in your personal grudge would be bad for business." He slid his seat back and shrugged. "I'm sorry, but I have standards."

"Yeah," she muttered to herself, watching him waddle away from the table. "Just not very high ones."

He was right, of course. She had no interest in the petty power-squabbles boiling in the vacuum of Sol System. She didn't care who came out on top in whose transplanted regional politics. All she wanted was someone to help her keep an eye on Morgan Roche—and more, if necessary.

De Bruyn shouldered her way back to the bar, where an orange-clad Exotic refilled her glass. She wasn't drinking anything alcoholic; she wanted to keep her head clear.

"I'm looking for Uyeno Lenz," she said.

The bartender gave her a noncommittal shrug as he took some empty glasses away.

"You don't want to do business with him," said a deep voice at her side.

She turned. Another Exotic leaned against the bar, green-skinned, a mug of clear liquid clasped in his large, oil-stained hand. His eyes were deep-set and red; two thick strands of black hair ran down his head from forehead to nape. He flashed her an amused expression which seemed strangely out of place on his otherwise hard features. He didn't have to say another word. She knew he was the mercenary called Lenz. Only a hack would try a line like that on someone.

"You're right," she said, walking back to her booth. "I don't."

An alarm went off in her implants before she sat down. Being fired from COE Intelligence hadn't meant the loss of equipment standard for upper-echelon agents. Her eyes and ears were artificial; much of her nervous system had been enhanced to run faster under stress, as well as to act as conduits for many different types of data; her skeletal strength had been increased by the addition of materials far stronger than Human bone. Although she could fight as well as most COE Intelligence operatives, she had not been trained for that; instead, she was wired to receive and transmit data—like a Human antenna, complete with two-way listening and viewing devices.

She recognized the alarm instantly; indeed, she had been expecting a call from this source for the last hour or two. Putting the drink carefully in front of her, she activated scramblers and ciphers and opened a link to her ship.

Kindling was stationed just inside the protective bubble of the *Phlegethon*, hidden by the big ship's camouflage and given clearance by her contact in the council. She had sent it there to act as a relay after catching a tug to the *Dark Stressor* compact habitat to look for allies. She'd been hoping for a little more time, though; if Roche was already on the move, she would have to hurry to keep up.

When the connection was made and secured, she spoke via her implants directly to her contact.

<What's happened, Trezise?>

<Nothing unexpected.> Via tightbeam, the lack of emotion in the man's voice was only magnified; she'd never decided whether it was an affectation or a genuine condition. <The worm is hooked and wriggling. Now all we have to do is wait for the fish. . . .>

The words came with an image of Roche's scutter leaving its dock and heading for the *Ana Vereine*, closely preceded by another ship—a long-range fighter of some kind, angular and harsh. The design was unfamiliar.

<Who's the escort?>

<That I am still trying to ascertain.>

<What about the other data I asked you for?>

<I have some.> An icon winked in the corner of her field of vision, indicating an attachment to the transmission. <The rest is on its way.>

<How long?>

<I can't be exact, Page,> he said. <We're a long way from home, you know.>

<I *know* that.> She hated it when people used her first name—a fact that wasn't lost on Trezise, she was sure. She forced herself not to rise to the bait, glancing instead at the data and searching for any of a handful of details she was hoping to find. One was there, as obvious as a nova now that she knew what to look for, and she smiled to herself.

She wasn't going to share her small victory with Trezise, though. <What about one of those ftl links? We'll need one if we're to keep in touch.>

<Can't help you there, > he said. <The best I can do is swing one by periodically, and give you the codes to call for one should you have the need. There are thousands all over the system. The longest delay you'll likely suffer is about ten minutes or so.>

<Then that'll have to do.> She looked up to see the green-faced mercenary still watching her. She caught his image and sent it to Trezise. <What Caste is this?>

<None I've seen before, but that's not surprising around here,> he said. <Where the hell are you, anyway? I thought you were in your ship.>

She smiled to herself. <If I wanted you to know where I was, I would've already told you.>

<Suspicious to the end,> he said. <Auberon always said that the feeling was mutual.>

<Auberon was a fool.> Her smile became a snarl. Auberon Chase, his boss and once hers, *was* a fool, but he was still head of COE Intelligence and safe in HQ, while she was out hunting among the predators. <What did *you* do wrong, Salton, to get such a lousy assignment?>

<Nothing,> he said. <I volunteered.>

<I don't believe you. Only a fool would want to come here.>

<Only a fool would fail to see the opportunity,> he said. <When I think of all that your friend Morgan Roche is doing to squander her unearned leverage, I can't help but want to kill her myself.>

Again, De Bruyn refused to rise to the bait. <And where is our little worm headed?>

<Who?>

She fought to contain her annoyance at his games. <Roche, of course.>

<Oh, did you think I was referring to Roche?> His voice was

smooth and amused. <I thought you knew me better than that. I was referring to a *much* bigger target than her.>

<What the hell are you talking about, Trezise?>

<My dear Page,> he said. <I'm talking about the council itself, of course.>

She broke the line abruptly when she saw the mercenary approaching.

"I heard you talking to Ken'an, before." The words rolled from somewhere deep in the back of his throat, sounding as though they were having to fight their way through food to get out.

"You have a problem with that?"

He sat down opposite her. "Not at all," he said. "But you should listen to him. Grudges are dangerous."

"I don't recall asking either you or Ken'an for your opinion."

"Well, make the most of it anyway," he said. "Advice is about the only thing you'll get for free around here."

"And what's the price of a little peace and quiet?"

"Quiet I can give you." He activated some sort of device in his jacket and a bubble of silence enfolded the booth. "Peace, however, will be more difficult."

De Bruyn's implants buzzed, warning her of the field-effect he was using to give them privacy. She ignored the alarm, doubting the bubble was anything more dangerous than a toy. Still, her right hand slipped to her thigh-holster and disengaged the safety on her pistol.

She smiled. "Okay," she said. "I'm looking for someone to watch my back while I go about my business."

"What sort of business?"

"*My* business," she repeated firmly. "For now, at least."

"In Sol System?" The words continued to rattle in his throat. "I wouldn't be here otherwise."

"For how long?"

"Until the job is done." De Bruyn kept her stare firmly on his gold-flecked irises. "It may require a bit of muscle."

"And how would you pay for this . . . muscle?"

"I have influence in the Interim Emergency Pristine Council. What I can't provide in credit, I can make up in IEPC clearance and access. The breadth of your clientele will increase overnight."

"*If* we survive." His lips tightened. "Perhaps Ken'an was right:

maybe you are a bomb just waiting to go off. Who's to say you won't take us with you?"

"There are ways to avoid that," she said. "And the right person working with me would find out how. But I'll need more than a handful of people to see this through."

"Promises and plans are easy to make," he said, his voice a low rasp. "So who is the target, anyway?"

She hesitated a second. Ken'an hadn't asked that, nor had any of the others. She'd been glad to assume it wasn't relevant.

"Morgan Roche—"

She was cut short by a hand under her chin, jerking her head back. She clutched at her pistol, but another hand gripped her wrist and yanked it away. She kicked, flexed, strained—then relaxed when she realized it was futile to resist. The hands were just too strong.

She cursed silently. The privacy field had kept her from hearing her assailant creep up behind her. But she wasn't at a complete disadvantage yet . . .

"Call him off, Lenz," she hissed. "Or I swear I'll blow this place apart."

The mercenary smiled calmly at her. "And how do you intend to do that?"

"With the nugget of turcite I slipped under the bar," she said. "One word, and it'll detonate."

"Blowing yourself up in the process," he said with a slight, forced laugh.

"A risk I'm prepared to take," she said. "But chances are this thug of yours will offer me some protection from the blast. As for you . . ."

The mercenary looked nervous and cast a glance at the person holding her. The grip about her neck tightened.

"Tell me why we should help you with this Roche person." This came from the man squeezing her neck.

"What—?" She attempted to turn around but was barely able to move at all.

"If I'm going to be doing business with you," he said, "then I want to know what's so important about her."

"*You're*—?"

Again the grip tightened. "Lenz," he said. "That's right." He released her throat and arm and pushed her facedown onto the table. She reached for her pistol, but he beat her to it and snatched it away, slamming it down in front of her. "Now, no more games; no more threats. You talk."

He moved a few paces from behind her to where she could see him. He looked much like the mercenary sitting opposite her, but broader, older, and without the hair.

"What do you know about Morgan Roche?" De Bruyn asked, sitting up and rubbing at her neck.

"Only what we've heard," he said. "There's a lot of stories going around about her. Her name keeps cropping up. Not many of the details match, though. The general impression is she's somehow relevant to everything going on here. Someone who might be dangerous."

"Yes, she is—but to whom? Us or the enemy?"

He frowned. "Meaning?"

"All those stories you've heard," she said. "They're all lies. Every one of them. The purpose of the stories is to hide the truth, and to keep attention focused on her—so that when she's ready, she can act."

His skeptical look didn't change. "And what is the truth?"

"I'm not sure," De Bruyn said thoughtfully. "But I think I can find out. All I need is a little more time, and"—she hesitated significantly—"some help."

He studied her for a long time. She looked patiently back.

"We have a ship," he said eventually. "It doesn't look much, but that's the idea."

"It's not your ship I'm interested in," she said. "What's your crew like?"

"Hand-picked."

"How many?"

"Eight."

"And you trust them?"

"With my life." He smiled. "But not my money."

She leaned back into her seat and returned the smile. "Okay, then. Let's talk business."

Lenz relaxed and moved around the table. His buddy slid over to make room. "You should know that we don't come cheap," he said. "For what you're asking—"

As soon as his hand came off her pistol, De Bruyn grabbed it and shot him through the chest. She shot his buddy too, before he had a chance to register what had happened. Screams erupted around her before the bodies had even hit the floor.

De Bruyn took the lights out with her next two shots, then slipped through the panicked crowd and out of the bar before anyone realized that she had gone. At the first sign of pursuit, she triggered the nugget of turcite with a quick burst from her implants. The explosion tore through pressure-walls and bulkheads, the shock wave hurling her and her pursuers through a locked door and into a storage room full of cartons. She sustained only minor bruising and temporary hearing loss, and was back on her feet in time to ensure that none of her pursuers would ever wake again.

The authorities believed her story about a clash between rival mercenaries. Using her IEPC pass, she was on the tug within the hour, and back on *Kindling* an hour after that.

<Let me guess,> said Trezise when she had reopened communications with him. <*Dark Stressor*, was it?>

<How did you find out?> she said with studied indifference.

<It wasn't difficult. There was a disturbance there, a few hours ago, involving a Caste much like the fellow you showed me. I looked into it, of course, to see if you'd come to any harm. The habitat's surveillance cameras caught a couple of good shots of you. Black suits you, my dear—much more so than a Commonwealth uniform ever did.> He paused for a moment. <Did everything go according to plan?>

She shrugged noncommittally. He knew damn well it hadn't, she guessed, and that ate at her. She was no better off than she had been the day before. But it was only a matter of time before she found someone suitable for her needs. There were many other places to look, and she would have plenty of other opportunities to do so while she followed Roche across the system.

Kindling's engines hummed softly through the walls of its cramped cockpit. In a way, she was glad to be on her own. Relying on other people was dangerous, albeit a necessary danger at times. It was much better, she'd always thought, to have them rely on you. . . .

<I hope you know what you're doing, Page,> said Trezise across the expanding distance between the two ships—one as large as a good-sized moon, the other barely a speck. There was still no emotion in the man's voice. <You seem to be expending a lot of energy on something that will ultimately get you nowhere.>

\<Is that what you think I'm doing?\>

\<I'm hypothesizing,\> he said. \<That's all.\>

\<And does your hypothesis explain why Morgan Roche's COE birth records have been erased?\>

There was a slight pause. \<I'm not sure what you mean.\>

\<The records you gave me,\> she said. \<Look at them yourself. Try to find her date of birth.\>

\<Why?\>

\<Just *do* it,\> she snapped. \<But you won't find it, Trezise. You won't find it because it's not there—along with a lot of other information that should be there too.\>

\<A woman without a past,\> he said, with the barest hint of dryness in his voice. \<Whatever will an intelligence operative come up with next?\>

\<Listen, you idiot. *We* didn't wipe those records. Someone else did. Someone's covering up. The same someone who got in the way when I tried to stop her. The same someone who sacked me.\>

Trezise sighed heavily. \<Listen to yourself, Page. Listen to what you're saying. This is ridiculous!\>

\<You think I'm crazy?\>

\<I think you're paranoid,\> he said. \<I think you *believe* you're making sense.\>

\<You're entitled to your opinion, I guess,\> said De Bruyn.

He acknowledged this with a nod of the head. \<And you yours, Page.\>

\<But only one of us can be right.\>

\<True,\> he said. \<And both of us could be wrong.\>

She shook her head. Trezise enjoyed arguing for the sake of it; she shouldn't let him get her worked up so easily. \<Do as I say. Look it up. You'll have to at least admit that it looks peculiar.\>

\<This whole thing is peculiar,\> he said. \<This entire *system* is. Did you know that the Heresiarch has advised all council vessels to avoid traveling in or near the ring after a probe found evidence of nanoware in the dust?\>

\<No, but—\>

\<And were you aware that rumors suggesting a cult worshipping the enemy arising among the more destabilized elements have been less ambiguously verified by no less than three council agents? And that—?\>

<Enough, Trezise.> She felt weary just listening to him. <If you think you have more important work to do, then just go. I'm not exactly here on holiday either.>

<No, you're not. If you do find anything out—something of note—please let me know.>

<Sure. And when the rest of that data comes through—>

<I will pass it on to you,> he said, cutting her short. <I know how much it means to you.> He almost seemed to smile as he added: <But be careful of the ring, Page. I wouldn't lie about something as important as that.>

Then he was gone, leaving De Bruyn half-smiling to herself. Trezise annoyed her, but he played a good game. She'd rather have one single adversary like him than ten allies of Uyeno Lenz's ilk. Not that Trezise *was* an adversary, she hoped.

Following the *Ana Vereine*'s trace at a discreet distance, she drilled deeper into the nugget of data Trezise had given her. What she found did little to put her mind at ease, and what she *didn't* find only added to her frustration. If only, she thought, she could get at the data directly and not worry about elements of corruption along the way. Or better yet, get her hands on *Roche*, and extract the data in a way that would leave no doubt at all. . . .

PART TWO:

PERDUE

5

Roche let Kajic pilot the scutter while she watched their new companion break dock. Defender-of-Harmony Vri flew a compact rapid fighter that looked like a cross between a throwing-star and a dagger. Roche didn't recognize it as a Surin military ship. Their designs were normally more hospitable. Only when the craft were attacked did they sprout numerous means of retaliation, suddenly taking on a more aggressive look.

Back on the *Phlegethon*, the warrior had spoken barely a dozen words to Roche before turning and moving off to where his ship was docked.

"Does he have a first name?" Roche had asked Nemeth, staring at the back of the receding warrior. On the back of his lightly furred skull was a triangle of darker hair, pointed upward like an arrowhead. Whether it was natural or dyed, Roche couldn't tell; and she wasn't about to ask him in a hurry, either. His wide-spaced, dark eyes had discouraged any personal questions.

"Not that I'm aware of," Nemeth had replied. "Or Vri might be it. Like your friend here, he doesn't seem to have a family name."

"Which would make him a renegade, right?"

<Soldiers who renounce their family line,> said Maii, <usually do so only to demonstrate that they are willing to die for the principle they embrace. In Vri's case, it is harmony.>

Roche caught an image from the girl of something that looked anything *but* harmonious. "So he's a fanatic?"

<No,> said Maii. <Just extremely dedicated.>

Roche couldn't argue with that. When introduced, Vri had nodded to Roche and Maii in turn and said: "I will defer to your instructions unless they conflict with the directives given to me by the Agora."

She could tell he would be a force to be reckoned with. Even from a distance he looked intimidating, with his sheer size—strange for his Caste—and the strange orange and yellow overlapping garments the Surin called ceremonial armor. It looked more like some sort of thick fungus.

"Is he any relation to Fighter-for-Peace Jancin Xumai?" she asked, thinking of the Surin who had threatened them earlier.

"Maybe," Nemeth said with a shrug. "We don't know exactly how many Surin there are in the system," he had said. "There could be numerous factions. You'd be more familiar than we are with how they operate."

The air-car had waited patiently for him while they talked. Vischilglin was watching silently and suspiciously on the sidelines. Roche had half expected Nemeth to say something more, but he obviously felt constrained by the woman's presence. He had bowed at Roche and Maii in turn, then climbed back into his seat.

"Perhaps we will meet again," he said.

"Perhaps." Roche didn't return his wave as the air-car sped off along the curving floor.

<He says to contact him when you're on the move,> said Maii.

<How?>

<Vri will tell you.>

"I must apologize for him," said Vischilglin. "If his behavior offended you—"

"No, it's all right." Roche suddenly felt sorry for the woman. If her hopes had been as high as Maii had said, then acting as Roche's guide must have been something of an honor. To see that hope dashed, then have that honor usurped by someone else, must have been disappointing.

Taking Vischilglin's hands in her own, Roche pressed them to her forehead, in the same way Vischilglin had done when they first met. "Thank you for your hospitality," she said. "I will do my best to prove that your faith in me was warranted."

Vischilglin looked in turn confused and embarrassed, then relieved. Then she smiled warmly. "Thank you, Morgan Roche. And you." She bowed to Maii. "My thoughts go with you."

She turned and walked away, leaving Roche and Maii to make their own way through the airlock doors and into the scutter. The same terse traffic controller as before guided them out of the dock in the same perfunctory manner, adding almost as an afterthought once they were clear: "Weryn guide you and keep you safe."

Vri's ship rapidly overtook the scutter, darting through space on jets of blue energy.

"How do you feel about him, Maii?"

<He means me no harm,> the girl said, her voice less strained than before. <But his definition of 'harm' is open to interpretation. If he feels that I am being mistreated by you, then he will try to take me back to my family.>

Roche shook her head. "But they *sold* you," she said. "Surely that's just an excuse to get a look inside your head."

<Possibly,> said Maii. <But *he* believes only what he's been told. He is very traditional and holds the Agora in high regard, as one would expect of anyone in the military. But how he came to be here, working with the Ulterior, I don't know. His thoughts do not reveal whether he thinks it an honor or a punishment.>

"Maybe it's neither," said Roche. "Maybe it's simply a chance to prove himself, an opportunity for advancement."

<Or an early death in defense of his principle.>

"That could hardly be regarded as harmonious."

<Perhaps not for us, Morgan,> said Maii. <But he is different.>

Roche couldn't argue with that. . . .

By the time the scutter docked with the *Ana Vereine*, Vri had placed the *Esperance* in formation nearby. Roche and Maii went straight to the bridge to debrief the others, and to open communications with the Surin warrior.

"I don't like it," said Haid. "He's potentially dangerous."

"His ship is no match for ours," she said. "Would you agree, Uri?"

"Without question. If he tried to attack, he would be disabled or destroyed with little effort."

"But if he catches us off guard—" Haid began.

"He won't." Kajic's voice was firm. "His every move is being monitored."

"But—"

"Enough," said Roche. "There's no point arguing about this. We can't do anything about it right now, so let's just accept that we're stuck with him and get on with it."

A signal came from the angular craft and Kajic put it through to the main screen.

"Commander Roche." Vri's elongated face was fuzzy with tightbeam static and hair. "I am instructed to accompany you on your journey and to lend assistance where I see fit. In order to do this, I will need notice of your destinations *and* intentions. I trust this will not be a contentious issue."

"Of course not," she said. "But as far as my 'destinations and intentions' go, I haven't thought that far ahead."

"Assistant Vice Primate Nemeth instructed me to advise you of the communication channels used by the Ulterior, and to ask you to call him immediately. A description of how to contact him accompanies this message."

Roche looked up at Kajic's hologram. "Got it," he said after a momentary pause.

"Thanks," she said, turning back to Vri. "We'll call him now."

The Surin warrior nodded slightly. "When you have decided what to do next, I may be contacted on this frequency."

He disconnected the line before Roche had a chance to say anything else. She shrugged and addressed the hologram once again. "Kajic, open a line to the Ulterior."

"Doing so now, Morgan," he said.

"I presume this will be a secure line?" she said.

"The content of the transmissions is encrypted, yes, but the transmissions themselves are not hidden. Signals in both directions travel in the same way the *Phlegethon* communicates with its ftl drones."

"As though we have nothing to hide, eh?" Roche could see the reasoning, but she didn't feel entirely comfortable with it. "I hope they're right . . ."

"Ah, Roche." Nemeth's voice and image simultaneously burst

from the main screen. "Glad to see you received my message in good faith."

She was in no mood for pleasantries. "Are you sure this is the best way to talk to each other?"

"No method of communication would be a hundred percent safe from prying ears," he said. "But this is certainly the safest option at our disposal right now. Just as I cannot possibly hope to safeguard against every security breach, so too are they—"

"Okay, okay," said Roche. "Just tell me what it is you've got to say. I presume you're going to tell me what you want me to do."

"More or less," he said, smiling at her impatience. "Rather than wandering all over the system in the hope of stumbling across something useful, we feel you would be better served having your own area to investigate. A file will follow this conversation; it maps out that area for you. Obviously it will change as ships arrive and leave, but it's a starting point. I have listed all major known Castes and alliances, and marked key congregation points. Infiltrate them and see what you can find, then move on to the next site. Report back as you are able."

"Anything else?" she asked, not even attempting to disguise her irritability. She listened to Nemeth with a growing sense of unease. She was becoming a lackey again, a pawn in someone else's game—something she thought she'd left behind with Intelligence HQ.

"You know the score, Roche," he said, suddenly serious. "Our main objective is to deal with the enemy, but first we have to know how to *find* them. There has to be a way of determining who they are—a test of some kind that can apply to *all* of them, collectively rather than just as individuals. Your reave might be able to help with that: if the enemy does possess a unique n-body signature, that might be a way we can distinguish between them and us. Our reaves have had no success at seeing what you've reported, but that doesn't mean you might not have better luck."

Roche nodded. "And once we have found a means of doing this, what then? How do you propose we deal with them?"

His shrug was both heavy and helpless. "That's a completely different issue," he replied. "And one we will address at a later date. But the matter of where they come from might assist us in this, just as why they're here might help us work out where to find them. They *must* be communicating somehow, so if you can work that out too, that would be excellent." There was a slight pause as the signal broke up momentarily. "Oh, and see if you can find out why so much energy is being wasted talking about you, too. The *Lucence-2* gives us a direct link between one of the enemy and the propagation of your name; it would be foolish to ignore the possible ramifications of this link. Clearly your Box wouldn't have kept you alive for so long if it too didn't have some sort of plans for you."

The mention of the Box threw her for a second. "I thought you didn't think the Box was important."

"Me? I said nothing of the sort. Even the council isn't so stupid as to ignore what it knows to be true—although it denies it in public. We've had some dealings with High Humans in the past months and years, but not as many as we would like. Two in particular—Aquareii and the Catiph—were quite frank until they suddenly stopped communicating with us." He paused again, as if in thought. "It's common knowledge in some circles that High Humans limit or actively suppress AI technology—except when it suits them, of course. That the Crescend runs a factory in Commonwealth space where you obtained this mysterious Box only supports your theory that it is somehow important."

"*Was* important," she corrected.

He shrugged again. "Anyway, one can only wonder what it would have thought of your situation now."

Privately she agreed, and promised to deal with that question as soon as possible.

"Is there anything else you'd like of me?" she said.

He either missed the sarcasm or didn't care. "That will be enough for now, I think. We can call each other another time, should something dramatic occur or some important need arise; otherwise we'll just get on separately with our work. Agreed?"

Again, she had little choice. "Agreed."

"Good. Until then . . ." With a curt nod he was gone.

Roche turned to face Haid and Cane, watching from the sidelines.

"I'm liking this situation even less, now," said Haid.

"It's better than nothing," she said. "We need *some* sort of contact with the council. At least this way we have a chance of making headway."

"Covert organizations can operate more effectively than their parent bodies," said Cane. "They can respond to changes more rapidly, and can work in areas prohibited to officials. I believe that this is a good sign, Morgan. Working for the council, you would have been just one agent among many; your voice could have been lost. Now you have a greater chance of gaining the attention of the entire Ulterior, and in time the council itself. Now, I believe we will start to make progress."

She couldn't remember the last time he had shown such enthusiastic support for one of her decisions. Her satisfaction was tempered only by the part of her that wondered if he was telling the truth.

"Well, I hope you're right, Cane, and Ameidio is wrong. No offense." She smiled at the ex-mercenary, who shrugged affably back. "Maybe we should look at the file Nemeth gave us, to see where we're supposed to go."

Kajic displayed a map on the main screen. It showed the entirety of Sol System, as mapped by the *Phlegethon*'s network of ftl drones over the previous days, with particular attention to a region beyond the planetary ring, one hundred and fifty million kilometers out from Sol. There, a moderately large collection of ships and habitats had gathered, including—if Roche wasn't mistaken—no less than five outrigger spines. Someone must have piggybacked them into the system, since they didn't use hyperspace technology. But why they were here at all, Roche didn't know; the system itself didn't even have an asteroid belt. She wondered if Nemeth had given her this region because she had worked with outriggers before. Certainly, there didn't seem to be any other reason.

"What does the file say about the people here?" she asked.

"There's a wide mix," said Kajic. "Some extremely Exotic Castes and some Pristines, with numerous variations in between. Some Castes segregate except to negotiate; others mix freely. There are three mobile habitats around which most of the activity takes place; the largest of these is called Perdue. There has been word of fighting from its vicinity, and remote observations of weapon-use. This is to be our first destination."

"How long will it take us to get there?"

"Twenty hours," Kajic replied.

"And does the file tell us what we're supposed to do when we get there?"

"No," said Kajic. "Nor in the other destinations we've been given, either."

"So I guess we'll just have to wing it," said Roche. "And no doubt stir up trouble in the process."

"I bet that's what Nemeth is hoping for," said Haid. Shaking his head, he added: "Look, if you really think this is the right thing to do, Morgan, I'll go along with it—but . . ."

"I know." She stood. "Uri, advise Defender-of-Harmony Vri of our destination, and let him know the course you set. Get us on our way as soon as possible. And keep us camouflaged. The less attention we draw to ourselves, the better."

She looked at the faces of the people in her charge. Maii, out of the hazard suit, seemed older, thinner, and paler beneath her hair than when they had first met. Haid's dark black skin and biomesh looked out of place against the warm browns of the bridge, lending him an air of discomfort. Neither Kajic nor Cane had changed at all—the former's image artificially generated and never looking as tired as he felt, the latter seemingly untouchable. The one and only time she had seen Cane at a loss had been when he was thawing from the coma Linegar Rufo had used to keep him contained on Galine Four. And even then, she had sensed dangerous aura around him—like a bomb that could explode at any time.

"Okay," she said after a moment. "We need to be fresh when we arrive at Perdue Habitat. Unfortunately we no longer have the luxury of the Box to keep an eye on things, so we're going to have to take shifts keeping watch."

"I am alert," said Vri, his face appearing on the main screen in response to Kajic's hail. "I'd be more than willing to keep watch."

"I appreciate it," said Roche, "but I'd like one of my own crew awake too. And don't you volunteer either, Uri; you can only run for so long on stimulants. *I'll* take the first watch. If something comes up that Vri and I can't handle, I'll sound the alarm. But until then, I want everyone to get some rest. That goes for you too, Cane."

"If you insist, Morgan," said Cane.

Roche had expected some objection from him, but was thankful it didn't come. Whether or not his obedience was offered in response to her earlier suspicions or for completely innocent reasons, she didn't know. Nor did she care. She was simply grateful not to be getting into an argument right now. She was just too tired.

She watched as Cane stood with his easy, smooth grace, and strode from the room without another word. Haid was close behind, with Maii in step beside him. They stopped at the doorway and Haid turned to face her.

"You *will* call, right?" he said.

She smiled. "You know I can't handle this ship without you or Uri."

The ex-mercenary returned the smile and then, with Maii using his eyes for guidance, left the bridge.

"Now you, Uri," she said to the hologram standing in the center of the bridge.

"I won't deny that I am tired, Morgan," he said. "But I am concerned that you are, too."

"Don't worry about me," she said. "I'll be okay. *And* I'll be watching your systems to make sure you're doing as you're told."

"Very well. I will rest for four hours, the most I need at this time. When I wake, it'll be your turn."

She raised her hand in mock salute. "Sweet dreams."

His image flickered out, and she was left with Vri's face on the big screen. "We'll speak if something happens," she said. "Otherwise, stay alert."

"I will," said the warrior, and closed the link.

Even then, she wasn't alone.

<Box, put a forward view on the main screen, along with a navigation chart. And dim the lights.>

Almost instantaneously a chart was displayed before her, showing numerous ships in a wide variety of orbits, none with any likelihood of crossing their path. Several were traveling in directions similar to the *Ana Vereine*, but that didn't necessarily mean anything; there was so much traffic in the system the chances were high that at any given time there would be such a coincidence.

<Any sign of the ftl drones?> she asked.

Two green circles winked around objects in the display. Neither was following them.

<I'm assuming they work by sending information through hyperspace to and from the *Phlegethon*.>

<That would be a reasonable assumption,> the Box said.

<You've seen technology like this before?>

<No, Morgan, but I am aware that it exists. There are many ways to communicate.>

<Does the Crescend use technology like this?>

<No.>

The simple response held a wealth of meaning. *No*, because the Crescend had far surpassed such simple beginnings. *No*, the Box wouldn't tell her any more if she asked. She tried to imagine what sort of communications a being thousands of years old and comprised of many millions of mundane Human minds would use. Instantaneous? She wasn't prepared to rule anything out. . . .

<Does the Crescend know you're still alive?> she asked.

<Yes.>

<Have you communicated with him?>

<After a fashion. We do not exchange information in the way mundane Humans do. It is more complicated than that.>

<Could you communicate with him now if you needed to? Could you ask him something?>

<Yes.>

<So you have access to the High Human's communications systems?>

<Some. For the most part, I am restricted to the means of communication you have at your disposal—namely those of the *Ana Vereine*.>

She thought for a few seconds before responding. <Would you be offended if I chose not to believe you?>

<Not at all,> the AI replied evenly. <Although I would stress that I have no reason to lie.>

She could think of plenty of reasons why the Box might not want that information freely disseminated. <Would you ask the Crescend a question for me?>

<If you wished it.>

<Would he answer?>

<I am in no position to speak for him, Morgan.>

<But you wouldn't rule it out?>

<No. He might.>

She nodded. <What you're saying, then, is that we could have contact with the High Humans at any time we want—or one of them, at least.>

<Potentially, yes.>

The admission didn't make her smile. <In other words, you made me lie to the council.>

\<You didn't lie, Morgan, because you didn't know the truth.\>

\<That's splitting hairs, Box, and you know it. Why don't you want the council to talk to the Crescend?\>

\<Because the Crescend has no desire to talk to them.\>

\<But *why*?\>

\<Because he doesn't believe that the council is relevant to the solution of this situation.\>

\<But they're the biggest force in the system. If *they* can't . . .\> She stopped, feeling cold at the thought. If the council, with the united forces of the four hundred plus Pristine nations behind it, couldn't fight back—who could?

The answer came to her almost immediately.

\<The High Humans,\> she said. \<The High Humans could wipe out the enemy any time they wanted, couldn't they?\>

\<It's not that simple, Morgan.\>

\<No? They have so much more experience, and their technology is better; there must be thousands, maybe *millions* of them—\>

\<*It is not that simple, Morgan.*\> the Box stressed.

There was a harsher tone to the Box's voice, but that didn't stop her. \<Why not?\>

\<You are extrapolating wildly. The High Humans are not super-Human. They too need to know *who* they are attacking. When the enemy as an individual looks like any other Pristine Human and as a group has become enmeshed in many Pristine governments, will any amount of higher thought or technology prevail?\>

She wasn't satisfied with this answer. \<So why can't they at least *talk* to the council?\>

\<Because the risks outweigh the benefits, Morgan. If the council has no contact with High Humans, the enemy will not know for certain that the High Humans are involved. Uncertainty may lead to indecision; indecision may lead to tactical error.\>

\<But how *are* the High Humans involved? As far as I know, you're the only evidence that they're showing the slightest interest, and even then, you're just a go-between.\>

\<Trust me, Morgan,\> said the Box earnestly. \<I am much more than that.\>

\<Then what are you? Why are you here, and who sent you? Is it just the Crescend, or are there more of them? And if they ever work out how to find the enemy, will we be able to rely on them to help?\>

The Box hesitated, then said: <I cannot answer these questions, Morgan.>

<You're saying you don't trust me?>

<I am saying that you are Human,> said the Box. <Nothing more.>

<*You* are saying that, or the Crescend?>

There was another slight pause. <I am in communication with my maker, yes.>

<He's listening right now?>

<In a manner of speaking, yes.>

That stopped her. The High Human was eavesdropping on them; the being that had grafted the Box to her very cells and sent her headlong through the galaxy was actually paying attention to what she said! The thought was unnerving. Nevertheless, she had the ear of someone a million times more evolved than she was; she knew she should use the opportunity while she had it.

Only one question concerned her at that moment.

<Does he actually care, Box?>

<What do you mean, Morgan?>

<Does he care what happens to us lesser Humans?>

<I would not be here if he didn't,> said the Box.

They had come full circle: the Box was proof that at least one High Human was interested in what happened on mundane levels—was, perhaps, even concerned—but beyond that refused to say anything at all. He had access to technology undreamed of, but wouldn't allow them to use it. He could step in at any time and be of great help in the struggle to understand and repel the enemy, but he did not. He preferred lurking in the shadows. . . .

Roche saw no point in pursuing the matter for the moment. She had more immediate things to worry about. Things she could actually do something about—or at least feel like she was doing something.

Once again, as the *Ana Vereine* powered its way across the solar system, Roche suspected that they were being followed. Not overtly; two ships hung back a long way and changed their trajectory several times, presumably in an attempt to allay suspicion by diverting attention away from their true activities. But their signature always reappeared on the navigation chart, and there was no doubt in Roche's mind why: they were in pursuit of the *Ana Vereine*.

They could have been Ulterior drones or ships making sure

she was doing the right thing; they could have been completely
unrelated to her situation in the system—security probes or free-
booter scouts, establishing the ship's status as either threat or opportunity. Regardless, Roche's first thought was to shake them,
but the difficulty of doing so outweighed the benefits; evasive
maneuvers were less effective at high velocities, and any change
in course at all would mean recalculating their orbit around the
sun. No large feat, but it would mean waking Kajic.

Her best chance of losing them would come when they reached
a relative halt at Perdue Habitat. That was just under a day's
travel. Until then she would simply have to try to ignore them,
and take action only if either ship made a hostile move.

<If I fall asleep,> she said to the Box, <make sure you keep
an eye on things, okay?>

<Of course,> the AI said. <And I will doctor the surveillance
records to show that you were awake. Kajic will never know.>

<And Cane?>

<He is in another section of the ship, exercising.>

Roche frowned. <Have you ever seen him sleep?>

<He has infrequently and briefly entered states that are sleep-
like, but that is all.> The Box's voice was soft in her mind, soothing. <I will ensure he does not intrude. If he were to find you
asleep—>

<He'd suspect something is up. I know.> She commanded her
first officer's chair to unfold, allowing her to recline more comfortably. Remembering everything Nemeth had said about the importance of finding the enemy, she asked one last question:

<You recognized Cane, and you knew Jelena Heidik's name.
Would you be capable of recognizing another clone warrior if
you came across one?>

<It is possible,> the Box said. <Either by name or face, if
neither had changed. However, I suspect that given time and opportunity, both would change to reflect the environment the clone
warrior is trying to infiltrate. Remember, Morgan, that both Heidik and Cane were recent awakeners; and remember also just
how effectively Heidik disguised herself as an outrigger.>

Roche nodded. <There has to be another way, then.>

<You may be right,> said the Box without conviction.

<You don't sound too confident, Box,> she said.

<I'm not, Morgan.>

The blunt and frank response surprised Roche. She had grown

accustomed to the AI's self-assurance, and despite feeling a certain trepidation at times, had come to take comfort in the idea that she could rely on the Box. To hear its uncertainty now was somewhat unsettling.

<Hey, who knows?> she said lightly, trying to reassure herself as much as the Box. <Maybe things won't be as bad as we imagine.>

<Maybe,> agreed the Box. <But I fear they will get much worse before they get better.>

6

Whether the Box's prediction had been specific to their journey or not, it turned out to be correct. Three hours after falling dreamlessly asleep, Roche woke to the sound of alarms: a Kesh interceptor was moving in to attack. The alarms brought the rest of the crew to the bridge, where Roche, still shaking off sleep, co-ordinated their response.

"How the hell did they find out who we were?" she muttered to no one in particular.

The interceptor—not one of the two ships she'd had her eye on earlier—was determined. Its relentless assault ended only when Defender-of-Harmony Vri dispatched it with a sustained blast from his A-P cannon. Before they could even begin to work out what to do next, an entire Kesh squadron slow-jumped to their location and opened fire.

"I have no idea," said Haid, operating the weapons systems with Cane as fast as he could. "But they want us *real* bad."

Roche glanced up from where she and Kajic were plotting evasion tactics and escape routes. "It's only one squadron," she said encouragingly.

"One could be enough," said Haid. "And to jump like that, at a moment's notice—they must've been waiting for the word. This didn't happen on a whim, Morgan."

Roche returned to the task at hand without agreeing or disagreeing. The sound of incoming weapons-fire was distraction enough without trying to have a conversation at the same time.

<They want revenge,> said Maii, lifting the information from the minds of their attackers. <Their war with the Olmahoi is going badly, and they blame us for getting them into it.>

"I can see why they'd miss the *Sebettu* at a time like this," Haid said. "Which they probably blame us for too."

"Forget the small talk, Ameidio," said Roche. "Stay focused! Maii, how did they find us so *easily*?"

<They weren't looking for us,> the reave explained. <Since we left the *Phlegethon*, they have been looking for Vri's vessel. He wasn't camouflaged. They simply deduced that any ship like his with a companion vessel was likely to be the target they were seeking.>

Roche cursed Nemeth's insistence that they take an escort— and herself for allowing this chink in their armor. "How's Vri doing out there, anyway?"

"Exceptionally well, actually," admitted Haid. "There are only six ships left. If I were them, I would've called off the attack long ago."

"They won't do that," said Cane. "Theirs is a suicide mission: it's a matter of win or die."

Roche didn't need him to tell her that. The Kesh pilots were fighting for their lives in the truest sense of the expression. Failure was not an option.

"Well, I hope they've made their peace with Asha," said Haid. "Because the way Vri's going out there, they'll be meeting her pretty soon."

"Kajic," said Roche. "Tell Vri to dock when this is over. I want him in *close* from now on, under our camouflage. He's going to be one hell of an inconvenience if he keeps on giving us away like this."

"Yes, Morgan," said Kajic.

"And Maii," Roche went on, "can you determine *who's* been leaking information to them?"

<Their orders came from superior officers. Beyond that, they know nothing.>

Roche cursed again, although the news wasn't all bad. Someone had set them up, yes—but that someone had only known who they'd be traveling with, not *where* they were headed. This at least put to rest her fears of an ambush at Perdue.

Nevertheless, it was frustrating. Word about her was obviously continuing to spread. The only time she'd been left alone since arriving at the system was while under the protection of the council. She wondered if the superior camouflage technology of the Skehan Heterodox alone was sufficient to explain that brief lull.

Cane exploited weaknesses in the engineering of three of the Kesh fighters, to cripple rather than destroy them. The remaining three were taken out by Haid and Vri with less compassion, or less skill. Roche plotted a high-energy course away from the area, which Kajic set off upon the moment Vri's ship was safely enclosed within the *Ana Vereine*'s camouflage field. Disguised as an innocuous freighter, they accelerated rapidly toward the sun.

"Our route takes us through or near several densely occupied regions—regions we know next to nothing about," Kajic warned. "We're battered but by no means unable to fight. However, I am going to require some time to do repairs."

"I understand," said Roche. "Vri, do you know anything about where we're going?"

"No." The Surin's stolid mien was unchanged by the battle. Despite being docked to the *Ana Vereine*, he remained locked in his ship, ready for anything. "I suspect that no matter where we go we will enter regions in which the risk of conflict is high. Such is the nature of this environment."

"All we can do, then, is keep our guard up." The two ships that had followed them from the *Phlegethon* seemed to have wandered off, but that didn't reassure her. If someone was still watching the *Ana Vereine*, their new attempt at camouflage wouldn't fool them, and neither would the change of course. And chances were that the Kesh probably weren't the only people who had known about the Surin escort.

Despite that, when they ran afoul of a minefield an hour later, then triggered a security alert two hours after that, the occurrences seemed unconnected to their mission. They were random incidents exacerbated by the tension and uncertainty in the system. As they traveled closer to the sun, then past it, the density of ships, and therefore the possibility of conflict, increased. Their sheer velocity was considered by some a serious threat, especially with so much debris already filling the system. They spotted two hulks in close orbit to the sun—strange spindly things that looked as though they'd been tied in knots. Roche couldn't tell how they'd been scuttled; she couldn't even imagine how they'd looked before being damaged.

They passed beyond the innermost regions and reached the domain of the ring. Ships seemed to avoid the dust-filled area, choosing orbits that arced out of the ecliptic or never crossed its aegis. Apart from the ablative effect of the dust on shields and hulls, Roche could see no good reason to take such dramatic steps, yet she did the same. There may have been a reason of which she was not yet aware.

The ring itself didn't look like much by visible light. Viewed in artificial colors revealing frequencies in the infrared and ultraviolet, and shown in rapid motion so that all the observations Kajic had made since their arrival in the system roughly two days before lasted only a fleeting minute, strange patterns swirled through the dust like standing waves in a torus made of water. What this meant, if anything, Roche didn't know, but it did give her something to look at apart from the endless parade of other vessels. Compared to Palasian System, Sol had very little to offer in the way of natural spectacles.

Beyond the ring, their velocity decreased. The number of ships in the region surrounding them decreased also, until they reached a distance from the sun similar to that maintained by the *Phlegethon*. Roche recalled how crowded it had seemed when they arrived; now it felt like a vacuum.

As a result, she was forced to concede the possibility that their close pass by the sun might have shaken off any pursuit. Fifteen hours into their voyage, and feeling the effects of another long, stress-filled stint on the bridge, she decided it was safe enough to call another break. Kajic, not knowing that she'd had little sleep while the Box kept watch, insisted that she retire to her cabin—or at least get something to eat.

The latter she couldn't argue with. Leaving the ship in Kajic's capable hands, she went to the mess and ate as much of a standard meal as she could stomach. Then, anxious about what lay ahead, she went to her cabin.

The whirring of thousands of electric scalpels disturbed her rest. Tiny machines, ranging in size from a pinhead to her thumbnail, were drilling somewhere nearby. They burrowed. They buzzed. The noise was maddening.

It seemed to be coming from inside her mattress, or possibly from under the bed. She got up and turned on the light to look, but there was nothing there. Nevertheless, the sound continued—but behind her now. She turned. The room was empty. Still the noise persisted, growing louder—whining, sawing, grating.

Then something tickled her ear. She flicked it away in irritation: a black speck, like a bug. Another ran down the back of her neck. She flicked it away too, and felt more. She shook her head violently as a sense of unease rushed through her.

The noise became louder. It was coming from behind her head.

In the mirror, she saw dozens of minuscule machines crawling through her stubbled hair, the area blurred and hazy from the frenetic movements of their razor-sharp mandibles. She brushed them away in fright, but others quickly took their place. She couldn't get rid of all of them; there were just too many.

With a growing sense of horror, she turned her head to one side to see the hole in the back of her skull, where hair, skin, fat, and bone had been carefully cut away, allowing the tide of machines egress from where they lived *inside* her. . . .

She woke with a start to the buzzing of her alarm.

Sitting up, she ran a hand across her scalp and tried to gather her thoughts. Her first concern was for the ship. A quick check of her implants showed that she had been asleep for almost five hours—the longest she could recall sleeping for ages. Presumably nothing dramatic had happened, or else she would have been awakened, but she'd be surprised if nothing had happened at all.

"Box?" She swung her legs out of bed and thought about standing. She needed a shower and a change of clothes. All she could smell was the sweat the nightmare had left on her skin.

"Box?" she said again. "Why the hell aren't you talking to me?"

<Because I was destroyed in Palasian System,> it said into her mind. <Remember?>

<Damn!> She cursed her stupidity. It was just fortunate that she hadn't made the mistake of speaking out loud to the Box with the others present. <I totally forgot.>

<You have to be careful, Morgan.>

She ignored the reprimand and headed off for the showers. <Any dramas while I was out?> she asked.

<Nothing of any consequence,> the Box replied. <We will arrive at Perdue Habitat shortly. Population eleven thousand, plus or minus a few hundred passers-through. Our IEPC clearance has taken us this far, but Haid suspects we'll be challenged once we're in range of their cannon.>

<Cannon?> A wave of hot water hit her skin. <What sort of habitat is it?>

<Ex-military. It's seen some service in the past, by the look of it, although it's not what you'd call serviceable now.>

<Who runs Perdue?>

<That has yet to be determined,> the AI said. <Kajic has spoken to three different people so far, each claiming to be the representative of the local powers-that-be. They don't seem to be exchanging information. I suspect Perdue may be in conflict with one of its neighboring habitats. The transmissions we are receiving could be coming from more than one source in the command chain.>

Roche exhaled heavily, and breathed in steam. <I assume Nemeth gave us *some* information on who to contact. A name, at least?>

<He did give us a name, yes: Atul Ansourian, the self-styled *éminence grise* to the Administer of this habitat and, by default, of the region. The Ulterior had come to some sort of arrangement with him, I gather, in which he traded resources for assistance when or if it was required. He was the one who was to have provided access visas and such support as we would require to carry out our mission.>

<*Was* to have provided?> said Roche. <Why past tense?>

<Because he is dead,> said the Box. <He was murdered yesterday.>

<About the same time we left the *Phlegethon*,> she mused.

<It would seem so,> it said.

<Do you think it's a coincidence?>

<I couldn't say, Morgan.>

She savored the last few moments of the shower. <*Éminence grise*, you said.>

<Yes. His rank was only adviser, but he wielded the real power. From isolation, apparently; according to the files he was something of a recluse.>

<It's a shame the two of you never got the chance to meet,>

she said, stepping from the cubicle. <You would have gotten along well.>

<Do I detect a hint of sarcasm, Morgan?>

Ignoring the remark, she began to dry herself. <So, let me guess,> she went on. <The murderer is still at large, identity unknown?>

<Far from it. She is in custody in Perdue Habitat and has already pleaded guilty to the crime.>

<Really?> said Roche. <Things aren't normally so cut and dried.>

<Indeed, Morgan,> said the Box. <There are several legal and ethical problems dogging the case. Although having said that, no one really expects her to escape the death penalty in the end.>

<What sort of ethical problems do you mean?>

<It appears that the girl is Ansourian's daughter.>

Roche wondered if any of this would prove relevant, but noted it anyway. <How do you know all this, Box?>

<I took the liberty of infiltrating the habitat's news services when we were first contacted. Once I had the correct frequencies, it wasn't difficult.>

Roche nodded thoughtfully as she finished toweling herself down. <Tell me about this Perdue Habitat, then,> she said, slipping into a simple, unadorned uniform. <Is it segregated or open?>

<The dominant Caste is called the Vax, but they allow free movement from the other two main habitats. Tocharia 13 is occupied solely by members of the Zissis Caste; Random Valence is an open space designed for trade. I would opt for the latter if I had the choice of destination, but there's no denying that Perdue Habitat has the influence over the region, and is therefore the main congregating point.>

<How long until we're ready to dock?>

<One hour. Cannon will come to bear, if Haid is right, in ten minutes.>

<Guess I'd better get moving, then.>

She took one last chance to be still, standing in the middle of the room and breathing deeply three times. Then, rubbing vaguely at the back of her head, she set off for the bridge.

"As I said, I don't *care* who you say you are," said the figure on the main screen. "You have *no* papers we recognize, *no* jurisdiction over us, and, as far as I can tell, no reason to even *be* here. Therefore, we have no reason to let you dock. So unless you change your orbit and move away, I will assume your intentions to be hostile and be forced to take appropriate action."

"And I've told *you*," Roche said. "We had private business with Atul Ansourian. He was supposed to meet us here!"

"I'm not stupid, Roche," said the official, his bald, yellowish scalp crinkling as he spoke. "Your ship is camouflaged, and you won't tell us what your business with Atul was. Yes, we've heard of you, but not through him. He never mentioned you at all."

"There has to be someone else there we can talk to, surely?" snapped Roche.

The man sighed tiredly. "I can pass your query through to the administer if I really have to, but I don't think it'll do you any good."

"I don't care what you think," Roche said. "Just get her on the line! I'd rather talk to her than waste my time with you."

The line closed without another word from the man. Roche vented her frustration by thumping the station in front of her.

"Maybe we should just try bribing him," said Haid.

"On an open line?" She shook her head. "That'd just give them another excuse to turn us away."

"And if they turn us away, anyway?"

She looked over at Haid and forced a smile. "*Then* we might give it a try," she said.

Five minutes later, the line opened again to reveal another yellow-skinned, bald male. Except that his face was rounder and his eyes more deeply set than the previous official, Roche would have had trouble distinguishing between them.

"I am Dockmaster Rench," he said, his voice smooth. "I apologize for the misunderstanding. Dock 14-B will be cleared for your approach—with the proviso that you drop your camouflage and declare your crew. Should you fail to comply with these conditions, access to this habitat *will* be denied."

"Agreed." Roche's response was immediate; she had little choice. She instructed Kajic to reveal the *Ana Vereine* and Vri's ship to the habitat; then she named each of her companions in turn. "Is that sufficient, Rench?"

The dockmaster studied something off-screen. "I don't recognize your configuration. Somewhere local?"

"Dato Bloc, a Commonwealth of Empires splinter government." She figured it didn't hurt to be open about some things.

He nodded. "Looking a bit rough around the edges for something clearly so new."

"We've seen some action," she admitted.

"Who hasn't?" He half smiled. "Prepare to dock, Roche. I'll have someone meet you down there."

Kajic followed navigation buoys into the crowded docks. Numerous ships of various types occupied most of the available gantries; some seemed to be undergoing repairs while others were idle, perhaps loading or unloading cargo and passengers. Most of them were support craft for the various military forces massing in the system. Roche recognized a COE Armada cruiser among them, although the name painted on its side—*Paraselene*—didn't ring a bell.

With a clang, the *Ana Vereine* docked with the massive structure. Shaped like a mutated sea anemone, the former military station had sprouted numerous access tubes and containers, crossing and recrossing, branching and rebranching away from a barely glimpsed central section. Its asymmetry reminded Roche of a coral, yet its angular edges and corners made her think of crystal deposits.

Outfitted with side arms and hazard suits, Roche and Maii stepped from their ship into the dock's grease-smelling antechamber. The entire area rang to the sound of metal striking metal, over the rumble of a thousand voices speaking at once. There was a striking contrast between the habitat and the vast empty spaces of the *Phlegethon*. It seemed to be full of crates, machines, and people of all shapes and sizes. None of it looked familiar to Roche, used to the homogeneity spread by the Eckandi Trade Axis.

From among the bustle, a woman stepped forward to greet them. Short and muscular, wearing a purple uniform with black trim and a close-fitting cap, she had the same yellowish tinge to her skin as the other two officials Roche had spoken to. She assumed that they were all members of the Caste the Box had mentioned to her earlier: the Vax.

"Hello," said the woman. Her voice was brisk but not unfriendly, and raised slightly to be heard above the clamor of the other voices around them. "I am Overseer Pacecca. Dockmaster Rench sent me to welcome you."

Roche introduced herself and Maii. Pacecca eyed the girl's blank visor for a second, then asked: "Your friend is blind?"

"Yes." That seemed the simplest answer. "Her suit's navigation systems are linked to mine; she won't get in the way."

"Very well." Pacecca looked around her, as though realizing for the first time just how busy it was. "Perhaps we should go elsewhere to discuss why you're here."

"I'd prefer to talk to the administer," said Roche.

"There isn't much chance of that, I'm afraid," said Pacecca. "She has taken the loss of Atul Ansourian very badly. You probably won't get to see her for a while, when things settle down."

The implication that the habitat failed to run without Atul Ansourian around backed up everything the Box had said. "Nevertheless, I'd like to try."

Pacecca looked at her evenly, patiently. "Very well. I shall see what I can do. My assistant—" The overseer looked around irritably. "Quare!" she barked.

A man stepped forward from the crowd, dressed in a uniform similar to Pacecca's, but green with gray trim. He looked like any number of faceless, middle-management lackeys Roche had seen over the years—slightly overweight, balding and stooped, yet with eyes that watched everything, keen to find an advantage.

"Yes, Overseer?" he said softly.

"This is Quare," Pacecca said to Roche. "He will take you somewhere quieter." She paused thoughtfully, as if considering her options.

"Perhaps Stateroom B?" the little man suggested.

She scowled at him. "Remember your station, Quare," she warned disdainfully. "However," she continued, turning her back to him, "Stateroom B *will* be fine."

"Yes, Overseer," said Quare, his head lowered.

Pacecca nodded, then faced Roche once more. "I'm sorry if we're not more hospitable," she said, distracted by something happening on the other side of the dock. "But what with the murder and the trouble with Guidon . . ." She shrugged helplessly. "Things have just been falling apart around here, I'm afraid. So, if you'll excuse me, I'll have to talk to you later."

Roche barely had time to nod before the woman was off. She didn't doubt that "later" meant "*much* later". . . .

<What was that she said they were having trouble with?> she asked the Box.

<Guidon,> said the Box. <A sibling-habitat that appears to have been recently destroyed. It seems that most of these people around you are refugees and survivors.>

Quare stepped forward. "This way, please."

Natural caution made Roche double-check: "Where did you say you were taking us?"

"Somewhere to wait," he said. "Away from all of this." He gestured at the chaos around them. His expression remained blandly pleasant, with a hint of indifference. "The overseer will report to the dockmaster, who will in turn report to his superior. Your request to speak to the administer will be forwarded to her in due course. I'm sure it won't take too long."

"How long, exactly?"

"No more than a couple of days, I'm sure," he said.

"A couple of *days*!"

He nodded. "Perhaps a little longer," he said. "If you'd care to follow me—"

"We don't have the time to sit around doing nothing while your precious administer decides whether or not to see us!" Roche was finding it difficult to keep her annoyance in check. "And even if we did, I'd do it on my own ship!"

"That is your decision, of course," he said. "We would not expect you to . . ." He stopped, suddenly turning his attention to Maii. "Why is your reave attempting to probe my mind?"

<Maii? What are you doing?>

<Trying to get in. He's blocking me.>

<How?>

<He has a very powerful, learned shield. I can't . . . quite . . . get through it—but I'm sure he can't keep it up forever!>

<Was Pacecca the same way?>

<Couldn't have been more different. She was as clear as glass.>

<Then he's hiding something.> Roche considered her options for a moment, then said: <Stop, for now, and we'll go with him. Try again later, but be more subtle if you can. I'd like to know why he can do it but Pacecca couldn't.>

Something in Quare's face relaxed. "Thank you," he said, to both of them. Then to Maii in particular: "Please do not try that again. It is considered by my people to be highly impolite." And to Roche: "Now, do you wish to return to your ship?"

"No, we'll come with you," she said. "For now, at least."

"Very well," said Quare, then turned and led them through the chaotic activity on the dock.

<Looks like we're wasting our time,> said Haid via her implants.

<Maybe.> Roche relayed what Maii had told her. <He might lead us somewhere.>

<And he might not. Maii can't even read him, Morgan. For all you know, he could be one of the enemy!>

<Now you're being overly suspicious,> Roche said, hoping Haid was wrong. <Why would the enemy clone someone who looks like him?>

<To fit in, of course,> he shot back. <I don't know. It's just frustrating to sit here and watch. Even if you do get past him, it doesn't sound like this administer is going to be much help.>

<But without her, we've no way of getting anything done.>

Quare took them through two large hangar doors, then along a corridor lined with a silvery metal. A hairpin bend brought them to another chamber, where it was at least quieter if still crowded. He waved them through some sort of security checkpoint, then took them deeper into the habitat.

<What exactly *do* you hope to get done?> Haid asked.

<Whatever Nemeth sent us here to do: spy, I guess. Look for the enemy. To do that, we need access to all areas and as much data as we can lay our hands on.> The Box would take charge of the latter, but she needed to put up a front for its behavior before she started producing conclusions based upon it. <With Ansourian gone, we don't really have anyone else to go to but this administer.>

<What about Ansourian's daughter?> said Haid. <She might know if he'd had anything planned for the Ulterior, should one of their agents come to town.>

<Yes, but I gather she's locked up somewhere. I doubt we'd get near her.>

Haid grunted his dissatisfaction with the situation. <One other thing I want to know is: what's the administer's name? The way they talk about her, she sounds like she's handling things pretty badly.>

<Her name is Inderdeep Jans,> said the Box to Roche. <It seems she inherited her position when her father, the previous administer of the habitat, died eight years ago.>

Roche couldn't pass that on without explaining where the information had come from. <Try hacking into the news channel,> she said. <Make yourself useful.>

Haid grunted again. <I'll see if I can find a map, for starters.>

<I have arranged the information so that it will be easy to access,> the Box whispered to Roche.

<Excellent.> To Haid she replied: <Let me know if you find anything unusual, Ameidio.>

She returned her attention to where they were going. The journey seemed to be taking a while, and had brought them to a relatively clean and quiet section of the habitat. White walls and ceiling and a gray floor made the area seem sterile, although the air smelled vaguely of Human sweat.

<I'm still not getting through,> said Maii. <But at least he's not sensing me probing at the moment.>

Roche remembered what Nemeth had said about using epsense to find a way past the enemy's natural camouflage—and Haid's half-serious suggestion that Quare might be a clone warrior. <Does his mind feel at all like Cane's?>

The girl sent a mental shrug. <There *is* something odd about him. I can use his senses, like I can with Cane when he lets me. But he doesn't *feel* like Cane. Then again, apart from Cane, I've never really studied another clone warrior, so who's to say they'll all be exactly like him?>

<What about the business of the black speck?>

<That was just the *irikeii*'s impression. He saw much deeper into things than I can. I can't see that speck in Cane at all.>

Roche mulled this over. <So although you don't think Quare is a clone warrior, you can't be certain, right?>

<That's right, Morgan.>

<Not very reassuring, Maii.>

<None of this is.>

Quare stopped at a door midway along the curving corridor they were following. He produced an old-fashioned key from his pocket and inserted it into a lock in the center of the door. It clicked open, and he gently pushed the door inward. It retreated a foot, then swung smoothly to one side, reminiscent of how some airlocks operated.

He took two steps inside, then gestured ahead of him. "Stateroom B," he said. "You will be comfortable here."

"Not if I have to wait two days, I won't be."

He didn't smile. "We shall see," he said, then urged them inside: "Please . . ."

Roche hesitated.

"I can stay with you if it will put your mind at ease," he said, seeing her apprehension.

"That's okay," said Roche. "Just leave us the key, and we should be fine."

"I'm afraid I can't do that," he said. "Besides which, it is ineffective from the inside anyway."

"In that case," said Roche, "after *you*."

He shrugged easily and stepped all the way into Stateroom B, which consisted of three connected rooms. From the comfortably furnished antechamber, Roche could see a conference room, with what looked like a small kitchen or toilet facility beyond that. There was a stale smell about the place, as though the air vents hadn't been cleaned for a while.

<No one here but us,> said Maii. <That much I can tell.>

Deciding that they could deal with him if he tried anything, Roche stepped into the antechamber with Maii right behind her.

"Would you like refreshments while you wait?" Quare asked. "A drink, perhaps?"

"No, I'm fine." Maii also declined.

"Then perhaps you would like to rest your feet."

Roche glanced around at the soft-cushioned chairs in the room, the legs so slender and graceful they looked as though they couldn't take so much as the weight of Maii's undersized hazard suit.

She laughed. "No, I really don't think—"

Movement out the corner of Roche's eye startled her: the door was sliding shut.

"Security," said Quare, catching her alarm. "We could not guarantee your safety if just anyone could get in."

"Nor the habitat's if we were to get out, right?" said Roche cynically.

The little man smiled briefly, but it didn't touch his eyes. The door clicked shut. "Now, about that seat . . ."

"It's not necessary," said Roche stepping over to the door to check it.

"We have something more practical through here," Quare said, waving them farther into the suite. "Come with me, please."

<Morgan!> Maii's sudden interjection was loud in Roche's mind. <The ship has lost contact with our telemetry feeds!>

<What?> Roche slid her helmet closed and studied its instruments. Sure enough, it hadn't received a return signal from the ship for almost half a minute. But Maii wouldn't have seen that: she must have learned from someone else.

<Uri?> she called. <Ameidio?>

There was no answer.

<I'm telling them we're okay,> Maii said, <but they don't know what to do.>

Angry, Roche drew her side arm and followed Quare into the conference room, where she grabbed him roughly by the shoulder and spun him around.

"What the hell is going on?" she demanded. "Why have we been cut off from our ship?"

He stared at her helmeted visage, visibly startled. "I don't understand—"

She wasn't in the mood for denials. "Just open that damned door now," she said. "We're leaving." When he hesitated, she snapped, *"Now!"*

He drew himself up in her gauntleted grasp. "No."

She pushed the pistol into his cheek: *"Yes."*

He flinched but didn't relent.

<Haid wants to know if you need reinforcements,> said Maii.

<Tell him . . .> Roche thought for a second. <Tell him to be ready just in case.>

"You won't be harmed," Quare was saying. "I promise you. This *isn't* a trap."

"You've locked us in here!" Roche said, her voice rising with her anger. "You've severed our communications with my ship! What would *you* call it?"

"An opportunity," he said, wincing as the pistol dug deeper into his cheek. "An opportunity to talk."

"I've got nothing to talk to you about. Let us out of here."

"Look, you can see I'm unarmed. Can't you at least put your weapon down? Please?"

"How do I know there aren't troops waiting just outside?"

"You don't," he said. "But I assure you there aren't."

Roche snorted derisively. "What the hell do I care about your assurances?"

"Don't be stupid, Roche," the man snapped. "Think about it! The administer wouldn't waste her time on a stunt like that."

"But *you* might," said Roche.

"I might consider it, yes," he said. "If I was truly desperate. But I'm not. Not yet, anyway. So again I ask you, please *hear me out.* If you've been cut off from your ship, then that only proves that I've done the right thing by bringing you here."

This took Roche aback. "What? Why?"

"This is a secure area," he said. "Electronically speaking, no one can get in or out. Once the door is shut, we're sealed in."

"And why is *that* so important?"

He stared at her then with a look that could not possibly be misinterpreted: it was desperation.

"Because my real name is Atul Ansourian," he said. "I need your help. Without it, my daughter—and maybe everyone else on this habitat—will die."

7

Perdue Habitat
955.1.32
0150

Roche held on to the little man for a while longer, searching his eyes for some sign of a lie. When she failed to find it, she let him go, saying, feebly: "But you're *dead*!"

"A necessary ruse, I'm afraid," he apologized. "I needed to disappear in order to survive. If I hadn't done that, the chances are I really would be dead right now."

"But Pacecca—"

"Doesn't know anything," he said, cutting her short. "To her I'm just another faceless drone to boss around. And that's what I want her to think. Her mind is weak. I couldn't trust the likes of her with the truth; she'd be too easily read."

Roche remembered how Maii had described the woman's transparency. Quare—no, *Ansourian*, if he was to be believed—was making sense in this respect, at least.

"How do I know you're telling me the truth?" she said.

"I'm not asking you to trust me," he said. "All I ask is that you hear me out."

"Why?" said Roche.

"Because I think we can help each other," he said. "At most I've only got another day or so before the truth comes out. And once that happens, there is every chance that *both* my daughter and I will wind up dead."

Roche was curious despite herself. "But if your daughter's going to die for killing you, why not confess to the truth so she'll be set free?"

"It's not that simple." Ansourian stepped over to the conference table and sat in one of the chairs. "Please," he said, gesturing to the chairs opposite him.

Roche glanced at Maii. The girl was still, concentrating.

<Maii?>

<I'm still not getting anything from him,> she said. <But there's definitely nobody waiting for us outside, Morgan. It seems that no one is too concerned about us being here.>

<Okay. Tell the others to sit tight. I want to find out what the hell is going on here.>

Roche took a seat at the wide wooden table opposite Ansourian. The roomy, low-backed chair creaked beneath her weight, but held. Maii positioned herself a couple of seats down.

"You've no doubt heard the official story," said Ansourian.

"That your daughter killed you a couple of nights ago and then turned herself in?" said Roche. "Yes, we had heard something."

Ansourian nodded, his expression earnest. "It's an open and shut case," he said. "Security has a body and a killer, with no evidence to suggest anything out of the ordinary. But for the fact that my daughter will almost certainly be charged with patricide if I maintain the fiction of my death, I would be content to let the situation rest. But obviously I cannot do this. In the next day or so the deception will be exposed, and my daughter will be forced to reveal the truth."

Roche was still wondering what she had to do with this. "And then what?"

Ansourian shrugged. "There is no legal precedent for this situation," he said. "Understand that we follow reproductive customs that are regarded as unusual by many Castes. The Vax do not have two parents as most do; we have just the one, who creates a child by combining his or her own genetic code with another's, sometimes chosen at random. The child, always the opposite gender of the parent, is gestated artificially, then released to its parent—and that parent is the sole caregiver for that child. But just as we have only one parent, so do we have only the one child. Perhaps you can appreciate that the bond between father and daughter or mother and son is *very* strong."

"So the murder of one by the other," said Roche, "would be considered one of the worst crimes imaginable."

"The most heinous of crimes," he said. "Punishable by death. It doesn't matter if the child is murdered or the parent, the consequences are the same: *two* lives are ultimately lost—and along with them is lost a long line of descent."

Roche could understand what he was saying, but she still didn't see the relevance of it all to herself.

"You say security has a body," Roche broke in. "Did you clone yourself and kill the clone?"

The look of surprise and disgust was genuine. "No, of course not!" he said. Then, seeing Roche's confusion, Ansourian took a deep breath and continued slowly. "Please understand that this is very difficult for me. Under normal circumstances, I am very much a recluse; I am uncomfortable with face-to-face contact. Only one person is allowed into my chamber and knows my face—and that is my daughter, Alta. Until two days ago, she shared my apartment in a high-security wing of the habitat not far from where the administer herself lives."

"Alta lived with you?"

"Yes, and would have until I died, with her son—should she have chosen to bear one, of course. But she is not as antisocial as I. Although she respects the lifestyle I have chosen, she does not feel the same need to remain isolated from the rest of the community. She works—or worked, I should say—in the Logistics Department, supervising the distribution of resources that pass through here to those who need it the most. Perhaps she was reckless in believing that the situation was not as dangerous as indicators suggested—and it does seem that my opinion on that score has been vindicated. But the fact remains that had she not gone out and returned when she did she would have died with me, or I would have died alone."

Roche listened closely. Again, the subtleties of Vax relationships escaped her. Did they take lovers from outside the family line, or was incest the norm? The question was irrelevant, yet it nagged at her just the same.

"Two nights ago," he went on, "Alta returned home late. When she came in to say good night, she found me asleep and another person in the room with me. This person, she says, was in the process of giving me a dose of poison that would have killed me in seconds and left no trace whatsoever." Ansourian stopped for a moment before going on. "Alta is a proficient fighter, Roche. Perhaps too proficient. She killed the assailant with little effort, but she did so before we could determine *who* he worked for."

"But did you at least find out who *he* was?"

Ansourian shook his head. "He carried no papers," he said, "nor did he have any DNA files in the habitat records. And I was not in a position to call security to find out, either. Disregarding the fact that I had already explored all the avenues they have open to them, my would-be killer had not broken into my rooms by force; he simply walked through my extensive security system as though it hadn't even existed. Someone *must* have shown him how to do that, and only a handful of people have access to that information."

"They're all high-up in the security chain, no doubt," Roche put in.

Ansourian leaned forward on the table, nodding. "I couldn't risk reporting the incident for fear of alerting whoever was responsible that they had failed."

"So you had to find a way to make the problem disappear, in other words," said Roche, wanting him to get to her relevance in this scenario.

He nodded again. "Smuggling the body out of the habitat was not an option, either," he said. "The moment I stepped out of my room, my enemy would have known something had gone wrong and would make sure security was watching every dock. And I couldn't keep the body in my rooms for any length of time for similar reasons. There seemed to be no avoiding the fact that I had survived by mistake; no matter which way I turned, that mistake looked likely to be rectified soon.

"The only way I could hope to find out what happened was to doctor habitat records to indicate that the body was mine, and convince whoever was responsible that I was dead. Under the cover of an alias I could watch to see what happened next: who would be looking to take over my position; who would advocate a speedy trial to see the matter closed quickly—"

"Basically," said Roche, "who would benefit the most from your death once the dust had settled on the whole unpleasant affair."

"Exactly," said Ansourian. "The most difficult problem to get around was the fact that Alta had left genetic evidence all over the body. But there was no avoiding that. We figured in the end that it would be best if she turned herself in and thereby forestalled a thorough inquiry. Her story wouldn't stand up under a detailed forensic examination, and no doubt my enemy is puzzled as to why my assassination didn't go quite as planned—it must have startled him to see Alta accused of the crime, especially if the assassin was supposed to report in, and has not—but I hope his acceptance of the situation will continue a little longer. While Alta is imprisoned, the thought that he might soon discover that the body is actually that of his assassin, and not mine, concerns me greatly."

"But surely he would be aware of that already?" Roche found this aspect of the story difficult to swallow. "I mean, didn't habitat files reveal a mismatch between your genetic profile and that of the body?"

Ansourian shook his head. "I had my own records removed a long time ago. It seemed a sensible precaution to take, especially for someone in my position. As far as preferring anonymity goes, doesn't it seem reasonable that the person who wielded the true power in this habitat should not seek recognition of any kind? The temptation to use it for personal gain would always be there. And the fact that I could walk the length of every corridor in this habitat and not be recognized by anyone but my daughter actually pleased me. As long as I could continue making the right decisions for Inderdeep to follow, *that* was the main thing."

"What about the administer?" Roche asked. "Doesn't she even know what you look like?"

"I couldn't take the chance." He shrugged. "I know this may seem paranoid to you, Roche, but if I *hadn't* taken such precautions, I might have died a long time ago. Everything I have feared appears to have come to pass. And now, I must find out who tried to kill me, and save my daughter."

Roche nodded her understanding. "This is where I come in, right?"

"I can't do this alone," he said soberly. "I need your help."

"Why do you think I should help you?" she asked. "It's not my brief to become involved in domestic politics."

"But you are," he insisted. "You are one of the Ulterior's

agents, and the Ulterior is dealing with a much larger enemy. Our goals may overlap."

"How?"

"A week ago, Guidon, one of Perdue's sibling-habitats, was destroyed."

"I heard about that on the way here," Roche half-lied. The Box had found the information en route, but hadn't told her until she arrived.

"No doubt," he said. "But what you wouldn't have heard is that Guidon Habitat was destroyed from within using security codes known only to a handful of people. Exactly *how* they were obtained remains a mystery, but I suspect that the enemy—*your* enemy—was involved. Perhaps he is my enemy too."

"Why?"

"Inderdeep tends toward a policy of indifference and non-intervention regarding the problems we left at home. It took a lot of convincing just to get her here. Ultimately, though, I wonder how much good we can do here, particularly now with Guidon destroyed—but I have always felt that it is important to at least try."

"So it was you who persuaded Inderdeep to come here?"

"Yes," he said. "And I've maintained a steady influence over her not to change her mind and return home. Maybe someone took offense at that, finally—this faceless man, pulling her strings so freely. Maybe that someone decided the war effort could do without me helping it along. But if that is the case, then this habitat has already been infiltrated, and we may all be close to the same fate that awaited those on Guidon."

"Let me get this straight," Roche said. "Someone in Guidon, working for the enemy, somehow managed to get the codes that led to its destruction, and now you believe this same person has turned up here on Perdue?"

"And is attempting to do the same thing again, yes," Ansourian said. "It would be easy to sneak on board right now. We're still collecting life-capsules from the wreckage of Guidon. In fact, we have inadvertently picked up a couple belonging to the enemy, but we disposed of them before they could open."

"You think someone in an ordinary capsule could have sneaked in unnoticed?"

"If they were carrying the right papers," said Ansourian, "there would be no cause to suspect anything. And once in, they could go about working their way up the chain of command. From there it would be a simple matter of working on Inderdeep to change her mind and go home. It would be an efficient way to get rid of the Vax."

"Efficient, yes, but that's not normally how they work," Roche said. "The more destruction and loss of life, the better for them—at least in my experience."

"Perhaps that is a generalization deserving examination," he countered. "The most destructive actions are the ones we see most clearly, and remember. There may be more subtle plots going on around us all the time."

<And remember Cane,> said Maii, privately.

"Perhaps," she said in response to both of them. "But I still don't know *how* you expect us to help. Your daughter's locked up somewhere. What do you want us to do? Break her out using brute force?"

"I'm not naive enough to think that would work—or that you would agree to such an action."

"What, then?"

"Your name precedes you, Morgan Roche. If my adversary hears that you have spoken to Inderdeep Jans, he may become anxious. If she can be reminded that the enemy may be whispering to her even now, she might take his advice less to heart. I may yet be able to come out of hiding in a way that will not place me or Alta in any more danger than we already are. I hope to use you, in other words, as a catalyst to change Inderdeep's mind."

Roche stared at him for a long time. He wanted to use her in much the same way the Ulterior and the Crescend both did: as a pawn in a personal power game. She wasn't sure she liked this role at all—but neither did she want to rule out the possibility that she could use it to her own advantage.

"You can get me to the administer?" she asked.

"I believe so, yes," he said. "I should be able to get you into her chambers without anyone knowing. You will have as much time alone with her as you need—as long as you can convince her to let you stay. You see, her chambers aren't monitored. Not even by me."

"And what's to stop her simply throwing us out?"

"She won't. She has heard of you, and I know her well enough to say that she will be curious."

"If that's so, then why would it take so long to get an *official* meeting with her?"

"Because the chances are she is unaware of your presence right now," said Ansourian. "Whoever is behind all of this is more than likely protecting her from you, making sure your request to meet her goes through official channels—which would ensure a delay of a couple of days, at least." Roche opened her mouth to object, but before she could speak, Ansourian jumped in with: "Believe me, Roche, this *is* the best option available to us at the moment."

Roche carefully considered what he was saying. "Okay, but once I've talked to her, then what?"

"That depends on how it turns out. If it goes as well as I hope it to go, there's a good chance I will reveal myself there and then in order to press home my case. If it goes badly, I will make other plans. I know of various flaws in security's prisoner-holding bays. I may still be able to set Alta free and find a way off the habitat."

Roche was under no illusions as to where she might fit into the latter part of such a plan. There was no way, though, that she intended to commit herself to anything but the most basic level of support for Ansourian—who was still, after all, a complete stranger whom she had little reason to trust.

<What do you think, Maii?>

<I think you should follow your instincts, Morgan,> the girl said. <I have little to go on, and would hate to mislead you.>

That was fair enough, Roche thought. She couldn't ask any member of her crew to give her advice when they didn't have enough information to decide; that was her job, after all.

Not that she thought of Maii as merely a crew member; she had become more than that in the previous weeks, especially after her capture and imprisonment by Linegar Rufo.

Roche had felt bad enough over that; she could only imagine what Ansourian had been feeling since his daughter's arrest.

"Okay," she said. "Let me talk to the administer and we'll see what happens. I can't guarantee you anything, but it's worth a try."

"Thank you." He smiled then. Surprisingly, it looked genuine. "Inderdeep will not be in her quarters for a couple of hours yet; I will endeavor to find out precisely how long. Also, Overseer

Pacecca will be expecting Quare back at some point and I don't want to needlessly arouse suspicion."

Roche nodded. "Can you give me some way to communicate with you?"

"I think it's best if you remain completely isolated in here," he said. "Even from your own ship." Seeing concern on her face, he added: "It really *is* the only way to be certain that you won't be discovered before time."

He seemed sincere, and his reasoning was sound, if a little overcautious. And she did have Maii, after all.

<Would you be able to find him if he leaves us here too long?> Roche asked the girl.

<Yes,> Maii said. <Or I could find someone else nearby and make them let us out.>

Roche nodded. The reave's power to influence those around her, not just read them, hadn't been necessary so far in Sol System. She hoped it wouldn't be necessary at all. At the very worst, though, Maii could force the administer to give them what they wanted.

"Okay," she told Ansourian. "I'll give you two hours. If we don't hear from you by then, the deal is off."

He nodded. "Don't worry," he said. "I'll be back before then."

They all stood, and he left the room. The door leading out of the suite hissed open, then clicked shut. There was no handle and no keyhole on the inside.

"I've got a bad feeling about this," Roche muttered to herself.

Maii slid her helmet back and sniffed the air. <Haid says that the inner defenses are fairly poor, now that we're past the perimeter cannon emplacements. He says he could probably blast his way in and get us out of here in under ten minutes.>

<Tell him he's being optimistic. It would take him at least fifteen.>

<He wants to know if that's a bet.>

<No, it's not.>

<He says: Then don't blame me if we arrive too late to save you.>

Roche smiled. <He would say that. He's probably just jealous he's not here himself.>

Maii didn't disagree.

• • • •

Time passed slowly. Roche hadn't realized how dependent she was on data from the *Ana Vereine*'s datapool to keep her occupied. The hazard suit's capabilities didn't include much in the way of sophisticated software. Even though the Box had access to vast amounts of data, she still didn't entirely trust the AI to give her what she wanted. There were too many ways it could exploit her ignorance.

<Do you believe what Ansourian is telling us?> she did ask it at one point.

<His story does match the data I have obtained through the news services—but that doesn't mean it is true. On the face of it, it is somewhat implausible. I do note, however, that Ansourian's security records have been skillfully tampered with, and that his relationship with his daughter has previously shown every sign of being exceedingly positive. If this is *not* Ansourian, then that leaves us with the original mystery: why did Alta Ansourian kill her father in such a brutal and apparently unprovoked way?>

<Not that it's any business of ours.>

<It is in the sense that it provides us with another reason to entertain this hypothesis a while longer.>

<Is that what all this is to you, Box: a hypothesis?>

<Naturally, Morgan. At present, all I *can* do is hypothesize.>

She gave up on that line of conversation. Talking to the Box for too long when it was bored could give anyone a headache. But she needed to do something, too, to stave off her own boredom. Sleep wasn't an option, and neither was eating; her stomach was too tense to make an easy meal of the concentrates stored in the hazard suit's compartments.

<Can you show me what's happening outside here?> she asked Maii.

<Sure,> said the girl. Her mind touched Roche's gently once, then again with more pressure. <Don't be alarmed, Morgan. I'm not going to take you over. I'm just going to give you a glimpse of how I see things.>

Roche forced herself to relax. After all, she had already done this a couple of times before—on Sciacca's World, before Maii had agreed not to go digging around in her mind. As on those occasions, when Maii touched a true sensory experience in someone else's head, that experience conveyed itself to Roche with the same vividness as if it had been her own. She could easily see how the girl survived on the senses of the people around her.

For a second, she seemed to see an echo of Maii, as she saw directly through her own eyes and *through her own eyes via Maii* simultaneously. But the effect was fleeting. Her own vision seemed to fold in on itself as Maii moved to another viewpoint.

They belonged to a woman who was performing repairs on an air filter somewhere along the corridor just outside the quarters they were in. Barely had Roche determined this when Maii skipped to another pair of eyes—these belonging to a courier on his way to deliver a package. A quick succession of viewpoints from various people followed as they moved ever deeper into the habitat, catching glimpses of people Roche didn't know doing things that didn't concern her. Maii never lingered for more than a few moments at a time; no sooner had they found an open mind than they were moving off in search of another. And none of the people seemed aware they had been touched by a reave, for Maii's mind was gentle and fleeting. But Roche knew that if provoked, the girl's butterfly touch could just as quickly become the sting of a wasp.

For a while, Roche forgot about Ansourian and their situation. As she and Maii danced across the minds of the habitat's populace, she became aware of another level situated beyond the sensory experiences she was receiving—or beneath it; it was difficult finding words to describe how she was feeling. Having never before gone along as the reave's willing passenger, she hadn't had the chance to appreciate the subtleties of what Maii did.

Each mind was separated by a moment of subtle dislocation, as old sights and sounds were replaced by new ones. In between, Roche felt Maii's mind searching, and for that split second she caught a glimpse of n-space—the theoretical realm in which the reave operated. It was like looking into the mind of a creature that used sound to echo-locate rather than sight to see. Maii was at the center of her universe, and the minds of everyone around her stood out like bumps on a flat plain—but in three dimensions. Some minds jutted out like peaks; others were no more than slight swellings on the surface. Roche understood intuitively that this impression bore no relation to the quality of the minds in the "real" world; they were no more or less intelligent, or epsense-adept, or Human for having odd-shape n-space contours. They were just different, in the same way that people's physical characteristics were different. Roche couldn't be sure from the brief glimpses, but every one seemed unique in its own way, like a signature or a fingerprint.

As they jumped from mind to mind, like someone circling an island on stepping stones, Roche became more and more intrigued by what she saw between the jumps. Eventually, she asked Maii to stop jumping entirely and show her the reave's world without any sensory input whatsoever.

It was wildly disorienting.

<I'm amazed you can see it at all,> Maii said. <In all the years Veden rode my mind, he never saw anything. And you've never shown any talent at epsense before.>

<Is this actually talent, though?> Roche wondered, not letting herself get her hopes up. Like most children in the COE, she had dreamed of epsense powers blossoming at puberty. The life of a trained reave was much better than average, orphan or not. To be in demand, to travel to different systems, to delve into minds for government or private business . . . Roche had dreamed but, also like most children, had never shown any promise.

<I guess not,> Maii admitted. <But I've never known anyone to be able to visualize n-space who wasn't able to access it too.>

<So I'm a freak?>

<A fluke, perhaps,> said Maii. <Sounds better.>

<Where's Ansourian?> Roche asked, curious to see a mind with a shield.

Maii guided her to the spot where the man's mind should have been. All Roche could see was a steep, circular lip, like the edge around a very deep crater. No matter how Maii tried, she couldn't get inside or even look over the wall.

<It's like a fortress,> Roche said. <This is fascinating, Maii. Keep going, please.>

Maii took her on a whirlwind tour of the habitat, showing her shielded and unshielded minds, minds with epsense powers and no epsense at all, minds that had been damaged by epsense attacks and minds that possessed strange outgrowths into n-space that the reave couldn't explain, except to say that she had seen their like before and that they didn't seem to serve any purpose. Roche tagged along for the ride, an eager student delighted to have discovered a new skill.

<Could this have anything to do with you?> she asked the Box, explaining briefly what she was experiencing.

<Impossible, Morgan. AIs, no matter how sophisticated, have never been able to master epsense to any degree.>

<Could the Crescend have knocked something out of whack when he was installing you?>

<Unlikely. I'm sure he knew what he was doing.>

<But—> Roche stopped, feeling a new pressure on her mind.

<Who are you talking to?> Maii asked.

Roche went cold. She hadn't thought that the link with the girl might expose the existence of the Box inside her.

She was unable to think of anything even remotely convincing. <No one,> she said lamely.

Roche felt a short, sharp probe penetrating deep inside her mind—then abruptly the girl was gone.

Roche rocked back into her chair, stunned by the girl's absence. The real world flooded her senses, dispelling the gray clarity of n-space.

<I'm sorry,> Maii said, reaching out and taking her hand, gripping it tightly through two layers of hazard suit glove. <I shouldn't have looked. But when I felt you talking to it . . .> A profound sense of remorse came with the words. <Oh, Morgan. I won't tell anyone—I promise!>

Roche didn't know what to do. Although the girl hadn't actually said it, there was no doubting that she now knew about the Box. That went against everything Roche and the Box had arranged; it could even jeopardize the Box's mission for the Crescend.

But it didn't *have* to be a problem. If Maii told no one, the secret stopped there—and unless Roche told the Box, it would never know either.

The simplest thing, she thought, might be to trust the girl.

<It's okay, Maii,> she said. <Keeping the Box a secret is only a precaution. As long as you don't tell anyone about it, it'll stay a secret until we're ready.>

The girl nodded. <But it's *inside* you!>

<Yes.> Roche couldn't put the girl's mind at ease on that score. <It's been inside me all along, Maii. I just didn't know. The valise was a backup, and a decoy.>

<You mean you dragged that thing from one end of the COE to the other for no reason?>

Maii's thoughts were tinged with an annoyance Roche could

relate to. But that was all history now; the present had given her a whole new set of problems to deal with.

<It doesn't matter anymore,> said Roche. There was a long stretch of silence which she ended with: <Are you okay about all of this, Maii?>

<Yes,> said Maii eventually. <Just . . . surprised, I guess.>

<I know,> said Roche. <But for now I don't want the others to know, okay? Even Ameidio.>

<I understand, Morgan,> said the girl. <And I am sorry for looking without—>

<There's no need to apologize,> Roche cut in quickly. Her attitude surprised even herself. A month ago when she had first met the girl, she would have been furious with what Maii had just done. But her time with the young Surin had tempered her hostility toward reaves—or at least toward this one.

<Shall we continue, Maii?> she said.

Maii hesitated for a second, then diffused once more into Roche's mind. This time they headed in a different direction, outward and away from their current location. As they traveled, the number of minds they passed slowly increased, then abruptly fell away to virtually nothing, until they were left facing just four anomalies in the n-space plain.

Three of them she wouldn't have recognized, but the fourth one she knew immediately. It was a sudden hole in n-space, as though someone had dropped a ball bearing made of neutronium onto a rubber sheet.

<That's Cane, isn't it?> she said.

Maii seemed momentarily taken aback. <How did you know that?>

<Just a hunch,> Roche said. <He looks so different from everyone else.>

<Different? How?>

Again Roche struggled for words. <He's not the way you describe him. I see him as empty and very deep—perhaps even bottomless.>

<Maybe you're seeing the hole the *irikeii* saw.>

<Or maybe I'm just imagining things.>

<Either way, it's strange.> Maii thought for a moment, then said: <From what you've said, I gather we don't see things the same way in n-space. You know how I saw Cane: like a complicated machine moving too quickly for me to grasp; to you,

he's a hole. It's the same with Ansourian: to me he's a slippery rubber egg, while you see him more like a cup. This isn't unusual; all people view n-space differently. And we do see *some* things the same way. Those odd outgrowths, for instance; I knew exactly what you were talking about when you mentioned them. And n-space itself; I also view it as a gray, smooth plain. So I wonder why the extreme examples should be so different?>

<It's what comes from being a freak, I guess,> said Roche. <Sorry, 'fluke.'>

<The *irikeii* called you an enigma,> Maii said thoughtfully. <It was curious about you. Maybe that means something.>

Roche nodded to herself, thinking: *An enigma* . . . <Do you think I could learn to do this on my own?> she asked.

<I doubt it. Your talent is reactive only. You can't see n-space on your own; a reave will always have to show it to you secondhand. Just like when we converse by epsense; it's not so much you talking as me hearing.>

<But why would I be able to see it at all?> Roche wondered, thinking aloud. <It seems a pointless talent to have.>

<Perhaps.> Maii drifted away for a second as she concentrated on something else. <Unless . . . Morgan, maybe now's not the right time to let you talk to Haid and Kajic. I'm taking you back to the habitat instead to have a proper look around. There are a lot of minds here, and you're new at this, so you're going to find this hard. But I'm going to sweep across as many as possible as quickly as possible. We won't be looking at individual minds, but rather at the landscape they create when combined— a bit like ignoring the trees in order to admire the forest. Let yourself drift with the flow, and let me know if you see anything at all that stands out.>

Roche did as the girl said, guessing immediately what she was after. If Roche could see one clone warrior so clearly, why not another? Ansourian had seemed so certain that there was another one on board the habitat. . . .

They swept rapidly over the population of the habitat. Minds blurred and merged into a strange landscape that dipped and fell around Roche. As she became accustomed to it, she started to find a sort of coherence to what she saw: there were few sudden dips or highs, as though minds that were alike tended to congregate even without being aware of it, or else individual minds were influenced by those around them. Only a few stood out, and then only because they were so tall among the others. She didn't know what that meant; possibly nothing. It wasn't what she was looking for, anyway.

She didn't know how much time passed before she saw something. Time seemed meaningless. Likewise, she had no idea where her mind might have been in the real world. . . .

<Wait!> she suddenly shouted. <I see one!>

Maii brought them to an immediate halt. <Where?>

<There.> Roche, unable to move of her own will, could only describe what she was seeing as best she could. <See that group of minds over there? A lot like Ansourian's all in a bunch? There are three in a line to one side. Next to them—yes, that one. It looks just like Cane.>

And it did. The same abrupt drop in n-space to a depth she could neither see nor imagine.

<This one?>

<Yes. And . . . Wait, pull back a bit—no, more . . .> Maii's mind roamed across the gray vista. <That knot of people. In there.>

<Another one?>

<Yes.> Roche's stomach fell at the sudden realization: there were two clone warriors on the habitat!

Maii seemed to be having trouble deciding which mind to look at. <I can't pin them down as well as you can, Morgan. Wait a second.> They headed back to the location of the first one. <No, I still can't see it. Here?>

<Close. Across a bit—yes! There.>

<And it's the same as Cane?>

<Exactly the same.>

<I can't imagine what else that could mean,> said Maii, <except that this person is a clone warrior.>

Roche's concern slipped back a notch as another realization hit home: <This is it, Maii! We can *find* them!>

<Maybe,> Maii said, jumping back to the place where Roche had spotted the second clone warrior. It had moved, and Roche had to keep giving Maii directions so they could keep up. <I can't enter this mind, Morgan, so we can't tell who it belongs to that way. Can *you* tell where this person is, precisely?>

<I, uh . . .> Roche realized then that it wouldn't be so easy. N-space bore little relation to the real universe, except in the broadest terms. She could tell that the clone warrior was one of

many in a group of people, and that that group of people was a
subset of the larger group that comprised the population of the
habitat. But beyond that . . .

<Hang on.> Maii let go of her for a moment. When she re-
turned a second or so later, she explained that she'd been exploring the scene more closely on her own. <Dragging you around
can be a strain if I move too quickly.>

<Sorry, Maii. I didn't realize.>

<No. This is interesting—and maybe important.> The girl
sounded alive in a way that Roche hadn't heard before; maybe
the thrill of guiding someone around on her own turf for a change
accounted for that. <It's hard to tell for sure,> she said, <but the
first mind you pointed out seems to be in an audience of some
kind. There are lots of important people nearby, most of them
with shields like Ansourian's. I touched a couple of ancillary staff
members who weren't as well protected. The audience *seems* to
be the one the administer is holding but I can't be absolutely
sure.>

<That would make sense,> Roche said. <That's where the
clone warrior would want to be—as close as possible to the center of power. Can you determine which one of them is the clone
warrior?>

<No.> There was both excitement and frustration in the reave's
voice. <To be honest, I can't even tell myself which one it is.
When you pointed it out, I could tell it looked different, but not
so remarkably different that I couldn't lose him in a crowd.>

<But *I* could spot him,> Roche said, confident in this new-
found sense. Cane's mind had been as different from the others
as a crater was to a mountain.

<I don't doubt that, Morgan,> Maii said. <But the other ones
you spotted *could* be unrelated. We need to get you face to face
with another clone warrior, alone, so there won't be any doubt
at all . . .> She sent a mental shrug. <Until then I guess we won't
know for certain if it really will work on the rest.>

Roche accepted that. The hope she had felt a moment before
was tempered by the thought that her gift might prove too unwieldy to rely upon. But it was a step in the right direction. If
the difference was a real one, and she could detect it, there was
always a chance that there were others like her who also had this
ability. Out of all the high-power reaves on board the *Phlegethon*
there had to be at least one who would replicate it.

The only trick would be proving it, and that meant coming into contact with another clone warrior.

As she and Maii lingered around the impenetrable mind in the administer's audience, Roche couldn't help but feel a little apprehensive about that.

8

Perdue Habitat
955.1.32
0330

Roche took the chance to speak to Haid and Kajic once she and Maii had tested her vague ability to its limits.

<Part of me still thinks you should tell the Ulterior to go to hell,> Haid said when she had finished bringing them completely up to date on the situation.

<Part of me agrees,> Roche replied. <But this is about more than the Ulterior. What's happening here could have a bearing on every habitat, every station, every ship throughout Sol System—throughout the *galaxy*. If we don't understand why and how it's happening here, we'll never be able to stop it elsewhere. Slowly, but surely. In that sense, I think Nemeth *has* done the right thing in sending us here.> She added: <Even if it does put us in the line of fire.>

<And I guess we're always going to be in the line of fire until this is over,> Haid said. <Or we leave the system.>

<Exactly.>

When she asked Kajic about the status of the ship, he was more relaxed. <Everything here is fine, Morgan. The repairs are complete, and we are completely restocked.>

<What's Vri up to?> Roche asked.

<Both he and Cane are keeping a very low profile,> said Haid. <Cane just watches the habitat. Vri just thinks. I suspect he's wishing he was with you, so he could keep an eye on Maii. I have to admit, though, he's a lot better at this waiting game than me. He stays in his ship at all times, always alert, always . . . poised, I guess.>

Roche pondered Haid's choice of word, and found it apt. He might exude calm and patience, but she knew Vri was wound like a spring. She wondered what it would take to make him snap.

<I'll see if I can convince Maii to send him some words of reassurance,> she said, knowing Maii would overhear. <I don't want him rushing in with guns blazing because he thinks I'm up to no good.>

<Good idea,> Haid said. <I imagine your radio silence isn't helping any.>

Roche dropped back into the real world while Maii conversed with the Surin warrior. They didn't talk long, and Maii's expression was sour when they were finished.

<He doesn't like my attitude,> she said. <He thinks I should be more responsible until I come of age.>

<How many years would that be?>

<Three. It's irrelevant, anyway. As far as I'm concerned, I became an adult the day my mother sold me for medical experiments.>

Roche didn't want to intrude upon that pain. She and Maii sat in silence for a long while, thinking private thoughts. It was odd for Roche after such mental intimacy to be alone again in her skull.

Or nearly so . . .

<Have you found a way to identify the enemy?> the Box asked.

<Not really,> she said. <I could probably pick them out face to face, with Maii's help, but that doesn't help us very much here.>

<It's something, though,> the Box reassured her, echoing her own thoughts.

<I guess so.> She was glad to be reminded that epsense gave her a way to converse with the others without the Box overhearing—especially at times like these, when she didn't feel like talking to the AI. She was afraid of letting slip that Maii knew

about the Box's survival. The Box probably wouldn't approve, and she couldn't help but wonder whether it would take any steps to ensure the girl's silence.

Very little time had passed when Maii lifted her head and said: <Ansourian is on his way back.>

<Alone?>

<Yes.>

Roche stood and shut the helmet to her suit. Maii did likewise. A minute later, the door clicked and opened.

"I'm sorry I took so long," he said as he entered, his voice loud as it filled the quiet of the room. "Pacecca's kept me busy, and Inderdeep is running behind schedule."

"Are we going now?" Roche asked.

"Yes." He started to lead the way, then turned back. "I do understand your need for security," he said, "but it would attract a lot less attention and suspicion if your visors were open."

Roche did as he suggested. The risk of physical assault was small, and the hazard suits wouldn't be as effective as combat armor anyway. If they were recognized, so be it; as it was, she had made no attempt to hide her identity when they arrived at the station. Someone looking for her would have found her regardless of an alias, or a visor covering her face.

Maii did likewise, and when Ansourian caught his first glimpse of her face, he smiled amicably.

"It's nice to see you properly," he said. "You have a very strong mind."

<You too. Where did you learn to shield like that?>

"The Vax were taught the technique by a senior adept passing through from Guo." Seeing no sign of recognition, he explained: "The Guo Sodality is dedicated to epsense training and study in the Middle Reaches; its senior adepts are renowned throughout our region for their strength and subtlety. The technique they taught us has been handed down along certain family lines in order to secure their places in the hierarchy of our culture."

"We noticed a lot of shielded minds in one particular spot in the habitat," Roche said.

He nodded. "That would be the audience chamber," he said. "That is where they would gather at this time." He half smiled. "Sometimes I wonder if there are any actual thoughts going on behind those shields." He shrugged. "But that's politics for you."

Roche debated whether to tell him about the two clone warriors, but decided to wait until she was sure. "Shall we go?"

"Yes, of course," he said, leading them out the door and into the corridor.

It was refreshing to be able to move again, and Roche relished the sensation of walking, even though it was in the cumbersome hazard suit. There seemed to be fewer people around than there had been earlier. Maybe that was because the habitat was between shifts, or the conservative Vax still maintained a consensus "night." Either way, Roche was glad for the relative anonymity.

They came to a major branching-point, where numerous corridors met at a wide variety of angles. The artificial gravity maintained in the habitat decreased slightly to accommodate the sudden shifts in orientation. Ansourian took them around a curved wall, then down into an undulating tube barely tall enough to accommodate Roche and her suit. This way was completely deserted; they passed no one, nor any doors or windows. But for her reopened link with the *Ana Vereine*, Roche would have had no idea where she was.

<You're heading deeper into the structure,> said Kajic, throwing a 3-D map of the habitat into her left eye. They were a red dot inching through a twisted tube that led, as Kajic indicated, to the heart of the habitat. <There's a junction up ahead. If he's taking the direct route, he'll turn left. But it doesn't seem likely.>

Ansourian turned right, taking them along a corridor that curved smoothly upward, then abruptly dropped 90 degrees in only a few meters. Roche negotiated the incline with care, trying not to let the wildly shifting gravity throw her off balance. The corridors from that point became decidedly cramped, with odd protrusions and corners and, overall, a makeshift air, as though they had been assembled from spare parts over many decades with little or no forethought as to their final function.

"Why don't you use transit tubes?" Roche asked.

"There are only a handful for freight," Ansourian explained. "Otherwise we don't care for them. There was a terrible accident a few years ago, and the previous administer discouraged their use."

"Where exactly are you taking us now?"

"Into the maintenance infrastructure. Security is relatively lax there, and we'll most likely pass as workers. The area is rarely monitored firsthand; only a basic AI checks for movement."

"We'll register, won't we?"

"Yes, but my Quare persona has clearance."

<Box, can you make sure of that?> Roche asked privately.

<I can disable the security systems in your vicinity, if you like.>

<Yes, do it.> She thought for a second. <I don't suppose you could get us to the administer more easily, could you?>

<Very possibly,> the Box replied. <But I feel you will have a greater chance of talking to Inderdeep Jans with Ansourian's guidance.>

<Do you think she'll listen?>

<That depends on what you have to say, I imagine.>

Roche had thought about that. She didn't have much to offer the administer apart from a vague hint about the enemy among her number and reassurances that the council was doing everything in its power (and more besides, in the form of the Ulterior) to rectify the problem. She was really only there to ask questions of her own, and if the administer was feeling uncooperative, then it was unlikely those questions would be answered.

"Is there a proper way to address the administer?" she asked.

Ansourian glanced over his shoulder. "I have no suggestions on how to get her to do what you want, if that's what you're asking." He shrugged and returned his attention to the way ahead. "Inderdeep is unpredictable at best, and can be willfully destructive at worst. Her father left me to keep an eye on things when he died. He never expected me to have to run things the way I have been. But if Inderdeep was left to act as she wished, the habitat would fall apart within months."

"What will happen if you're not going to be there?"

Again, he shrugged. "Maybe things will go well when you talk to her and I'll be able to reveal myself," he said. "If not, there are a couple of options still available. Oren Quare may prove to be eminently suitable for an advisory post closer to the administer's office. I know enough to work my way back in; given time, I could regain lost ground. But time is something I do not have, I'm afraid."

Roche knew what he was referring to. "How long do you think Alta has?" she said.

"Not long," he replied. "The evidence alone would have been

enough for a guilty verdict. Her confession will hasten the legal proceedings. Only the fact that I was so close to Inderdeep is keeping her alive right now. Who knows? Sentence may already have been passed. The matter was bound to come up in the current round of audiences, so Inderdeep may have already signed the execution order."

"She has power of life and death in the habitat?" Roche said, shocked that so much authority could reside in one person—especially one such as this Inderdeep Jans seemed to be.

"Indirectly she has *some* power," Ansourian explained. "She ratifies the decisions of the judicial system. Without their approval she can't impose the death penalty, but she can overturn one at will. I am hoping she will do this in Alta's case."

"Why should she do that?"

He faced Roche again. "Because you are going to ask her to," he said. "Tell her you came here because Alta and I called you. Tell her you're here to help, but you don't know how. Only Alta knows, now that I'm dead. The habitat may be riddled with the enemy for all anyone can tell, but with Alta's help you might be able to ferret them out."

"That's ridiculous," Roche scoffed. "She won't believe that."

"She might," he said. "Besides, it's not so far from the truth. Someone did try to kill me, after all."

Ignoring the obvious—that someone might've killed Ansourian simply because they disagreed with him—Roche said, "Is there anything else I'm supposed to be asking her? Anything else I should know?"

He thought for a long while as he continued to lead them through the habitat's maintenance labyrinth. "Just don't take her for an idiot," he eventually replied. "She's not stupid. She's just . . . wayward."

Roche absorbed the comment as they walked. Since Ansourian had worked with the administer so closely for so long, Roche had to assume that he would know her better than anyone else would. If he said she wasn't an idiot, then Roche had to accept that she wasn't—even though it was difficult to believe, given everything she had heard.

"How much farther?"

"We're practically there," he said, negotiating a narrow pass between two large ducts that intruded on the passage. "Just around this corner."

"Good, because I'm getting claustrophobic." That wasn't exactly true; she was just tired of squeezing through the tiny spaces. Her suit scraped the ducts even when she turned sideways to slip through.

<Could you get us out of here if we lost Ansourian?> she asked Kajic.

<Absolutely,> came the confident reply, echoed a split second later by the Box, privately. <Why, do you think that's likely?> Kajic went on.

<Anything is possible,> she said.

"Here," said Ansourian, taking them up a short corridor that ended in a cul de sac and bringing them to a halt. "I prepared this entrance in secret when Ehud Jans, the last administer, was still alive. It was intended as an escape route only, but it can work both ways, of course." He produced some silver tape from the pocket of his uniform, along with what looked like a small battery. "This will only work once," he said, affixing a length of tape to the wall at head-height and another down by his feet. The tape slowly changed in color from silver to red. "It may look like an ordinary section of wall, but it's not. It's barely solid at all: enough to fool a rapping knuckle, or even a gentle punch, but barely more than that. When I run a current through it, the alignment of its molecules will change, and it will dissolve completely. You'll be able to walk through without any trouble at all."

"And then?" said Roche uncertainly.

"Inderdeep will be on the other side," he said, meeting her gaze squarely. "I'll wait here and listen. The less she knows about me, the better—as her old friend Atul, or Oren Quare."

Roche nodded, and drew her side arm in readiness.

"That won't be necessary," he said.

"No?" She didn't put the pistol back into its holster. "You told me not to trust you before. Why should I start now?"

He smiled. "Just don't shoot *her*, whatever you do."

She smiled in return, but there was no humor to it. "I'm not stupid either, Ansourian."

He turned back to the wall.

<Can you sense her?> Roche asked Maii.

<There's someone there, yes> said the reave, <and it matches the echo I perceive in the minds of those who know her. Those I can read, at least. She's shielded too, though.>

<Naturally,> said Roche dryly. So much for her backup plan of forcing the administer to do what she wanted.

Ansourian reached up to affix the battery to the top strip of tape.

"Get ready," he said.

Roche tensed and watched expectantly. Little happened at first, then the red plastic seemed to soften and run. As though it was composed of grains of sand slipping through a person's fingers, the wall simply fell away. After barely ten seconds, all that was left was a spreading accumulation of dust on the floor, and a smell like ozone.

"Right," Ansourian whispered. "In you go. Good luck."

Roche nodded and, with Maii following, slipped through.

Roche's first impression of Inderdeep Jans was that she looked older than she'd expected. Her skin was paler than that of the other members of the Caste whom Roche had met, and she actually had hair: a long ponytail of perfect white that hung from the back of her skull and was bound in three places with bronze clasps. She wore a simple yellow robe adorned with a stylized sun—a motif echoed throughout the room.

She was seated on a wide couch, drinking deeply from a glass containing a pink liquid. She stopped drinking the moment Roche stepped from behind the wall hanging that hid the secret entrance, and turned coolly to face her.

"Who are you?" she demanded, seemingly unsurprised by the sudden intrusion. She put down her glass calmly but didn't rise from her seat. "How did you get in here?"

Roche kept her distance, not wanting to alarm the woman with any gesture that might be construed as hostile. "I apologize for the intrusion, Administer, but I—"

"What are you *doing* here?" Jans said with a hint of irritability when she saw Maii emerge from behind the wall hanging, also.

"We mean you no harm," said Roche. "I assure you."

The administer snorted. "Why should I believe you?"

Roche hefted her side arm. "We could have killed you already, if that was what we really intended."

A sly look passed across the woman's face. "Then what *do* you want?"

Before Roche could answer, the administer raised a hand and said: "Wait. I know you, don't I?" Roche opened her mouth to speak again, but again never got the chance. "Roche!" she said, clicking her fingers and nodding her head triumphantly. "I was told about you barely an hour ago. They showed me footage of your arrival and said you wanted to talk to me."

This surprised Roche, given what Ansourian had said about how her request for a meeting with the administer would probably be deliberately delayed.

"Yes, Administer," said Roche. "And I apologize for the manner we went about it, but—"

"This must be your blind companion." The woman stood now, and Roche realized with a shock that Jans was almost as tall as she was, hazard suit included. The administer took a step closer, scrutinizing with some fascination the bandages about Maii's eyes.

"This is Maii," Roche said. The girl nodded in greeting.

"I don't recognize her type." She looked at Roche. "Local, I assume?"

"The Surin are neighbors of the Commonwealth of Empires."

"Ah, yes, I've heard of them." The woman nodded with private satisfaction. Then, as if remembering something, she said: "You were meant to be in Stateroom B, waiting to be granted an audience."

"We were, but we were told it could take up to two days for us to see you . . ."

"Very likely," Jans said. "I am a busy person, you know." She glanced away for a second, her expression sad. "A dear friend will be consigned to the sun tomorrow. And *that* is more important to me than anything you or anyone else might have to say at this time."

The sorrow on the woman's face seemed completely genuine. Roche would have liked to reassure her on that score, but knew she couldn't do that just yet.

"I understand that, Administer," she said. "But please hear me out. My mission is of the gravest importance, and I need your assistance to complete it. In two days, it might be too late."

"Too late? For what?"

"For me to make a difference." Roche was loath for the moment to stoop to the story Ansourian had suggested. She had to at least see if something closer to the truth would work first. "I've been sent here by the Interim Emergency Pristine Council in response to claims that your habitat has been infiltrated by agents working for the enemy. With Atul Ansourian's help, I had hoped to investigate these rumors and, if they proved to have some foundation, determine precisely who among your staff could no longer be trusted."

"Atul knew you were coming?" Jans turned easily and returned to her seat.

"Yes, he did."

"And he was going to help you?" she said, leaning back and looking over at Roche with some suspicion.

"Yes."

"How?"

"I'm not sure exactly. All I know is that he was to be my contact here."

The administer's expression became one of distaste and annoyance. "But Atul is dead now," she said. "Killed by his own daughter."

Roche nodded. "We were told," she said. "I'm sorry. Perhaps . . ." Roche vacillated regarding how much to say. "Perhaps there is more to it than meets the eye."

"What are you saying?" Jans studied Roche. "Are you implying she might *not* have been responsible?"

"It is a possibility, Administer."

"But why would she lie?" The woman looked confused.

"She could be covering for the *real* assassin," suggested Roche.

The administer's confusion deepened. "The person you came here to warn me about?" she said. "Why would she do *that*?"

"I'm not sure," said Roche. "But if you would allow me to talk with her, perhaps we could find out just how much she knows."

"And what makes you think she would tell you anything?"

"Maii, here, is a reave," said Roche. "She could read her mind."

"Really?" Jans turned to face the girl. "Can she read mine?"

Maii shook her head.

The woman looked smug. "So why assume she could read Alta's? She was Atul's daughter through and through, and *his* shield was perfect. I should know. I once hired a reave to crack it, just to see if she could. She failed."

"Be that as it may, Administer, I do feel it is worth a try."

The woman shrugged, and with it Roche knew the possibility had been dismissed. "It doesn't really matter anyway," said Jans. "Alta is guilty of *something*. I signed her execution order barely an hour ago. Whether she is interrogated or not, she will be dead this time tomorrow."

Roche took a deep breath. That closed off that line of inquiry, for the time being. "Even so, that doesn't change what I have come here to tell you."

"No? Without Atul, what can you do?"

"I can still *try*."

"How?"

"With your help."

"*Mine*?"

Roche tried to contain her impatience. "Administer, I am not exaggerating when I try to impress upon you the urgency of my mission. The council needs the help of the Vax, and in return I will try to help you. Atul Ansourian freely offered us his assistance. It continues to be my hope that you will decide to offer us the same."

The administer looked bored. "Why should I care about your Pristine Council? The Vax can take care of themselves."

Roche recalled the number of ships in the habitat's docks, at least one of them—the COE's *Paraselene*—a Pristine vessel. "You already lend support to the IEPC's campaign. And I note, without meaning to offend, that you yourself are of different stock from the other Vax I have met. With such diversity—"

"Mind your words, Roche." Inderdeep Jans stood abruptly, taking one menacing step forward. Even with her side arm, Roche felt threatened and instinctively stepped back. "How *dare* you suggest that—"

"That's not what I meant, Administer," said Roche quickly. "I was merely trying to reinforce the fact that different Castes *can* work together for a common good—be they Vax, Pristine, or any other. If you—"

"If *you* hadn't come here, maybe Atul would still be alive."

The sudden shift in topic caught Roche off guard. "What? That's ridiculous! There is no evidence to suggest that—"

"Really? Atul calls for your help, and within days he is dead. The coincidence seems striking, does it not?"

"Then surely you must see that *your* life is at risk also?"

"Why should *that* be?"

"Because if your chain of command has been compromised by the enemy, then their ultimate aim will be to dispose of you too."

"I don't see why they'd want to do that," Jans said, gesturing dismissively with one hand. "I don't even want to be here. It was Atul who talked me into it, and see what it cost him! Besides—" She took another couple of steps forward, her relaxed expression belying her words, "the only person who has even remotely threatened me to date, Roche, is *you.*"

"That's not true, Administer," said Roche defensively. "I pose no threat to you whatsoever!"

"No? You break into my private chambers and exhort me to assist you in your mission—a mission, I might add, that requires turning my staff upside down to search for a hypothetical spy—while muttering vague suggestions that if I don't, my life will be forfeit. That sounds like a threat to me, Roche."

"Everything I have said is true," Roche stated patiently, although she could feel her patience crumbling. "Your life *is* in danger, and inaction on your part only increases that danger. But I'm not the one threatening you. It is the enemy—our *common* enemy. It's this person, and many more besides, that we should be fighting—*not* each other."

"So you say," Jans remarked dubiously.

"Because it is true," insisted Roche.

"Then show me the proof."

"It's all around you! The death, the destruction, the distrust, the disorganization . . ." She struggled to remember the name she'd heard just hours before. "And what about Guidon?"

"The cause of that accident has yet to be verified." The administer looked uncomfortable, but was unwilling to take the point. "None of this is proof. Your words are empty, Roche. Why should I believe you over one of my own advisers?"

"Because one of your advisers may well belong to the enemy!"

The administer smiled wryly. "As might *you,*" she said. "Your reputation precedes you, Roche. It is said that wherever you go, trouble follows. If I were to give you the help you request, how could I be sure that the Vax won't become your next victims?"

"Nothing could be further from the truth!"

"So you say." The administer held a palm outstretched, silencing Roche, who had opened her mouth to object again. "I have no desire to put my people at risk on such flimsy evidence! A few disputes and the threat of war, an accident, and a failed assassination attempt closer to home—it will take more than *this* to convince me, Roche. And if you *cannot* convince me, you might as well leave."

The administer's words sent a chill down Roche's spine. She knew, then, that there was no chance of convincing the woman to change her mind—not on that score, and especially not on the matter of Alta Ansourian.

"Very well, then," Roche said, backing away toward the secret exit. "We'll trouble you no further, Administer."

The woman watched them leave, a wary expression on her face. "Wait," she said, just as Roche pulled the sun-motif wall hanging aside. "Who told you about this entrance?"

Roche thought fast. She really had only two options, given that she didn't want the administer to know the truth. She could refuse to answer, or she could lie. How to do the latter convincingly was the trick.

<Box?>

<Tell her it was Gurion Egarr, one of her senior councilors. She will want to believe that. The news reports them as being old antagonists.>

"It was Councilor Egarr," said Roche a second later. "And I tell you that now only to demonstrate my openness and honesty with you. His intentions were good, I assure you."

The administer's broad smile was cut with cynicism. "I bet." Then she nodded. "Go now," she said. "I shall allow you five minutes grace before I send my guards after you. And I do this now to demonstrate *my* magnanimity."

Her smile dissolved as she glared at Roche.

Whether she was serious or not, Roche could not tell. But she couldn't afford to take the chance. With Maii ahead of her, she slipped behind the wall-hanging and back into the cramped confines of the maintenance infrastructure.

9

Ansourian led them quickly through the tunnels, taking them by a different route from the one they had followed on the way in. Maii was directly behind him with Roche close on her tail, glancing back uneasily now and then to see whether they were being pursued.

<Please stop doing that, Morgan,> said Maii. <It's hard for me to see where I'm going when you keep looking over your shoulder.>

<I'm sorry, Maii,> Roche said. <It's just . . .>

<Trust me, there's no one following us,> said the girl. <The administer seems to be keeping to her word so far.>

Ansourian stopped suddenly, ushering both Maii and Roche through a hatchway; he closed the heavy bulkhead behind them.

"That'll stop them," he said, belligerently punching some commands into a keypad. "I've let the air out of the tunnels we just came through."

"I don't think it'll stop them," said Roche. "At best it will only slow them down."

The small man shrugged but said nothing. Roche could see the hurt in his eyes.

"You heard what she said, didn't you?" she asked.

He didn't need to reply; his expression spoke volumes. *Failed assassination attempt*, the administer had said. Roche could believe that she had guessed it was an assassination rather than simple patricide—but how could she have known it had failed if she hadn't been a party to the attack in the first place? At the very least, she had known about it.

"I'm sorry," Roche said.

"Don't be," he said. "It has made my decision easier. Escape seems the surest course, now."

"What about Alta?"

"As I said earlier, there are blind spots in the security system. I will try to get her away first."

"More secret doors you put in place?"

"No, just exploitable flaws," he said. "Even the best security system has its weaknesses—I simply have the advantage of *knowing* what those weaknesses are. I am confident that I can get into the holding cells. Getting out will be more difficult, but not impossible."

Roche followed him along the corridors while conducting a conversation via her implants with her crew back on the *Ana Vereine*. <Ameidio, Uri—have you been following this?>

<Of course,> said Haid. <Are you thinking of helping him?>

<We'll need him if we're to have any chance of fixing the situation here. The administer is going to be worse than no use to us, since the enemy has obviously gotten to her and turned her against him; they're aware that he runs the shop, and that they couldn't influence him. With him out of the way, or with his daughter as leverage, they figure they have control.>

<But why should they need leverage if they think he's dead?>

<They're not stupid; they might at least suspect that he switched bodies, especially when their assassin hasn't turned up since. And when the administer tells them about our little visit, that'll probably just confirm their suspicions.>

<How can we help him, though?>

<The old fashioned way, I guess,> she said.

<A show of strength?> asked Haid.

<We haven't got time for subtlety here, Ameidio,> Roche replied. <You and Cane—or Vri, even—can act as a distraction while we make a move on the holding cells. Do you think you

could organize something big enough and fast enough to attract everyone's attention?>

<Undoubtedly.>

<Feel like some action?>

Haid laughed. <I can't deny that I could use the change,> he said. <And I'm sure Vri would be up for it. One mention of you putting Maii on the firing line and he'd move for certain.>

<Okay. You and Vri it is. We'll leave Cane to mind the ship with Uri. Are they both listening?>

<We're here, Morgan,> said Kajic.

<Do either of you have any reservations about this?>

<It's your decision,> said Kajic. <I am confident we can pull something like this off successfully. But there are no guarantees.>

<There never are,> said Roche.

<I agree with Uri,> said Cane. <However, I feel that I might be more use to you alongside Vri in the diversionary attack.>

Roche paused before replying. <I appreciate what you're saying, but—>

<But you need to have someone there that you can trust,> he said with no hint of indignation. <I understand this, Morgan. I felt I should voice my feelings just the same.>

Roche smiled to herself. <Thanks,> she said. <Okay, I'll talk with Ansourian and see what he thinks. Then we move—as soon as possible. The longer we take, the more chance we give the enemy to be ready.>

<And we don't want to do that,> said Haid. <They have enough advantages as it is. . . .>

Ansourian looked surprised when she offered to help.

"Why?" was the first question he asked.

"Because if I just let you rescue Alta and leave, it's tantamount to handing the enemy this station along with everyone in it. The same if I let you try and you fail. You'll be dead, and that doesn't serve anyone. If we're to stand any chance of fixing this, we're going to need you alive."

"What difference does it make to you, either way?"

That wasn't so easy to answer. "It makes a difference to how I feel about myself," she said. "It's a matter of pride. This mission is a test, if you like; maybe metaphorically rather than literally, but a test all the same." She shrugged. "I don't want to fail."

He nodded slowly. They had stopped to rest in an unlit stores cubicle; the only light came from the necks of Roche's and Maii's hazard suits, lending their heads a surreal, disembodied look.

"So your crew will create a diversion while we get Alta," he said. "Then what?"

"Then you help us get back to the *Ana Vereine*," she said. "You know your way around this place; I'm going to need a less obvious way to get off the habitat than the main docks. The ship will have to cast off once things heat up, but it can send a scutter to get us when we're ready. Just name the place and we'll head for it."

"Okay," he said. "There *is* a way, but it will be tricky. And I'm going to need pressure suits for myself and Alta. There are—"

<Morgan.> Kajic's voice broke in sharply; Roche raised her hand to silence Ansourian. <There's been a development.>

<I'm listening.>

<I've been monitoring traffic to and from the docks. Exactly twenty minutes ago, every commercial and military vessel from the Random Valence habitat disengaged and retreated to a safe distance. Now a contingent of ships has arrived from the same habitat and is demanding to dock.>

<How many ships?>

<Fifteen, all armed.>

<A takeover force?>

<It seems likely, striking while the chain of command here is uncertain.>

Roche relayed the information to Ansourian, who simply nodded. "It doesn't surprise me. Frane Yugen has been itching to move on Inderdeep since she rejected his offer to form a partnership against Tocharia 13. With me out of the way, it's a perfect opportunity."

"Can she hold him off?" Roche asked.

"That depends. I've kept the defenses well-stocked over the years, and made sure the staff know what to do. If she doesn't interfere, they'll manage well enough."

That sounded ominous. "Can you guess how she'll respond?"

"Again, it depends on what the enemy are telling her. If they want to increase conflict, they might feed her inappropriate advice."

"Then we can't assume things will go well," said Roche. She switched to her implants. <Uri, where are Haid and Vri?>

<In the habitat,> he said. <Preparing for the distraction.>

<It doesn't look like we'll need them, after all,> she said. <Recall them and disengage. I don't want you caught in the crossfire.>

<Understood.>

"How far is it to where they're keeping Alta?" she asked Ansourian.

"Fifteen minutes or so, going the back ways."

"Then let's get moving before things start heating up."

"Not without the pressure suits," he reminded her.

Roche nodded and indicated that he should lead the way. They left the cubicle and headed off through the labyrinth.

<He's worried,> said Maii.

<You can tell that? Good. That means his shield must be slipping. Can you pick up anything else?>

<No, nothing. Whoever those people from the Guo Sodality are, they taught the Vax a good technique.>

<What about the administer? Did you get anything at all from her?>

<A few stray thoughts; most likely just planted to fool a casual glance. The core of her mind is impenetrable, like Ansourian's.>

<You said you thought you might be able to break into his, given time.>

<I'm sure of it,> said Maii. <But this is hardly the time to try. At the very best, I would distract him; at the worst, I might seriously injure him. The Guo shields are deep-rooted; cracking them would probably have consequences for the mind beneath.>

<Maybe I should set you loose on the administer anyway. It's not as if we have much to lose.>

<That wouldn't be ethical, Morgan.>

<Maybe not, but it is an option.>

A siren sounded in the distance, echoing along the winding corridors like the baying of an enormous beast.

"What's that?" Roche asked Ansourian.

"Security alert, level 5. Ambient gravity will drop by twenty percent to conserve power."

Even as he said it, a wave of dizziness rushed over Roche, leaving her feeling somewhat lighter after it had passed.

"Does that mean the habitat is under attack?"

"No, not yet. You'll know if that happens. Perdue is designed to absorb the energy of an impact and spread it across its structure."

"Meaning we'll feel it regardless of where we are?"

"Yes, but it shouldn't be too bad. Habitats like these tend to absorb almost anything up to a point, and fall apart completely only if you cross that point. That's what happened to Guidon; it was pushed too far. Since a ruined habitat will be of no use to Yugen, he'll play it fairly safe."

"And if he *does* want a ruined habitat?"

Ansourian looked sharply at her. "You think the enemy might have got to him, too?"

"It's a possibility we can't ignore."

They stopped at a locker, from which Ansourian produced two transparent pressure suits. "We call them OSFA suits," he explained, slipping one over his uniform. "One Size Fits All. They're designed to maximize survival through a wide range of conditions—heat, cold, vacuum, pressure, etcetera; they'll even stop a measure of coherent light—but they won't last long in combat."

"Do you have access to weapons?"

"They'll be in the armory. We won't get in there at a time like this."

Roche touched the pistol at her side. An identical weapon rested on Maii's hip; unlike most reaves, the girl had proven herself more than capable of killing on Sciacca's World. By looking through her victim's eyes and aiming along the barrel from the other end, she made quite an effective fighter.

"We'll have to make do, then," Roche said, hoping the distraction would be enough.

Ansourian finished sealing the suit, leaving only the hood open, then continued to lead them along.

<Are Vri and Haid back on board yet?> Roche asked Kajic.

<Vri is unwilling to leave until Maii has returned,> Kajic replied.

<But it's unlikely we'll be able to exit that way.>

<He's aware of that.>

<Then what does he think he's going to do?>

<Find you and take her himself.>

<Damned fool!> Roche snapped irritably.

<As Maii pointed out, he's quite dedicated.>

A deep vibration rippled through the tube surrounding them. Ansourian placed a hand against one wall.

"It has begun," he said. "That one hit the shields. Maybe nothing more than a warning volley. If there are more, then we can assume Inderdeep isn't going to give in without a fight."

<Dockmaster Rench has ordered all docks sealed,> said Kajic. <Haid and Vri are still not aboard.>

<Okay,> she said. <Disengage. Tell them to sit tight. We'll just have to work something else out.>

They headed off along the corridor. The floor still moved slightly as the energy of the attack ran through the entire habitat and dissipated, ultimately, as radiant heat. In theory, Roche could see how such a passive defense might pay off; she could also see, however, how disastrous it might be. One sustained attack could ruin everything, decisively.

<Disengaging now,> said Kajic. <Cane will fly the scutter when the time comes to pick you up.>

<Fine.> She didn't have much choice, really. With Vri and Haid stuck on the habitat with them, and Kajic potentially dodging fire, there *was* no one else. Even with Ansourian's help, the chances of finding a ship and breaking the dockmaster's embargo had to be almost zero.

She explained what had happened to Ansourian. "We'll need a rendezvous point. Can you give us one away from the docks?"

"Yes, but it's too complicated to explain how your friends should get there. They can access a map using Quare's security code." He rattled off a string of letters and numbers, which Roche memorized. "They want to reach the maintenance airlock at the end of corridor 14 in Sector Green-D. It's not far from the holding cells in Sector Blue-J. Tell them to wait for us there. We shouldn't be more than an hour."

Roche relayed the information through Maii, using the girl as a medium the way she had earlier.

<You be careful,> Haid said, via Maii.

<You too.> She could clearly taste the worry in his mind, and the tangle of plans and counterplans as he mentally prepared for any contingency. <I'll call if we need help. What equipment do you have?>

Using mental shorthand, he sent her a list that included shaped charges, compact percussion rifles, pressure mines, and flash-bombs—anything that would fit into the relatively low-key armor the two men had donned in order to enter the habitat. Dock security hadn't been especially tight, not since they'd been given approval to disembark, but cannon and full combat suits would have attracted attention.

<I wish we had some of that,> Roche said, <but there's no helping it, I guess. Make sure you're at the rendezvous when we get there.>

Haid mentally nodded and went back to studying the map Vri had accessed via a wall terminal. That left Roche with half a mind on where Ansourian was leading them, and the other half in n-space. Again she experienced a moment's disorientation as she simultaneously saw through her own eyes and those of Maii, who was also looking through her eyes.

<Could the Box help us?> Maii asked.

<It could probably open the docking bay doors, but that would be too obvious. All it's good for at the moment is gathering information and keeping automatic security off our tails.>

<It seems to be doing a good enough job at that, anyway.>

Another vibration rippled through the corridor, followed quickly by another. The wailing alarm changed pitch, becoming more shrill and urgent. <It's a shame it can't do anything about the Random Valence ships. . . .>

"*That* was no warning shot," said Ansourian, steadying himself against a wall.

Roche forced herself to keep walking even as the floor moved beneath her feet. <Box, are they firing back?>

<All A-P cannon emplacements have been ordered to retaliate. Nine free vessels have sided with Perdue and are joining the fight. However, more vessels are on their way from Random Valence.>

<Who has the advantage?>

<Perdue should hold. Its structure is more than capable of bearing the brunt of such an attack, and given the extra ships, I doubt the attackers will be able to board at any point.>

<What about our scutters? Could one of them make it through the defense?>

<If it declares for Perdue's side, then it will most likely be allowed into the fray.>

<Okay. I'll get Cane out there now, to save time later.>

She got Kajic on the line and instructed Cane to take the scutter as the Box had suggested. Kajic didn't ask how she had found out about the battle; she hoped that he simply assumed that she had learned about it via Maii.

Still linked via n-space, she noted that the reave was occasionally glancing away from where they were headed in the tunnels to the people surrounding them in the habitat. Even in the maintenance infrastructure, they weren't completely alone. The ones that weren't shielded were mostly thinking about what was going on: curious, concerned, frightened, angry . . . Only a handful were hoping the attackers would win, and none of them had any specific thoughts about the enemy. If there was a connection between the attack and the clone warriors, Roche had yet to find proof of it.

<Any sign of the enemy?> she asked Maii.

<I still can't pinpoint them the way you can. Want to try?>

<It couldn't hurt.>

Roche tried to concentrate on walking as well as the mental landscape of the habitat. The rapid progression of minds was as disorienting in its own way as the incessant but irregular grumbling of the walls and floor. Mind after mind rolled by, until—

<There's one! Back up. *There*.> The pitlike mind was in a group of three or four others, all stationary. <Where is it?>

<Hard to tell,> said Maii. <I think it's the same place we were looking before.>

<The administer's audience chamber?> Roche asked.

<Possibly. Or maybe even her private rooms.>

Ansourian brought them to a halt when they came to a closed door.

"On the other side of this bulkhead is the corridor leading to the holding cells," he said. "I don't know what's waiting for us there. It *could* be messy."

<Box?>

<It's empty. Two guards are at the entrance to the holding cells, though not in line of sight.>

<Good. Keep me posted as we get closer.>

<There is one thing, Morgan,> the Box said, before she could turn her attention back to Ansourian. <I have just intercepted a coded security bulletin. Inderdeep Jans is dead. She was just found in her chambers with her neck broken.>

<Who killed her?>

<That is the curious thing. Obviously the crime scene is awaiting a thorough forensic examination, and no firm conclusions should be drawn without—>

<Come *on*, Box!>

<It would seem that you are the main suspect, Morgan.>
<*Me?*>

<All available security officers have been advised that you and other members of your crew are presently on the loose and, according to the security bulletin, quote, required to assist the investigation, unquote. They have been instructed to use force to bring you in.>

<*Lethal* force?>

<If necessary.>

<Damn!> Until now, it had just been necessary to keep a low profile. Now they were suspects and would be hunted through every corridor of the habitat until caught. Or killed.

Her face must have shown something. When she focused once again on Ansourian, he was staring at her.

"What's happened?"

"The administer . . ." Roche began, then hesitated, debating for a moment whether or not to tell him. The news had the potential to distract him, a distraction she couldn't afford right now. Nevertheless, he did have the right to know. "The administer is dead," she finally said. "Assassinated, it would seem."

His expression flickered, and for the briefest moment she glimpsed a grief that surprised her. Even knowing that Jans was involved in the attack on him, Ansourian still felt compassion for the woman.

Catching Roche's surprise, he said: "For all her failings, she didn't deserve *this.*"

Roche nodded. "I understand," she said. She allowed a moment's pause before gesturing to the door. "I'm sorry, Ansourian, but we have to keep moving."

All trace of sadness vanished from his expression as quickly as it had appeared. "Do you want me to go first?" he said, jerking a thumb at the door in front of them.

Roche flipped her helmet closed. "No, I'll go. The suit will hold for a second or two, if it has to. You just open it."

He nodded and stepped back. The lock glowed green, and the door slid aside.

Roche stepped into the corridor, confident that the Box knew what it was talking about but wary of any new developments it may have overlooked. As promised, though, there were no guards in sight.

"Clear," she whispered.

Ansourian stepped out of the tunnel with Maii. The girl's visor was also closed, and she kept one hand close to her pistol at all times.

Ansourian indicated the passage to their right, and they walked that way. Two guards came into view thirty seconds later, one on either side of a door two meters wide. They seemed alert but not especially concerned at seeing Ansourian and his companions as they approached.

<What's on the other side of the door?> she asked the Box.

<A rectangular grid thirty-five meters across, with ten corridors in two groups of five crossing at right angles. There are normally twenty guards, one at each end of each corridor, but half have been reassigned during the attack. There are one hundred cells in all. Alta Ansourian is in number 77.>

<Are the guards shielded, Maii?>

<Neither of the ones ahead,> said Maii. <But there are two on the other side of the door that are.>

Roche didn't know what Ansourian had planned, so to forestall anything precipitous, she said to Maii: <Tell Ansourian his daughter is in Cell 77, in case he doesn't know. We'll take care of these guards.>

<Okay, Morgan.> There was a brief pause as Maii relayed the message. <He sends his thanks,> she told Roche.

Roche nodded. <Now, what about these guards, Maii?>

<Already taken care of,> she said.

<Okay, then let's move.>

Influenced by Maii's powers, the guards stepped aside as they approached and waved them through; then, when the heavy door had closed behind them again, they promptly forgot they had ever seen the intruders.

Ansourian automatically took off along the nearest of the black-gray corridors. He seemed unconcerned by the strong jolts that occasionally rattled and shuddered through the walls. Roche followed him, keeping a close eye out for the two shielded guards. They turned right, then left, passing sturdy-looking doors with numeric keypads instead of locks. There was no way to determine whether the cells were empty or not, however, as the window in each door was shuttered closed.

When they reached Alta's cell, Roche noticed a guard standing motionless at the far end of the corridor. She assumed he was unshielded and controlled by Maii, since he didn't seem too concerned about the presence of visitors to the cell block.

Ansourian quickly tapped the appropriate code into the keypad of his daughter's cell. Nothing happened.

"They've changed the codes," he hissed. "We'll have to blast our way in. Is your pistol up to it?"

"It'll have to be." She removed it from her holster and took careful aim. <Box? Help me out here, okay?>

<The door is already unlocked,> it said.

<Thanks.> She fired, and the door sprang open. Roche looked up. The guard hadn't reacted to the noise, but she could hear the inquiries of someone who had.

"Inside!" She pushed Ansourian and Maii into the cell, followed them in and shut the door.

Alta was sitting on a low bunk. She looked up, surprised, when she saw them enter.

"Father!" A smaller, female version of Atul Ansourian, with dark eyes and a small tattoo on her throat, sprang to her feet to embrace him.

"Shhh!" Roche waved for silence. Footsteps were coming toward the cell.

<One guard is approaching your location,> said the Box.

<I hear him.> She waited, pistol at the ready. The smell of energy-fire would linger for a while. If it was strong enough, the guard might realize immediately where they were. If it wasn't, he might just keep walking, which would at least give them an extra minute or two. As far as Roche was concerned, every second was valuable.

The footsteps stopped directly outside the cell.

Roche didn't hesitate: she opened the door and fired her pistol. The bolt of energy caught the guard on the shoulder of his armor, spinning him heavily into the wall. While he was distracted, Maii penetrated his shield and rendered him unconscious.

He fell to the ground with a thud, his weapon sent clattering along the floor. But Roche didn't dare hope that he would be the last of their problems. There was one more unshielded guard in the complex, and she had now fired two shots.

"Quickly!" said Roche back over her shoulder. "Get her into that suit!"

Without a word, Alta slipped into the OSFA suit her father had brought.

Roche edged back out of the corridor, using the Box to scan the corridor of the holding cell grid. Aside from the unconscious guard outside Alta's cell, she counted eight others: five along one wall and three along the other, all subdued by Maii. One was missing.

<Any guesses, Maii?>

<He must've slipped out to get help.>

The Box thought otherwise. <The checkpoint door has not opened since we came through it.>

<So check the cells, then,> said Roche. <He must be in one of them.>

<The cells do not have surveillance cameras,> it said.

<You didn't *see* where he went?>

<I was distracted by the guard approaching you,> the Box confessed. <The resources I have available here are hardly what I would call optimal, Morgan.>

She shrugged off its excuses. They would just have to hope the guard planned to lie low while they made their exit.

Alta had finished donning her suit and stood, slightly stunned, with one hand on her father's shoulder.

"We're leaving here?" she asked.

"Yes," Roche said. "The sooner the better."

They filed out of the cell and into the corridor, Roche leading, keeping alert for any sign of the missing guard. They made it around the first corner, then the next. The checkpoint appeared ahead of them, its doors invitingly open.

Roche had barely passed the last cell door when it burst open. The guard managed to get off three shots before Roche brought him down with two shots from her own weapon—the first bolt hitting his side and spinning him away, the second taking him in the back and throwing him forward onto the cell's bunk, which collapsed noisily beneath him.

Roche ignored him and went to check on Alta and Ansourian instead. The woman, clutching an injured arm, was scrambling her way to her father who had taken two direct hits, one to the chest and one to the stomach.

Roche checked Ansourian for broken ribs, but couldn't feel anything through her glove and the blackened material of his OSFA suit. Even unconscious, he winced with pain as she probed.

"I can carry him," she said to Alta, "if you want to take that risk."

The woman nodded, all expression gone. "He needs medical attention," she said, "and he's not going to get it here."

"He'll be all right if we can just get him back to the *Ana Vereine*. But before that," she said, remembering Ansourian's instructions to Haid and Vri, "we need to find corridor 14 in Sector Green-D. Do you know where that is?"

"Yes, of course," she said. "But why do we need to go there?"

"Because that's our escape route," Roche explained hastily. "I'm arranging a pickup at the maintenance airlock there."

Alta frowned. "'Maintenance airlock'—is that what Father said?"

"Yes, why?"

"It's not a maintenance airlock," she said. "It's an old refuse dumper."

Roche stared at the woman for a second. Dumpers were little more than chutes designed to fire pellets of unreclaimable material at a suitable disposal site—be it the atmosphere of a dead world, the nearest sun, or anywhere the waste would do little harm. They would be lucky if it had even the most primitive airlock facilities, let alone somewhere to dock.

"This just gets better and better," she said, shaking her head. "But it doesn't matter. If it's the only way out, we're going to take it."

She rose slowly to her feet, bringing Ansourian with her. The suit gave her the strength to carry him, and the fall in ambient gravity helped, but he was still going to be a burden—especially if they encountered any more guards and she had to use her pistol.

<I'm going to need as much warning as I can get if there are any signs of guards approaching—okay, Box?> she said. <I don't want to have to drop him like a dead weight at the last moment.>

<You've got it, Morgan,> said the Box.

She staggered as the floor shifted under her; then, regaining her balance, she headed for the checkpoint. They passed through unhindered, and headed off along the corridor.

<I presume you can't read her,> Roche said to Maii.

<Not at all.>

<Trusting bunch, aren't they?> She shifted Ansourian's body to a more comfortable position. Alta took them along a series of wide, curving corridors, many of them ringing to the sound of sirens, but each as deserted as the last. The vibrations seemed to

lessen when they stuck to the main routes, and Roche was grateful to be able to forget about not banging her head on the maintenance tunnels' low ceilings. She did feel exposed, though, and would be glad when they reached the exit point—even if it was just a refuse dumper.

<Is Cane going to be able to find us, Box?>

<He and Kajic are monitoring our progress through the habitat, and the egress point is clearly visible from the outside. That is probably why Ansourian chose it. Once we get close, there won't be a problem.>

<How far away are Ameidio and Vri?>

<They are a little farther away than you.>

<And any word on the situation with the administer?>

<No change, Morgan. You are still wanted, and I am still blocking security's attempts to trace you electronically.>

<Well, that's something at least.>

A further violent judder swept through the habitat just as they turned down another corridor, this time forcing Roche to one knee in order to keep herself from falling.

"What was *that*?"

Alta looked frightened as she helped Roche to her feet. "We've been holed!" she said as a sudden shift in air pressure made everyone's ears block. The sirens took on a new note of alarm. "Pressure-doors will be up all over the station."

"We have suits," said Roche. "Do you know the override commands?"

Alta shook her head. "My father would have."

Roche felt trapped. Keeping the Box's existence a secret was becoming harder and harder. <Box, give me the codes!>

The Box complied and she quickly relayed the codes to Maii. <Give them to Ameidio. Tell him Ansourian told us what they were. Hopefully they don't know he's down.> Via implants again, she said: <Box, give us some interference on the line to the *Ana Vereine* and open those doors for us when we reach them. We'll just have to bluff our way through this one.>

<Yes, Morgan.>

Roche nudged Alta on. "Come on, keep going. We're going to make it, okay?"

They continued through the vibrating corridors of the habitat, though now with more pace and urgency. There was still no one around, and Roche assumed the nonessential Vax personnel were holed up in their pressurized compartments. If the majority of the security personnel were down at the docks or elsewhere in the habitat where the defense was concentrated, that at least decreased the chances of their being found. But it wasn't enough to help Roche relax. Not until she was standing on the bridge of the *Ana Vereine*, with the habitat far behind her, would she allow herself that luxury. . . .

They passed through two open pressure-doors, then a third. Roche could see the puzzlement on Alta's face at the blatant lapse in safety precautions, but there was no time to explain. The only time they stopped was when a particularly violent attack shook the habitat so badly that Roche was flung into one of the walls, and Maii and Alta were thrown onto the shuddering floor.

Steadying herself, Roche asked: <How far now, Box?>

<Two more junctions. The way is clear. Haid and Vri are two corridors over, barely a minute behind.>

<Uri? Tell Cane to start moving in. We're almost there.>

From the *Ana Vereine*, Kajic said: <We have the location. I'll let you know when he's there.>

They passed through the first junction, taking a little-used passage that obviously connected to the maintenance tunnels they had left earlier. The second junction took them to a wide, straight corridor that seemed to stretch for miles. In the distance, loping toward them, were two figures, one dressed in black, the other in gold.

Alta started when she saw them.

"It's okay," Roche assured her. "They're with us."

Yet another violent shudder ran through the walls and floor.

"Quickly," said Roche, stepping over to the dumper's enormous steel hatch. "Get that thing open!"

"We haven't used the dumpers for years," explained Alta, tapping at a keypad. "Father kept this one in commission to use as an emergency exit, if he ever needed it. It was used occasionally, but not regularly. But the codes should still work."

Thinking of the dissolving door in the administer's chambers, Roche said: "If we do get out of this in one piece, we'll have your father's devious mind to thank for it."

Haid and Vri arrived in a clatter of armor and heavy footsteps.

"Any problems?" Roche asked

"None," Haid said. "Which only makes me more nervous."

"It would," she said. Alta glanced up but there wasn't time for introductions. "Cane should be waiting for us out the other side of the dumper. If they're designed like others I've seen, we should be able to crawl into the induction tube and out into vacuum easily enough. Then we'll have to jump to the scutter."

"And then . . . ?" Haid prompted.

"Then we wait to see what happens here," said Roche. "The administer has been killed, so it'll be easier to deal with things here if we can reinstate Ansourian somehow. It might be worth sticking around to see if the habitat survives the attack."

Alta had looked up again when Roche mentioned that Inderdeep Jans was dead, but returned quickly to her task. Seconds later she had finished tinkering with the keypad and tried to open the hatch. The hinges were stiff; with Haid's assistance the hatch finally came open a little.

<Morgan,> asked Kajic via her implants, <is everything okay?>

<As much as it can be. Why?>

<Cane is reporting something unusual on the hull near the dumper outlet.>

<'Unusual'? In what way?>

<An object of some kind. He can't make it out yet, but he's concerned you might be about to walk into a trap.>

A trap. Roche watched as Haid and Alta continued to pull at the dumper's hatch. Haid might have been right to be nervous, after all.

"Just blow it, Ameidio," she said. Then to Maii: <Maii, link up! I want to see what's ahead.>

<I can sense nothing, Morgan.>

<Let's do it, anyway,> said Roche. <I want to make sure.>

She stepped back from the recalcitrant hatch as Haid positioned the charges to blow it open. She closed her eyes as she lowered Ansourian to the ground, allowing the gray vistas of n-space to unfold around her.

<Cane is in position,> said Kajic. <But the object he saw has gone.>

<Wait . . .> Roche's mind drifted with Maii's, leaving the cluster of minds that were Haid, Vri, Alta and Ansourian. She had trouble seeing herself, and Maii.

Not far away from them, though, she clearly saw the distinctive dip of a clone warrior.

<Who's that?> said Roche. <Is it Cane?>

<I *think* so,> said Maii, uncertainty stressing the word. <He's closer now than he was.>

<That would make sense. Can you see anything else?>

<No . . .>

The corridor rocked beneath them as the charges blew open the hatch. Roche opened her eyes on a cloud of smoke obscuring everything in the corridor. Haid stepped to the hole in the wall where the hatch had been.

<No, wait!> said Maii, her mental voice urgent. <There are two of them!>

Haid hesitated by the entrance to the refuse dumper, startled by the mental shout. The gray of n-space overwhelmed Roche's ordinary vision—and she too saw the second hole in the field that meant a clone warrior. At first she didn't realize how Maii had known there were two, but then it all fell into place. The second one was farther away and moving gradually closer. It had all the hallmarks of Cane's mind.

The first one they had seen was *inside* the refuse dumper.

Before anyone could move away, there was a second explosion, this time from the other side of the open hatchway. A hurricane of air roared past them as the atmosphere inside the corridor was sucked out the open outlet, into space. Roche braced herself, and grabbed Ansourian's body as it slipped toward the hole. Pressure doors slammed closed along the corridor; alarms screamed, fading gradually as the air pressure dropped.

<Check your seals!> she shouted via her implants. <Make sure your suits will hold!>

Then, out of the hatchway, moving easily against the whirlpool currents of air, her white ponytail whipping in the wind, stepped Inderdeep Jans.

10

Jans was wearing an OSFA suit not dissimilar to the ones An-sourian and his daughter had on, except her face mask wasn't in place. That she had blown the dumper outlet without sealing her suit first surprised Roche, but she didn't have time to dwell on the matter—the clone warrior was advancing toward her. Jans didn't appear to be armed, but that didn't lessen the potential threat. There was a spark of malice in her eyes, and her atten-tion was fixed firmly upon Roche.

Before Roche could react, Haid grabbed Jans's shoulder from behind and spun her around. Jans used her momentum to kick out and up, throwing him with ease across the corridor. Then, with a single, fluid motion, she was at Vri's side, disarming him of the rifle he had leveled at her only a second earlier. One shot blew a hole in the far wall as the weapon was wrenched from his grasp and turned on him. In that same instant, Roche man-aged to snap off a shot from her own pistol, knocking the rifle out of Jans's hands. The warrior didn't seem the slightest bit fazed; instead, her free hand now struck out twice at Vri's head. The third time she lashed out at him she grabbed the Surin's arm and spun him around, hurling him at the nearest wall. He bounced off the gray-black surface heavily and fell back to the floor, his body prostrate and writhing.

The warrior now turned to face Roche. For the briefest moment their eyes met.

Then the clone warrior pulled her mask closed and took two running steps toward Roche—unbelievably fast. Roche fired just as her assailant jumped. Jans's suit flared mirror-bright for an instant; then she was on top of Roche, forcing her down and knocking the pistol out of her hands. Roche struggled, but two incredibly strong hands lifted her from the ground and threw her across the floor. She slid into a wall; even through the hazard suit, the impact knocked the breath out of her. She raised her hands to ward off another blow, but none came. It wasn't *her* Jans was after.

Placing her feet on either side of Atul Ansourian's prone body, Inderdeep Jans thrust down with her left fist, penetrating his suit, rib cage, and heart with one, smooth punch.

Even in her dazed state, Roche knew what the clone warrior was doing: she was finishing the job. Now there would be no easy way that the situation in Perdue Habitat could be fixed.

Inderdeep Jans rose to her full height now and looked around, her hand dripping red. The drop in air pressure cast an eerie half-silence across the scene. Roche could hear her own breathing loudest of all, over the calling of voices in her implants. Vri's roar of defiance from behind the clone warrior went unheard entirely, as did Alta Ansourian's cry of horror.

Roche felt a wave of giddiness wash over her as Maii leveled a spear of mental force at the clone warrior, and thrust with all her strength. Jans didn't even react. She just stood there for a couple of seconds, as though contemplating what to do next. Then, having made a decision, she stepped away from Ansourian's body and over to Roche. Without wasting time, she steadied Roche with one hand to the chest and raised her bloodied fist to strike. There was no emotion in the woman's eyes, just cold detachment. And in the seconds that Roche looked into those eyes, part of her felt a fear deeper than any she had known before. But another part of her was just tired, and the breath she released at that moment was almost a sigh of relief that it was finally over. . . .

Then the clone warrior's fist fell.

A flash of white, and the fist missed her helmet and embedded itself in the corridor wall.

Roche sagged, her legs turned to water. Only Jans' hand on her chest held her upright as the clone warrior turned, eyes flashing at Cane standing in the open dumper hatch, a pistol steadied in both hands, still aiming the shot that had knocked Jans' punch aside.

<Morgan, get the others out of here while you still can!> Cane's voice traveled via his pressure suit through the *Ana Vereine*, then to Roche's implants. <The scutter's holding by the outlet. I'll take care of this.>

Jans's face became an angry sneer and the hand on Roche's chest tightened.

Cane shot her again. The suit's reflective powers had been compromised by the two shots it had already received, and this time the reflective flash was more purple than white. Jans recoiled from Roche, then sprang forward so fast that her figure became a blur.

Cane didn't waste time firing again. The pistol had hardly begun to fall when her lunge met his defensive crouch. Their limbs moved too rapidly for Roche to make out anything clearly. One would strike, the other would defend and counterstrike—the exchange almost too quick to follow. There was a dizzying effect to the battle as each whirled, ducked, and thrust, with no indication as to who was gaining the upper hand.

After a few moments the two of them came apart, as if thrown from each other by a small and silent explosion. Cane bounced back into a wall as Jans skidded along the corridor. Quicker than it would have taken Roche to blink, the two were poised again, ready to attack.

<Move, Morgan!> The inside of Cane's pressure mask was spattered with fresh blood.

His call brought her to life and, as the two clone warriors clashed again—with Cane leaping forward to prevent Jans getting any closer to the hatch—Roche reached for Alta, who was crouched over the body of her father.

"Come on!" she shouted. But Alta ignored her, whimpering as she pulled ineffectually at her lifeless father, as if trying to drag him to his feet. "We have to *go!*"

Roche dragged her to the hatch. Maii followed, clutching the back of Roche's suit as though it were a lifeline. Once there, Roche took Alta's face in her hands and forced the woman to look at her.

"I need you to help Maii through the hatch. Do you understand?"

Alta blinked back tears, sniffed, nodded.

"Okay, *in*," said Roche.

The floor bucked beneath them as first Alta, then Maii, climbed through.

"Help Maii into the scutter at the end of the outlet," she said to Alta while their suits were still touching. "I'll follow in a second."

Vri was standing over Haid, his gold armor dusted with frozen water vapor. Haid was out cold, his armor heavy and inert. Roche helped Vri drag him toward the hatch, each taking one leg. She briefly considered using one of the weapons in his suit pouches to shoot Jans again. But when she glanced up the other end of the corridor, she knew there was no way she would get a clear shot.

The two clone warriors were a blur of motion with only occasional, unpredictable pauses. There was a strange beauty and grace to their movements, almost balletic. Each was as superb as the other at combat, each forced to rely on subtleties and surprise rather than brute strength to gain the edge. Roche had never seen anything like it, and knew that in such a conflict she would have barely lasted a second against either of them. And in realizing that, she also realized just how lucky she was to be alive right then. Had Cane reached her a second later . . .

"Lift," Vri grunted, returning her attention to her injured friend. She bent her knees to slide Haid's body into the hatch. The floor shifted beneath them again, and Roche distinctly felt the ambient gravity dip. That was a bad sign, even if it did make Haid easier to carry. Somewhere, something was going terribly wrong for the station.

<Uri, what's happening?>

<Reinforcements have arrived from Random Valence,> Kajic replied. <They're concentrating fire in several areas, including power generators and life support. The habitat is taking a beating in the process.>

<I can feel it,> said Roche. <Do you think it'll hold?>

<Unless their tactics change, I have no doubt.>

<I bet that's what they thought on Guidon, too.>

With Haid through the hatch, Vri also went through, and lent Roche a hand. Together they maneuvered Haid along the chute and to the open end. The hatch there was blackened and bent open from the outside. Seeing it, Roche realized that *Cane* had blown the outer door on the outlet, not Jans, thereby forcing the other clone warrior to attack before she was ready. Had he not done this, it was unlikely they would have survived so long.

The scutter hung tethered two meters from the outlet. Vri jumped the gap, easily negotiating the change from gravity to zero-g. A quick glimpse of the local region of space revealed several ships accelerating brightly across the starfield, some of them under fire from cannon out of sight behind the tangled bulk of the habitat. Gas clouds, glowing and expanding, hung in numerous places between the ships, although Roche couldn't tell whether they were the remains of destroyed fighters or missiles that had missed their targets. Another shudder rocked the section of the habitat she clung to while leaning out to pass Haid's body to Vri. Looking back along the length of the outlet chute, she could actually see the structure flexing.

When Haid was safely aboard the scutter, Vri reached out for Roche's hand.

She shook her head. <Give me a rifle,> she said. <I'm going back for Cane.>

He turned away, returned a second later with two weapons pulled from Haid's armor, then jumped across the gap. Handing one to her, he said: <I'm coming with you.>

<You don't understand,> she protested, waving the weapon under his nose. <This isn't to help him; it's for self-defense!>

<I know, but I'm still coming.>

She shrugged, turned, and began crawling back along the chute. She didn't have time for arguments.

Neither Cane nor Jans had followed them, so they had to be still inside—unless one or the other had forced their way through the pressure doors at either end of the section of the corridor.

<Be careful,> she said as Vri approached the open hatch.

He nodded, shifting the rifle into the optimal position and taking one side. Roche took the other.

Peering out of the hatch, to the right along the corridor, she could see nothing. Vri, on the other hand, nodded, and she shifted over to his side.

Cane and Jans were still fighting furiously, although both had sustained injuries now. During one standoff, Roche noticed that one of Jans's fingers stuck out at an odd angle, and that she seemed to be favoring the hand in combat too. But the blood on Cane's face mask was thicker and darker, and it had to be obscuring his vision.

Jans lunged again; Cane parried her blows with familiar grace. But this was different from the fights he'd had before. Then he had been fighting almost for the fun of it; now he was fighting for his life.

<Box, is there nothing we can do?>

<No. We can only watch.>

And learn, she thought to herself, hoping it was worth risking a companion's life in exchange for such knowledge.

The two combatants separated and maneuvered for position. Jans caught sight of Vri and Roche in the open hatchway and kicked off for them immediately. Taken by surprise by the move, Cane was a split second slow in jumping after her. Roche recoiled as Jans's hands reached out for them, but the clone warrior rolled at the last minute and kicked off the wall. Cane was caught mid-leap and flung across the room.

Jans was on him before he could recover, rolling him over so he was between her and Roche, with an arm firmly around his neck. Cane's spine bent backward, and he twisted to look into Jans's eyes. As Roche aimed her rifle on the slight chance Jans miscalculated and gave her a clear shot, Roche saw their eyes lock.

Then, with a sickening lurch, gravity failed entirely. Using the sudden shift to his advantage, Cane pushed away from the floor and kicked Jans into the ceiling. As she rebounded, he was ready with a second kick that sent her spinning into a wall. He followed, catching her around the throat and wrenching her backward. It was her turn to be pinned from behind.

Jans writhed, managing to twist her hands behind her and pull Cane's mask off. He hung on even tighter, provoking a grimace of pain from the woman. Roche could see air puffing out of his suit, around his cheeks and jaw, but he seemed oblivious. Jans screamed silently into the vacuum, and for a moment Cane's grasp seemed to relax. Only slightly, but enough to allow Jans to twist her own head around to look at him. He leaned into his sibling, then suddenly tightened his grip once more. With one savage twist he snapped her neck.

Her body went limp, but he waited a further minute before letting her go. Then he collected the face mask dangling about his throat and carefully replaced it. The exposure to vacuum didn't seem to have harmed him at all.

Roche climbed out of the hatch, followed by Vri. Cane looked up. His face was black with frozen blood.

<Are you okay?> she asked, kicking closer to him through free-fall.

<Are *you*?> His voice, even via implants, sounded weary.

<Yes, but we should get out of here.>

He nodded and let Vri take him by the arm.

<The body,> said the Box. <You must take the body with you.>

Roche eyed the corpse of Inderdeep Jans with distaste; it was one of two in the corridor. <I presume you mean hers, not Ansourian's.>

<It will contain important data,> said the Box.

<Yeah, I know.> She approached it cautiously, afraid that even now Jans might be dangerous. The clone warrior's skin was much paler than it had been only seconds ago, and mottled with hundreds of odd-shaped bruises.

<Guards are coming,> the Box nudged her.

She grabbed the body with both hands and pushed it toward the hatch as Vri and Cane passed through. With considerably less difficulty than she'd had with Haid—for Jans was smaller and unarmored—Roche got her through the hatch and dumper chute and into the scutter. She sealed the airlock behind her, glad to be in familiar territory once again.

Maii and Alta were already braced and ready in the cockpit. Alta looked up as Roche brought Jans's body inside, then glanced away, her eyes watering.

Vri helped Roche stow the body in the rear hold, where the Box could keep an eye on it. Then she went back to the pilot's station, which Cane had left vacant, and took control of the scutter from Kajic.

<Where are you, Uri?> she asked.

A chart appeared on the console, with major concentrations of fire and wreckage marked. <I've marked the optimal course.>

<Thanks.> She glanced around the cockpit. Everyone looked shell-shocked. She supposed she looked the same. Surprisingly, Cane looked worst of all; his skin was pale and his cheeks were hollow. He looked sick, something Roche would never have

thought possible. And it wasn't just exhaustion, either. It was something much more.

With a simple series of commands directed through her implants, she fired the scutter's thrusters and moved them away from Perdue Habitat.

The scutter was attacked the moment it disengaged. Fighters and cannon converged on it, urged on by reports that they were responsible for the death of the administer—which in essence was true. Roche guessed that the remaining clone warrior was behind it, continuing the ploy that had begun with the report that she had assassinated Jans—only this time it was for real.

Surprisingly, the Random Valence ships joined in, local rivalries forgotten for the moment—or perhaps directed by another clone warrior among their own numbers. Roche wondered what lies they might be being fed, but it was impossible for the Box to access their command network.

Barely had they managed to evade pursuit long enough to dock with the waiting *Ana Vereine* when something exploded in the habitat behind them. They couldn't tell what it was—maybe a major power plant, or a weapons store. Roche could only watch with a sinking feeling as the great tangle of corridors began to disintegrate, unraveling like a knot and breaking into chunks as local stress points flexed too far and snapped.

Pursuit abruptly fell off as all the ships in the area retreated to search for survivors. Roche wanted to assist also, but Haid—awake but concussed—talked her out of it.

"Even if they don't shoot us out of the sky," he said, "they probably wouldn't let us get close enough to do any good. Remember: one of them is still in there, and they're *not* going to make it easy for you."

By "them" he meant the clone warriors. Roche was beginning to think that 'they' were everywhere.

As the *Ana Vereine* retreated from the vicinity, injuries were attended to while everyone discussed what had happened. Haid was still recovering. Alta Ansourian was under sedation; Roche didn't know if she would ever be united with the habitat survivors, or indeed any of her people, but she would do her best for the woman. Vri was back in his ship. Maii was resting on a bench on the bridge, where Roche and Kajic went over the small amount of data they had managed to gather.

Cane was asleep in the medical unit.

<He's genuinely unconscious,> the Box informed Roche.

<How can you be sure?> she said.

<I coopted the diagnostic AI to my service,> it replied.

<So his injuries were severe, then?>

<I don't believe his need to rest has anything to do with his injuries or his being tired, Morgan. At least not a physical tiredness.>

She knew what the Box was implying. She herself had done little else but think about it since leaving the habitat, and even now the significance of what had happened was still difficult to fully appreciate.

<He killed one of his own kind,> she said. <He killed her in order to save us—at no small risk to his own life, either.>

<Yes.> Even the Box seemed to be caught on that simple fact. Why would Cane be prepared to do something like that if he wasn't worthy of their trust? She should have been glad now to finally have proof that he was in fact on their side. So why was she still suspicious of him? Because he had hesitated at the end? She wasn't sure she could blame him for that. . . .

<What about the dead warrior?> she asked needing to think about something else. <Anything there?>

<Some developments I've not seen before. The cellular composition of her skin is changing at a rapid rate, returning to a decidedly more Pristine appearance rather than that of the Caste she was impersonating. The chameleonic abilities of these creatures is literal, it seems, to a degree.>

Roche added that to the list of things they'd learned. <So you've studied their bodies before?>

<Others have, and I have access to some of their data. Most bodies are found in capsules or ships destroyed by energy fire. Very few intact remains in other words. Never has one been studied so soon after death.>

<Well, that's something,> she said. <At least we know how she managed to look so much like the Vax, even if it wasn't perfect. What I don't understand is, how could she have fooled Ehud Jans into believing that she was his daughter?>

<She didn't have to.>

<What do you mean?>

The Box hesitated for a second. When it spoke again, its voice was contrite. <It is easy to see in hindsight, Morgan. The data

was in the habitat records all the time. Despite their strict laws controlling breeding, the Vax do have adoption policies. A parent may adopt a new child if their first has been killed by accident, or died of a disease. In such circumstances, they may take a parentless child as their own, in order to continue both lines. In the case of Inderdeep Jans, she is recorded as an orphan recovered from the wreckage of a mining vessel that drifted into Vax space. She was taken in and became a close friend of Ehud's real daughter, Eir. Not long after, Eir Jans was killed in an accident, and Ehud adopted Inderdeep as his own.>

Roche remembered something Ansourian had said about the previous administer discouraging the use of transit tubes after "a terrible accident," years ago. <All arranged, I imagine.>

<It seems likely,> said the Box. <Since then, she simply bided her time until she could do the most damage, doing her best in small ways to impede progress against the enemy.>

Roche could see that, too. Ansourian had also mentioned that Inderdeep Jans wouldn't have agreed to come to Sol System at all if he hadn't pressured her into it. Certainly her odd moods had kept the efficiency of the habitat at a low ebb. And ultimately, with Roche on her way and Ansourian a genuine thorn in her side, she had been forced to make her move.

Roche couldn't help but wonder what might have happened had they realized the truth earlier. Maybe she could have saved the lives of Ansourian and everyone else on the station, or maybe it would've turned out as it had. There was no way of knowing.

<And what do we do now?> Roche mused. <Turn around and go back? Proceed to the next place on Nemeth's list? Return to the *Phlegethon*, perhaps? We could even just head off on our own.> She sighed tiredly. Despite the options, she still felt trapped. She wanted a clear goal—or even better, a decisive way to strike at the enemy. The ambiguity was driving her crazy. <Or maybe we could just do nothing at all,> she finished.

<It is up to you now.>

<Yes, I know,> she said irritably. <But what do *you* think?>

<I believe proceeding to the next place on the list would be the best course of action right now.>

<There's no guarantee it'll be any better than where we've just been.>

<Of course not.>

<No, and that's the point, isn't it?> Perdue Habitat had been

ready to explode, and Roche had been the lit fuse Nemeth had thrown at it. The chances were high that the other places on the list would be equally volatile.

<Now that we know that the enemy is able to pose as members of marginally Exotic Castes,> said the Box, <we can at least be more careful in future. And we've also learned that they can be patient for years before cutting loose.>

<That only makes them harder to find, though,> said Roche.

<Not for you,> returned the Box.

<But that doesn't do me much good when I have to stand practically face to face with one to be certain!> They hadn't spent much time examining her newly found talent. When Cane was awake, perhaps, they would look at it more closely. When they could find a way to fix the precise locations of people in the real universe from the impressions they left in n-space, maybe there would be a chance. Maybe.

She sagged back in her seat. If Kajic wondered why she was no longer showing much interest in the data they were supposedly examining, he said nothing at all. Maybe he just assumed she was tired like everyone else—which she was. It was made worse by the fact that she knew she wouldn't be getting the chance to rest any time soon.

<What *is* next on the list?> she asked.

<We have a choice of two. There's either an out-station maintained by the Drys or a loose collective known as the Katajalin Serai. Both are slightly out-system from our present position. We can be at either place in approximately fifteen hours.>

Roche's weariness intensified at the thought. In just fifteen hours they could be going through it all again.

<First, I suppose I'd better put together some sort of report for Nemeth,> she said, feeling no enthusiasm at all for the task.

<I can do that for you, if you like,> said the Box. <At least the first draft. You can look at it when I'm done, and send or amend it as you wish.>

<Thanks, Box.> As always, she was unsure how far she could trust the AI, but the offer was a welcome one.

Speaking aloud, she said: "Uri, I'm sorry. I'm really not up to this at the moment. I'm feeling a little tired and distracted. Let me get a couple of hours' sleep and we'll finish up then, okay?"

"Of course, Morgan," Kajic said. "Is there anything you'd like me to get on with while you rest?"

Roche thought for a second. "Yes. Plot a course for the Kata-jalin Serai and get us under way. Its location is in the file Nemeth gave us. Send a drone to check things out first, though; this time I want to know exactly what we're getting ourselves into."

"Understood." As his holographic image began to dissolve, he added: "Sleep well, Morgan."

"I will," she said to the suddenly empty space before her.

<I can make sure of that,> said Maii softly into her mind.

For once, Roche was tempted. All the other times the girl had made that offer, she had turned it down out of fear that the reave might tamper with her mind. She'd had plenty of opportunities now to see that Maii's intentions were innocent. If Roche could trust her with the knowledge that the Box had survived the de-struction of the *Sebettu*, then she could probably feel safe in her hands for a couple of hours.

But the thought still nagged at her that she would be defense-less. It would take longer still for her to get over that feeling.

<Okay,> she said. <Just get me to sleep, though, and I'll do the rest.>

The girl radiated warmth. <Of course, Morgan. Gladly.>

Later, though, Roche would regret that she hadn't given herself wholly over to the girl's care. Her sleep was disturbed by dreams that left her frightened, bewildered, confused, and sad. Most un-nerving was a recurring image in which she was floating gently over a flat gray landscape in which there suddenly appeared a circular hole. First a pinprick, then a gaping mouth, then a yawn-ing chasm, it sucked her into its lightless maw—and she fell, much as she had in the dream that had haunted her through COE Armada Military College and before her arrival in Palasian Sys-tem. Only this time there was no bottom. This time her fall went on forever.

PART THREE:
PHLEGETHON

11

TBC-14 (a.k.a. IND *Kindling*)
955.1.33
0390

"Who is the enemy, Page?" Salton Trezise asked via the ftl link with the *Phlegethon.*

De Bruyn didn't answer immediately. She was too busy watching the recording of Perdue Habitat disintegrate. It was the third time she had sat through it; this time she was paying special attention to one particular section of the structure.

Signs still remained of where Roche's tame clone warrior had blown his way in through the outer hatch of the refuse dumper, and where the ex-Dato scutter had left distinctive exhaust marks upon its departure. Unfortunately, that portion of the habitat had been one of the most severely damaged, and De Bruyn's recording was the only remaining proof of what had taken place there.

"Someone got rid of the evidence," she said, watching again the puff of energy that tore apart the section of the habitat, atomizing anything that might have remained within and slagging the dumper itself. "There's nothing left at all."

"Are you listening to me, Page?" he said. "I asked—"

"I heard you," she said. And indeed she had: she had switched to an ordinary audio link, tired of his voice insinuating through her implants. After a session with him, she felt as if her brain had been soaked in oil. "I'm busy."

"Busy doing what?"

"The work you and your ineffectual council should be doing."

"We have enough on our hands without wasting time pursuing grudges."

"Is that really what you think this is?" She made no attempt to hide her anger. She'd had enough of that sort of talk from the mercenaries on *Dark Stressor*.

"You haven't given me sufficient evidence to think otherwise, I must say."

"*Must* you?"

His sigh was audible over the link. "Page, you're acting like a child."

"I'm investigating every possibility," she said. "*That's* what I'm doing."

"No you're not," he countered quickly. "You're investigating just *one* possibility from every possible angle."

"And what's wrong with that? It's still a possibility."

"A remote one, at best," he said. "Really, Page, what have you to go on? A suspicion; a scrap or two of barely circumstantial evidence—"

"*More* than a scrap! We know Roche was in the habitat. One of your own agents lifted her image from security. But no one saw her leave." She indicated the image before her, speaking as much to herself as to Trezise, mulling over the problem again. "This whole area was blacked out at the time. We have no hard evidence of anything!"

"We *do* know she escaped, Page. She sent a report to Rey Nemeth ten hours later."

"*Someone* did. We can't be sure it was her."

His laugh held more exasperation than amusement. "You think she stayed behind?"

"Maybe. Or maybe the scutter acted as a distraction while she went elsewhere."

"Where?"

"I don't know."

"Why?"

"I don't know."

"With *whom*?"

"I don't *know*." Her fists clenched.

"So in the absence of any alternative theory, do you *really* believe it wasn't her?"

"All I'm saying is that it pays to be careful. She's slippery, and she's not stupid. If she thinks she's being followed, who knows what lengths she would go to to avoid me?"

"Possibly," he muttered. "But you have to admit that these lengths would be ridiculous."

She opened her mouth to protest, but decided against it. The evidence overwhelmingly suggested that Roche *had* been on the scutter when it left the habitat, and that she had therefore been aboard the *Ana Vereine* when it left the vicinity of the disaster. If De Bruyn could allow herself to feel satisfied on that point, she could move on. There were other, more immediate things to worry about.

She killed the recording, deciding that she did in fact agree with Trezise. She would not, however, give him the satisfaction of knowing that she had given in.

"Have *you* learned anything of note?" she challenged him as she checked local space. Still no sign of the ship she was waiting for.

"Things are moving apace," he said. "The Kesh-Olmahoi conflict has ended as expected, with the Kesh decisively routed. Surprisingly, no evidence has been found of enemy involvement. But the council is lending its support to those attempting to clean up the mess."

No evidence, De Bruyn repeated to herself, disappointed that he should be so blind.

"We've been investigating the cult I mentioned earlier, the one purported to worship the enemy," he went on. "They have caused a moderately large amount of damage and their influence appears to be growing. It seems there are several splinter sects. Their devotion is quite genuine, albeit misplaced and lacking any foundation. We have interrogated a number of devotees and found that they possess no more knowledge about the enemy than we do ourselves. If the enemy *does* have any involvement with them at all, then it is purely symbolic. They share no information with their worshippers, and no plans, and seem to bear them no sympathy at all when they are purged. Five pockets of the religion have been flushed out of as many fleets, and not once has the enemy raised a hand to stop us.

"The interesting thing, though, is that the cults believe, as do some of us, that the enemy has been sent to rid the galaxy of Pristines. While this does conflict with some of the evidence we have gathered, it *is* suggestive. There might yet be a grain of truth to that belief, after all."

De Bruyn let him ramble on. She didn't know whether he was talking for her benefit, or his own, but she doubted he would be telling her anything simply because he thought it would help her. Maybe he thought she knew something about the cults and might let it slip if he encouraged her. She did, but she wasn't going to let him know.

The near-space screen was still empty.

"There have been a few setbacks," he continued. "One of the council's major allies, the Espire-Mavrodis Coalition, was struck from within just hours ago. A group of military officers attempted to capitalize on discontent in the lower ranks, and mounted a coup that might very well have been successful, had not one of their own had a change of heart at the last moment and turned against them. The debacle cost the life of nearly every person we had come to rely on in that quarter, and has left the Coalition in complete disarray. They'll be no use to us in the short term, I'm afraid—and maybe never, as there is talk of them pulling out to regroup. Unfortunately, the defecting officer has not been found."

"Has the Commonwealth of Empires been affected?" De Bruyn asked.

"No. That continues to puzzle me. It is such an easy target, and so close to the focus of things. I would've thought it would be riddled with the enemy."

De Bruyn nodded to herself, agreeing with him about the COE's vulnerability but not really surprised that it seemed to have been spared.

"And I hope you've taken my warning about the system's ring," he said. "We've lost five ships in there, that we know of. Four others are incommunicado. With the little information we've had to go on, it's hard to say why this is happening. Given the conflict within the system at the moment, the likelihood of a ship being attacked simply because it is not recognized by another Caste has risen dramatically. It is possible that the ships were attacked out of paranoia. It's hard to know for sure." He paused. "It may not have anything to do with the ring itself at all. Still, it doesn't hurt to be cautious, and until we *do* know for certain what's going on, I advise you to stay away from it."

De Bruyn had been doing just that, not because of Trezise's warning, but because Roche herself had stuck to more distant regions of the system.

"Could the enemy be hiding within the ring?" she asked.

"No, it's too thin—thinner than even the most meager of atmospheres. Add it all together and you get enough for a medium-sized gas giant or two, but spread out so far it amounts to practically nothing at all. The Heresiarch still hasn't worked out where it came from, but that's a low priority at this point. He's only concerned because he's obsessed by navigational anomalies. With a ship that big to look after, even the slightest snag could be disastrous. You know, I think he spends all his time—"

"Look, Salton," she interrupted, "was there an actual *reason* for this call?"

"I always have a reason, Page. You know that."

"Would it have anything to do with the information I requested?"

"No," he said. "But I do happen to have that as well."

She gritted her teeth. "Can I have it?"

"It should be coming through with this transmission." She could hear the smile in his voice, but kept her annoyance in check.

"Thank you," she forced herself to say, but not without a hint of sarcasm, and not before checking that he was telling the truth. He was. As soon as the data transfer was complete, she would get rid of him.

"But before you go," he said, irritating her still further by seeming to read her thoughts, "can I ask you a small favor in return?"

Here we go, she thought. "Which is?"

"That idiot Murnane is thinking of letting Exotics onto the council. Obviously that would be a dangerous idea, even if they were allowed only an advisory or associate status. Things are complicated enough without adding more interests into the mix. If we can't guarantee our own safety—as the downfall of the Espire-Mavrodis Coalition demonstrates all too well—why should we make ourselves responsible for anyone else's?"

"Unless they can help you more in return."

"Which is exactly what I think Murnane is hoping for. But I for one am skeptical."

She refrained from commenting on his motives. "What does any of this have to do with me?"

"Well, I'm presuming that you are following Morgan Roche as she gallivants across this forsaken system. That seems to be your mission in life, after all."

"You could presume that," she said, thinking: *But you'd be wrong*.

"And I happen to know that her mission is to reconnoiter the Exotic Castes to see how they are faring against the enemy. But we both know this is a waste of time. *Everyone* is performing badly against the enemy—be they Exotic or Pristine."

The data had arrived. "What's your point, Salton?"

"I need a reason to keep the Exotics off the council, Page. You can help me find that reason."

"I can?"

"You're out there, among it all. You're seeing it firsthand. You can give me the flip side to Roche's reports. She makes it sound like the Exotics are suffering as much as we are—which may be true, but I'd prefer if it wasn't quite so obvious."

"Why not, if it's the truth?"

"That's just the point I'm trying to make. We should ignore it *because* it is true. It *has* to be deliberate. What's the biggest problem in Sol System at the moment? It's not the enemy—although I don't doubt their presence is being felt in a thousand small ways: disrupting communications, sabotaging procedures, corrupting information, and more. Even without the enemy, even if everything ran smoothly, there'd still be chaos: there are simply *too many people*! And when these people start fighting among themselves, the situation inevitably worsens. We're balancing constantly on the precipice of all-out mayhem; only the most super-Human effort stops us from doing the enemy's job for them."

"So you figure that if there are less people, things might improve?"

"Of course! Reorganize and integrate our resources, limit the number of governments to a manageable number, reduce the council's active concerns to a feasible few, and *maybe* we'll prevail. Given that the majority of people here are Pristines, and that apart from a few exceptions the enemy seems to target Pristines, wouldn't it be better if everyone else left and let the Pristines sort it out?"

"With you in charge, no doubt."

He laughed lightly. "I knew I could count on you to see my reasoning," he said. "And if my proposal goes through the council, hopefully others will too."

"So you want me to lie about what's happening to the Exotics?"

"No; I just want you to balance the scales."

"It amounts to the same thing," she said.

"It's all about *how* you put it, Page. How else do you think politics works? Give me the right words and I could move entire solar systems."

"Not if there isn't anyone listening to you." She found it hard to imagine greasy Salton Trezise, known for so long as Auberon Chase's lackey, being a force in his own right in something like the IEPC. "*Is* anyone going to be listening to you, Salton?"

"I have the ear of several councilors," he said. "Enough to make a difference."

"Why do you need me, then? Why not use the council's own agents?"

"Because *your* reports will help discredit Roche's. That's a cause to which I know you will apply yourself." He chuckled softly to himself for a second. "Look, even discounting personal grudges, Page, this will benefit us both. Think of the enemy—the *common* enemy. *They're* the ones we're ultimately after—not Roche, not Murnane. If we can do what we want to do while at the same time achieving what we need to achieve, then we approach success. Ultimately the ends do justify the means, and, as we're in this together, we might as well use each other to the best of our abilities. I'm not naive, Page; I *know* you've used me to suit your needs."

"I would never call you 'naive,' Salton," she said soberly.

"Good," he returned. "Then let's start working together, because together we *can* do some damage—to the enemy, and to those who oppose us."

And to each other, she thought. But all she said was: "Okay, Salton. I'll see what I can do."

He was silent long enough for her to suspect he might have gone, even though the line was still open. That suited her. A beacon had begun to flash on the fighter's main display, indicating that a ship had just entered her region of the system. She didn't know if Trezise could tell where she was by tracing which ftl drone had detected her replies to him; maybe the broadcasts traveled from drone to drone in a complicated chain, not just via a single one direct to the receiving stations on the *Phlegethon*. Either way, she was glad he seemed to think she was still hot on Roche's heels. If he knew where she actually was, he might reconsider his deal.

The Hurn ship drifted smoothly toward *Kindling*, looking like a cross between a sailing ship and processional barge, its bulky, bullet-shaped body almost completely obscured by tapering instrument spines, crisscrossing antennae, and curved flanges that seemed to serve no actual purpose. This far from the sun, out where an Oört cloud might once have existed, there was very little light to view anything effectively. In artificial color, the vessel looked like it was painted electric blue, with highlights of bright orange and green. Its vividness was unsettling enough without its contents to consider.

It decelerated to a relative halt and hung there, waiting.

"I have to go," she said to Trezise.

"Understood," he replied without any appreciable lag. "We'll speak again soon, Page."

For once, despite herself, she hoped that this would be true.

The circular bridge of the *Apostle* was dimly lit and smelled of steel. De Bruyn sat at the lowest point of the cavernous space, surrounded by ranks of instruments like steps in an amphitheatre. Tall figures moved among those instruments, but the light was too faint for her to make them out. She half-glimpsed robes and cowls; very occasionally, eyes glinted at her.

"We know who she is," said the shadowy figure sitting opposite her. His face was completely obscured by the hood of a black combat suit that had been modified to give it a more ceremonial air. "But do you know who *we* are?"

"You are the Disciples of Evergence," she said.

"And what does that name mean to you?"

She hesitated. "I'm not sure," she said finally. "The word 'Evergence' doesn't appear in any language I have access to. It's not a name, it's not a code—"

"It has no meaning of itself," the hooded figure interrupted her. "It could be said to be a confluence of many essences: of convergence, forever, emerging, divergent, evolution, emergency, and even vengeance. But 'Evergence' is none of these things. It is a word for something that has, until now, needed no words. It has existed in silence, and will return to silence when the need for words is gone." The ominous figure inclined its head as the echoes of his voice faded. "But I feel you do not understand."

"No, I'm afraid you've lost me," she admitted with a shrug.

"It doesn't matter. Your comprehension is neither essential nor desired. We simply wish to ensure that you bring with you no misconceptions about our purpose here in Sol System."

"You worship the enemy," she said softly. The words carried much more significance when said in context.

"So it has been said," the figure observed. "And if that is what you choose to believe, so be it."

"You're telling me you *don't* worship them?"

"We do not *worship*," the figure intoned. "That is all I am telling you."

"But you are on their side?"

"Yes."

"And Morgan Roche is your enemy." She didn't need to phrase that as a question.

"Yes, she is."

"Then I believe I can help you," De Bruyn said, feeling a catch in her voice that surprised her.

"Really?" Was there a hint of mockery in his voice? She couldn't be sure.

"Yes," she said, the word emerging as little more than a croak. What was wrong with her? Finally she had found people that suited her needs, and she seemed to be having second thoughts! But she wasn't about to back out. Not now. She *couldn't*.

"I *can* help you," she said more assertively, adding: "If you help *me*."

"Ah, I see." The figure nodded thoughtfully. "And what is it exactly that you want from us?"

"A deal," she said. "We work together and we *both* get what we want."

"You would serve us?"

"No," she said quickly. "I would work with you. For a time."

"How?"

"I am alone, here. My resources are meager. But I know what I'm doing, and I have access to information at the heart of the

IEPC. Give me one of your cells to command, and I will do your job for you."

"Which job do you think that would be?"

She leaned forward. "With my knowledge and your Disciples, we can trap Roche. I *know* we can. All we have to do is cooperate, and she will be out of your hair forever. It's that simple."

"Nothing is ever that simple," he said darkly.

"Look, all I need is to get my hands on her," De Bruyn said. "I don't even care if she's alive, just as long as I have her body."

"Why would you want her body so badly?" he asked.

"Because it contains the truth," she said. "The truth of who she is."

"I've told you once that we already know who she is," he said. "Why not just ask?"

De Bruyn didn't state the obvious: how could he know anything more than *she* did? The rumors she'd heard—and which, she was sure, comprised the bulk of the Disciples' knowledge— were wild and contradictory. Some proclaimed Roche as a savior, others as a traitor. De Bruyn lent none of them credence, just as she wouldn't waste her time listening to the views of a religious fanatic.

"Because I want to see the truth with my own eyes," she said.

The robed figure pondered this for a few moments, then asked, "And what *exactly* do we receive in turn?"

"Apart from Roche out of the way?" She leaned back into the seat and shrugged. "What do you want?"

"You say that you have access to the Interim Emergency Pristine Council."

"I have a contact—"

"Will you give us information?"

She hesitated. "What sort of information?"

"The information we require."

She waited for him to elaborate, but he said nothing more— and he obviously wasn't going to until she had agreed or disagreed. An icy silence filled the air of the bridge, and again her doubts returned.

She shook herself free of them by reminding herself why she was here. This *wasn't* a grudge-match. This was about justice. Everything she had unearthed suggested that she was doing the right thing. If she was doing this for herself, why was she going to such lengths? Any sane person would have given up weeks ago—and there could be no question of her sanity.

She was *so close* to the truth. . . .

As she waited for docking instructions to arrive from the *Apostle*, she'd used the time to scan the data Trezise had given her. A cursory glance had been all she needed. The records weren't complete, but they did fill in portions of a bigger picture. They had come from the second moon around Bodh Gaya, the former capital system of the Commonwealth of Empires, where the Armada housed its Military College. Morgan Roche had served there during her training for COE Intelligence, years ago. Trezise had managed to get his hands on various reports, assessments, essays, and test scores that demonstrated how average a student Roche had been. Only in one area had she excelled, and that had been the handling of AIs. She had preferred to grapple with artificial minds rather than those of the people around her.

Perhaps, De Bruyn thought, that might explain why she'd had so few friends. It certainly explained how she had been selected as a courier for JW111101000, the Box that had ultimately helped her escape from Sciacca's World and the clutches of the Dato Bloc. That was one AI De Bruyn was glad to see the end of.

But that information was not specifically what De Bruyn was after. The information she sought hadn't been there at all. And in some ways, the gaps were more telling. All of Roche's physical records were unavailable. Not missing or deleted: *unavailable*. When Trezise had asked why, he had been told that access to those records was restricted by special order VSD5278.

De Bruyn recognized that order number. It was department shorthand for the COE's previous Eupatrid, Enver Buk. Eupatrid Buk himself had specifically ordered those records kept secret, no matter who asked for them.

That in itself might not have been significant. Trezise had dug back a little further, not just trying to find a birth date but *any* physical record at all, prior to Roche's enrollment at Military College. Her name was recorded at an orphanage on Ascensio, but there was little else of note: no medical records, no education reports, no informal recollections. Her application scores were on file in Ascensio's COE Armada recruit database, along with the form she must have filled out to apply for the test, but the results of her medical exam were missing. Special order VSD5278 had cast a cloak over them, too, it seemed.

It had taken De Bruyn only a minute or two to confirm what she already suspected: that the details of Roche's early life were being kept secret by the government of the COE, and that this secret had been ratified by the Eupatrids past and present who had issued the special orders required to ensure that no one ever found out the truth.

What that truth was, though, she wasn't yet entirely sure. But she had suspicions. She had been chasing those suspicions, along with Roche, across Sol System and half of the COE in the hope that they might be verified. If Roche's early life was being kept secret, it was entirely possible that the details Trezise had uncovered were completely fictitious. Where had Roche come from before Military College? Out of thin air, it seemed—which made her suspiciously like the clone warriors the IEPC were trying to fight.

As soon as the idea occurred to her, De Bruyn had been caught by its ramifications. If it was true, Roche *must* have been planted by the enemy to seed chaos and disorder the way that they had in so many other systems. The fact that she had not, until recently, shown any destructive or even subversive tendencies did not necessarily invalidate this theory.

De Bruyn noted that at about the time Roche enrolled in the Military College the High Human known as the Crescend had joined the COE in a partnership designed to foster trade and joint industry between the Caste echelons. Maybe the Crescend knew about Roche and had decided to see if she could be contained rather than destroyed. Maybe he hoped to bend her to his will, or at least make her an ally rather than an enemy; that might explain why he was so keen to keep her existence a secret, to the point of penalizing those who came even close to the truth, like De Bruyn. Maybe he didn't care what happened to the COE at all, and was only interested in seeing what happened at firsthand when the time bomb called Morgan Roche finally went off.

Maybe he wasn't involved at all, and the giant shadows De Bruyn saw on the wall before her were cast by shapes much tinier. Either way, she had to be sure. Something odd was going on, and she had been caught up in it. Now that she was close to finding proof—of *anything at all*—it was finally time to act. But she couldn't do it on her own; she was going to need powerful friends if she was to see justice served.

She needed to fight fire with fire.

"I'll give you information," she said to the man in black, "if you give me Morgan Roche."

His posture didn't change, but in the shadows that hid his face she thought she had seen him smile.

"Good," he said. "In that case, *God's Monkey* will meet with you in precisely seven hours. Its pilot and contingent of Disciples will obey your commands—unless, of course, those commands are contrary to the goals of our movement. You may use them as you will until such time as our mutual obligations have been discharged. Does that suit you?"

She swallowed with relief. "Thank you, yes," she said. "But where exactly will I meet them?"

He gave her the coordinates. "They will know you as 'Reverence,' " he said. "Use them well, Page De Bruyn."

He stood. She stood too, although her muscles felt weak. The gray-clad Disciples who had led her to the bridge stepped out of the shadows to stand by her side.

"Wait," she said to the figure in black. "You know my name?"

He turned to face her, but said nothing.

"Couldn't I at least know yours?"

"Mine is not relevant," he said.

"If you're worried that I will tell the council—"

"The thought would never cross our minds," he said, taking a step toward her. "Nor should it cross yours again."

De Bruyn swallowed. "I assure you," she said nervously, "I wouldn't tell anyone—"

"Oh, I know you won't," he interrupted her. "Not just because I tell you that should you betray us by divulging anything that has passed between us this day, we would hunt you down, Page De Bruyn, and we would kill you. Of that *you* can be certain."

He took another step forward, into the light, and smiled as she recoiled a pace in alarm.

Even with the hood up, there was no mistaking the face of Adoni Cane.

"I know," he said, "because we have a deal . . ."

12

AVS-38
955.2.12
1770

Defender-of-Harmony Vri carried the injured girl over the threshold of the airlock, ignoring the gunfire that insistently peppered the back of his combat suit. Once he had safely passed the girl to the armored figure waiting for him, he turned and fired four shots in rapid succession in the direction he had come.

There was an explosion. Immediately, the gunfire stopped.

The scutter shuddered noisily as the airlock closed with a hiss.

Vri steadied himself. The scutter lurched away from the station and weathered a battering on its way back to the *Ana Vereine*. He walked the short distance to where the girl had been strapped to a stretcher and attached to a portable autosurgeon. The shot had taken her in the shoulder, piercing her hazard suit and making a mess of the flesh beneath, then exploding messily out the back. Only the suit's small first-aid facility had kept her alive while Vri and Haid fought their way back to the scutter through near-endless waves of Fathehi custodians.

The autosurgeon's display was blinking red: the girl needed the full version on the main ship before she would begin to recover.

Vri stood. His faceplate clicked open, swinging up and back

to reveal not just his face but most of his head too. Even through the light hair that covered every inch of his features, his anger was obvious.

"It was too close," he said. His voice was deep, and every word perfectly enunciated.

Haid too had shucked the helmet of his combat suit. "We were unlucky," he said, wiping sweat from his hairless black forehead with the palm of his glove. "Even when they sprang the trap, we thought Maii had it covered. But all it took was one lucky shot . . ." He looked down at the girl, rocking in her stretcher as the scutter endured another battering. "Maybe we weren't so unlucky. At least we managed to get out."

"It was too close," Vri repeated with the same, slow precision to his words.

Haid looked at him. "So you keep telling us."

"It is not *you* I am telling." His intense eyes were as golden as his armor, and focused on the back of the person piloting the scutter.

"I hear you," said Roche. She didn't need to turn to know he was referring to her. Nor did she particularly care what the Surin thought at this moment; there was too much happening to worry about that. Besides, she had been watching via the suit monitors and the Box's patch into the consulate's security channel; she knew better than either of them just how narrow their escape had been. Another ten seconds in the dock and a full squadron of custodians would have pinned them in a crossfire from which none of them would have emerged alive.

"I'm taking her back," the Surin warrior said. His firm tone conveyed more than the words themselves.

Roche did turn, at that. "You're not taking her to Erojen." Her voice was as hard as his.

"No, of course not," he said. "I meant to the *Phlegethon*."

Roche was silent for a long moment; then her expression softened slightly. "Okay," she said. "The *Phlegethon* it is. But if you don't let me fly this thing home first, we won't be going anywhere at all. . . ."

The Surin nodded, and Roche turned back to the controls. He took the seat closest to Maii's injured form.

Sensing Haid's eyes on him still, he turned to face the ex-mercenary. They stared at each other for a few seconds.

"You fight well," Vri said finally, adding: "Despite your handicap."

Haid's eyes flashed. "As do you, despite yours."

Vri frowned a question, and Haid indicated the girl.

"I do not consider my protecting this child to be a handicap," said Vri indignantly.

Haid raised one arm, indicating where an energy bolt had passed clear through his arm and out the other side.

"Nor do I consider this to be one, either," he said.

Vri pondered this for a moment, then turned away and was silent for the remainder of the trip back to the *Ana Vereine*.

Earlier, they had argued about the mission to the Fathehi Consulate.

"It is too dangerous," Vri had insisted.

"Dangerous, yes; *too* dangerous, no," Roche had shot back. "The junior consul herself has assured us that we will have free passage through the station."

"And you *believe* her?"

"Why shouldn't I?"

"After all that has happened, I find your naiveté disturbing."

Roche felt her face turn red. "We are more than capable of handling anything they might throw at us."

"We are a handful of people against an entire station!"

"Maii can—"

"Yes, she can. And she *has*. You rely on her too much. You are *using* her! You are using her as I would use a percussion rifle—to be tossed aside when its usefulness has expired."

"That's not true!" Roche was finding it difficult containing her emotions, and a blast of anger from the reave in response to Vri's accusation only enhanced her irritation. "We rely on her help, but that's *not* the same as using her."

"She is a child that is—"

"That is still capable of making up her own mind!" snapped Roche. "If you want to talk about people being used, then take a good look at yourself!"

This caught the Surin warrior by surprise, and he frowned in confusion.

"You're just a stooge of the Surin Agora," Roche went on. "They don't care about the truth, and they don't care about Maii!

They just want her back so they can take her apart and see how she works. And you're helping them!"

Vri had reared back in the screen. "Be careful what you say, Morgan Roche."

"If you're threatening me," Roche spat, "I swear I'll have you shipped back to the council faster than you can say 'mindless pawn'!"

"Easy, you two," said Haid, putting a hand on Roche's shoulder. "This is getting us nowhere."

<I agree,> put in Maii herself, her emotions back under control. <I don't require either of you to argue on my behalf.>

Roche took a deep breath and looked down at her feet. Maii was right; she was as guilty as Vri of assuming that she knew what was right for the girl.

<I will go into the consulate,> Maii said. <And if you so desire, Vri, you may accompany me as my bodyguard. Would that be acceptable?>

For a moment, Roche thought Vri would argue with her, but instead he simply nodded. "It is a reasonable compromise," he said.

<Good. And Haid will go with us while Morgan stays with the scutter.>

"But—" Roche began.

<Morgan, you need a rest from the front line. Let someone else take the risks for a change.>

"She's right, Morgan," said Haid, smiling. "It's my turn to be the hero."

Roche knew he was only joking, but she couldn't help feeling slightly stung by his words. She was reluctant to lose control because she was desperate for something to go right—just once! The fact that nothing had gone right for anyone in Sol System didn't change things. She still felt like it was *her* that was somehow getting it wrong.

And Maii did have a point. She *was* tired of facing hostile envoys and suspicious security forces. This could be a good way for Vri to save some face, and to relieve the restlessness eating at Haid. Besides, she and Maii had swept for clone warriors upon their arrival and the place seemed clear. That made it safer than any of the other ports they had visited.

Or so it had seemed. Roche had become so used to looking for clone warriors that she had blinded herself to base Human treachery. When the junior consul decided that Roche had extended herself far enough into her station, she ordered her custodians to open fire—on the boarding party and on the *Ana Vereine* itself, forcing the ship to retreat to a safe distance and leaving the others to scramble for their lives through the station. Had the scutter not already docked, and had the Box not been available behind the scenes to keep the custodians at bay, the situation could have been a lot worse than it was.

Even without knowing what lay ahead, Roche had approached the mission with apprehension. Before leaving, she had gone to see Cane.

He had taken up residence in an observation blister on one of the *Ana Vereine*'s seven nacelles. The curved window allowed him an unobstructed view of the space around the ship. Not that there was much to see. The only object visible to the naked eye was the crossed rings of the Fathehi Consulate, tumbling slowly against the starry backdrop.

The Box had observed him there on numerous occasions over the previous two weeks, since the events on Perdue Habitat. When Roche didn't ask for him specifically, that was where he went. She suspected that he was avoiding her.

"Will you tell me why you're doing this?" she had asked.

At first he hadn't answered, his brown skin soaking up the light from distant stars.

"Cane?"

"I am thinking."

"What about?"

"About what it is like to be alone."

Roche had glanced at the stars, at the galaxy around them. All those systems, all those worlds, all the Humanity filling them up: High and Low, Pristine and Exotic, old and young—and almost a thousand of those Castes were now crammed into Sol System. She didn't feel alone anymore. Not at all.

And that didn't even take into account the AI sharing her body.

"Why?" she had asked.

"I killed one of my own kind," he said. He turned to face her.

"You still have us." She had attempted a smile, then regretted it. "I'm sorry. I didn't realize it was bothering you this much."

He had shaken his head and returned, expressionlessly, to watching the stars.

"Nor did I," he said quietly.

"You mightn't be the only one in this position, you know."
She didn't want to take his black mood with her to the consulate;
if there was anything she could do to crack his reserve, she would
try it—even if it meant inviting him to join the landing party to
the consulate in Haid's place. "Your siblings don't seem terribly
indiscriminate. We only know of one time when they cooperated,
and that was on Perdue. Maybe *that* was the exception. Maybe
they kill each other as easily as ordinary Humans do."

But he hadn't responded.

Eventually, she had left him alone and gone to see Alta Ansourian. Another mistake. The woman was still grieving for her
father and for all the friends destroyed with her habitat. Since
coming on board she had barely emerged from the stateroom
Roche had given her—not even to see what was going on when
the *Ana Vereine* had come under attack.

"Do you think I'll ever get back to Vacishnou?" she had asked
Roche.

"I'll do my best," Roche told her, hoping the words didn't
sound as empty as they felt. The homeworld of the Vax was on
the other side of the galaxy and seemed far removed from their
current situation. "That's the most I can promise, I'm afraid."

"I understand." But if she truly understood, it hadn't given
her any comfort. And that more than anything made Roche wonder if Alta Ansourian was wiser than she looked.

<Are you sure this is the right thing to do?> the Box asked Roche
as she rested in her cabin, the disastrous sortie to the Fathehi
Consulate fresh in her mind.

<What do you think?> She scratched absently at the back of
her head. <Despite recent history, running away really isn't my
thing.>

<You know that it's not what you will be doing.>

<No, but it feels like it,> she said. <And I don't like it.>

<That much is obvious. But ask yourself, Morgan, who you
are most angry at—and why.>

She thought seriously about the question. Was she angry at
Rey Nemeth for giving her a mission she couldn't finish? Or at
Vri for forcing her to face the inevitable? Or at Maii for being
shot?

The last was ridiculous. If anyone, she should resent the person who had shot the girl. That in itself was tempting, but not

as tempting a target as the junior consul who had ordered the attack. Or the lieutenant who had turned them away from the LaGoc barracks that had been their previous port of call, as had leaders of the three previous habitats they had tried to contact. Then there were the Noske saboteurs who had planted a bomb on their usual scutter, nearly killing everyone on board; the clone warrior in the Katajalin Serai, responsible for triggering a mass riot that had torn the normally tight collection of vessels apart within a day of Roche's arrival; and finally Inderdeep Jans and her unknown enemy cohort who, together or apart, had brought about the appalling failure that had been the very first of Roche's missions for the Ulterior.

She could hate the council for not helping her, but that was pushing the boundary too far. She might as well hate the COE, or the Crescend, or the galaxy itself.

Except the Box hadn't asked about *hate*, had it? It had asked her about her anger, and once she separated the two, the answer came to her.

<I'm angry at myself,> she said in the end.

<And why is that, Morgan?> he pressed.

<Because I'm losing control, Box. I'm losing control of it all.> She paused as a dream image momentarily flashed across her thoughts. <I'm falling.>

<Morgan, you never *had* control.>

<But I had a direction! At least that was *something*.> She rolled onto her side, into a fetal position. <Now . . .>

<Now you just have momentum.>

She couldn't tell if the Box was being facetious or not. <What good will *that* do me when it comes to the crunch?>

<Perhaps a lot of good, depending on what you hit.>

<If it's the council, they're not likely to give.> Vri had been pestering her ever since they left the volume of space the Fathehi Consulate controlled, but she hadn't yet confirmed the order to return to the *Phlegethon*. <Come on, Box, what do you think? I want your honest opinion.>

<I would give you nothing less, Morgan.> The AI seemed pleased that she had asked its advice. <I think the *Phlegethon* is as good a place as any.>

<For what, though? What do I do once I get there?>

<You can see what happens. Maybe the Ulterior will not re-

gard your mission as a failure at all. You have, after all, learned some things.>

<And got my name blacklisted from every station this side of the system.>

<That's something, too. One would have to assume that was deliberate.>

<I considered this. Why else would everything fall apart just when I arrived?> The destruction of Perdue had taken less than two days; the Katajalin Serai had dissolved in half that time. By the end of the week, no one in their right mind would let Roche on board their stations—except the Fathehi Consulate who, it turned out, had planned a trap. <It's not me doing it, so it must be someone else hoping to make it *look* like me. Unfortunately, it seems to have worked.>

<No doubt the Ulterior will guide your return to the *Phlegethon*.>

<I hadn't even thought of that! What happens if they don't let us in? What if—?>

<Morgan, you don't have to worry about that. They will let you return; you have something they do not.>

She rolled onto her back again. <Such as?>

<Two things, actually. The most obvious being the experience you have gained.>

<Half as much as their usual agents, I'm sure.>

<Possibly—but none of their agents have discovered a means of identifying the clone warriors, have they?>

She was about to protest that the talent was so vague as to be almost useless, except to sweep a large number of people to make sure they were clean. But then she stopped herself. The council didn't need to know about her talent's limitations—not initially, anyway. The very fact that her ability existed would at least guarantee her a hearing.

<So I become their test subject while people like Nemeth get all the credit,> she said cynically. <Sounds like a lot of fun, Box.>

<But at least you'll have some direction again,> the Box responded.

She thought about that for a few seconds.

<That's true,> she admitted. <And somewhere to channel that momentum.> She forced herself to let her eyelids close and her muscles relax. The last thing she wanted right now was to move *anywhere*.

<How many more stops were there on Nemeth's list?> she asked.

<Two—outposts run by the Saa-hurod and Yemena Castes.>

Neither of the names rang a bell. <Does either look likely to tell us anything new?>

<Impossible to say, from here.>

<Does Nemeth highlight either as being especially important?>

<No.>

<Then we can safely ignore them, I think. And without Maii to help me sweep for clone warriors, I wouldn't feel comfortable in approaching them.>

<Her prognosis is good, Morgan. She will be conscious within twenty hours.>

<That's not the point,> Roche said, recalling the accusation leveled at her by Vri about using the Surin girl. <I don't want to push her unnecessarily. She needs rest.>

Roche was silent for a while, on the verge of making the decision but still balking. It would only take a call to Kajic to put them on their way. She wanted to make absolutely certain—as certain as she could be, anyway—that she was doing the right thing.

<Have you heard from the Crescend?> she asked.

<If you are asking me whether he would approve of your return to the *Phlegethon*, I can tell you that he would.>

She hadn't dared ask the question so blatantly, so to hear the reply threw her off balance for a moment. She didn't want to push her luck by asking *why* he approved.

<He's told you that?>

<Yes.>

<When?>

<While we were just talking.>

The ramifications of that information were profound. <So you and he are communicating by ftl, like the council does?> she said. <Why didn't you tell me?>

<It didn't seem necessary. Should I have?>

<Well, no. It doesn't make that much difference, I guess. I just assumed . . .> She wondered how much else she had assumed about the Box's relationship with the Crescend that would one day turn out to be wrong. That was the problem in dealing with the AI: without asking exactly the right question, she couldn't be entirely sure she was learning what she needed to know.

And yet it had offered the Crescend's advice on the matter of the *Phlegethon*. That was out of character. Either it had a hidden agenda—which was all too possible—or the High Human had finally decided to become involved.

She wasn't sure if the latter would be a good thing or not.

Yawning, she rolled back onto her stomach. <Box, open a line to Vri's ship. Audio only.>

The AI did as it was told, making sure to maintain the illusion that Roche herself had placed the call. When Vri responded, she said:

"Vri, it's Roche." The Surin didn't respond, so she kept talking. "I need to ask you something. About Maii."

"Which is?"

"Do you know the name of Maii's mother? Or even her family name?"

There was a pause. "No. Why?"

"Would the Agora know?" she said, ignoring his question.

"I would assume so."

"And would you think it unreasonable of me to ask for that information before I even consider handing Maii over?"

He paused again, then answered, "No, not at all."

"Good, because that's as far as I'm prepared to compromise at the moment. Unless you can convince me that the Agora knows what it's doing—and is doing it for the right reasons—then you will never complete your mission. If, however, you *can* convince me, then your chances of convincing Maii will improve. Ultimately, *she* is the one you have to deal with. Unless she agrees, you'll go home empty-handed."

There was a third pause as he seemed to consider this. "I understand," he said finally.

"*Do* you, Vri?"

"I am not stupid, Roche. There is a bond between you and the child; that is indisputable. I may question the nature of the bond on your side in the same way that you question the sincerity of my superiors—but, as you have pointed out, neither of us can do anything without Maii's consent. We are not monsters, you and I."

Remembering the concern with which he had brought the injured girl back to the scutter, Roche could only agree.

"Then let's leave it at that," she said. "We'll go back to the *Phlegethon*. She'll be safer there. You can contact the Agora, or their representatives in the system, and we'll talk about it. Openly, and *with* Maii. She'll be conscious by the time we get back, and she'll be able to tell if anyone's lying. When we've all talked it through, she can decide what she wants to do, and we'll abide by her decision. Can we agree on that?"

"We can." Through his gruff reticence, she sensed a certain satisfaction. "I will contact my superiors as soon as we arrive and advise them of our decision."

"Good." She went to close the line, but stopped at the last second. "And Vri? Thanks for everything you did for her today. You saved her life over there."

"Your thanks are not necessary. I was doing my duty."

"I know that," she said. "But to you, duty is everything, isn't it?"

He didn't reply. A second later, the line closed.

Roche smiled to herself. <Box? Get me Uri. I want us under way as soon as possible. And draft a report for Rey Nemeth describing what happened with the Fathehi.>

<What else would you like me to tell him?>

<Just that. Let him assume we're going on to the Yemena Caste. I think I'd like to surprise him by turning up unannounced.>

<Yes, Morgan.>

<And . . .>

<Yes, Morgan?>

<The next time the Crescend thinks I should do something, ask him to tell me himself. I think it's about time we dispensed with the go-between.>

<I hope you mean that metaphorically, Morgan.>

She smiled again as she closed her eyes. <Of course, Box,> she said. <Of course.>

13

The conference room was conical in shape, its walls tapering smoothly up from the circular floor to a point far above, from which shone a single, bright light. A round table filled most of the floor space, cut, like the walls, from heavy gray stone. Apart from the table, the light, eight chairs, and a single door, the room was featureless. Roche had been assured that it was completely secure: no information could get in or out by any means, including epsense, without the knowledge of the room's inhabitants.

"We hardly expected you back so soon," said Esko Murnane. Roche had been surprised to see him at the meeting of the Ulterior, but not as surprised, it seemed, as Rey Nemeth, whose customary charm—superficial though it might have been—was still clouded by a scowl. There were four others at the table Roche hadn't been introduced to.

"I thought it best to return, for a number of reasons," she said, feeling extremely uncomfortable. Even though she was dressed in full combat armor and armed to the point where even the hospitable Skehan Heterodox had thought twice about letting her aboard their ship, she still felt vulnerable. "There's something you need to know."

"Is it related to your mission?"

"Perhaps indirectly," she said. "I might not have found out about it if I hadn't gone."

"I have her reports," said Nemeth, attempting to reclaim some power in the assembly.

"I'll read them later," said Murnane dismissively.

"You won't find anything in the reports about this," Roche said. "It's not information I'd like to go public with just yet."

"What is it, then?"

She glanced at Haid, who had accompanied her this trip. Maii was still in the *Ana Vereine*'s medical center, conscious but weak. Haid caught her look and shrugged.

"You have a problem," she said slowly. "There are five of the enemy on board the *Phlegethon*."

Startled mutterings broke out among those gathered, but it was Nemeth's voice which rose above them all: "Are you sure?"

"I have no doubts whatsoever," she said. "In fact, there may be even more. You have too large a crew to scan all of them effectively and quickly. But I can tell you that three are amidships, one is down in the crypt and the other is up near the minaret."

"*Where* exactly?" pressed Nemeth.

"I can't tell," she said with a slight shrug. "I just know they're there."

The mutterings continued among the other members of the Ulterior. Except for Murnane, who hardly reacted at all.

"How could you possibly know this?" he asked calmly.

"It's hard to explain," said Roche.

"Nevertheless," said Murnane smoothly, "you're going to have to try. We have no intention of taking you at your word."

"I understand that."

"Is there *any* way to get a precise fix on them?" said Nemeth.

"Only by looking for them in person," she said. "By coming face to face with them."

"At grave personal risk, no doubt," said Murnane, leaning back in his seat.

She met and held Murnane's icy blue eyes. "Yes," she said.

"Do you expect the council to sanction such an undertaking?" There was a hint of a smile at the corners of his mouth.

"She hasn't come to the council," said Nemeth.

"The person I *should* speak to is the Heresiarch," Roche said. "It's his ship, after all."

Murnane dismissed this with a wave of his hand. "How long have you known?"

"Little more than an hour. We swept the ship on the way in to dock."

"And how do you know that one of *us* isn't a clone warrior?" asked a woman to Roche's left.

"I checked before you sealed the room." Although Maii was on the *Ana Vereine* and physically resting, her mind was still strong. The n-space link was harder to maintain over a distance, but still viable.

"That's not to say, of course, that one of us couldn't be in league with them," said Murnane, glancing around the table. "The Ulterior is an organization designed for covert dealings, after all." Then, returning to Roche, he said: "Perhaps it's time you told us exactly how you came by this knowledge."

She agreed and proceeded to describe how her chance link with Maii had brought to their attention Roche's ability to detect the minds of the enemy in the way they distorted the fabric of n-space. She still couldn't explain what those distortions meant or why it seemed she alone possessed this ability, and was as open about this as she was about her inability to pin down a clone warrior's precise location.

"Despite this limitation," interrupted someone from the end of the table, "you are certain you *can* identify them?"

Roche nodded. "It enabled me to identify Inderdeep Jans as one of the two clone warriors on Perdue Habitat," she said. "And of the seven locations we visited, I was able to scan them prior to boarding and determine which of the locations had been compromised by the enemy and which of them had not been."

"How many hadn't been?"

"Just one."

This provoked another round of muttering, until Murnane broke in.

"Would it be possible to replicate this procedure with another reave?" he asked.

"I don't know," she admitted. "But I'm willing to try."

"Good." He nodded. "We've been looking for a way to use epsense to reveal the enemy. This might just be it."

<You are taking a risk doing this,> said the Box into her mind.

\<Less of a risk than a full probe.\> Then, heading off an argument, she said: \<It's a risk we have to take, Box.\>

The conference room was unsealed for a moment, to summon one of the high-grade reaves warding the room—one of the many Maii had observed in the fane during their first visit. She was a short Pristine woman dressed in white robes and a ceremonial headdress wrapped about her eyes, ears and mouth.

\<You are allied to the Surin Abomination,\> she said to Roche. It wasn't a question.

Roche colored slightly. Answering in kind, via epsense, she said: \<The Olmahoi have permitted her existence.\>

\<They *suffer* her existence,\> the woman said, taking a seat vacated by one of the Ulterior. \<I am Stryki of Taborca. You are shielded. I cannot help if you will not open yourself to me.\>

Roche felt the faintest suggestion of Maii at the back of her mind; before Roche had left the *Ana Vereine*, the reave had installed a shield guarding the knowledge that the Box had survived Palasian System. She forced herself to think of something else.

The woman entered her mind like a sheet of silk sliding into water. There was no sensation of invasion or penetration; she was suddenly *there*, among Roche's thoughts, as though she always had been.

\<How does the Abomination access n-space?\> the woman asked. \<Like this?\>

Roche felt her mind swept up by the woman's and tugged into another place—a place where there were no walls, no boundaries, just the faintest suggestion of lines all around them, some intersecting, others stretching out to infinity. Where they met, they glowed white.

\<No,\> Roche said. \<It wasn't like that.\>

\<This, then?\>

Roche was suddenly pulled in a thousand directions at once—as though her skin had been plucked by fishhooks and stretched like the fabric of a balloon to the breaking point—

\<No!\> she managed.

The reave made no apology for the obvious discomfort she had caused, but the sensation vanished and Roche found herself floating over the familiar gray field of n-space.

\<That's it,\> she said, unable to keep the relief from her voice.

\<Ah,\> said the reave. \<A simple two-dimensional Nyberg rep-

resentation. I should have anticipated something unsophisticated like this. It's often the way with the self-taught.>

Ignoring Stryki's disdain, Roche forced herself to look around with the woman.

<What do you see?>

She described the congregation of shielded bumps that she guessed was the meeting. A steep ridge surrounded the gathering—the shield, she presumed, that kept outside observers at bay.

<Can you see yourself?>

<Not clearly, no.>

<And me? Can you see me?>

<The same. You're indistinct, kind of fuzzy around the edges.>

<That's because our minds are linked,> explained the reave. <Were we to disconnect and you to look at the view on your own, or with the help of another mind, I would spring back into focus.>

<Can you look at yourself?>

<Of course,> Stryki said. <All reaves are taught to do this before they learn to examine another's mind. But we do not see ourselves as you would see us.> The woman paused. <Your mind has an unusual flavor, Roche. One I have not tasted before.>

Roche recalled what Maii had said about the *irikeii* calling her an "enigma." The possibility that it might be Maii's block confusing the issue didn't occur to her until the reave went on:

<I can sense the Abomination's hand in your mind. You are aware of this?>

<Yes.> Wary that the reave might penetrate the block, she automatically withdrew.

<I would not violate your privacy,> the reave assured her. <I am not here to probe you, and I would not do so without your permission. That would not be ethical.>

Although leery of the woman's intent—and tired of her incessant insinuations regarding Maii—Roche did allow her back into her mind. She had little choice but to trust the reave if she was to get anywhere.

<Okay,> said Roche. The woman's gaze began to wander, through a short-lived gap in the barrier around the meeting and out into the *Phlegethon*.

<Do you know where we are?>

<No.> Within seconds, Roche had become completely lost. <Do you?>

<More or less. Fixing spatial coordinates to n-space equivalents is one of the hardest things a reave must learn to do,> the woman explained. <It is only complicated when the real-space environment is unfamiliar or inconstant. Fortunately, I am both trained and familiar with this environment.>

<So pinpointing the clones shouldn't be too difficult, then?>

<Theoretically.>

Roche allowed Stryki to whisk her through the concatenated minds of the crew of the *Phlegethon* for a minute or two before asking: <Have you studied clone warriors before?>

The reave hesitated a second. <No, but I do have a great deal of experience with Exotic and near-Transcendent Humanity.>

Roche would have been interested to hear more about the latter. She was, however, forced to concentrate on the task before her. The sea of thoughts was rushing by much faster than it had with Maii. It was all she could do to keep up.

Then she saw it: a dip representing a clone warrior.

<Stop! Go back!>

The reave retraced the way they had come, more slowly. Now Roche could tell that the concentration of people was less dense than it had been before.

<Where are we?> she asked.

<Find the one you are looking for, and I will tell you.>

Roche swept invisibly among the crew of the *Phlegethon* until the dip reappeared.

<There. No, there! Can you see it?>

<I see nothing out of the ordinary.>

<Look at that group of five minds,> Roche said. <The bottom right-hand individual—that's the one!>

<Are you sure?>

<I'm positive,> said Roche.

The reave was silent for a moment. <I can't read the person you have identified. That in itself is not unusual, but it does lend some credence to your story. Other reaves have reported difficulty reading the enemy's minds. They seem to be totally impenetrable, if they so desire. They may, at times, allow a reave to access sensory data, but little else. . . . > She paused again. <The people speaking to the person you have indicated know her as Advocate Janil Coriett. They are in compartment 43 on Deck 25B of the minaret.>

The view of n-space disappeared and Roche found herself back in the meeting, facing the hooded reave.

"Are you okay?" asked Haid, his hand resting on her armored shoulder.

She blinked and looked around, dazed. "Fine, I think." She turned to Murnane. "We found one."

"So I am hearing." The councilor listened to the reave's mental voice a moment longer.

"We need to handle this very delicately," said Nemeth, leaning forward.

"Obviously," said Murnane. "What do we know about this person?"

"Advocate Coriett has been with us for six months," said the woman who had spoken before. Her eyes were out of focus; she was obviously studying information through her implants. "She came from Ceyle's Hub and, as well as taking a position in Environment Control, helped us negotiate a settlement with the H'si F'ta."

"The Hub was destroyed not long before she arrived here," said Nemeth. "The H'si F'ta didn't last much longer before they were decimated by a rival Caste. The settlement encouraged them to drop their defenses." He shrugged. "At the time, we thought it was just a bad call."

"That makes her a prime candidate, then," said Roche. She faced Murnane. "Do you believe me now?"

Murnane turned from Roche to the others. "Until we have definitive proof—" he began.

"What sort of proof do you need?" said Roche sharply. "Her body on a slab?"

Murnane ignored her.

"We'll *have* to move in," said Nemeth.

"No," said Murnane firmly. "That would only alert the others, and that could be disastrous. If one can bring down a civilization, imagine what *four* could do to this ship!"

"Then perhaps we should we tell the Heresiarch," Roche said.

"I disagree," said Nemeth. "The fewer who know about this the better—at least until we've dealt with the situation."

"And how do you propose we do that?" asked Roche.

"Well, first, you're going to have to find the others," said Murnane. "We can keep track of Coriett. Once we have all five, *then* we can act."

"And I repeat, *how* do you propose to do this?"

Murnane glanced away for a second, then returned. This time, the fear in his eyes was obvious. Roche didn't need to be a reave to know what he was thinking. It was all very well to contemplate a nebulous, almost unreal enemy, but to actually come directly in contact with them was another matter altogether. . . .

"We'll deal with that when the time comes," he said. But the uncertainty in his tone did not inspire confidence.

It wasn't difficult to find the other four, but it was time-consuming. By the time Roche had helped the reave pinpoint the location of each of the five clone warriors on the *Phlegethon*, she felt weary right down to her bones. Her brain ached in ways she had never imagined before. When she was released from n-space for the final time, she sagged back into her chair with a groan, and only Haid's hands under her armpits stopped her from slipping to the floor.

With a whine of servo-assisted joints, he helped her upright. "Morgan, this is crazy."

"No, it's done now." She turned to Nemeth for confirmation.

He nodded. "We have the identity of the fifth. He's a fusion technician, of all things."

"In a prime location to sabotage the power core," said Murnane. "Roche, if you're right about these people, you have undoubtedly saved the lives of everyone on this ship."

"They're not safe yet," said Roche.

"Quite," said Nemeth. "I suggest we move on all five simultaneously—send multiple containment teams to pin them down; then, if they resist—or if there's even the slightest chance they'll get away—neutralize them permanently."

Murnane nodded slowly. "That at least gives them a chance to prove their innocence," he said. "A blood test would be enough to reveal the truth."

"They've obviously managed to avoid blood tests before now," objected Nemeth.

"And if they do come quietly and are guilty?" Roche asked. "What then?"

Nemeth glanced at Murnane. "Execution."

"No," said the older man. "We're not barbarians."

"They would kill *us* out of hand!"

"But we are not like them, Nemeth," said Murnane severely.

"And I have no desire to become like them, either. There *must* be some way to subdue them."

Roche described the crystalline cocoon Linegar Rufo had used to neutralize Adoni Cane. "He was in a coma," she said. "There was no way he could escape."

"We could easily implement something like that," said Murnane thoughtfully. "Later, higher authorities could decide what to do with them."

Nemeth still didn't look happy, but dropped the argument. "What happens after this?" he said. "Can we replicate these results? Can we use this process to keep the *Phlegethon* clean?"

He was addressing the white-robed reave, whose posture stiffened as she replied.

<I do not understand how Morgan Roche is able to identify these individuals—assuming they are what she says they are. To me, they stand out from a crowd no more than anyone else. In the same way that mandatory blood tests have not isolated them, detailed scans of the crew might not turn up more of those we seek. We need more people with Roche's ability.>

"And to find them," interrupted Nemeth, "we need to know *how* she is doing it in the first place. We're back where we started."

"Not quite," said Murnane. "We have a test. Bring in those five, or attempt to. Once we have ascertained whether or not we're on the right track, *then* we can work out what to do next." He turned to the other members at the meeting. "I want those containment teams in place in half an hour. Prepare for any contingency, no matter how unlikely. Advise the Heresiarch by epsense that an exercise is about to take place, but that he is under no circumstances to alert the crew. Everything proceeds as usual until the operation commences. No one leaves here until it is concluded. Is that understood?"

There was a chorus of assent. Nemeth offered his last of all, still clearly displeased at the way Murnane had taken over his operation.

"Can I talk to my crew?" Roche asked.

"A brief message relayed via epsense only," Murnane conceded. "When everything is concluded here, you may converse freely."

Roche and the reave put together a short message for Maii explaining that they would continue to be incommunicado for an hour or so. After that, they would know if it was safe to bring Maii aboard the *Phlegethon*, as Vri insisted they do. Should they receive any unusual communications from the *Phlegethon* at all, Kajic was to move to a safe distance and wait for news.

The reave sent the message and, a moment later, confirmed that it had been received.

As they waited, the mood around the conference table became increasingly restless. How arrangements were being made, Roche couldn't tell exactly, but she noted the far-off expressions of those using implants. She worried that word might somehow get to the clone warriors, warning them of what was to happen, but as she could see no way to organize things without taking that risk, she said nothing.

Haid tapped her on the shoulder and indicated for her to close her faceplate. Roche nodded, and instructed her suit to seal. The people around the table looked up as her visor and Haid's hissed shut, but when she and Haid made no other move they returned to their work.

"What do you think?" asked Haid over the private link between their suits. "Is this actually going to work?"

"It had better," she replied. "Because if it doesn't, we're really in trouble. If we can't fight them individually, even when we know who they are, then there's no point even trying. We either give up, or we advocate extreme solutions like completely destroying habitats and stations that we know have been infiltrated. And even then, we could never be certain that we've wiped out the last of them. There could always be one capsule left in deep space, or one survivor hiding out in the Far Reaches. And where there's one . . ."

Haid grunted. "No one's mentioned the alternative to killing them."

"Which is?"

"Conversion."

"Like Cane?"

"Maybe."

She frowned. "It would be hard to trust them after what they've done—or what their kind has done."

"I know. But not impossible, surely?"

She shrugged the suit's heavy shoulders, thinking of Cane and her own uncertainty. "Only time will tell, I guess."

"Speaking of trust," Haid went on: "Why's Murnane being so

chummy all of a sudden? You were definitely persona non grata last time you two met."

"I don't know. Maybe something's happened to change his mind. I'm sure he doesn't trust me too far. At the most, I'd say he's decided I'm useful."

Roche examined the councilor while she talked. His face seemed more deeply lined than ever, and the faint wisp of hair at the back of his skull had faded almost to invisibility. He looked older, more tired, and less inclined than ever to tolerate fools.

"How desperate do you think he is?" Haid asked.

Very, she thought, but said nothing. After a moment, she unsealed her suit and leaned back into her chair with her eyes shut, thinking.

They waited another twenty-five minutes. Then, finally, everything was ready. Security in the conference room was eased slightly to allow data to flow in and out as the five containment teams moved into position. The teams, consisting of fifteen security officers each, had strict instructions to use lethal force at the slightest sign of resistance. Protecting the lives of bystanders was considered a lesser priority than ensuring the death or capture of the targets.

Roche watched via her implants as the containment teams closed around the areas where the clone warriors were situated. It was a complicated display, showing all five teams simultaneously. There was no way she could follow all of them at once, so she focused on the team advancing on Coriett.

The woman was in one of the uppermost levels of the giant ship, sitting in a room with four other people. To all appearances she seemed an ordinary Pristine dressed in a plain shipsuit, discussing the day's activities with colleagues. They chatted amiably, laughing now and then, and sipping occasionally from their mugs. It all seemed so innocuous to Roche, which paradoxically lent the scene a sinister air—because she *knew* what this woman was truly capable of.

"Pull out two of those people," she heard Murnane say.

"Why not pull them all out?" said Nemeth. "It would make it easier to deal with her."

"Because we risk arousing her suspicions," said Murnane.

Through her implants as well as the ship's internal intercom system, Roche heard the names of two of the people being summoned. They exited the room a minute or so later with smiles and polite bows of the head, leaving just Coriett and the two others behind.

A joke was made by one of the remaining colleagues; Coriett smiled politely and sipped from her cup. As she did so, she glanced up at the room's monitor.

Roche went cold: for the second it lasted it seemed as though the clone warrior was looking directly at her.

"She suspects something," she said. "I'm sure of it."

"What?" It was Nemeth. "That's impossible . . ."

"Move your team in now," insisted Roche.

The security guards entered the room just as Coriett made to stand. All three guards took position around the woman, leveling their weapons carefully at her. The two other people present in the room leapt up from their seats in alarm, spilling their drinks.

"Advocate Janil Coriett," said one of the guards loudly, firmly, "by order of the Interim Emergency Pristine Council, I am placing you under arrest. Please put your hands together behind your head and step away from the desk."

"What is the meaning of this?" said one of the other women angrily. "This is an outrage!"

Instead of answering, one of the guards indicated that she should step away from Coriett, out of the line of fire. With a weapon leveled directly at her, the woman's indignant protest became alarm.

Coriett, meanwhile, had responded to the orders, but not before coolly appraising the three guards.

"Don't I at least deserve some sort of explanation?" she asked.

The guard didn't respond, and her two companions were ushered from the room by one of the other guards. When the room was cleared, another guard produced a set of handcuffs and approached the clone warrior.

"Surely I have rights?" she said, holding her hands to be cuffed. But it wasn't to the guards she was speaking. She was looking again at the monitor. Even from this safe distance, Roche couldn't help but feel unnerved by the woman's unflinching confidence.

At the same moment, the sound of secondhand gunfire came from inside Haid's helmet. Clearly, one of the other missions wasn't going as well as this one. Roche was about to switch viewpoints when a subtle change in Coriett's expression caught her eye. It was as though she too had somehow heard the gun-fire, and knew what it meant: that one of her siblings was in danger—and that this was therefore much more than an administrative error or a mere suspicion she could talk her way out of.

Coriett pulled back from the cuffs and elbowed the guard in the face. As he went down, she grabbed him by one arm and swung him in front of her. The two other guards in the room contemplated shooting through him to get to her, but in the second they hesitated, the warrior had found the stock of the rifle and brought the weapon up firing.

The rifle was set on rapid repeat; all she had to do was swing the barrel to cut down the guards and the two other people in the room. One of them was half out the door when the shots took him in the back, throwing him forward into the hall with enough force to disrupt the formation of guards waiting there. Coriett followed a second later, capitalizing on the surprise. Roche watched with mounting alarm as the guards recoiled in confusion, only a few of them managing to get off even a single shot before Coriett targeted them herself.

Her shots never missed.

But killing the guards wasn't her main priority. Escape was more important, and there would always be more guards if she stayed in one spot too long. Roche could only watch anxiously as the warrior paused to evaluate her position: she was in the middle of a long corridor with an open elevator at one end and a junction at the other. If she could reach the elevator, she could go anywhere on the ship. Security would be hard pressed to catch her. And once she had slipped through the net, she would have the entire ship to hide in.

Roche wanted to cry a warning to the remaining guards as Coriett strafed them with one wild wave of her gun, then sprinted for the elevator. Behind her, amid the tangle of wounded and dead, only one guard had the forethought to guess what she was doing. He pushed a limp body aside, raised his rifle, and fired.

At first, Roche thought the woman wasn't going to stop. Round after round struck her in the back, propelling her onward through a mist of blood. She was still running even when she hit the back wall of the elevator cab, her speed unchecked. With a sound like the crack of bone, she rebounded and fell to the ground.

As she fell, her hand struck the access panel on the inside of the cab, and the doors slid shut.

Roche quickly changed her view to the inside of the cab. Surely there was no way Coriett could have survived so many shots at such close range. Hitting the switch *must* have been an accident.

The cab slid silently away from the carnage, taking the immobile and bloody body of Coriett with it. The gun was on the floor where she had dropped it, a crimson puddle quickly pooling around the barrel.

A map in the side of the channel tracked the cab as it traveled out toward the hull of the ship and down to the docks. Another team was being sent to meet the cab at its destination.

Roche watched. Coriett didn't move.

Satisfied that the clone warrior wasn't going anywhere, Roche skipped to the other channels. Only one was still active. Another clone warrior—a male with close-cropped red hair, the fusion technician—had managed to get his hands on a weapon and taken a hostage to use as a shield. His containment team had hesitated long enough to allow the clone warrior to regain the initiative. He shot five, and the hostage, while they were making up their minds, then slipped away before they could regroup.

The point of view of the channel followed him easily, however—jumping crazily from camera to camera as he ran headlong through what looked like a cargo section of the ship. Guards converged on the area from all directions; blast doors slammed shut in his path. But he seemed to know what he was doing. The area was riddled with accessways and maintenance shafts. Where he couldn't run, he crawled; where he couldn't climb, he jumped. Roche didn't know the big ship well enough to guess where he was headed, but she didn't doubt he had *somewhere* in mind.

In the end, though, his luck ran out, and a stuck hatch forced him into another team's path. When he realized his mistake, he tried to double back on his pursuers and take them by surprise. They realized just in time, and the concentrated fire from three security guards finally brought him down.

Roche took a deep breath. That made four confirmed kills. As Coriett's cab came to a halt, she felt sure that it would soon be five.

The team were ready for anything as the doors slid open. From the viewpoint of one of the guards, Roche watched as they inched forward, weapons at the ready, until they were within meters of the woman.

She didn't move.

One guard reached gingerly forward to slide the still-smoking gun out of arm's reach.

Still she didn't move.

More confidently, another approached to test for vital signs while the others kept their weapons trained on her. If she was conscious, or even alive at all, she gave no indication as his fingers sought for a pulse in her throat.

The diagnosis wasn't one Roche expected to hear.

"She's alive," the guard called.

The containment team had begun to relax in the face of her lack of response. Now they tightened formation again and began to inch away nervously.

"What do we do with her?" said one of the team anxiously.

"Restrain her," came the response. "Bring her in for examination and interrogation if you can. But shoot her if she so much as moves. Whatever you do, *don't* let her get away from you. If she—"

A siren began wailing through the ship. Distracted from the view through her implants, Roche looked up. Murnane's eyes were flickering rapidly, intent on an internal feed.

"What's happening?" she asked.

"Overheated life-support module," said Nemeth.

The siren grew louder and more strident.

"Is that all?" she said.

He stared at her. "You still haven't grasped how big this ship is, have you? Each of those modules is bigger than a small moon, and there are *five* of them. If one blows, it could start a chain reaction through the ducts that'll tear the whole place apart."

"What's causing it?"

"The Heresiarch is trying to find out. Something is interfering with the module's normal operation. A virus of some sort, perhaps, triggered from the outside."

"Sabotage?"

"Could be. We don't know yet. But it's going to blow in thirty seconds if we can't get control of it, so hope for both of us someone works out quickly what the hell is going on."

Roche's attention was drawn back to the channel in which Coriett was being dragged out of the cab. The woman was limp, unprotesting, to all appearances completely unconscious. And as she watched, a sudden realization brought with it a sense of terrible panic.

"Tell your team to shoot her!"

Nemeth's eyebrows shot up. "*What*?"

"It's *her*!" Roche found herself shouting. "*She's* doing it."

"Don't be ridiculous," said Nemeth, but the uncertainty was evident in his tone.

"Didn't someone say she worked for Environment Control? She would have been in a perfect position to set something like this up. If she has implants, and if she's faking unconsciousness . . ."

Roche didn't need to go any further. The alarm blossoming in Nemeth's eyes matched her own.

He turned away to rattle off orders to the containment team and to the councilors around him. The siren wailed on as the guards readying Coriett for mechanical restraint looked up at their superior and listened to the new orders coming through their armor's communication links. They let go of her and backed away.

But even as they did this, Roche felt it was too late.

The warrior's eyes snapped open, and in an instant she had rolled toward the nearest guard and grabbed him by the legs, blood squirting from her injured back in a high-pressure jet. Confused, surprised, frightened, the guard didn't have time to react, and fell heavily to the floor. His head hit the ground with a sickening thud.

Coriett seized the fallen guard's rifle and raised herself up on one knee, leveling it effortlessly at the others. But three members of the containment team had managed to raise their own weapons first and had already targeted the injured woman.

A volley of shots flung the clone warrior back into the cab, and they kept firing until her body stopped moving altogether . . .

Nemeth acknowledged the woman's death only in passing. He didn't relax until word came that the interference with the life-support module had ceased. Its operations were being normalized, and the threat to ship integrity would soon pass. He sagged visibly as the siren decreased in volume and then fell silent.

"That's it," he said. "I think we can call this operation a success."

"Bring her body," said Murnane. Outwardly he seemed unaffected by the events. "I want *all* of the bodies in for postmortem examination. Then we'll know for certain."

"We already know," said Nemeth.

"We can take nothing for granted," said Murnane evenly.

"How could you even doubt it? Look at them! They ran and they fought—they fought even when there was no chance they could win! If they weren't the enemy, then what were they?"

Roche looked, and knew what he was feeling. Five of the clone warriors lay dead on the *Phlegethon*'s decks—killed by the Pristine Humans they impersonated. *That* was progress.

"Now we're getting somewhere!" Nemeth gloated.

But as the surviving security guards picked themselves up and saw to their injured colleagues, and as the casualty reports came in listing thirty dead guards and fifteen dead civilians, Murnane's face grew grim.

"At what cost?" he asked, perhaps of himself.

Roche looked down at her trembling hands and wondered the same thing.

14

Within the hour, chaos had erupted all around the system. Border skirmishes broke out and became firefights; grudges became battles; enemies forgot diplomacy, along with the greater good, and exchanged open, sometimes devastating attacks. Within three hours, virtually every Caste present in Sol System was engaged in some form of dispute.

"I don't understand." Nemeth watched the screens with a growing confusion. Perhaps, Roche thought, he was watching his new-found position of dominance in the council dissolving before his eyes. She hoped he had more Humanity than that; she herself saw nothing but lives wasted, nothing but more death and destruction—with the potential for it to become worse than anything she had witnessed in Palasian System. Worse, even, than anything she had ever imagined.

"I don't *understand*!" Nemeth said again, hitting a console with the palm of one hand. Roche could appreciate his frustration, but his anger was serving no purpose. A feeling obviously shared with the Heresiarch, who turned to Nemeth and said:

"If *you* don't understand, then who does?"

The question was clearly rhetorical, for the Heresiarch didn't wait to hear what Nemeth would say next. Instead he returned to the business of running the ship, turning his attention to the influx of data coming at him from all the monitors about the room.

He was standing in the center of the small room adjoining the fane to which Roche and Haid had been moved following the Ulterior's apparent success with the five clone warriors. The room was fifteen meters across, at most, with glowing blue walls that looked as though they had been fashioned from crystal. Set into the walls and floor, and even the ceiling, were consoles and stations for dozens of crew members. The air was full of whispered instructions, burbling data, and an impression that everything was running perfectly to order. Busy yet not chaotic, the adytum hummed to its own driving rhythm.

In this space, the Heresiarch did the real work involved with the running of the *Phlegethon*, rather than the ceremonial. Roche knew that being permitted here, among the highest officers and critical decision-makers, watching the information pouring in live from tens of thousands of ftl drones, was something of a privilege. Also a high honor, if Nemeth's expression upon arriving was anything to go by.

"We killed those five easily enough," persisted Nemeth, turning now to Murnane with his concerns. "They had no chance to warn the others. All this . . ." He gestured at the mess on the screens. "It *has* to be a coincidence." He searched the room now, looking for support but finding none. "It's always been at flashpoint," he insisted. "The whole system was unstable from the moment we arrived—and it's been getting worse every day! There have been skirmishes, conflicts, even small wars, before. This is just more of the same. Only worse."

"Much worse," the Heresiarch said dryly, leaning against the steel rail surrounding his station. He seemed to be completely hairless; his eyes were a deep brown, like his skin.

"It's a chain reaction, that's what it is." Nemeth began pacing and gesticulating agitatedly. "Civilization A attacks civilization B, who calls in C as an ally. That would be fine, except D has been waiting for the chance to move on C and ropes in E and F to stack the odds. G is caught in the crossfire, and H and I come to its rescue. And so on. Perfectly sane and comprehensible." His words trailed off as he stopped and looked up at the screens. "What we did has nothing to do with this," he finished more calmly. "It *can't* have."

"I fear it did," said Murnane.

The elder councilor didn't waste energy posturing as he talked. He simply stood, composed, on the other side of the Heresiarch. "The timing is too precise. Every new conflict was initiated within moments of the deaths of those five. Medical tests confirm that they were the enemy, so their exposure and attempted capture *have* to be connected. The others, the rest of them"—his eyes flickered for a second to the screens—"the ones that are still alive are fighting now because they know that we have learned how to find them. They feel vulnerable—perhaps even afraid. We were able to kill those five because we managed to take them by surprise; the others are not going to allow the same thing to happen again."

"But *how* did they know?" Nemeth's frustration was palpable.

Murnane shrugged. "I'm not sure," he said. "But the information *must* have been transmitted by either an epsense or hyperspace signal. There's no other way it could've spread so quickly."

Roche remembered the black speck at the heart of Cane and Jelena Heidik's minds, as viewed by the *irikeii*, and the look on Janil Coriett's face as firing broke out on the far side of the *Phlegethon*.

"It was epsense," she said.

Nemeth rounded on her. "How can you know that? None of our reaves have ever detected anything."

"Neither have we," she said. "But look at the recordings: Coriett suspected she'd been discovered, but she didn't know for sure until someone opened fire on one of the others. She wasn't anywhere near any sort of hyperspace communicator; there's no way we know of to hide one inside a Human body—and we would've found it if one had been there. So it must have been epsense."

"That's not proof," Nemeth said.

"It's all we have to go on," said Murnane. "We need to recall our field agents and warn anyone who might not have realized what's going on. Without extensive ftl communications or epsense on *our* side, word might take time to spread that the disturbances aren't local. We have to save as many people as we can, starting with our own."

"And then what?" Nemeth asked.

"Then we wait and see what happens." The elderly councilor suddenly looked very tired. "This might blow over; it might just be a warning. We might receive some sort of communication, at last. Who knows? If they are that concerned that we have the ability to find them now, we might even be able to negotiate a settlement."

"What *have* we got to negotiate with?" The short bleat of a laugh from Nemeth was cynical and derisive. "If we don't find someone else who can do this, it'll take us months to sweep the entire system. Maybe forever, if Roche is killed!"

"The enemy doesn't *know* that!"

"How long do you think it'll take them to figure it out?" said Nemeth. "They're not stupid, you know."

"Exactly—they're not. They know they can't afford to take too many chances while they're so outnumbered."

"But what if they can?" continued Nemeth. "What if they *don't* negotiate?"

Murnane shrugged. "Then we save what we can," he said. "That's all we can do."

"There is another alternative." A new voice entered the discussion, this one hauntingly familiar to Roche.

Murnane looked up. "Yes, Trezise?"

The senior aide to Auberon Chase stepped into the center of the adytum. Roche hadn't noticed him there before, but recognized his narrow, almost equine features immediately.

"Roche claims to have among her crew one of the enemy."

"Yes; the council decided Adoni Cane was a fake," Murnane said.

"What if he isn't? What if he *is* as tame as Roche suggests? Surely his opinion would be worth seeking at this juncture."

"Bring another one of the enemy onto the ship?" objected Nemeth. "We've just killed a lot of people clearing out the first lot! If he is a clone warrior, it would be insane to allow him on board."

"What other means do we have to decipher the enemy's intentions?" Trezise opened his hands in supplication. "If an epsense link *does* exist, he might be able to tap into it."

"*If* he is genuine," Murnane said.

Trezise nodded, agreeing calmly. "If he is genuine, yes."

Murnane turned to face Roche. "What do *you* think?"

She wanted to say that this was what she'd wanted to do two and a half weeks earlier, that if they'd listened to her the first time, then maybe everything that had happened since then might have been avoided.

But she didn't. She was too conscious of the fact that this could be her last opportunity to speak to the council. She couldn't afford to miss that chance.

"On two conditions," she said instead. "One: you will grant any member of my crew asylum on this ship should they seek it. And two: you will make me a participating member of the council, effective immediately."

Murnane chuckled softly. "*I* have no objection to either condition," he said. "Obviously, though, the granting of asylum would need to be ratified by the Heresiarch." He nodded to where the Heresiarch stood at his station, preoccupied with the running of the ship. "I'm not sure he would extend the honor to Adoni Cane, enemy or not. And your membership in the council would have to be on a *pro tem* basis, to be ratified by a formal sitting—"

She raised a hand to silence him. "Okay, okay, you've made your point," she said, and sighed. "Just give me your assurance that you'll *listen* to me, at least."

He nodded once. "Make arrangements to transfer Adoni Cane across and we'll prepare for the interview." He swept his gaze across the room. Nemeth looked relieved, but said nothing. "If there are no further urgent issues to be raised, we will adjourn to await further developments. The Heresiarch has work to do, and our being here can only be a distraction."

Even as he spoke, a bell chimed loudly, sending the assembled officers to their stations. A raiding party from a small but aggressive government had stumbled into the *Phlegethon*'s camouflage field and opened fire on the middle decks. Roche turned to the monitors, watching as hundreds of pod-shaped fighters swarmed out of the giant ship's many docks to repel the intruder.

The council moved out to the fane. Hue Vischilglin took Roche's arm, nodding recognition but saying nothing. As she and Haid were led away, Roche caught a glimpse of Salton Trezise, who could barely contain his look of triumph.

From the safety of another conference room, Roche made arrangements for Cane and Maii to cross by scutter to the *Phlegethon*. She also instructed Kajic to assume a close parking position under the big ship's shadow. While the raid had in no way threatened the *Ana Vereine*, it did highlight the potential for conflict nearby. If things did get too hot, Kajic had permission to seek protection in the *Phlegethon*'s larger docks.

Once that was organized, Roche had nothing else to do but observe. Even as only a *pro tem* member of the council, the information she now had access to was overwhelming. What had once been chaos had now become a slaughter. Traditional alliances dissolved; defensive agreements were torn apart; like fought like as intra-Caste conflicts expanded to consume entire fleets. Conservative estimates put the number of ships and stations lost in the first three hours at twenty thousand. That only amounted to barely two percent of the million or so ships known to have entered the system, but the sheer loss of life could not be ignored.

<I hope you're watching this, Box.>

<Indeed I am, Morgan. This is an unexpected development. The ability of the enemy to mobilize such a response so quickly is unprecedented. Few could have anticipated this sort of capability—or this sort of generalized conflict so early in the endgame.>

Its choice of words made her frown. <I hope this is more than just a game to you, Box.>

<Of course it is, Morgan. Of course.>

She couldn't decide whether the AI was being insincere or patronizing. Perhaps it was both. <Do you see any biases toward any particular Castes?>

<None at this stage. Taking regional peculiarities into account, the targets are randomly distributed. There doesn't even seem to be any broad trend, either—such as Pristine versus Exotic, for example.>

<Does that blow your theory?>

<No. I may need to see more data before a trend emerges.>

<*If* a trend emerges,> she said, thinking of the twenty thousand ships destroyed already and wondering how many more it would take to give the Box enough data.

<Naturally, Morgan.>

She went back to watching the screens. Sitting beside her, heavy and brooding in his black combat suit, Haid was as silent as she was. He kept his emotions carefully hidden, only a slight tightness to his jaw revealing anything of the tension he must have been feeling.

After a few moments, she addressed the Box again. <Box, someone mentioned being able to identify the enemy by blood test. Do you know how they do this?>

<It's a genetic analysis,> the AI replied. <As Rufo and I previously noted, the enemy has an unusual genetic structure. Where normal Humans possess long stretches of 'junk' genes called introns, Cane and the others have sequences that *appear* to serve a purpose, yet result in no known proteins. Whatever else they might do remains a mystery, but these stretches can be used to distinguish a clone warrior from any other ordinary Human.>

<That's why Rufo wanted us to look at Cane's introns more closely?>

<Yes. He suspected that an important clue to the origins and/or purpose of the enemy would lie within.>

<Do you agree?>

<I agree that it's a possibility.>

<What about the council? They obviously knew about the introns when I mentioned them at the first meeting. Have they learned anything new in the time they've had?>

<Well, if they have, it hasn't explained anything about the enemy we didn't already know.>

Roche absorbed this. <What about the Crescend, then? What does *he* know?>

<If he knows anything conclusive about this, he hasn't told me.>

Tired of repeatedly butting the same brick wall, Roche fell silent. A few minutes later, Kajic reported that Maii and Cane were ready to leave. Roche switched her implants to a view of the scutter's cramped interior. Cane sat in the pilot's seat, his face expressionless. Maii sat beside him, still somewhat pale, but looking better than she had been earlier; the medicinal pack covering her wound was less bulky than it had been, indicating that its healing work was almost done. Behind her . . .

<What's *he* doing there, Uri?> she asked Kajic.

<Defender-of-Harmony Vri insisted on coming,> he replied.

<But we're getting Maii to safety,> she said. <That's what he wanted, wasn't it?>

<He seems determined to keep an eye on her in person.> Kajic sounded almost amused. <It wasn't my place to stop him.>

<No, of course not. Nor mine.> Roche found the Surin war-

rior's persistence admirable, if a little obsessive. <But are you going to be okay there by yourself?>

<Everything will be fine, Morgan. Now that normal channels are open again, I'll be able to watch what you're doing. Besides,> he added, <I'm not completely alone. Alta is still here. And there's still plenty of work to do shipside. I think everything must be perfectly in order if we're to get out of this one.>

Roche agreed. Part of her was still nervous about giving the ex-Dato captain the chance to escape with the ship, but the rational side of her knew that this was simply unjustifiable paranoia. Had he wanted to, he could have killed or lost them dozens of times already.

<Vri will attempt to make contact with the Surin delegates in the system,> Kajic went on. <That is one thing you haven't been able to do as yet.>

<It's not as if I've had the time!>

<He realizes that. He just wants to resolve this issue once and for all.>

Roche nodded to herself. She couldn't do everything—especially when this particular job held little appeal. <How long until they arrive?>

<They should be there in about half an hour.>

<Okay. Thanks, Uri.>

The scutter disengaged from the *Ana Vereine* and arced smoothly toward the larger ship. Cane flew the small craft with competence and ease. He was a natural at everything he turned his hand to, even a complicated task such as flying a space vessel. Somewhere in his lost memory, Roche supposed, was the knowledge he needed, accessible at will. How it had got there in the first place, though, was the question—one question among many. She could only hope that some of them would be answered when he came under the council's spotlight.

There had been no mention of the Ulterior outside the sealed conference room where Roche had revealed her knowledge concerning the five clone warriors. She assumed that it was still considered at best to be an informal group by most of its members—although Murnane's presence at that meeting was a strong indication that its activities were partially sanctioned by its parent, or would be gratefully absorbed into the greater body of work if things went well.

How long her partial acceptance by the council would last she didn't know, but while she *was* a member, she resolved to take full advantage of it. She couldn't just sit by and watch while everything was potentially falling apart around her. Even if the council ended up dismissing her again, then at least she could say that she'd tried.

"Ameidio?"

Haid turned to face her.

"If you were the enemy, and this was your doing"—she indicated the images of destruction displayed on the monitor which was built into one wall of the conference room—"*why* would you be doing it?"

He faced the monitor and contemplated the question for a few moments. "To reduce the resources of the enemy," he said at last.

She shook her head. "No," she said. "They're far too outnumbered. Even a ninety-nine percent reduction in our capability would leave them way behind."

"To disorganize the enemy, then?"

She considered this for a short while before offering another shake of the head. "That's a hell of a lot of effort for so little gain."

"Depends on how you look at it."

"Not really," she said. "Wouldn't any sensible campaign concentrate its energies here, on the *Phlegethon*? That's where the potential for organization exists. Even if it's the only surviving ship, it'd stand a chance of victory against a small enough enemy force."

He shrugged. "This could just be a smoke screen, then, and they are already working on us. We just haven't realized it."

"We got rid of their agents; they don't have anyone else to work through."

"You heard what Murnane said: the council is recalling its field agents. How many of the enemy do you think will slip in with that lot?"

She nodded. "I've considered that," she said. "And who's to say the enemy *has* to be a clone warrior at all? There are bound to be collaborators we'll never detect, small-time operators who might slip past even high-grade reaves because they aren't aware that what they're doing is even wrong."

His dark eyes watched her closely. "You could be right about the agents," he said. "But there's something else on your mind, isn't there?"

She half-smiled, then sobered. "This mass killing," she said slowly. "It's a message of some sort."

"A message?" Haid frowned. "Saying what?"

"I'm not sure," she said. "I'm not even sure for whom it was intended."

"It would have to be for the council, surely," said Haid. "Who else could it be for?"

She didn't answer that, because were she to voice her suspicions, she was sure that Haid would think her totally paranoid. Nevertheless, she couldn't shake the feeling that the message was aimed at *her*. It was as though they somehow knew that *she* was responsible for having located the five clone warriors, and that now they were making her pay the price. If so, this was retaliation on the largest possible scale; they were warning her not to do it again. . . .

But that all presupposed the existence of the epsense link Cane had already denied knowing anything about. She doubted the council could decide in a single sitting whether he was telling the truth or not, but she was looking forward to seeing them try.

On the screen, a habitat shaped like a spinning top broke up under centrifugal forces, spraying fragments into the small flotilla arrayed against it. Roche couldn't even begin to imagine the scale; the habitat could have been home for dozens or thousands of people, and the ships may have been fighters or cruisers. There was no way to tell the scale from the display on the screen alone.

She stood abruptly, turning from the destruction to face Haid. "Come on," she said. "I'm going to get Vischilgin to take us to the docks to meet Cane and Maii."

"You don't trust the council to do it for you?" said Haid.

"That's not the problem," she said. "The last time I sent those two somewhere on their own, I very nearly didn't get them back."

"What about Vri?" Haid said, getting to his feet.

She had forgotten the Surin. Vri had been with them for twenty-four days, but had never integrated into the group. He kept apart, following his own agenda, only working with them when their goals meshed. The moment their goals came into conflict, she had no doubt whose orders he would follow. On the *Phlegethon*, he would be close to getting what he and the Surin Agora wanted. She didn't entirely trust his ability to compromise if his superiors didn't follow suit.

"All the more reason to go down there." She turned to leave.

"Morgan?" Haid said suddenly. She stopped and faced him again. "Do you think you could handle Vri?"

The question startled her.

"If you had to," he went on quickly. "One on one."

"I've no idea," she said. "Probably not. I've never even thought about it, to tell the truth." The soldier had performed very well in the Fathehi Consulate. Not as well as Cane, but better than anything Roche could ever hope to perform. "Why do you ask?"

He shrugged. "Just curious."

"And what about you?" she said.

"Me? I wouldn't stand a chance." His smile was disarming. "But both of us at once . . . ? Well, that would be a different story."

She smiled slightly and patted the ex-mercenary's shoulder. "Let's just hope it doesn't come to that."

The scutter was delayed slightly by an unscheduled course-change undertaken by the *Phlegethon* in order to avoid a cloud of debris too extensive to tackle head on. Even with the enormous ship's shields, the chance of a large fragment slipping through was too great to risk. Changing the ship's orbit gave a certain tactical advantage too: camouflaged or not, the more it moved, the less chance someone hostile had of tracking it from its last known location.

Apart from a containment team already in position when they arrived, the civilian docks were virtually empty. Of all the airlocks Roche could see, the one through which Cane and Maii disembarked seemed to be the only one in use.

"You don't get many visitors here, I take it?" she said to Vischilglin, who waited with them by the inner door.

The tall woman shook her head. "Security is very tight at all times, and especially so now. I am told that docks like these are usually a hive of activity when consistory vessels return to their home system. With such a large crew, the reunions can go on for weeks. The Heterodoxies are renowned for their devotion to family as well as to faith."

The woman spoke quickly and with animation, but never meeting Roche's eyes. It seemed to Roche that she was nervous, anxious—trying, perhaps, to suppress an uncomfortable thought.

"Something's bothering you?" Roche asked.

Vischilglin kept her gaze on the dock's inner door. "I've lost contact with my superiors back home," she said softly. "Signals stopped arriving three days ago."

Roche nodded slightly, but didn't know what to say. She was saved from having to by the inner door hissing open. The suits of the containment team whirred as they stood at the ready.

Cane stepped out first, followed closely by Maii. She wore a new hazard suit with additional armor provided by Vri that lent the normally gray exterior an air of gilt decoration. Cane wore nothing but a typical brown Dato shipsuit. There was a tension in his posture which only heightened when he saw the containment team.

Maii looked tired; her lips were thin, her pale features drawn. She stepped over to Roche and lightly touched her arm.

<I'm not going to seek asylum,> she said, her mental whisper directed at Roche alone. She sent a picture of herself standing on the top of thick battlements.

The image might have been meant to make the girl look strong. To Roche, it made her look very small and alone.

<I'm glad to hear it, Maii,> Roche said, quashing her impression. <But I don't think Vri will be.>

The Surin girl touched her mind with a mental shrug.

Vri was the last to step from the airlock. His visor was in place and his eyes were hidden, but Roche could tell from the way the helmet moved that he had scanned the containment team, Vischilglin, Haid, and herself with one appraising glance. He knew what had happened on Galine Four and was obviously prepared for anything.

He stopped just behind Maii and waited silently.

"The council will convene in fifteen minutes," said Vischilglin, stepping forward. "Transport has been arranged."

As she spoke, a large, flat vehicle slid quietly to a halt nearby. The containment team reorganized itself to create a clear space leading from the airlock to the transport.

"Do we all go together?" Roche asked her.

"That would be simplest."

Roche nodded, but instead of heading for the transport, she moved to face Cane.

"Do you know why I've brought you here?" she asked.

"To testify before the council," he said.

"Are you ready for that?"

He returned her stare evenly. "Are you?"

The question was a challenge, although she didn't know why it should be. "I have nothing to hide," she said. "And I'm assuming that you don't, either—that you've been telling the truth from the start."

"Why would I do otherwise?"

"Because . . ." She faltered in mid-sentence. There were no words to frame the suspicion she still felt, deep in her gut. "Because you *could.*"

Because I stand to lose everything if you haven't been telling the truth. . . .

"Having the potential to do something is not the same as intending to use it, Morgan. You of all people should know that."

"What do you mean?"

"I mean that five of my people died today as a direct result of your involvement in this conflict. Uri showed me the footage. Now that you know for certain that your ability works, you have the potential to track down and hunt every one of my kind and bring them all to their deaths. Whether I agree with them or not, whether you think I might be one of them or not, whether I am lying to your or not—it's all irrelevant. Ultimately, all that matters is your *intent*, isn't it?"

She took a step back from his intense gaze. "Killing all of your kind would be genocide."

"Exactly. And since I know that this is what you would call it, you have nothing to fear from me." He reached out and put a hand on her shoulder. "Morgan, any intelligent being can only do what it thinks is right. Have faith in my ability to do that, and everything will *be* all right."

His eyes never once left hers. His hand gripped her shoulder tightly. She felt he was pleading with her, trying to make her understand something important—but she couldn't quite grasp it. Genocide? Was he talking about the destruction of the Caste that had made him and his kind over half a million years ago? Or was he just using that possibility to illustrate a more general point?

"If you have any surprises in store for me," she said, "you'd better let me know now."

"I'm not the one with the surprises, Morgan," he said.

Turning on his heel, he stepped through the containment team and onto the transport.

15

The fane was full. By the time Roche and her party took their places in the front row, with a clear view of the font and the small group of people around it, she had lost count of the number of unfamiliar Castes mixed in with the thousands of Pristines: short ones, tall ones, broad ones, thin ones, Castes that required filters to weed out atmospheric irritants, and Castes that, judging by the thickness of their skins and protective coverings over their eyes, could have survived just as comfortably in a vacuum. She recognized only three types: a Surin not far from where they stood, an Eckandi toward the rear, and a robed Hurn looming to one side. Where they had come from, she couldn't guess.

<Some people aren't happy about this,> Maii's voice whispered to her.

<Anyone in particular?> asked Roche, continuing to scan the crowd.

<No,> said the girl. <It's just a general feeling, underlying the tension.>

The "tension" sprang in part from the news that the Heresiarch had placed the ship on red alert. The conflict in the system showed no signs of abating; if anything, it seemed to be spreading. All peripheral civilian ships, including the *Ana Vereine*, were to dock, and a protective sphere of fighters would patrol the space between the camouflage and the body of the *Phlegethon* itself. If anything got through, it would be instantly dealt with.

When the time came, Esko Murnane stepped forward and bowed respectfully to the Heresiarch. He raised his hands and, gradually, silence fell about the fane.

"We have taken the unprecedented step," he began, without preamble, "of inviting our non-Pristine guests to join us today. We intend this as a sign of solidarity in these difficult times, when *all* of Humanity seems endangered, not just the Pristine Caste. For many of us, this meeting could well be the first time we come face to face, knowingly, with the enemy."

Although Murnane had made no gesture nor mentioned any names, heads began to turn toward Roche and her party.

"We have among us again a person you all know at least by reputation—a person who was initially rejected by this council but who has, despite that, worked for us in an unofficial capacity for the last two and a half weeks. The information distributed immediately prior to this meeting explains how Morgan Roche has stumbled across a means of identifying the enemy. If this ability is unique to her, it may be of little long-term benefit in our fight with the enemy. But if it is not, if there are others among us who share this ability, then we have a very real chance of victory. To overcome the enemy we must explore *every* possible avenue—and at this moment in time, this is the best option available to us."

Roche couldn't tell from Murnane's expression whether he believed what he was saying or not, but the triumphant glint was back in Nemeth's eye. It probably wouldn't matter from his point of view if Murnane believed it at all, as long as the council gave *him* the credit.

"The sudden and unexpected escalation in conflict we've seen around us," Murnane went on, "may be connected to the death of five clone warriors earlier today on board this very ship. Immediately following their deaths, fighting broke out around the system, and it has not stopped or even eased since. The speed with which the news spread suggests that some sort of epsense link might be involved, and so we have asked Morgan Roche, here, if she will help us in determining whether or not this might be the case."

The whispers around the fane became slightly louder, and in the general murmur Roche heard her own name being mentioned over and over again. She wished that she could shut the helmet of her combat suit to block the voices out; the attention focused on her from those present in the fane was almost suffocating.

Murnane stepped back to let Nemeth take the floor.

"I have been declared chairperson for this meeting," said the younger man. "As someone who has recently worked with Morgan Roche, I am in a unique position to guide the council to the conclusions it *must* reach. As my colleague has just told you, this development may prove crucial to the success of our defense of the galaxy against our enemy. Indeed, it may prove critical to our very survival."

The murmurings rose in pitch again, threatening to become a clamor of alarm.

"Please!" Nemeth raised both his hands, gesturing for calm. "There is no need for panic!" he called out over the noise. "We mustn't be unnerved by what the enemy has done this day! Don't allow yourselves to think that they have the measure of us. What you are seeing is merely the winnowing of the weak—of those corrupted and influenced by the enemy! Those seduced by evil have died by evil's hand! But the same fate does not await us. We are equal to the task ahead. *We* are strong; we *will* prevail!"

He lowered his hands and cast his gaze across the crowd. If he expected cheers, he didn't get them, but he did get the crowd's full attention. After a while, relative quiet returned to the enormous room.

Roche wondered how many people had allies, friends, or family among those already killed in the chaos. She didn't think that any of the Castes she had encountered deserved to be labeled "weak" or "evil" simply because they had been destroyed by the enemy before the others. After all, only chance might have spared the *Phlegethon* itself from the five clone warriors that had infiltrated it.

But this was politics, not reasoned debate, and the reminder was a timely one. In order to get what she wanted, she would have to score points, not make them.

When he had finished scanning the crowd, Nemeth faced

Roche's party. "Morgan Roche and Adoni Cane, please step up to the font."

Cane waited for Roche to move before stepping out of the crowd. Together they walked the twenty-odd steps to the heart of the fane, where Nemeth and Murnane and a dozen other people waited for them. The gaze of the council was almost unbearable now: as heavy as a planet and no less impersonal. A subtle prompt from Maii buoyed Roche slightly, made her feel that she could actually face them successfully.

<You've tackled worse than this,> said the girl. <Many of them are more scared than you are, Morgan.>

<Yes,> she sent back, <but it seems they're more scared *of* me than *with* me.>

<That's only natural, Morgan.>

<I'm not sure it helps me much, Maii . . .>

Nemeth's nod to each of them was formal and perfunctory. His only interest was in beginning the interrogation.

"Morgan Roche, why are you here?"

"To determine the origins of the enemy," she said briskly; she was tired of answering the same old questions over and over. "And, if possible, to find a way to stop them."

"Who sent you?"

"No one sent me," she replied. "I used to work for the Commonwealth of Empires, but I am now independent."

"Is it not true that your mission has been sanctioned by at least one of the High Humans?"

"I am unable to answer that question," she said after some consideration, "because I'm not sure myself of the truth." That much, at least, was honest. "There have been times when I was convinced of High Human intervention, but I've never had the evidence to prove or disprove this." That, also, was true; she only had the Box's word that the Crescend was involved. "The fact that I once had in my possession a fully conscious artificial intelligence—something far beyond the capabilities of mundane science—was all I really had to suggest that I was being helped by someone in the High Human ranks."

"And this AI is now destroyed," said Nemeth. "Is that correct?"

"Yes." Having been said so many times now, the lie came easily.

"Do you claim that your companion here is one of the enemy?" He looked at Cane as he said this.

"Yes."

"We'll come back to this in a moment," he said, returning his attention to Roche. But first I'd like to address something else." He paused, posturing loftily. "The last time you came before us," he said, "you refused to submit to a genetic test. Why was that?"

"At the time I was unaware of your reasons for wanting me to," she said. "The thought simply hadn't occurred to me that you wanted to determine whether or not I myself was one of the clone warriors. Having said that, however, I should point out that I will *still* resist such a test, because I believe that I have clearly demonstrated my allegiances in this last week. Even if I *was* a clone warrior, I have given the council information on the whereabouts of five others. Why would I allow my own kind to be killed if I wasn't on your side?"

Nemeth nodded—approvingly, she thought. He knew what she was doing. She was setting up her argument for the acceptance of Cane. If she could convince the council that the matter of her genetic origins was irrelevant given that she was clearly working for them, not against them, then it would be easier to convince them about Cane.

"Neither would you submit to an in-depth epsense probe, though," he went on.

"Because I believe such probes are invasive and unnecessary," she responded calmly. "*And* they are open to misinterpretation. My actions should be taken into consideration, not what takes place in the privacy of my own thoughts."

He nodded again. "And do you speak for Adoni Cane, here?"

She glanced to her left, to where Cane stood patiently, awaiting his turn to speak.

"In what sense?"

"Would *he* allow himself to be genetically examined or probed by an epsense adept?"

She shrugged. "That's up to him," she said. "But I've already given you his genetic data. As for probing him, I don't believe it's possible. The reave in my crew finds his mind impenetrable—"

<In both senses of the word,> interrupted Maii. <His barriers are naturally strong; he himself might not be able to dismantle them. Even the surface levels of his mind are too complicated

for me to interpret; the impressions I receive are in no way typical of any minds I have known.>

Nemeth turned to face the girl, whose thoughts had easily filled the fane, relayed by the other reaves around them. "Your testimony is not called for at this time, child," he said, "The council will address you if and when it is required."

<Squt,> the girl sent to Roche alone. Roche suppressed a quick smile, recognizing the Surin word for a closed-minded fool.

"Your reave is young and inexperienced," said Nemeth to Roche, "although I am told she does possess a formidable raw talent. It's possible she may be right, but I would prefer to trust the judgments of the high-grade epsense adepts the council normally employs." He turned to Cane. "So I ask you now, *would* you allow such an examination?"

"Your reaves have been attempting to read my mind ever since I arrived on the ship," Cane said. "They have not been able to."

A flicker of a smile crossed Nemeth's face. "Then will you at least drop your barriers for them?"

"I am not able to do that," Cane said. "The barriers I have around my mind are not artificial. They are part of me. I am as unable to remove them as you are unable to remove your skin."

"You realize that this will make it difficult for us to trust you? After all, we have nothing but your word that this is the case."

"I understand that," said Cane implacably, as though daring the entire council to change his mind.

Nemeth shrugged helplessly. "Then all we can do is proceed," he said. "Do we at least have your permission to take a genetic sample, to confirm the data Morgan Roche gave us earlier?"

He didn't hesitate: "Yes."

Nemeth waved forward two of the people standing by the font. Cane held out his hand as one produced a small device designed to take a blood sample from his thumb. There was a small *click*, and the two women stepped away.

A few moments later, the results were displayed for all the council to study. In a giant hologram hanging above her head, Roche could see a stylized representation of Cane's genetic code alongside the data she had given the council before. She recognized the scientific shorthand standardized by the Commerce Artel across the galaxy: chunks of code common to all Humans, no matter how divergent their Castes, lay scattered through Cane's genes like islands in an otherwise unfamiliar sea. For the first time, she saw the vast stretches of introns laid bare, incomprehensible patterns of base pairs lined up like words in a language she completely failed to understand.

"They are the same," observed one of the women who had taken the sample. One of the two patterns disappeared, allowing the remaining to be seen in more detail.

"He possesses the features we have come to associate with the enemy?" Nemeth asked.

"There can be no doubt." Several of the unknown sections were highlighted in red.

"You are convinced that this man is one of the enemy, then."

"Genetically speaking, yes." The woman stared balefully at Cane. "I am convinced."

Nemeth turned away from her, but Roche cut him off before he could speak.

"Wait," she said, addressing the woman. "What can you tell me about these features?" She indicated the sections highlighted in red.

"Nothing, I'm afraid." The woman seemed unsettled by the question. "They don't correlate to any known Human code."

Roche raised her eyebrows. "What does that mean?"

"Just what I said."

"That he's not Human?"

"No . . . no, of course not." She frowned at the question. "What else *could* he be? I just meant that the features we find in his introns are not seen in any other Caste."

"But why is that so unlikely? Every Caste is different. Surely there must be some that stand apart from the rest?"

"*No.*" The woman was emphatic. "There has been much genetic intermingling between the Castes since the Primordial strains speciated, five hundred thousand years ago. One always shares *some* common features with another, no matter how different they might appear in the flesh."

"Then what happened to Cane's introns? Where are the sequences that should be there, and where have the new ones come from?"

"The only way the common features could be missing was if they were somehow removed and replaced with new, maybe random, sequences. But I can't see why anyone would want to do that. The introns are ignored, for the most part, since they serve little or no function."

"But if someone *did* have the capability to do this, might they want to do it to conceal the origins of a new Caste?"

"They might." The woman shrugged. "But, again, I can't see why. Only the High Humans have this sort of technology—and why would they create a new Caste just to kill us? There must be many more certain ways to do that."

Roche nodded. The woman had raised an interesting point, and allowed Roche to assert her presence in the meeting. Satisfied that the council knew that she was not going to sit back and let Nemeth railroad her to whatever conclusion he was hoping for, she indicated for him to continue.

He nodded with exaggerated politeness. "Thank you," he said. "Now, having ascertained that Adoni Cane is in fact one of the enemy, several questions arise that cannot be easily answered. Why he chose to ally himself with Morgan Roche at all is one such issue; why he chose to risk his own life to save hers and that of her companions would be another. These were key sticking points at Roche's last appearance before this council, and they have yet to be resolved. The possibility also remains that he is in fact still working for the enemy—a possibility which cannot be completely discounted, and *must* be the context within which his replies to our questions are considered.

"Do you understand what I am saying, Adoni Cane?"

"Of course I understand you." Cane's expression didn't change, but Roche noted the contempt in his tone.

If Nemeth heard it, he ignored it.

"Very well," he said. "We'll proceed. Tell me, Adoni Cane, *do* you possess epsense abilities?"

"In the sense that I can make myself heard to a reave? Yes, I do. But if you are asking whether I can actually read minds or stop people's hearts—then no, I don't."

"And you are certain of this?"

"I would hardly be unaware of such an ability," said Cane.

"Morgan?" Nemeth turned to her, asking her to corroborate Cane's statement.

"Obviously I don't know what goes on inside his head," she said, "but I haven't seen anything to suggest that he's a reave of any kind."

"His shield?" Nemeth suggested.

"It *could* be innate. I've never seen him hurt anyone that way, or even been addressed by him that way. He has never tried to influence my decisions—"

"Are you sure of that?" Nemeth was quick to jump on this.

"Positive." She was certain Maii would have alerted her to any mental tampering, had it occurred.

"Then what makes you think an epsense link could be responsible for the chaos that has broken out around us? Either the link exists, and therefore Cane has it, or it doesn't exist and he is as mute as he appears to be."

Roche remembered the conversations she'd had with Maii and Cane immediately prior to coming to the *Phlegethon* the first time. "Like his shields, the link could be innate. Before his death, the Olmahoi *irikeii* expressed the opinion that the clone warriors were like him: absorbers of thought—*all* thought, from all around them. This would include each other's thoughts, of course, assuming they can penetrate each other's shields. That would turn an innate ability to absorb thought into a means of communicating with each other."

Nemeth frowned. "Wouldn't this make them some kind of collective mind?"

Roche shrugged. "I raise it merely as an hypothesis to be tested."

"But how could we possibly test it?"

"Maybe we already have, inadvertently," she said. "By alerting one clone warrior to the knowledge that we can now find them, we may be alerting the others and—"

"You cannot produce the phenomenon you are attempting to explain as evidence to support your hypothesis," said a voice from the crowd.

Roche looked around and saw Salton Trezise stepping forward to confront her.

"How do you plan to prove your argument?" he continued. "We need more data. How do you propose we go about getting it?"

Roche glanced at Nemeth, who looked furious at the interruption but didn't himself in turn interrupt. An intrigued sussurrus spread through the fane.

"I have no specific experiment in mind," Roche admitted. "That's why I'm here, to talk to the council."

"Well, maybe it's time the council started asking the right questions, instead of skirting the issue. Tell me, Roche, have you personally ever seen anything in the time that you have known Adoni Cane to suggest that he shares a connection with the other clone warriors?"

Roche thought about this for a second. "Only once," she said. "When we arrived in Sol System. Jelena Heidik, the clone warrior we were following, knew exactly when we would arrive and where we were headed. That information could have been transmitted through such a link."

"But is it possible that this information could have been obtained through other means?"

"Yes, it's possible—"

"Then such evidence is circumstantial, *not* conclusive, and comes from a source one might describe as unreliable: *you*."

He smiled broadly, but Roche didn't respond. Nemeth stepped forward to regain control, but Trezise refused to stop.

"And what about you?" Trezise asked, turning to Cane. "Do you share a connection with the others?"

"No," said Cane bluntly.

"You're not aware of any such a connection? Or are you saying that such a connection does not exist?"

"It doesn't exist."

"Good, because I'd hate to think the enemy was listening in on us." He turned to Roche again. "Did you think about that when you brought him here? That if such a link *did* exist, he could broadcast every word we said to the enemy in this system?"

"*You* suggested it," she said.

"Yes, I did—and not because I believed your crazy theory, but rather to clear this matter up once and for all. It's time this nonsense was laid to rest and we returned to serious business."

A dissatisfied mutter from the crowd echoed his words. Rey Nemeth took advantage of the slight pause to break in:

"What are you suggesting, Trezise?"

"I am suggesting that we are wasting our time here!" he said loudly. "That *Morgan Roche* is wasting our time, and that you, Nemeth, are letting her!" He turned to the crowd. "It is not any mysterious epsense link which will allow the enemy to win; it is meetings such as this! While we stand around here listening to *her* outrageous claims and *his* pontificating, we are doing the enemy's work for them!"

Nemeth drew himself up. "What exactly are you accusing me of, Trezise? Collaboration with the enemy?"

"I accuse you of nothing more than incompetence, Councilor. Morgan Roche came to us with vague hints and rumors and she was rightly rejected. *You*, however, took it upon yourself to pursue her cause in another forum. Perhaps at the time the gamble seemed justified, but her reports now reveal how disastrous that course of action was."

Roche felt Maii's anger boiling over, but she forced herself to remain calm as Trezise ranted on.

"Then she returns, spouting even more wild allegations. They serve no purpose. Worse—they actively impede any progress we might make toward ascertaining the truth! Word about today's 'exercise' could just as easily have spread by means of ordinary Human spies and hyperspace communications. There is no need to hypothesize beyond that. All we have to do is look for those spies and the problem will be solved. But no, instead we're off in search of phantoms, while the very real enemy continues to work among us!"

"Not any more," said Nemeth. "The five she helped us locate *were* clone warriors. There is no doubt of that."

"I don't dispute this," said Trezise. "But how many *more* might there be, that she *hasn't* told us about? We have only her word that the ship is now clean."

"There has been no overt move against us—"

"*Yet*." Trezise turned to Esko Murnane. "And *you*! Bad enough that Assistant Vice Primate Nemeth should already have wasted so much of the council's time—but you had to give him more. You encouraged this 'exercise' which has brought the entire Sol System to war. Do you call this progress? Thousands are dying every minute!"

Trezise turned to address the council as a whole. "I call for a vote of no-confidence in the leadership and guidance of Esko Murnane and Rey Nemeth!"

Roche understood, then, why Trezise had asked for her to appear in front of the council.

She glanced at the Heresiarch, who was watching the proceedings with a frown. The crowd was unsettled; she heard confusion and anger in the mingled voices surrounding her. How a no-confidence vote would go she couldn't guess, but the fact that it had been called was bad enough. Even if it failed to get rid of Murnane or Nemeth, it had placed Trezise firmly in the minds of the councilors, and it would disrupt normal proceedings for some time.

This was his chance to seize power, and he wasn't going to waste it. He wasn't interested in her testimony one way or the other. She was just a tool to help him get what he wanted.

She was being used yet again—and the worst thing was that she had to go along with it. Regardless of who ran the council, it was still her best chance to do any good in the system. She knew the ship was clear of the enemy, and she also knew that whether Cane was himself telling the truth, he was still their best hope of learning anything new about the enemy.

<Box, can you do anything to stop this?>

<If you wish, Morgan.>

<Nothing too drastic. I just want it postponed until after we've dealt with the real problem.>

<I understand. Give me a minute.>

Roche returned her attention to Trezise. His expression was guarded, outwardly restrained, but she could see the delight behind his eyes. He was pleased with his work, was relishing the growing dissent about the room. The council wasn't entirely on his side—but he had upset the balance; he'd had a direct effect on its mood. Where Nemeth had been simply power-hungry, Trezise looked like he was enjoying the disruption purely for its own sake.

Murnane tried to quiet the crowd, but to no avail. There was too much tension in the air now for it to be so easily quelled. Even when Nemeth added his voice to the call for calm, the racket continued. Trezise took a step back and smiled openly at the chaos.

Then a single, clear chime cut through the noise. A Heterodox officer ran through the crowd to talk to the Heresiarch, whose face instantly became grim.

The bell chimed a second time. As the Heresiarch headed for the adytum, the officer came to the font and spoke to Murnane. Roche wasn't close enough to hear what was being said, even though the noise of the crowd was finally ebbing.

After the third chiming of the bell, Murnane stepped forward to address the council.

"We are under attack," he said simply. "The Heresiarch has

been called to attend to the vessel. This meeting is therefore adjourned until the emergency is past."

The crowd erupted once again, thousands of voices shouting out in a mix of fear and anger. Robed officials stepped into the fane and moved among them, trying to get the people to head toward the exits. Roche saw scuffles break out in a number of places.

<Thanks, Box,> she said. <A little dramatic, perhaps, but effective nonetheless.>

<This has nothing to do with me, Morgan,> the AI said. <We really are under attack. A large fleet previously stationed several million kilometers from here just slow-jumped to the edge of the camouflage field and launched base-line probes. No shots have been exchanged yet, but that is only a matter of time. Fighters have been launched by both sides.>

She tried to call Kajic, but a precautionary scrambling system was in place. <What about the *Ana Vereine*?> she asked, concerned. <Is it okay?>

<It is docked and safe.>

<Good. I—>

A hand came down on her shoulder. "We should leave," said Cane.

She looked around. Haid, Maii, and Vri were being herded toward an exit on the far side of the fane, and the containment team was closing in around the font.

<We'll meet you back at the ship,> Maii called, her voice faint through jamming of a mental sort. The council's reaves, it seemed, weren't taking any chances, either.

"You go back to the ship too," she told Cane. "You're not a prisoner. They'll take you there and let you go." She directed the words at the leader of the containment team, who nodded. "Wait for the others. I won't be long."

Cane hesitated for a moment, then nodded and was led away by the squad of soldiers.

Roche approached Murnane, who stood, looking stunned and confused, with one hand on the font supporting him. Trezise was arguing loudly with him.

"This is exactly what I said would happen if we allowed Exotics into the council meetings! We've become caught up in someone else's dispute!"

"Our ftl drones are being destroyed across the system," Murnane said. "This is a coordinated assault, not a random skirmish."

"All the more reason to resolve this issue *now*—"

"*No!*" Then, more calmly, meeting Roche's eye, Murnane said: "I don't think talking will resolve anything anymore."

He turned and walked away. Trezise glared at her, then followed.

Roche was at a loss for a moment. She had hoped to find out how she could help, but the fane was rapidly emptying. Nemeth had gone with the others. The only ones remaining were a handful of Exotics trying to get closer to her, and a ring of guards around the central area keeping them at bay.

<What now, Box?>

<We watch,> it said. <This is an interesting development, Morgan. Before, the attacks were random and local. Now they have a target. The enemy is moving against the council in a manner that cannot be disguised as anything but purposeful and destructive. At last, we have confirmation of their intent.>

<But what can I *do*?>

<Nothing for the time being. You are safer here than you would be anywhere else in this system. Even if the *Phlegethon is* overcome, you will have ample warning, and therefore time to escape.>

<Has the firing started yet?>

<No. The Skehan Heterodox will not initiate the conflict. They would rather avoid it if possible, since it is likely that such an exchange would result in the deaths of many innocent people.>

"Roche!" Vischilglin's voice echoed in the emptying space. "What are you still doing here?"

Roche turned to face the tall woman who had breached the ring of guards and now stood on the far side of the font.

"I don't know," said Roche. "I feel like I'm missing out on something important."

Vischilglin came closer, until she reached the font. Then she did as Murnane had done during the first council meeting Roche had attended: she dipped her hand into the water and sipped it.

"The Heterodoxies say it brings clarity of thought," she said, wiping her hand lightly on her robe. "Something we could all use at the moment."

Roche nodded, willing to accept the superstition but not to indulge it. "There's nothing for me here," she said. "I should get back to my ship."

"I'll take you," said Vischilglin.

"No, that's all right. I can find it."

"Please," she insisted. "I have little else to do while the warriors blunt their swords on each other."

Roche acquiesced, and was led out of the fane via the same exit Murnane and the other senior councilors had used. It opened onto a series of featureless white corridors that could have come from any center of bureaucratic power anywhere in the galaxy—a far cry from the streams and valleys she had witnessed on her first trip to the fane.

Thankfully, Vischilglin seemed to know where she was going. She said nothing as she guided Roche through the warren. The only sounds were the soft pad of her footfalls, almost entirely drowned out by the heavy footfalls of Roche's combat suit.

<The battle outside has commenced,> the Box announced matter-of-factly. <The first shot was fired forty seconds ago. Another fleet has moved into position alongside the first, and the Heresiarch has ordered a course-change.>

Roche didn't respond. The news wasn't good. With two fleets now engaging the *Phlegethon*, the possibility that more might join in was very real. How long the Skehan Heterodox could last against a sustained assault she didn't know—and she didn't want to have to find out the hard way, either. She just wished there was something constructive she could do to ease the situation.

Instead, she was stuck in a warren, led by a woman whose silence was starting to make Roche nervous.

<Do you know where she's taking me?> she asked the Box.

<You are on an administration level directly beneath the fane.>

<That's not what I asked,> Roche said.

They turned a corner. Ahead was a row of doors that suggested elevators or some other intraship conveyance like the one they had used on her first visit. Vischilglin took her to the nearest and pushed a button. The door opened with a hiss and they stepped into the small capsule. Vischilglin selected a destination and the doors hissed shut again.

<She is taking you to the docks,> the Box confirmed.

<As expected.>

Roche didn't know why Vischilglin's behavior was bothering

her. All she knew was that there was something odd about her, something not quite right. . . .

Although she hadn't felt the capsule begin its journey, she did feel it decelerate. Before it could come to a halt, Vischilglin tapped something into the pad by the door, and the capsule coasted a second before recommencing its braking.

<Something's wrong,> said the Box. <She's overshot the level you need.>

Roche didn't give herself time to think. Her combat suit was sealed and a weapon in her hand just as the capsule slid to a halt.

"Any sudden moves and I won't hesitate to pull the trigger," she warned Vischilglin, her voice booming via the helmet's speakers into the confined space.

The woman's eyes widened. "How . . . ?"

Then the doors opened, and Roche saw the welcoming party intended for her: five tall figures dressed in a mixture of spiky Hurn armor and robes, all with weapons raised and aimed directly at her.

"Put the weapon down, Roche," said one. "You can't possibly hope to fight us all."

She hesitated, ready to fire. They all had heavy-duty rifles, and she didn't dare doubt that they were all equipped with armor-piercing ammunition. If she so much as raised a hand, they would cut her down where she stood.

<Box?>

The lights went out. In the same instant Roche dropped to the floor and switched to infrared. Her welcoming committee was slow to respond, giving her the few precious split-seconds she needed to get out of their sights. She took one robed figure in the throat and another in the hip before any of them returned fire. When they did, the elevator exploded with light. Vischilglin's scream was short-lived.

Roche used the suit's attitude jets to propel herself along the floor. Sparks flew from her stomach-plating as she fired at another of her attackers. The first two she had shot were down but still moving. The armor of the remaining three was tougher; the third one she hit barely flinched.

Their heat-images were turning to follow her. She scrambled to where one of the fallen figures lay and wrenched the rifle out of its grasp. Rolling, she fired at the other three. The recoil of the rifle took her by surprise, even through her suit. One of her attackers flew backward into a wall. The two others split up and darted away.

She took the opportunity to look around her. In infrared, the scene was confusing. Airlocks glowed red with flashing lights above them; floors, walls, and ceilings were lukewarm gray; energy from the shots splashed the area around the elevator with bright swaths of white-yellow. Her attackers were green-blue on either side of her, trying to pin her between them.

She turned and ran as fast as the suit would allow her.

<Box, I need a way out!> she said quickly. <An elevator, an open lock—*anything*!>

Something red flashed in her implants to her left: another elevator. She headed toward it. Energy flashed past her and blossomed on a far wall: her attackers were firing at her. She crouched to decrease her profile, dodging as much as she could without lessening her speed.

She switched to visible light for a second to judge the distance. The elevator doors hung invitingly open, barely fifteen meters ahead. Yellow light shone from between them. Gunfire flashed past her again, and she realized that she was silhouetted against that light, giving her assailants a perfect target.

<Box, kill the light and get ready to close the doors! Warn the others!>

<I've already told Kajic.> The Box's calm voice was in almost surreal contrast to her mad dash for safety. <He says—>

Something smashed into her from behind, throwing her forward, sprawling. Pain exploded in her right shoulder and back. She skidded helplessly along the floor, moving fast enough to reach the elevator but missing the doors by a meter and crashing heavily into the wall. She tried to move, to stand, but her suit only whined ineffectually at her. She could smell ozone and smoke and burning blood.

Lots of blood.

<Box?> Through the pain, she managed to tip the dead weight of her suit onto its back.

Someone was running toward her with a rifle trained on her stomach. She tried to raise her own weapon, but her hands wouldn't respond. Her attacker came closer, slowing to a cautious walk. The weapon's aim didn't waver for a second.

<Box! Help me!>

One of the other suited figures appeared, asking, "Did we get her?"

"Don't ask stupid questions," said the first. "Call the others. We're going to need help getting her on board—and make sure the surgeon is ready!"

The other nodded and turned away. The first suited figure approached closer still, until it was an arm's length away. Reaching out with a boot, the figure tapped Roche on the chest. She could do nothing but grit her teeth on the pain.

The light spilling out of the elevator seemed to be fading.

Somewhere in the distance—or perhaps from deep inside her—she thought she heard a voice calling her. A girl. She knew she should respond, but she didn't have the strength.

In the fading light, the first figure crouched on one knee beside her. "Morgan Roche." It was a woman's voice. "At last."

Roche had barely a second of consciousness to realize that she knew that voice.

Then a wave of darkness broke over her and took her with it.

PART FOUR:
THE CRESCEND

16

Page De Bruyn watched closely as three Disciples carried Morgan Roche into the Hurn cruiser. Roche's face was red-lit through the blood-spattered visor of her damaged suit, painted oddly by warning lights and alarm signals from within. She was very pale beneath the blood. De Bruyn caught herself thinking that Roche was lucky to be alive—although from Roche's point of view, 'lucky' was hardly the right word.

They hauled the injured woman through the cramped, convoluted crawlspaces of the ship and placed her on the autosurgeon's table. Cutting devices flared as they stepped away. Something in De Bruyn's stomach dropped as the cruiser disengaged from the *Phlegethon* and accelerated into the battlefield, broadcasting clearance codes to ensure their safe passage. De Bruyn waited anxiously for any sign of attack, but none came. The besieging fleets ignored them as the Disciples had assured her they would.

Bit by bit, Roche's suit fell apart down her right side, exposing the woman within. De Bruyn was surprised at how small she was, but supposed that was only in contrast to the sheer bulk of the suit. They were approximately the same height, and De Bruyn was taller than most men she knew. Or maybe it was just Roche's vulnerability that made her seem so small—lying there now, finally, helpless and alone. Without her crew of freaks around her, she wasn't as impressive as the rumors would suggest.

Roche's body was covered with gore. The shot had taken her low in the right shoulder and gone straight through her, leaving a hole easily a hand's-breadth wide. Shattered bone, torn muscle, and liquefied organs filled the hole. Blood still pulsed weakly from it, even through the cauterized ends of veins and arteries. De Bruyn could have pushed her hand through the mess and out the other side had she wanted to.

But the torment could wait. The important thing for now was keeping the woman alive. It was inconceivable that Roche could have survived such an injury. She should have died on the spot.

Hissing and licking sounds emanated from the autosurgeon as it went to work on Roche. De Bruyn faced the Disciple who had fired the wounding shot.

"You're very fortunate," she said quietly. "Had she died, I would have killed you myself. As it is, you'll just be disciplined."

The Disciple paled, but bowed in deference and backed out of the room. The others followed, sensing De Bruyn's mood. She didn't bother to hide the fact that she was displeased, even though the mission had, in almost every respect, been a success. But the Disciples didn't respond as well to reward as they did to punishment.

When they were gone, De Bruyn unsealed her own suit and slipped out of the helmet. While she watched the autosurgeon stabilize its patient, she patched into the command network via her implants and summoned the pilot of the vessel.

<Wamel, how long until we're out of here?>

<A few minutes. The Rebuli have given us a mine-free vector taking us up the long axis of the camouflage shield. That will mean a slight delay, but less risk of—>

The ship lurched. De Bruyn grabbed for support as the deck fell out from underneath her and the lights flickered.

<What the hell was that?> she asked.

<I don't know.> She could hear a racket in the background as the pilot fought for control of the ship. <We're changing course!>

<What?>

<The instruments—> There was another lurch, more violent than the first. Voices shouted at each other over the command

network. <I'm shutting down the main drives and going to aux­iliary. Hold on!>

Free-fall came suddenly, and just as abruptly ended. De Bruyn's feet lifted off the ground for a second, then slammed back down with twice her normal weight. She slipped and fell, skidding across the floor as acceleration sent the ship into a tight turn. The lights flickered again, and didn't return to their full strength. Red emergency lighting came on, and stayed.

<I don't understand it!> the pilot shouted. <The instruments are giving me readings that don't make any sense, and the con­trols aren't responding—>

<Don't be a fool,> De Bruyn snapped, gripping the lip of the autosurgeon's operating table and scrambling to her knees.

<We're being dragged back to the *Phlegethon*!>

<Call the Rebuli!> she ordered.

<I can't! We're broadcasting something but I can't tell what it is. It's like the ship's been taken over!>

A chill ran the length of De Bruyn's spine. "This can't be happening," she muttered. "Not again . . ."

The last time she'd had Roche in her grasp, something much like this had occurred. The AI that Roche had babysat *too* well had somehow taken over a Dato Marauder and COE Intelligence HQ, bending them to its will as easily as De Bruyn used the Disciples. But a recurrence was not possible. That particular AI had been destroyed back in Palasian System. Or so she had thought.

De Bruyn clambered to her feet, leaning over the operating table, studying its patient intently. Despite all the power fluctuations, the autosurgeon's work on Roche continued unabated.

Roche's lips were moving. It was hard for De Bruyn to hear over the racket in her implants, but Roche was definitely trying to say something. De Bruyn leaned in closer still, and in doing so heard one word being repeated over and over again. It was faint, but unmistakable:

"Box . . . Box . . ."

De Bruyn stood upright, aghast. *How* it was possible, she didn't know, but she couldn't afford to have any doubts. Not now, when she was so close.

<Shut down the navigation and communication systems!> she ordered. <Hit the manual override! Shut down *everything*—even life-support! Do it now, before it's too late!>

The ship lurched beneath her again as the pilot obeyed.

<Control system not responding—trying module overrides. Drive module not responding. Navigation down. Communication not responding. Life-support down.>

The emergency lights went out completely for a second. De Bruyn could hear noises from the bridge that sounded like panels being opened. <Attempting physical disconnection.> There was a pause and then: <Drive module out.> Gravity disappeared completely. <Communications—>

The line died, and everything went quiet.

De Bruyn anchored herself on Roche's table. Her suit had closed automatically, and she had just enough light to see by. Roche's face was in shadow, but parts of her body were visible under the autosurgeon's lasers. It was still operating, using its internal emergency power. Roche's lips had stopped moving.

De Bruyn grabbed a cutter and began to slice away the remaining fragments of Roche's suit. The autosurgeon resisted, especially as she cut at the glove encasing Roche's right hand—where Roche's standard COE Intelligence implants provided her with an external data link. But the autosurgeon had nothing strong enough to cut living armor, and as the glove came free, its resistance ceased.

De Bruyn heard someone moving toward her, through the crawlspaces.

"Reverence?" called a voice. "Reverence!"

"Here," she replied, turning from Roche.

"The interference has ceased," said the pilot, climbing into the room. His robes fluttered like the wings of a giant moth. "But we are drifting blind and vulnerable!"

She heard reproach in his voice, and didn't rise to it. "Bring the systems up slowly," she said. "One by one. Keep automation to a minimum. If that means doing without communications and life-support for the time being, then that's what we do. Navigation, too. All we really need is a working drive to get us away from here. Once we're out of range, everything will operate properly again, I'm sure."

"Out of range?" The pilot frowned. "Of what?"

Of the damnable Box, she wanted to tell him, but couldn't bring herself to say it. She hardly believed it herself.

"The *Phlegethon*," she said instead. "They must be interfering with us somehow."

It was only a half-lie. If the Box still existed, then it had to be broadcasting from the big ship. Roche's suit was in pieces, now, and it wasn't anywhere to be found on her, so it *had* to be somehow communicating via her implants. If they could just get away from its influence, they would be able to continue their work. With the only possible link between Roche and the Box severed, now that she was entirely free of the combat suit, it would have no way of communicating with her when she awoke. Or so De Bruyn hoped. Her only alternative was to try the "Silence between thoughts" shutdown code again—although Roche had ordered the machine to ignore De Bruyn if she said it, and there was no guarantee it would listen to any of their transmissions anyway.

The pilot looked doubtful. "Reverence, I—"

"Do as I tell you, Wamel." Her tone was smooth and cold; argument would not be tolerated. "I want those drives working even if you have to stoke them with coal. Take us away from the *Phlegethon* as quickly as possible. We can discuss what happens later. Just get us moving before someone decides to do it for us."

"Yes, Reverence." He bowed and left the room.

De Bruyn returned her attention to Roche. The sight of her lying there in the dark, so near to death, filled De Bruyn with a sense of satisfaction. Finally, Roche was in her hands. Finally, she would know the truth. And *nothing* was going to keep her from that.

The lights flickered weakly. Gravity came and went. Deciding that the Disciples needed all the help they could get, she left the autosurgeon to its work—confident in the knowledge that, at least for the moment, she and the machine were on the same side. . . .

God's Monkey limped through the battle zone and out of the *Phlegethon*'s camouflage screen on the tip of a fluttering, poorly tuned fusion flame. An hour later, when the need for accurate navigation overrode De Bruyn's sense of caution, she allowed the pilot to risk switching on some of the ship's higher functions. Gradually, when it became apparent that nothing untoward was going to happen, all of the systems were reconnected. When the ship was fully operational again, she sent it along an orbit that would take them close to the sun, then out to the system's dark fringes, where they would linger in the lesser-populated regions until they had to return.

Within another hour, the embattled *Phlegethon* was far behind them, along with the council, the Rebuli, and Siriote fleets, beyond even Salton Trezise and his devious little schemes. Originally, his price for letting her and the Disciples into the *Phlegethon* had been a disturbance that would justify his push to get the Exotics off the council. But events turned out to be a little more dramatic than anyone had anticipated, what with the Hurn kidnapping *and* the attack of the Rebuli at once. Nevertheless, from De Bruyn's point of view, the outcome had been more than satisfactory.

Separating Roche from her friends had been ridiculously easy, and Trezise had happily turned Hue Vischilglin to his will, filling her head with the notion that Roche was consciously working for the enemy and convincing her to set Roche up. Whether it was true or not, De Bruyn neither knew nor cared. She had what she wanted, and that was all that mattered.

When she was certain they weren't being pursued, she returned to the operating room to see how her captive was doing.

Hurn autosurgeons were notoriously simple-minded in their relationships with Pristine Humans, and this one was no exception. It took her much longer to access Roche's medical data than it should have, and even then it didn't make much sense.

Roche was stable. Her wound had been cleaned and sealed, and tissue regeneration had begun. It would be days before she was able to move again, and it was still a mystery how she had survived such enormous blood-loss and trauma, but at least she was out of immediate danger.

Trezise had given De Bruyn the council's information on the enemy, and she ran Roche's genetic code past it, to see if there was a match. She was half surprised to receive a negative response: Roche was *not* a clone warrior. But she wasn't normal, either. Roche's code was riddled with irregularities that neither De Bruyn nor the autosurgeon could explain.

She patched into the command network. <Wamel? Send Lemmas down here.>

<Yes, Reverence.>

When the reave arrived, De Bruyn was busy programming the autosurgeon to remove Roche's implants.

<You summoned me, Reverence?> The man's voice in her

mind was like a smooth dark fluid, yet conversely sharp and penetrating at the same time. The first time his mind had touched
hers had been disturbing, but she had quickly accustomed herself to this epsense adept's "tone."

"Yes. Wait a moment."

Lemmas waited patiently behind her, his arms at his sides in
the folds of his black robes. No ordinary reave, he was unskilled
at long-distance communication or remote sensing but frighten-
ingly precise at close range. His specialty was the extraction of
information from unwilling subjects, and his methods were notoriously effective.

The autosurgeon whirred and set to work, prepping several
places on Roche's body for surgery. De Bruyn turned to face
Lemmas, folding her arms across her chest. In doing so, she felt
a stickiness there and looked down; some of Roche's gore had
made it onto her, perhaps during the brief free-fall when the ship
had been drifting.

Not that it mattered. Undoubtedly there would be more in the
hours to come.

"Lemmas," she said, absently wiping Roche's blood off her
uniform. "I have some work for you to do."

The man nodded slowly, his hairless face, like most Hurns,
finely boned and long. He wore his ritual mutilation openly: ears
removed, eyes sewn shut, tongue gone. His skin was bluish in
the harsh light; through it, De Bruyn imagined that she could see
not just his veins but his bones as well—yellow and decayed,
like his teeth.

<I am yours to command, Reverence,> he said.

"I want you to take her apart," she said. "Slowly. I don't want
you to kill her. Just break her open so I can look inside."

<What is it you are looking for?>

She looked over to Roche on the table and shook her head.
"I'm not entirely sure."

<That will make it difficult.> There was an unhealthy relish
to his voice.

"Just do what you have to do."

The reave inclined his head. <You will be required to observe,> he said.

"Naturally. You need my eyes."

<I will also need you to tell me when I have found the in-
formation you seek.>

"I can assist you in other ways, if you like."

<That won't be necessary.> He paused. <You are not squeamish, then?>

The thought of Roche being tortured didn't bother her at all. Not that she could have hidden it from the reave even if it did. "That's not something you have to worry about," she said.

His smile was an open wound between his cheeks.

<When shall I begin?>

"By epsense, immediately," she said. "You will have full access to her body once the autosurgeon has finished. In theory, you will have as much time as you need. In practice, however, I think you should proceed as quickly as you can. There's always a possibility that we'll be traced." She was still nervous about the Box. However it had survived, and whatever it was doing on the *Phlegethon*, the fact that it was out there at all made her anxious. The one thing she couldn't take into account in her plans was a rogue, hyperintelligent machine.

<I have her shielded,> said the reave. <Unless someone knows where she is, she will not be found.>

"Be that as it may, I'd still like you to hurry."

Lemmas moved closer to the table and rolled up the sleeves of his robe. His hands were as slender as the rest of his body; his right hand possessed six fingers. He had no fingernails, and below each knuckle were tattoos like rings. He stood for a moment with his head bowed over the operating table, uncannily as though gazing at Roche's face.

The autosurgeon whirred as it unwound artificial nerves from Roche's arm.

De Bruyn wondered when and how Lemmas would start.

<I have already started,> he said.

He reached out with one hand to stroke Morgan Roche's face and, even though she was unconscious, she flinched from his touch.

It was less crude than De Bruyn had anticipated. Barely minutes after the autosurgeon had finished—leaving Roche with several wounds across her body, one hand crippled and an empty eye socket—Lemmas began in earnest. All he did was touch her. De Bruyn couldn't tell whether his mind had powerful psychosomatic effects, or if his nail-less fingertips held hidden tools, but his slightest touch pierced skin, parted fat, and slit through muscle with disturbing ease.

Roche remained unconscious throughout the procedure. De Bruyn didn't ask if that was Lemmas's decision. The autosurgeon might have been keeping her sedated while she recovered from its ministrations. A couple of times De Bruyn had to override its attempts to intervene in Lemmas's work, but she resisted turning it off completely; she didn't want Roche dying from shock before she had learned everything there was to learn.

<Ask.> Lemmas held one hand over Roche's mouth as though he were trying to keep her silent. A tiny line of blood trickled down her cheek and onto the table.

"Where does she come from?"

<You already have that information.>

"That's not the point. I want to know what *she* thinks."

<Ascensio,> he said, with the faintest hint of irritation.

"When was she born?"

<Day thirty-six of the eighth month, '933.>

De Bruyn nodded. That accorded with COE Intelligence and Armada records, but still had not been verified independently.

"Who were her parents?"

<She doesn't know.>

"There are no deep memories at all?"

He paused for barely a couple of seconds; Roche's body stiffened. <There are vague recollections,> he said. <But they could just as easily be memories of her early caregivers at the orphanage or her host family. It is impossible to say.>

"So she does remember her childhood?"

<Yes,> he said, as if at that very moment his mind was caressing those particular memories from Roche's past. <Vividly, at times.>

"Give me an example."

<She had a nightmare when she was four,> he said. <It was raining so hard that she couldn't see through it. She was trying to get home but was unable to find the back door to her house. Something large and hairy brushed her—>

"Not dreams," snapped De Bruyn. "Are there any *real* memories?"

Lemmas didn't hesitate: <She had a favorite toy in the orphanage. It was a talking book called Paz. It was yellow, with a round display, and specialized in M35 children's stories. It—>

"Enough of that," she said. "Tell me what she was afraid of."

<She was afraid of being alone,> he said. <Of having no one to talk to.>

"Was that why she put her name down for the Armada intake?" De Bruyn asked.

<Partly,> said Lemmas. <But she also disliked being poor and felt that her options on Ascensio were limited. She believed joining the COE Armada would give her more opportunities. One of which was to be able to look for her parents.>

"Did she ever find them?" De Bruyn was suddenly very interested in this line of questioning.

<No. She never looked.>

De Bruyn nodded thoughtfully to herself. "Was she ever sick before joining the Armada?"

There was another slight pause. <She contracted a severe viral infection at the age of ten,> he said. <And she broke her leg at fifteen.>

"She was treated on Ascensio?"

<Yes.>

De Bruyn noted that treatment of neither condition appeared in Roche's official records. "Go back to the orphanage," she said. "Does she remember any of the caregivers' names from there?"

<Yes.> Lemmas rattled off five names, two of which De Bruyn recognized from her research.

"And did she have friends in the orphanage, or outside?"

<Both.> More names followed. De Bruyn consigned them to her implants; she would check them later.

"What about emotional or physical intimacy?"

<What do you mean, exactly?>

De Bruyn couldn't help a slight sneer. "Was she ever in love?"

Lemmas didn't reply immediately. <She did not seek such relationships.>

"That doesn't mean there weren't any," said De Bruyn. "I want someone who will remember her—somebody who couldn't possibly forget her. Caregivers can forget, and even friends might with time—but a lover never forgets."

Lemmas recounted several instances that, on the surface at least, suggested a willingness to open up to friends and colleagues—a willingness that De Bruyn knew Roche had not shown in Military College nor any time after graduating. She had always been considered aloof by those who came to know her—emo-

tionally distant and efficient, very much like the machines she had
once regarded as friends. Yet what Lemmas recounted now of
Roche's past portrayed a woman who at least had dabbled with
the idea of sharing life with someone else, but who had ultimately
rejected it—maybe because it made her feel vulnerable; maybe
because her sexual needs simply weren't that great; maybe because she was self-sufficient within herself. For whatever reason,
there were only a handful of people, male and female, who featured in Roche's memories as ones who might have been regarded
as "lovers."

De Bruyn had hoped for more, but she was content with anything at all. She at least had more knowledge, now, of Roche's
life on Ascensio, and that knowledge could be verified in time.
All she needed was one person to say that they recalled Roche,
and De Bruyn would have the proof that the official information
had been covered up.

She was still missing the *why*, though. *That* would be much
harder to find, she was sure.

At her instigation, Lemmas dug deeper. A life as unremark-
able as that of any other orphan from an out-of-the-way world
presented itself: her hopes, her fears; her delights, her disap-
pointments; her ambitions, her failures; her dreams, and her everyday anxieties. The COE was full of people like her.

So why, then, De Bruyn wondered, had she been chosen? And,
more importantly, for *what*?

After four hours, they took a break. De Bruyn was tired and,
although he displayed nothing but cool aloofness, she suspected
that Lemmas was also feeling the strain. Roche's condition was
a concern, too. De Bruyn couldn't tell exactly what the autosurgeon's data meant, but the patient *was* showing signs of extreme
stress. That was the idea, of course, but it was possible to push
too far too soon.

<Do you know now what you are looking for?> Lemmas
asked.

"No." She didn't feel inclined to discuss her quest with the
reave; the fact that he could reach into her mind and pluck out
the information himself only made his asking all the more insincere. "How deep can you dig?"

<As deep as required,> he said with unfaltering confidence.

"Is it possible to hide information from you?"

<Conceivably, but not permanently,> he admitted. <She is already doing it.>

"How?"

<There is a block in her. I touch it whenever we talk about her mission for Intelligence.>

"Which aspect of the mission?"

<The AI.>

"What about the AI?"

<I don't know. That's what the block is for.>

She ignored his sarcasm. "Can you break through it?"

<It is crude but effective. I suspect the girl, Maii, put it in place at Roche's request. Given time, it will unravel.>

"Could it be that she doesn't want anyone to know that the Box still exists?"

<Perhaps.>

She studied Roche's face in silence for a moment. Bruised, missing one eye, encrusted with blood, the woman was barely recognizable. Fleetingly De Bruyn wondered if she might be wrong—if Roche wasn't as important as she had first thought. What would she do if all this had been for nothing?

But there was no getting past the enemy's fixation on her: the way they had disseminated her name and interfered with her work among the Vax, the Fathehi, and the Noske. And what of Adoni Cane? It all had to fit together somehow. If she wasn't herself a clone warrior, then there had to be another explanation.

De Bruyn glanced again at Roche's genetic code. The unidentifiable sections remained just as mysterious as they had been before, different from those of the clone warriors *and* any known Caste. Random mutations? She didn't know. But at least now she had that data.

<Reverence?> The voice came from the command network, not the reave. <We've spotted a ship that looks like it might be matching our orbit,> said the pilot.

She felt a tiny shot of adrenaline. <Are you sure?>

<Not one hundred percent. It could be chance . . .>

<Unlikely,> she said. <Any stray emissions?>

<A few. It might be the *Apostle*, but we haven't been signaled yet.>

A slight apprehension tightened her gut. The idea of the Disciples' leader arriving made her uneasy. <They wouldn't announce

themselves too soon for fear of detection,> she said. <Keep an
eye on the ship and let me know if there's any change.>

<Yes, Reverence.> The pilot went back to his work with no
mention of Roche. That side of their mission was not relevant
to him.

But cracking Roche *was* relevant to De Bruyn, and she was
conscious now of time running out.

"Let's continue," she said, approaching the table.

The reave inclined his head. <As you command, Reverence.>
Earlier, he had removed the pack covering the great wound
through Roche's chest. Smoke came from where his index finger now brushed the stump of her shattered clavicle. <What is
it you wish to know now?>

She only had to think for a second; there were so many questions to choose from. "Find out if she knew anything about the
enemy prior to her meeting with Adoni Cane."

He probed Roche's mind at the same time as he sent her nerves
jangling with pain. <No.>

"Then did she know anything unusual about the Box prior to
commencing her mission on the *Midnight*?"

<No, nothing at all.>

"Has she ever had any contact with Eupatrid Gastel or his
predecessor?"

<No.>

"Does she know why I was sacked?"

<No. She doesn't even know you've *been* sacked.>

De Bruyn sighed. She hadn't really believed it would be so
easy—but it would have been nice.

She tried another tack: Did Roche know how the clone warriors communicated among themselves? Did she know why Cane
was helping her? Did she know who made him? Did she know
why she seemed to be the only one who could find them?

The answers came as rapidly as De Bruyn fired the questions,
and each time the response was the same: *No*.

Her questioning became bolder, and Lemmas's probing blunter:
Was Roche aware of any plan to the engagements in Sol System? Was the fact that they were in Sol System in the first place
significant, or was that just chance? To her knowledge, was the
planetary ring as dire a navigation hazard as the Heresiarch
feared—and if so, why?

But again, Roche had no knowledge of these things.

De Bruyn moved down to details. Had Proctor Klose, captain of the *Midnight*, known anything about Cane? What about Uri Kajic, ex-captain of the *Ana Vereine*? Why did she think Cane's introns were so important? Did she know where Jelena Heidik was hiding, or how many of the enemy were still at large in the system? Did she know anything *at all* about the movements of the enemy?

Within fifteen minutes De Bruyn guessed that Roche in fact didn't know anything about the big picture; two hours more and she was convinced of it. Nevertheless, she persisted, digging for what she suspected might remain behind a veil she hadn't pulled back yet, working through her own fatigue and the continuing fluctuation of Roche's condition. If the reave's finer efforts weren't successful, maybe sheer persistence would win the day.

The trouble was, she was running out of questions. Since the only area she had taken steps to avoid was that of the Box, it was there that De Bruyn finally turned. She didn't know why it was important, but Roche clearly thought so, and that was enough for her.

"What can we do about that block?"

<We can try two things: break it down, or circumvent it.> The reave was weary but still compliant.

"How difficult is the latter?"

<Less difficult than complicated. No knowledge can be completely hidden; even when removed from conscious thought it leaves echoes. Locating those echoes, those secondary and tertiary iterations, is a time-consuming task. But it can be rewarding.>

"Give me an example."

<Well, I can't tell you whether Roche thinks this Box is destroyed or not, but I can tell you that she thinks that she has talked with it in the recent past.>

"What about?"

<That I cannot tell you.>

"Then where is it?" De Bruyn said, then added: "Or where does she *think* it is?"

<That I cannot tell you either. But I do know that the valise that once contained it was a decoy, and that *was* destroyed in Palasian System.>

"What has the Box been doing since?"

<Specifics are hidden in regard to this.>

"Does anyone else know about it?"

<Her reave friend, presumably: Maii. No other name is mentioned, except that of the High Human you refer to as the Crescend.>

"Really? How is he involved?"

<Again, I have no access to information regarding that.>

De Bruyn felt her frustration growing. This was worse than getting nothing at all. However, she was beginning to see how it worked. Direct questions would get her nowhere; she had to go around the issue and tackle it from behind. "Can you tell me why the Box is important?"

<No.>

"Is it connected to the Crescend somehow?"

<Roche seems to think so.>

"How?"

<Not connected so much, perhaps, but *part of*. Her understanding of the situation here is particularly vague. It has troubled her—hence the leakage around the block.>

De Bruyn pondered this with interest. The Box and the Crescend *were* connected, it seemed—perhaps more intimately than anyone could have guessed.

"Where is the Crescend?"

<She doesn't know.>

"What is he doing?"

<She doesn't know.>

"Is she working for him?"

<If she is, she isn't aware of it.>

"Has she at least spoken to him?"

<Through the Box, perhaps, although that also is vague.>

"Why is he so important?"

<She doesn't know.>

"Why is *she* so important?" Frustration gave De Bruyn's voice a bitter edge, one she instantly regretted. Even though Lemmas couldn't actually hear it, he would certainly read the emotion behind it.

The reave stiffened slightly, but didn't reply.

"What? Have you found something?"

<No. I was simply listening—>

<Reverence?> broke in the pilot.

<What, Wamel?>

<We have received orders to dock with the *Apostle*. It has as-

sumed an approach vector and will be in position in ten minutes.>

She closed her eyes, annoyed. The timing couldn't have been worse. <What do they want?>

<They have not said, Reverence.>

<Are they waiting for a reply?>

<No. Confirmation is not necessary.>

That was a polite way of saying that nothing would stop him from obeying that order to dock—not even De Bruyn.

<Give me an airlock and I'll meet you there.>

<Deck 4, Reverence.>

She killed the line.

"We're done here for now," she told Lemmas. "Maybe it's not a bad thing. She'll have a chance to heal." She glanced down at Roche's broken and bloodied body on the table and nodded to herself. "We'll resume later."

Wamel was at Deck 4 ahead of her, straightening his robes. They watched together through the command network as a singleship detached from the many-spined *Apostle*. Again, their environment was dark, so the images were either gloomily portentous or painted in surreal colors. De Bruyn remembered the first time she had encountered the cruiser, and felt a similar dread.

The singleship approached with bright flares from its thrusters, moving confidently across the gap between the two ships. Its approach took barely two minutes, during which time De Bruyn did her best to maintain her composure. She didn't have any doubt who would be in the singleship.

It docked with a bump heard clearly through the rigid bulkheads of *God's Monkey*. Via the command network she saw it anchor firmly in place not far from her own fighter, *Kindling*. There was silence for a moment, then came the sound of the outer door of the airlock opening. There was another pause, followed by a hiss as the door shut again. Then the inner door was open and Cane's twin walked through.

<Master.> Wamel bowed at the sight of the black-robed figure.

The clone warrior didn't acknowledge him. His face was exposed, and his eyes sought De Bruyn. "You have her?"

"Yes." As uneasy as he made her feel, she refused to defer to him the way the Disciples did. "How goes the campaign against the *Phlegethon*?"

He smiled. "The arrangement has been profitable for both of us."

She thought of Trezise for a moment, and wondered if her old colleague had any idea what had happened—if he even suspected just how thoroughly she had betrayed him.

"What are you doing here?" she asked.

"I want to see her. Is she still alive?"

"Of course."

"Good," said the clone warrior.

De Bruyn frowned. "Why? What does it mean to you?"

"We are curious."

"About what?"

"That is not your concern."

"I disagree," said De Bruyn. "Everything to do with her is my concern."

"I think the truth would appall you."

"But *the truth* is exactly what I'm looking for."

"Very well," he said. His smile widened. "Morgan Roche may yet be the key to our defeat. In her lies the potential for our destruction. She alone could be the undoing of all we have worked for."

De Bruyn paused to digest this. "Do you expect me to believe that?"

"I expect nothing of you."

"Could you explain—"

"No. I will not," he said. "We appreciate your efforts in neutralizing this threat to us. With Roche out of the way, our work can continue unchecked."

De Bruyn felt suddenly cold. Whether he was merely posturing or not, the thought was sobering. "And what *is* your work, exactly?"

"What do you see?"

Her laugh was humorless. "I see nothing but destruction."

"What you fail to see is *justice*." There was no mistaking the passion and anger in his voice. "There is no higher aspiration, De Bruyn. You should know that."

His smile was gone. And something in his expression warned her not to push any further.

"Take me to her," he said. "I want to see her with my own eyes."

She turned and led the way to where Roche was being held. Cane's twin followed her silently, with Wamel bringing up the rear. Along the way, De Bruyn turned over in her mind everything the clone warrior had said. What if he was telling the truth? What if she had somehow ruined any hope at all of defeating the enemy?

The autosurgeon had tended to Roche's minor injuries by the time they reached her. Her skin was a patchwork of healing strips and salves, and the pack was back on her shoulder wound. Her readings had stabilized slightly, although they still seemed odd to De Bruyn.

The clone warrior stepped up to the table and looked down upon the patient. "What have you learned so far?" he said, his dark eyes studying Roche's embattled body with dispassionate interest.

"Very little," De Bruyn confessed. "Perhaps if we knew what to look for—"

"You still wouldn't find it." Cane's twin faced her. "Because you're looking in the wrong place."

"But . . . *you* said she was the key."

"*May yet* be the key, is what I said. Even if she is, the key itself holds nothing. What the key is *for* is the important thing, and to know that you must have everything else: the lock, the door, the room beyond . . ." He seemed to be enjoying her discomfort.

"You're talking about Sol System, aren't you?" she asked, riding a hunch. "That's where I should be looking?"

"Yes."

"And that's why you've come here: you're looking for something too."

"In a sense," he said. "If Roche *is* the key, and Sol System is the lock, then the room beyond contains the justice we seek."

Remembering his metaphor, she asked: "And what is the door?"

His smile returned. "That is the one remaining issue we must deal with," he said. "Then our business in the galaxy can truly begin."

His expression was relaxed enough, but De Bruyn sensed a terrible energy radiating from him. She felt like a moth flying into a furnace, only slowly realizing just how dangerous her environment was becoming.

If the enemy's work in the galaxy hadn't even begun, where would it stop? When every Pristine Human was dead? Every mundane, including the Exotics? When all that remained was High and Low Humans?

It was all very well to think in abstract terms about the enemy and their apparent desire to destroy Humanity, but De Bruyn found it disturbing to be confronted with the possibility that it might actually come true.

Or was he just bluffing? She clutched at this thought. Maybe he was trying to put her off balance. And if that were so, then she would have to find some way to regain control of the situation. . . .

"We did find something unexpected," she said.

His stare was cold and penetrating, his silence demanding she continue.

"The Box," she said. "It still exists. Roche was lying when she said it had been destroyed."

His eyes narrowed. "How do you know this?"

"It interfered with our escape from the *Phlegethon*," she said. "It infiltrated the ship's systems and tried to take us over. We very nearly didn't get away. If I hadn't guessed what was happening and shut everything down in time, we wouldn't have made it a thousand kilometers."

"Are you sure you're not mistaken?" said the clone warrior, suddenly alert and interested.

She bristled at the question. "Of course I'm sure," she said. "I've seen it in action before."

His gaze drifted back to Roche. "But it's not possible," he mused aloud. "It couldn't be . . ."

He stepped back to the table, leaning slightly over Roche's helpless form. In a loud and clear voice, he said: "*Silence between thoughts*."

The readings on the autosurgeon instantly changed, going haywire for a moment, then settling down into a new pattern. Roche shuddered; her mouth opened, gasping for air; her one good hand clutched at nothing. . . .

Then she relaxed. The readings changed again, returning to how they had been previously, as though nothing at all had happened.

De Bruyn watched in amazement, her jaw hanging.

"It's inside her!" The clone warrior's hands gripped the edge of the operating table, knuckles slowly whitening. "There's no other way to explain it! The Box's shutdown code affected her physically, and that could only happen if it was interfering with her in some way. And given there are no signals passing between her and any part of this ship—"

"That's why she didn't die," De Bruyn muttered incredulously. "It's been keeping her alive!"

"Perhaps. But did you note how her readings returned to normal so quickly? Something or someone must have countered the shutdown code, and the only person that could have done that is Roche herself. She must be aware, on some level at least, of what is happening around her." His gaze was fixed on Roche's face, as though daring her to wake and contradict him.

"But . . ." De Bruyn shook her head. Another realization had come to her while he talked. *How could he have known about the shutdown code?*

<Lemmas?> She broadcast her mental summons as loudly as she dared. <Lemmas!>

The reave answered her from the far side of the ship. <Yes, Reverence?>

<Have you detected any interference from the *Apostle* since it arrived?>

<No, Reverence.>

<Were there any unusual events before then?>

<None.>

<Is there anything going on now?>

<I will check, Reverence.>

Cane's twin had glanced up, and was looking at her closely. "Something is troubling you?" he asked.

"Nothing." She shook her head. <Quickly!> she urged the reave.

<I detect no interference.>

<Nothing from the ship at all?>

<No emissions of any kind, Reverence. Why do you ask?>

She didn't have time to answer. The clone warrior had returned his attention to Roche and the autosurgeon.

"I will be returning to my ship immediately," he said. "I will, of course, be taking Roche with me."

"No, wait—you can't!"

"Do not defy us, De Bruyn," he said, gesturing for Wamel to disconnect Roche from the autosurgeon. The pilot moved obediently forward to help his master.

De Bruyn backed away a step. She had to decide, and fast. Roche had theorized about some sort of connection between the clone warriors; that would have explained how Jelena Heidik had known when she was arriving in the system. Perhaps it explained now how this clone warrior had known about the shutdown code for the Box—codes known only by a handful in the COE, but which Cane had heard used before the Box had taken over Intelligence HQ. Maybe she was overreacting.

Or maybe there was some deeper treachery at work.

The clone warrior watched as Wamel disconnected Roche from the autosurgeon. As the last of the contacts fell away, he indicated that the pilot should swing her around so the two of them could lift her. They seemed to have forgotten all about De Bruyn, or perhaps their ignorance was deliberate. She had played her role. She was no longer important. She had become irrelevant.

She sent a command to *Kindling*, instructing it to prepare for launch, and drew a pistol from her suit's thigh compartment.

"Put her down," she said, aiming the pistol at the clone warrior.

Wamel stopped, looking to his master for guidance. Cane's twin simply stared at De Bruyn, totally expressionless.

"Put her down," she repeated, lowering her aim. "Or I'll shoot *her*."

"Don't be ridiculous, De Bruyn," said the clone warrior. "Think what you'll be throwing away. Think of how hard you've worked for this."

"I *am* thinking of how hard I've worked for this," she spat vehemently. "That's why I can't let you take her."

"But to kill her would mean never learning the truth," he said.

"I've learned nothing anyway!"

He shook his head. "But you would have found out eventually," he said. "This way, you'll never know."

"Just put her *back* on the table!" De Bruyn waved the gun nervously toward the bloodied tabletop.

Wamel let go of Roche's legs and went for his weapon. De Bruyn had a split second to think that he would have been on her side—if only she'd had time to explain—before she shot him. He fell back onto the operating table, smoke sizzling from the hole in his chest, and slid to the floor.

An alarm rang. De Bruyn guessed that Wamel must have sent a warning through the command network before he died. Already she could feel Lemmas batting at her mind, trying to find out what was going on. Once the Disciples learned that she had threatened their leader and killed one of their own, it would be as good as over.

"I want to know the *truth*," she hissed. "Or I'll kill her now!"

The clone warrior raised an eyebrow. "You wouldn't believe me if I told you."

"Try me!"

His eyes shone from his dark complexion. "If my people do not receive the justice we deserve, we will eliminate every Human in the galaxy."

De Bruyn was taken aback for a moment. Although she had considered the possibility before, stated so boldly it sounded almost ridiculous.

"That's—"

"Inhuman?" he offered.

"*Insane*," she said.

Something moved in the doorway behind him—the other Disciples had arrived—and De Bruyn was out of time. She had nothing else to bargain with.

"Let me go," she said, trying anyway.

The clone warrior shook his head. "No," he said. "I couldn't possibly allow that."

She fired: the shot took Roche in the hip and spun her off the table.

Then, moving impossibly fast, the clone warrior was upon De Bruyn, pushing her off balance onto the floor with her arms pinned beneath her suit. His face was close to hers; she could feel his breath as she vainly attempted to break free. A hand in her hair twisted her backward, making her gasp. The air was full of the sound of footsteps as Disciples rushed into the room—but all she had ears for were the words he spoke to her as her neck twisted—

"You would have been right the first time," he whispered. "And *that's* the truth."

With her last strength, she instructed *Kindling* to blow its antimatter fuel reserves.

She never felt the explosion.

17

JW111101000
955.2.14
1380

Morgan Roche was dreaming.

She had never considered herself a terribly imaginative person. Through most of her life, her dreams had consisted of everyday things and simple imagery, easily interpreted. They reflected the logical and rational person she was, and demonstrated a lack of creativity—something COE Intelligence appreciated in their agents. They wanted them to be reliable and thorough, not innovative.

But in accordance with the dramatic change to her life in recent weeks, her dreams had become much more disturbing and vivid, the symbolism darker and more profound. It had gotten to a point where she almost became reluctant to close her eyes for fear of what images she might meet in her sleep.

More often than not the images fragmented and disappeared soon after she awoke, leaving her with just a vague impression of the emotions that the dream evoked—and even this tended to dissipate as the day progressed. But now and then a dream would be too powerful, too provocative, to ignore and would stay with her long into the waking hours.

Two dreams she'd had in Palasian System alone would stay

with her forever: the lizard she had been trying to trap, which had in turn caught her, and the meeting with the twins on the deck of the stone boat. There had been other dreams that had left impressions, but none like these. These were dreams she would simply never forget.

As with the dream she was having now. It hadn't even finished yet, but she knew it would be a dream she would not be rid of in a hurry. It felt so real, and the fact that she was unable to wake herself up from it disturbed her terribly.

She was standing inside a hollow sphere barely ten meters wide. Gravity pointed outward from the center of the sphere, with no odd tidal effects arising from the height difference between her head and her feet. No matter where she walked, the sphere was the same: white and featureless. Light seemed to emanate from all around her; there was no obvious source.

But something was wrong. She could feel it. Something terrible was happening outside the sphere. Something wanted to get in to where she was. No matter how hard she tried, she couldn't see beyond the sphere to make out what was trying to get her, and that just scared her all the more. She didn't know even vaguely what would happen if *it* penetrated those walls, if it did get inside, but she knew it would be horrible.

The unspecified threat made her cold, and she wrapped her arms about herself. She didn't know *anything*. All she remembered was being shot in the back and falling, calling for the Box, hearing Maii calling her ... and the suited figure that had approached her. There had been something about that figure's voice. Something familiar. She had heard it before. But where?

She couldn't remember. It was hard to concentrate while trapped in the bubble, cut off from the rest of the universe with no way out, and something terrible lurking just outside wanting to get in.

"Hello?" she called, for what felt like the thousandth time. Her voice echoed dully in the chamber.

She bent down and touched the floor. It was warm and yielded slightly, like rubber. Underneath it, though, was something firm. She reached into the pockets of her shipsuit in the hope of finding tools of some description, something that might have helped her dig her way out. But her pockets were as empty as the sphere itself. Nothing in them but *her*.

<Box? Maii?>

As when she had called their names before, there was no reply.

She resumed pacing. There was nothing else for her to do. Eventually something would happen. The bubble would burst and the thing outside would break in, or she would simply wake up.

She wanted the latter more than anything.

Was it possible to sleep within a dream? Possible or not, she woke with a start. Her entire body spasmed, recalling the shot she had taken in the shoulder. And the face leaning over her, the voice speaking to her . . .

"This isn't over yet."

No. Those weren't the words—but it *was* the same voice.

The words rolled around in her thoughts. She reached for her shoulder, feeling for the wound, but there was nothing there now. She was undamaged; there was no blood whatsoever. All she had were the memories of pain, a pain worse than any she had experienced before; a pain too huge to comprehend. And the tide of darkness which had followed, pulling her into its depths.

A shudder passed through her. She had dreamed during her brief sleep, and it came to her now with a viciousness that stung. She had been lying on a slab somewhere, in a dark space, and someone had been looming over her, hurting her. There was pain all through her body—her left arm, hand, and eye; her right shoulder; her face and throat. And in her mind. Someone was cutting into her, slicing her thoughts open, piercing the inner depths of her psyche—and behind that someone, behind that pain, standing in the shadows, was *Page De Bruyn.* . . .

A door seemed to close in her thoughts; images faded. She found herself on her side in the sphere, mouth slack, nose running. She sat up and wiped her face. Her hands were trembling.

"This isn't over yet." Page De Bruyn, of course: the woman who had betrayed her on Sciacca's World; the words De Bruyn said to her the last time they'd seen each other . . .

Outside, the terrible thing was still trying to get in.

She wasn't so sure she was dreaming anymore.

<Box?> Her voice shook slightly. <Box, answer me! I *order* you to talk to me!>

The sphere seemed to tremble beneath her.

<I can't talk right now, Morgan,> came the reply.

Relief washed through her. Although it was unable to disobey her when she issued a direct order, she'd feared the worst. "Box! I thought you'd abandoned me!"

<I can assure you that I have not, Morgan,> it said. <I am doing everything I can to help you. Please be patient for a little longer. I will return to you soon.>

Then it was silent again, and she was alone with the echoes. She listened to them uneasily. The Box had sounded weary, strained. She had never heard it like that before.

The sphere was solid as it had ever been. A stab of pain in her left eye reminded her of her dream's dream, and of De Bruyn. . . .

She wrapped her arms around her legs and waited for the Box to speak again.

A long time passed before the sphere trembled beneath her again. She woke immediately and looked around.

The light had changed. She had a shadow pooling beneath her now. Above her, in the exact center of the sphere, was a point of light too intense to look at directly. She glanced away, blinking.

<Box? Is that you?> she said, rubbing at her stinging eyes.

<Not as you would understand it, Morgan,> it said. <But yes, it is me. Or at least the part of me that believes itself to be conscious. The part that *lives*.>

She looked around again at the sphere, avoiding the light. <So where am I?> she asked. <And why am I here?>

<You are inside me; inside my mind.>

<*Inside* you? That's not possible!>

<It is difficult to explain,> it said. <Your mind is attempting to interpret sensory inputs of types it has never encountered before, and the only way it can do that is by analogy. The truth is that our minds are cohabiting cognitive spaces I normally reserve for myself and my creator. Or to use another analogy, we are thinking with the same mind in the same way that two programs might run simultaneously on the same processor. Just as I have infiltrated your cells in order to exist within you, your mind is now operating within me. Does that make things any clearer?>

She fought an image of two Klein bottles constantly filling and emptying each other. It wasn't helping.

<I guess,> she said, sitting up. <This place isn't real, but it isn't a dream, either?>

<It is *like* a dream in that it is an unreal construct of your subconscious mind comprised of real images. Its details might be wrong, but it does contain some truth. It would be wrong to dismiss it as a complete fabulation.>

<So you really are talking to me right now?>

<Yes, Morgan. I am.>

<Then you can tell me why I'm here. What's going on—and how is Page De Bruyn involved?>

The Box paused for a long moment. When it spoke, its voice was softer than before, almost tentative.

<I must confess to having miscalculated, Morgan,> it said. <Page De Bruyn was somehow able to infiltrate the *Phlegethon* and ambush you on the way to the *Ana Vereine*. You were shot in the process.>

<*That* much I remember.>

<You should have died. Shock very nearly killed you instantly. Only by my sacrificing part of myself were you able to survive long enough to make it to an autosurgeon.>

<You 'sacrificed' yourself?> she echoed. <What does that mean, exactly?>

<The function of many of your cells has been subverted in order to maintain my existence. By reducing the number of such cells in critical places and thereby allowing them to return to normal duties, or by enhancing their activity in others, I was able to stabilize your condition long enough for you to receive treatment.>

She didn't know what to say at first. <And now that I've been treated . . . ?>

<The capacity I sacrificed is beyond immediate recall. Too many cells have died. And there is a complicating factor.>

<That being?>

<You are being tortured, Morgan. The damage to your body is continuing at a rate too great for even the autosurgeon to contain. Far from reclaiming my lost components, I am forced to sacrifice more to ensure your continued survival. I am only able to talk with you now because they have temporarily ceased with the torture.>

Roche felt something much like sadness welling in her. But she wasn't sure who it was for: herself or the Box.

<How long can you keep this up?> she asked.

<A while yet, Morgan. Once this crisis is past—or once it has

overtaken my capacity to maintain this refuge—you will be returned to your normal mode of being. If you are allowed to recover, I will eventually regain my former stature. All we need is time—time to *heal*.>

She nodded. <But that's not all, is it? That doesn't explain why I'm here. If your capacity is reduced—and running *me* must be taking a large chunk of what's left—why are you going to such trouble? It's not just to keep me alive, surely?>

<No.> Again the Box hesitated. <You are here because your torturer is a reave.>

Realization dawned. <And reaves can't read AIs,> she said. <If my mind is running on your components, then I'm safe from him, right?>

<That is approximately correct, Morgan. In fact, minds as complicated as mine *can* be partially read by a reave, but he simply does not know where to look. That makes all the difference.>

Roche remembered her fuzzy self-image in n-space. <So are *you* a reave?>

<No—although I can, at times, read your surface thoughts. That is not my purpose. My purpose is—and has always been—to protect you.>

The Box had said something very much like this before. She still wasn't sure she believed it, even in the current circumstances. <So if I'm in here,> she said, <who is the reave torturing?>

<You, still. Although the essence of you is in here, everything else remains outside. To him you appear unconscious, and he has free access to those memories of yours not blocked by Maii. Eventually, though, these blocks will fall, but for the moment everything you do and say in here will be safe.>

<If the block fails, they'll know you weren't destroyed!>

<They already know that. I was able to take direct action only once you were stable in the autosurgeon; even so, I was too late to prevent our kidnap. Since then, I have had no chance to subvert De Bruyn's command. She ordered your implants removed; I no longer have access to the outside world, except by the passive observation of your sensory input.>

Her thoughts were reeling, and she found herself wishing this really had been a dream. <Okay,> she said. <So what are we going to do?>

<Before De Bruyn realized what was going on, I managed to broadcast a brief call for help. I also programmed the ship to

broadcast a tightbeam beacon back the *Phlegethon* every hour. If someone has followed us here, there may be a chance of rescue.>

<And if not?>

<Morgan, there is much I must say to you, and I fear we don't have a lot of time. When your torturer resumes, I must return to the maintenance of your body and will not have the capacity to hold a conversation. Do you understand?>

She nodded. <You have to talk now, while you can—and I don't have a problem with that. It's about time you told me what's going on.>

<I can hardly blame you for feeling this way, Morgan, but do try to see why the truth was withheld from you. It was not that you couldn't be trusted, but that it could have been got at. Had you known prior to your capture what you are about to learn, your torturer would have already extracted it. For that reason, also, I have brought you here, with me. Were we to discuss this in your normal state, your torturer would access those memories instantly.>

<So let's get on with it.> She lay back on the curved floor of the sphere, closing her eyes against the Box's glare. She was tired, apprehensive, even scared. But her curiosity overrode all of these. <Before you're called away.>

<Very well,> the AI said. <The first thing you should know is that you were partially correct in regard to what you said the other day about the High Humans. They *could* destroy the enemy at any time; they possess the technology to do so with ease. What they lack is the inclination.>

As vindicated as Roche felt to learn that she had seen through at least that part of the conspiracy, the conclusion she had avoided disturbed her deeply.

<You mean they'd rather let us all *die* than help us?>

<Morgan, you have to understand that High Humans like the Crescend are rare. Most of them follow a strict anti-Interventionist path—not out of any profound principle, but because they have little interest in the affairs of mundanes. They are as different from you as you are from an insect. Would you save one species of insect over another invading one? Maybe not, unless your interest happened to be myrmecology.>

Roche could tell where it was heading. <So the Crescend is a myrmecologist?> she said dryly. <It studies ants?>

<Essentially, yes. He is concerned enough about mundane Hu-

manity to become directly involved in this situation. The Crescend—perhaps alone of all the High Humans—has considered ridding the galaxy of the threat you face.>

<So why doesn't he?>

<It's not so simple, Morgan. As we discussed earlier, there are many issues he must face before coming to such a decision.>

<Like finding the enemy,> she remembered.

<That, and reaching consensus with the rest of the High Caste. At present, there are four thousand and seventeen High Humans active in this galaxy. Approximately thirty are Interventionists and willing to support the Crescend. The majority has ruled that it is not the Interventionists' place to decide whether or not to destroy the enemy. They will not allow a massacre of mundanes to occur with the help of the High Caste—even though inaction might well allow a greater massacre to take place. For the time being, the Interventionists can only observe and assist in the decision-making process.>

Roche fought the urge to argue that the anti-Interventionists' stance neither made sense nor was fair. <That's where you come into it, I take it—on the information-gathering side?>

The Box didn't sound as smug as she might have expected. <Suffice it to say that the Interventionists' role is *mainly* passive, for the moment. They have access to the little information available regarding the enemy, and although they are not, strictly speaking, allowed to spread that information, they can ensure that the right people come across it at the right time.>

<Is that what you're doing now?>

<Yes. The Interventionists are on the brink of finalizing their plans. The decision whether or not to assist in the eradication of the enemy is about to be made—and the High Caste majority *will* support it, if it is made in the agreed fashion.>

Roche thought of the thousands of people dying every minute in Sol System, and wondered what was happening outside the system. <Is there any way we can hurry them along?>

<Not at the moment, I'm afraid. Our options are decidedly limited.>

<Well, what *can* we do, then?>

<In a moment, I will give you access to much of the information gathered in recent weeks about the enemy. It will help you decide whether you want to be a part of this process.>

<Why wouldn't I want to be part of it? If I don't kill the enemy, they'll kill me!>

<I feel obliged to point out, Morgan, that your life is at present in more danger from one of your own kind than from the enemy.>

She conceded the point. <Well, all right, Box. I'll look at this information, whatever it is. But then what? Where do we go from there?>

<That remains to be seen, Morgan, and it depends to a large part on what happens to you—your body outside of this shell. If no one rescues you and you die at the hands of De Bruyn's torturer, then all our plans are undone.>

<And if I fall into the enemy's hands?>

There was a lengthy pause. <Then there is no telling what might happen.>

The Box's tone made her nervous again. <But *why*, Box? Why am I so important?>

<Ask yourself one question, Morgan, and think about the answer while I am gone: why can you detect the enemy when so many who have tried before have failed?>

<How the hell am I supposed to know the answer to that, Box?>

<Just think about.>

<But I *have* thought about it!>

<I'm sorry, Morgan, I can't explain. You must work it out for yourself. Your torture has resumed, and I must attend to your physical well-being. I will return as soon as I can, even if it comes to the worst. Be assured that I am—>

The light above her suddenly went out, and the Box fell silent. Roche sat bolt upright, looking in alarm to where the Box's light had been. It was suddenly very quiet, and the sense of threat from beyond the sphere returned.

Her skin tingled all over as a patch of air one meter in front of her clouded over, as though a self-contained mist had suddenly formed out of nowhere. It swirled around itself for a moment, becoming thicker and darker, then faded to reveal a three-dimensional tank not dissimilar to the instrument displays on the *Ana Vereine*. Inside was a single, flashing icon, shaped like a gold key.

There being no other visible way to interface with the display, she reached in and touched the key.

It turned into an embedded document containing numerous chapters and headings. The glossary was full of references to things she had never heard of before. There were links to diagrams and charts, statistics and formulae. There were texts from the fields of biology, sociology, anthropology, and archaeology. There were maps of regions long since distorted by millennia of stellar movements, and others so up to date that they included the destruction of Palasian System. There was even a mention of her, although when she touched the link, the display returned a message saying: "Access Denied."

She sat back with her legs crossed, the display following her every move. Then when she was relatively relaxed, she began to browse. . . .

The second name she recognized was that of Adoni Cane. There were several Canes listed, and some with aliases; one was the Cane she knew, his activities extensively chronicled thanks to the Box's proximity. Other Adoni Canes had appeared in diverse parts of the galaxy, always to sow chaos, then to disappear. One had left a swath of disorder from the core to the Middle Reaches, his path pointing directly to Sol System. Where they were now was not listed, although the anonymous authors of the text speculated that at least some of them had made it to Sol System already.

She followed two links from that article. One led to the original Adoni Cane. The other explored the history of Humanity, as near to its origins as the High Humans could get. She was amazed to learn that even they didn't know for certain where their progenitors came from. She had always assumed that there was nothing they didn't know—or couldn't find out, if they wanted to. But clearly that wasn't the case.

Humanity had diverged from the original, Pristine genetic strain somewhere between five and six hundred thousand years ago. Its dispersal throughout the galaxy could be plotted by studying the aging of certain anchor points known to have been constructed at that time. Anchor points didn't decay like matter; over hundreds of thousands of years, they dissipated back into the universe's natural background vacuum fluctuations in gradual, known ways. The remnants of the network that had first allowed Humanity to spread outward into the galaxy later gave archaeologists a rough guide to how that expansion had taken place.

By following it backward, a vague approximation could be made as to where it had all started.

The study of the propagation of the four known Primordial Castes suggested that the original Human homeworld had once been located near the space currently occupied by the Commonwealth of Empires. This region itself was now totally empty, with any ruins that might have existed long since removed or destroyed. No hard evidence remained to isolate a single system out of the many possibilities, but around twenty had been singled out as likely possibilities.

Sol System was one of them, despite its emptiness. The proponents of this theory raised the history of the system as their main evidence. Time and time again, it had become the focus for fringe groups or obsessive cults as though a subconscious collective memory guided them there. The Sol Apotheosis Movement was just one of many that had used the empty system as a home base, free from observation and interference. The system's name had accrued a certain notoriety among the High Caste observers, and the current convergence only added to that.

From Roche's point of view, the difficulty lay in knowing whether the convergence occurred because of the system's history, or regardless of the fact. The Box had admitted that the Crescend sowed rumors of the enemy's origins in order to draw people to the system, but the reasons for his doing this were unclear. Roche wasn't sure whether the rumors had been started *because* the enemy was already converging there, or whether the enemy had been lured there by the rumors, along with everyone else.

The history of the system itself, though, did intrigue her. It had once possessed a number of planets—at least eight, if the records were accurate, plus a large number of dark bodies, an asteroid field, and a cometary halo. Their fate was a mystery, although one observer grimly hypothesized that the composition and mass of the ring suggested that the entire system had somehow been ground to dust and put in orbit around the primary. Why anyone would want to do this remained unknown.

Among the ancient records that did remain from the older days of Humanity were scraps pertaining to the present situation. The name Adoni Cane was among those scraps, as were the other names the Box had mentioned in Palasian System. They had once been real people.

On a list of military honors, Field Admiral Adoni Cane of the Old Earth Advance Guard had received a Military Star for extraordinary acts of valor against the enemy. General Jelena Heidik distinguished herself against the same enemy in a place called Alpha Aurigae and received a Mars St. Selwyn Medal for her trouble. Vani Wehr was a civilian whose quick thinking on the Clarke Cylinder thwarted an enemy incursion and earned him an Honorable Mention. Captain Sadoc Lleshi was one of many Ground Corps officers posthumously recognized for excellence in battle after the long and bitter campaign had ended with the enemy's defeat. And so on.

Although there was no explanation for the names of the medals awarded or places mentioned, and nothing placing the battles in any context, Roche recognized the pattern immediately. The names used by the present enemy were all taken from those distinguished in the battle against them in the distant past. No doubt it was intended as an insult or a grand irony. That lent credence to the theory that the "enemy" referred to but never actually named in the old records was indeed the source of Adoni Cane and his siblings—but it didn't really tell her anything new about the enemy, past or present. There were still no recognizable names or locations, no descriptions, no clues at all as to where they came from or what they had looked like.

There were some tantalizing snippets, however. One concerned the command language Linegar Rufo had used in his attempts to communicate with the clone warrior in Palasian System. It appeared to be an actual language, not specifically restricted to military applications—although, again, its origins were clouded. Whether the Box had lied when it denied recognizing the language upon first hearing it, or whether this was new information added since then, Roche couldn't tell. Either way, its unique syntax and dissimilarity to any tongue currently in use marked it as enigmatic. Why it remained when so little else did was not explained, and Roche had a feeling that if she pursued the matter, she would run up against another Access Denied warning.

When she hunted for a genetic reference to the ancient enemy, she also found no data available. That didn't surprise her as such—if the records didn't contain even a name, then a DNA record was too much to hope for—but it did disappoint her. Hard evidence of a connection between the ancient enemy and the new would have been good. It would have silenced the doubt that nagged at her even now, asking her how it was possible for a connection to exist across such a gulf of time.

But then she remembered that to people like Adoni Cane, no time at all had really passed. The capsules that had created them had been drifting through the galaxy for over half a million years, their contents frozen, waiting for the moment to loose a new clone warrior. Their creators had programmed them and set them loose, then been destroyed forever. The legacy of their clone warriors was all that remained.

As such, their own genetic code was of particular interest to the High Humans. Were the unique intron passages somehow responsible for the unusual structures in Cane's brain that had baffled Sylvester Teh on Sciacca's World? These in turn might have been related to their odd n-space impression. But how? Minds greater than hers had grappled with these problems and had come to no firm conclusions. All were convinced that the introns of the enemy contained important information or played a critical role, but no one knew exactly how.

After what felt like an eternity browsing through the file, Roche closed her eyes and leaned back on the yielding floor of the sphere. She really wasn't learning terribly much. Yes, there had been a war in the distant past, whose losers had seeded this peculiar revenge. And yes, Adoni Cane was one of them. But she still didn't know who the enemy was, and she still didn't know how she fit into it all.

The Box had asked her to think about why she alone could detect the enemy. She was no closer to the answer than when she had started, and she suspected that no amount of random browsing would find it, either. But if she knew that, then the Box knew it too. It obviously hadn't meant that she would find the answer there.

But where, then?

She got up again and began to pace. The misty screen followed her for a while, then collapsed to a fuzzy point and fell behind. There was nothing else in the sphere. It was as featureless as ever, its air perfectly breathable and temperature perfectly comfortable. Her only distraction was the occasional urge to sleep, which she resisted. Even if such urges meant that the Box was having problems running her on its components, she didn't care. Its components were part of *her*. She had every right to use them, too . . .

She stopped in mid-pace, struck by an idea.

Was *that* what the Box had meant? Could it be so simple?

The galaxy she knew was about to be destroyed by a relatively small number of superior warriors partly because Humanity lacked the ability to tell these warriors from their own. If the High Humans did in fact possess the ability to wipe out the enemy, then presumably they also knew how to find them. But if the Crescend wasn't allowed to intervene directly, he also couldn't stand back and let Humanity be slaughtered. He therefore had to find another way to help.

One way would be to provide Humanity with a means of detecting the enemy. Since mundane Humanity already had access to epsense abilities, a slight enhancement of those abilities could be enough to give them an edge. If it could be done subtly, without obviously interfering, all the better. In short, the ability Roche had could be a "gift" from the Crescend. It might have been implanted within her along with the Box.

If it was true, she had been tinkered with yet again.

And now she was a *tool*.

She began to pace again, angrily. It all made perfect sense. The Surin had learned how to engineer for epsense abilities, and the High Humans surely had superior abilities. Why not give her the ability to perform this feat and allow her to discover it by accident? No one could accuse the Crescend of creating a weapon designed explicitly for retaliation: after all, she was unable to access n-space without the help of another, and her ignorance of the ability meant that it might never have been found. From the outside looking in, it could even be mistaken for a fluke of genetics.

But why *her*?

She cursed aloud and strode on, working her anger out. She hadn't asked for this! What was she supposed to do? Devote what little of her life remained to the hunting down and destruction of the enemy? She didn't even know how many there were in the galaxy; there might be millions! High Executioner wasn't a role she relished playing alone, and without respite—and, ultimately, with little chance of success. It was too much for one person.

Unless, she thought, there were *more* like her. . . .

But there was little she could do except stew over it until the Box returned, and she had no idea how long that might be. She walked around the sphere to where the reduced display wavered in the air, and passed a hand through it. It returned instantly to its full size, displaying the key once again. She sat down on her haunches and searched every link she thought might be even remotely promising. Anything to distract her.

She learned some things she hadn't known before. The Crescend wasn't the most powerful Interventionist. One called Aquareii—whom Rey Nemeth had once mentioned in passing—coordinated that faction in the High Caste. The Crescend's value, it seemed, lay in his close proximity to the convergence—to Sol System—although his precise location was never specified. Roche didn't know whether members of the High Caste retained a physical component when they Transcended; for all she knew, they might have written their minds on the fabric of space itself, never to be erased. But if they did have components that could be damaged or even destroyed, she could understand why they kept their locations a secret, even from each other. When one's potential for life was equal to millions of mundane lives combined, death was a tragedy only comprehensible in the same terms.

There were other details, too, that she couldn't see connected in any particular way to the matter of the enemy. One struck her as being so far afield that it couldn't possibly be right: the discovery in a distant part of the galaxy of several anchor point remnants that appeared to be older than Humanity itself. Either the dating of their decay was wrong, or Humanity was simply older than first thought—

The sphere suddenly and violently vibrated, flexing as though it had been struck by a giant hammer.

The display dissolved as an inrush of sensory data flooded through Roche—pain, fear, nausea, paralysis . . .

Almost buried beneath it, she heard two words:

". . . between thoughts."

She knew instantly what had happened. Someone had used the Box's shutdown codes! She hung on desperately as the sphere threatened to unravel beneath her. Clutching for the appropriate response before she lost herself totally to the overwhelming sensations, she called out as loudly as she could: "The game begins! The game begins!"

As the rush ebbed slightly, she fell back with a gasp. The sphere was still unstable, but at least the pain had relaxed its grip on her.

A flash of light above her heralded the return of the AI.

<Box! What's happening?>

<I don't have time to explain,> it said, its voice thin and strained, its light weak. <And I won't be able to protect you for much longer, Morgan.>

<But—> she began.

<There isn't *time*,> it snapped. <Tell me now: do you *know* what you are?>

<The Crescend made me like this, didn't he?>

<Yes, but why?>

She paused, reluctant to say what she knew to be true. <I'm a weapon,> she said finally.

<That's right, Morgan.> The Box sounded almost relieved. <You are. And it is important that you contact the Crescend as soon as you are able.>

<What?> Roche felt confused. <*How?*>

<With the code phrase 'Dawn comes,'> it said, its voice growing softer. <The High Caste has agreed to abide by your judgment on the matter of the enemy. When you have weighed up the information you have learned here, contact the Crescend and let him know your decision. He will act immediately.>

The sphere shuddered around her. <What are you talking about?> she said, fighting down panic.

<On its own, the High Caste will not sanction the eradication of a weaker enemy, but it *will* if the decision is made by an ordinary Human. That is the way they have resolved to break the moral dilemma. The decision is yours, Morgan, and yours alone.>

For a moment she couldn't speak. This was far more than she had guessed. The Crescend was putting the lives of Cane and all his siblings in her hands!

The light of the AI flickered, then returned at a reduced intensity. <You must decide, Morgan,> it repeated.

Stunned, Roche closed her eyes. This wasn't what she wanted to hear. <I don't believe you, Box,> she said.

The sphere seemed to be unraveling again beneath her, and the Box's voice grew fainter every second. <Yes you do, Morgan; I feel it. You *have* to believe. It is why you are here!>

<I . . .> She shook her head. Her thoughts were becoming fuzzy, as though whipped by a rising wind.

<*Please*, Morgan!>

Something caved inside her. She had never heard the Box so anxious, so desperate.

<But I don't even know where he is!> she said, her panic rising steadily as the Box's voice gradually faded.

<Just aim for Sol, Morgan. Use the words I gave you. Use the—>

Before it could finish, the sphere was torn apart by forces beyond her comprehension and the Box's light faded completely. Pain exploded through her. Her skin was afire and every cell of her being cried out in agony. She dimly heard voices—someone shouting her name—and felt hands roughly on her shoulders.

She opened her eyes to a darkness broken by the faint flicker of light.

"Box?" she said weakly.

But all she saw, looming from the shadows, was Cane's face.

18

After the solitude of the sphere, his voice struck her like a whip.

"She's alive!"

Roche reached for him with hands bent into claws. "Help . . ."

"Don't move," he said, putting his arms beneath her to lift her up. He placed her down again on something hard and cold.

"The Box . . ." The world grayed for a moment, and she clutched at consciousness with the last of her strength. "Don't let me die!"

"Trust me," Cane said. "I have no intention of allowing that to happen."

She felt an incredible pain surge through her as he stretched her out. Her gut heaved and she tasted blood—just as something exploded nearby and she was flung back onto the floor. Someone called out in pain; she didn't recognize the sound of her own voice.

"That idiot blew her ship!" Cane said loudly. "We'll have to manage as best we can."

Was he talking to her? Roche couldn't tell. But her mouth moved feebly in response anyway.

Robed figures suddenly loomed over her, trying to pick her

up. She recoiled from them, confused. Was she still back on the *Phlegethon*, trapped by Page De Bruyn? Was all that had gone before merely a dream, and the nightmare proper only just beginning?

Wanting to cry out, she let her body go limp. She was simply too weak to resist.

Her head lolled back over her shoulder, and she glimpsed a body dressed in a black uniform lying in one corner, its head twisted at an impossible angle. The face had once belonged to Page De Bruyn. It didn't seem to belong to anyone now.

She heard Cane's voice as though from a great distance, ordering the robed people to move faster. She thought he sounded different somehow, but was unable to be sure with the wailing of alarms and the pounding of machines booming through the bulkheads. He sounded colder, more efficient perhaps. He sounded *dangerous*.

Her body spasmed as the terrible realization spread like burning ice through her mind: *it wasn't Cane!*

"Where"—Her mouth was full of blood. She tried her best to spit it out—"are you taking me?" she managed.

One of the robed figures turned to face her. Beneath the cowl, the woman's skin was pale-blue and waxy. Her eyes were red.

"To Hell," she said matter-of-factly.

Roche closed her eyes; despair threatened to overwhelm her. She could feel it gathering like the black clouds of a dust storm on the horizon. If she let it in, it might never leave. She had to fight it.

<Box? Box—can you hear me?>

Nothing.

<*Box!*>

Silence.

<*The game begins,*> she tried lamely, but even as she spoke the words she knew it was pointless.

Her bearers slowed and she heard the hissing of an airlock.

"Through here," she heard Cane say. "On the acceleration couch. Careful!"

She was brought forward and laid gingerly on a reclined, cushioned seat. The sound of alarms faded slightly. She tried to look around, but her vision was blurred and hazy. Her left eye was completely blind.

The hands that had held her fell away, and a series of footsteps led out of the room. Then there was a voice:

"Master?"

"What is it?" Cane snapped.

Roche could hear the speaker's obsequious tone; she imagined him bowing, but couldn't see to be sure. "Master, I would accompany you to safety."

"That is not necessary. The *Apostle* is only minutes away—"

"Allow me to serve you, Master."

"You have served me," he said. "But now you must return to the others and tend to repairs."

"But our pilot—"

"Another ship shall be summoned," he said, his patience wearing thin. "You will be rescued."

"Master—"

"I *command* you to wait." The frost in Adoni Cane's voice could have cooled stars. "Leave me now, or invoke my displeasure!"

"Yes, Master." The owner of the voice didn't believe he would be rescued; that much was clear. Yet he obeyed. His footsteps slowly shuffled away, then were cut off by the closing of the airlock.

The baying of alarms ceased, and for a second all was silent.

"Fools." Cane's voice so close to her made her jump.

"Where . . . ?" she tried, then: "Why . . . ?"

"Don't talk." His strong hands strapped a harness around her broken body, tying her hands together in the process. Then a medical pack was pressed against her hip. "I only have one of these, I'm afraid. I didn't think you'd be this bad."

The pack attached itself with a slight sting.

Why do you want me alive? It was nothing more than a thought. She was unable to control her voice enough to do anything other than moan.

"That's it," he said, his tone almost encouraging. "Keep fighting, Morgan, and you might even make it."

She shuddered, feeling a strange coldness in her mind. She wanted to succumb to the physical and mental exhaustion, wanted to sleep. But that was a luxury she couldn't afford just yet. For now she only had grief to distance her from the pain. . . .

•   •   •

Gradually, as the medical pack took effect, the pain began to ease. The sharp edges in the world softened. Blinking, she could make out flashing lights around her, blurred as if she were looking at them through rain over a pane of glass. Cane sat not far away, his back to her.

Instruments chattered briefly; she felt a gentle nudge of acceleration. Then something clanged, and the acceleration became more insistent. She clutched the sides of her couch as the pressure mounted. It might have lasted only a minute or so, but seemed like an hour.

As the minutes ticked by, she found her vision clearing even more. Not very much at first, and only in her right eye, but she appreciated any improvement.

She was in an ordinary-looking cockpit, with Cane operating the pilot's station. All she could see was his scalp and the lights reflecting from it like multicolored stars in a chocolate sky.

"Where are you taking me?" she asked eventually.

His chair swiveled to face her. He pointed to a display. In it she could make out, vaguely, a large Hurn ship against a starry backdrop.

Despair rippled through her. "Am I going to die?"

"Not yet," he said, returning to his console. "That would be counterproductive."

"If you think I'm going to help you—"

"Conserve your strength, Morgan. You're going to need it."

Something in his voice made her look at him again. *Was* he the Adoni Cane she knew or not? He looked and sounded exactly like him, apart from the coldness in his tone. But that was the whole point: the enemy was composed of clone warriors, many of them identical. He could very well be one of Cane's siblings with the same face, but with the killing instinct intact.

Regardless of who he was, he was right about conserving her strength. She felt weak right down to her core, and the coldness was still in her mind. The pain was manageable now, thanks to the ministrations of the medical pack, but that meant she could look down and see how badly she had been injured. When she did, she instantly wished she hadn't.

The Hurn ship grew larger in the display. Cane had mentioned something about "the *Apostle*" being only minutes away. Presumably they were one and the same. Although she had never seen this particular ship before, the connection between it and the black-robed figures they had left behind seemed clear. Some sort of organization staffed and supplied by Hurn backers had obviously assisted Page De Bruyn in hunting her down. Why, she didn't know, but the presence of a clone warrior high on the command chain seemed ominous. If this *was* her Cane, how could he have infiltrated such a group so quickly?

Her wrists chafed where he had tied her hands together. Her left hand in particular ached as though stiff from a half-healed wound. The back of her head felt like someone had hammered a nail into it, and the vision still hadn't cleared in her left eye. When she blinked, the socket itself even felt odd, unnatural—

Empty. The Box had said that her implants had been removed. The harsh reality of that fact was only now sinking in. Without them, she felt hollow, incomplete.

"Why did you rescue me?" she asked.

He turned again to face her. "If you can't answer that question, then perhaps I have wasted my time."

Him and the Box, she thought to herself. "Maybe you have."

He shrugged. "It might change nothing."

She winced as another wave of pain swept through her.

He came over to check her medical pack. "I haven't come all this way to watch you die," he said dispassionately. "You'll be treated properly when we arrive."

Her words came through clenched teeth. "How much longer?"

"Not long. We're almost in range." He turned back to the display. "It'll be over soon."

He adjusted something on the pack and warmth rushed through her. At first she resisted it, wanting to remain alert. Maybe all hope was not quite lost; if a chance came to escape, she had to be ready.

But then she remembered what she had seen when she had looked down at her body. There was nothing she could do. She closed her eyes and let the warmth caress her pain, blunt the icy coldness inside her.

A moment later, it disappeared completely. In its absence, she felt strangely light, as though it had been tying her down. In its wake, she felt almost free. . . .

That was crazy, she thought. She was half-dead, the captive of an unknown organization with links to the enemy. Not only had she no way of escaping, but she wouldn't even live much longer if they chose not to help her.

Cane cocked his head as though listening to something.

"That's close enough," he said, turning back to her. "Morgan, I have someone who wishes to speak to you."

Roche steeled herself for another grim surprise, glancing around the cabin to see if anyone else had entered.

Then she heard the voice—loud and clear in her thoughts.

<It's so good to feel your mind again, Morgan,> said the reave. <We thought we'd lost you for good!>

<Maii?> Roche tried to sit, but pain forced her back. <Maii, is that you?>

"Look at the screen," said Cane.

Through her one remaining eye, Roche watched as they passed through the fringes of a camouflage screen and the Hurn ship became the *Ana Vereine*.

"It really *is* you?" There was both uncertainty and relief in her whispered words.

He smiled. "Does that surprise you?"

<We couldn't let you know until you passed out of range of Lemmas, their reave,> Maii said. Her voice hinted at dark truths Roche didn't want to explore. <I'm sorry we kept you hanging.>

"But *how* . . . ?"

She felt Cane's hand on her left shoulder, pressing gently but firmly. "This can be discussed later, Morgan. Right now I want to dock and get us out of here before anyone back there suspects what has happened—before their *real* contact shows up."

She nodded weakly. Maii filled her mind with a radiant warmth. She felt as though she had been dipped in a bath of light, and the cold, dead touch of the Hurn reave faded like ice in the sun. For the first time, Roche allowed herself the luxury of really *believing* that she might live long enough to see her friends again.

Anything beyond that could wait.

Haid and Vri met the scutter with a fully equipped stretcher. Barely had she been placed in its embrace than her treatment began. The autosurgeon dictated the list of her injuries all the way to the medical center: beginning with her shattered hip and pelvis, her punctured lung and blood loss, and working its way down to relatively minor muscle damage and gashes. It was still droning on when Haid cut off its output in order to let her rest.

At the same time, Kajic sent the ship accelerating back in-system, away from Roche's captors. She was conscious just long enough to learn that the *Phlegethon* was still under intense attack, so was not considered a safe port. Kajic had plotted a relatively innocuous orbit instead, bypassing the major concentrations of fighting in the system and skimming close to the outer edge of the ring where traffic was light. The ship would travel under heavy camouflage and in a constant state of alert. If they *were* spotted, they would be ready to defend themselves.

Haid was sitting with her when the autosurgeon put her under, his black skin and artificial eyes gleaming in the medical center's bright lights.

"Don't worry, Morgan," he said, touching her arm lightly. "We'll still be here when you come back."

"How long?" The anesthetic was already beginning to work; her voice sounded like it was coming from kilometers away.

"As long as it takes, I guess."

"Two hours," she said. "There's something . . . something I have to do."

Haid glanced at the autosurgeon's holographic display. "It'll take at least six to clean you up, not to mention fitting the new eye."

"Forget the eye." She could barely keep her remaining one open. "Make it three, or so help me I'll—I'll—"

—*send you back to Sciacca's World.*

She never found out whether she finished the sentence.

When she woke, the pain was gone. That more than anything else convinced her that survival had been worthwhile.

She couldn't move, though. The autosurgeon had her carefully encased in a body cast that allowed the use of her right arm only. When she tried to sit up, it correctly interpreted her feeble movements and tilted the entire bed instead.

"It won't let you out of its clutches just yet," said Haid. He was sitting with his feet up on one of the other operating tables with his back to the holographic "cybercorpses" rotating slowly in one wall.

"You're still here?" she asked. "Haven't you anything better to do?"

"It's not as if I've been sitting around idly waiting for you to wake up." He smiled at her warmly. "You said three hours, and it's been exactly that. I just had to be here on time."

She smiled also, envying him his mobility and fitness—even with his cybernetic mesh and patchwork limbs. "How am I?"

He swung his feet off the table, but didn't stand. "Much better. Not one hundred percent by any means, but at least you look"—he shrugged—"*better.*"

"Is there a mirror in here?"

"No, but I'm sure Maii can arrange something."

Roche felt the girl's featherlight touch in her mind, and full stereoscopic vision poured through her, from Haid's eyes. She saw a white-wrapped corpse half in and half out of a gleaming sarcophagus. One eye was covered with a patch. Her mouth was swollen; yellowing bruises spread down one cheek to her jaw. Her head had been shaved and half-covered with bandages.

<It's a vast improvement,> said Maii.

<Is it? Show me.>

"That's not a good idea," Haid warned.

<It's therapeutic,> Roche insisted. <If this is better, how bad was I?>

A flash of red passed before her secondhand eyes, but it didn't really register. The naked woman curled up in pain, the one arm nearly severed and vertebrae visible through wounds at the back of her neck, the messy crater on her right hip, the blood . . . surely this couldn't have been her?

"Enough," she said, swallowing. If the Box really was dead this time, at least she knew why. Nothing else could have kept her alive through such mistreatment. She tried shaking the image from her mind by changing the subject altogether.

"Where's Cane?"

"Up in the observation blister," said Haid. "He's been there since we got you back."

"I want to talk to him later." She couldn't help the tiredness in her voice. She was alive, yes, but there was still so much to do. "First, tell me *how* you got me back. How did you know where I was?"

Haid stood, frowning, and stepped up to her. "I'm not sure I understand all of it myself, Morgan. We knew something had gone wrong almost immediately, when you didn't arrive at the *Ana Vereine* and Maii couldn't find you. There'd been a disturbance in the docks below us, and security arrived just minutes too late. Automatic monitoring in the area had been shut down somehow during the ambush, so we never did get a good look at what was going on, and the ship they had you on had detached and hot-launched before anyone could work out it was involved. Things were pretty messy in the area because of the attack. It wasn't until we received a tightbeam squirt from the ship that we guessed."

"What did the message say?"

"It was fairly short, telling us basically that you were aboard and injured and that a pulse would be sent every hour telling us where the ship was, but it didn't tell us who it was from. The Heresiarch picked it up and passed it on. I wanted to follow straightaway but Cane was adamant we shouldn't. Quite apart from getting through the siege around the *Phlegethon*, he felt there was also the matter of the people who captured you to take into consideration. We couldn't afford to take the chance that they might kill you if we came in with guns blazing. So we kept track of the ship and thought of another way."

"By masquerading as one of them."

"Basically, yes."

"And who *are* they?"

He looked uncomfortable. "To be honest, I don't know."

"So how did you know what to do?"

"I didn't. It was all Cane's idea. He got us through the blockade and gave us the specifications of the ship we were to impersonate. When we caught up with the ship you were on, he gave us the codes to broadcast to convince them that we were who we said we were. And when we were in range he insisted that he should go aboard alone. He didn't tell us what he was going to do, just told us to trust him. I didn't know whether I should, but couldn't think of anything better to do. He seemed to know what he was doing, and if it got you back . . ." Haid shrugged. "It worked out in the end, I guess."

She was silent for a while, remembering Cane's tone, remembering how he had dealt with the groveling Hurn. And she thought of the epsense link that possibly connected the clone warriors. . . .

"He was different back there," she said. "For a while there, it was almost as if he *was* the enemy, you know? I think he was close to becoming one of them."

"That's what I was afraid of," Haid said, concern etched deeply in his face. "I couldn't help think that if he went too far, he wouldn't come back to us." He shrugged again. "I didn't want to lose him as well."

"I don't believe he was ever ours to begin with."

"You know what I mean," he said. "We need him here."

Perhaps a little too much, she thought, but said nothing.

"Alta Ansourian is still with us, by the way," he went on. "She refused to disembark when she had the chance. She's still in her quarters."

"Doing what?" Roche asked.

"Staring at the wall as far as I can tell," he said. "Cane has tried talking to her a couple of times, but to no avail. She just won't snap out of it."

"Give her time, Ameidio," she said. "She just witnessed her father being murdered. It's going to take more than a few days to snap out of that."

He nodded wearily. "Who knows?" he said. "Maybe she has the right idea. At least she doesn't have to worry about . . . everything."

He pulled his gaze away from hers; Roche realized he was embarrassed.

She reached out and took his hand lightly in hers. "If it's any consolation, Ameidio," she said, "I think this will all be over soon."

His hand squeezed hers back. "Not soon enough for my liking." He forced a smile.

"Have we heard anything from the council?"

"Nothing yet. There's an ftl drone following us, though. We can call them when you're ready. If the fighting's done at their end, they might be willing to reconvene."

It felt like weeks had passed since the last meeting. "How long was I gone?"

"Just over thirty hours," he said. "You still haven't told us what happened to you."

"I'm not sure I'm ready to." Her scalp itched, and although she wanted to scratch it, doing so would mean letting go of his hand. She wasn't ready to do that, either, even though she'd already held it longer than she'd intended to.

As though through a fog she saw Page De Bruyn's face as it had looked, lifeless, on the deck of the Hurn ship. She still had no idea what her former superior had been doing to her, and why. If the Box had been around, she could have asked it, but this time it seemed to be irrevocably gone. Having lost it once before, she found it hard to believe that it wouldn't come back to her again—but she could *feel* its absence all through her body. It was gone forever.

"Hey," Haid said, letting go of her hand and wiping her cheek. "I'll go and let you get some rest."

She took a deep breath. "How about *you* get some rest? I'll bet you haven't slept for two days. Besides, I want to talk to Uri. Then Cane. I need to sort this out now, before I convince myself it was all a bad dream."

"The surgeon says—"

"I don't care what it says, Ameidio," she cut in. "It's keeping me comfortable enough in here, and I'm not planning on going anywhere for a while."

He nodded reluctantly. "Okay, but you call if you need anything, all right?"

She assured him she would, and watched as he turned and strode from the room.

When he was gone, she turned her eyes to the ceiling and asked: "Okay, Uri, what *does* the autosurgeon say?"

"That you are responding unexpectedly well to treatment." The voice of the ex-captain of the ship came from one side of the room, not all around as she'd expected. She glanced around to find that three "cybercorpses" had disappeared. In their place, Kajic's hologram reclined comfortably in a standard bridge chair, affecting a warm and slightly amused expression.

Her bed rotated to face him.

"Your fractures have already knit," he went on, "and all tissue grafts are proceeding ahead of schedule. Although the autosurgeon doesn't anticipate your returning to full mobility for at least two days, I wouldn't be surprised if you were out of the cast in eight hours or so and walking within the day."

"That seems unreasonably fast," she said.

"As I said, you are recovering quicker than expected. I've had a quick look to ascertain why and found some evidence of nanotech tampering here and there. It looks like you were being helped along. Not so much now, but certainly when you were first brought here."

She nodded slowly, not wanting to say anything in case it made him suspicious. "I guess I was lucky."

He smiled then. "It's okay, Morgan. I guessed the Box was

still around after Perdue Habitat. You had too many lucky es-
capes that could not have occurred any other way. And since it
wasn't anywhere on the ship, it had to be on you—or inside you.
It helped you escape from the destruction of the habitat, it sent
the message when you were kidnapped, and it somehow kept you
alive long enough to reach here. Am I right?"

"Yes," she said. "But it's dead, now."

"Are you sure?"

"You said the evidence of nanotech had faded. That's the only
way you would have picked it up—and that's why it didn't want
me examined back on the *Phlegethon*. A thorough search would've
found signs of it for sure. Since you can't find it now, it must
be gone."

"I'm sorry, Morgan," he said.

She brushed aside his sympathy, genuine or not. "Don't be,
Uri," she said. "It lied and it manipulated me and I'm still not
entirely sure what its hidden agenda was. Maybe in the long
run I'm better off without it."

"Maybe." He paused for a moment, the light from his hologram flickering minutely. "Was this what you wanted to talk to
me about?"

Roche sighed. "Uri, I need to make a decision," she said. "One
that could affect millions, maybe even trillions of people."

"Regarding the enemy?"

"Yes." She cast about for a way to phrase her question, but
in the end decided to be blunt. The chances were he would take
it for a metaphor, anyway. Not even she could take the idea seriously yet.

"If you found a way to wipe them all out," she said slowly,
"would you do it?"

"That depends," he said.

"On what?"

"On why I was doing it, of course."

"Because if you didn't do it, there is every chance that Pristine Humanity could wind up extinct!" She blurted it out, and,
having done so, realized how ridiculous it sounded. She sighed
again, this time in annoyance. "There's only a few of them, Uri,
but their method of turning us against each other might actually
work."

"But why are they doing it, Morgan? Ask yourself that. They
might have good reasons—or think they have, anyway. Whoever

created them may have felt justified in unleashing them against us."

"Justified half a million years ago, maybe—but *now*? So much time has passed; Humanity has moved a long way since then. Surely we shouldn't be held responsible for the crimes of our ancestors? There must be another way for them to achieve retribution—or whatever the hell it is they want."

"I agree. But if they're programmed to attack—"

"Exactly: they're *programmed*. There *is* no other way, for them. But does that make it *right*?"

"There is no right and wrong in war, Morgan. There is only expediency, efficiency, and capability—all untainted by emotions or morals. Nearly all wars are won or lost without regard for Human values. As a result, the right side loses as often as the wrong. Only when the odds are stacked highly in favor of one side can such qualities be called into play. Mercy, after all, relies on the certainty that one party can kill another any time they wish. Without that certainty, mercy is meaningless. Only the most powerful can afford the luxury of forgiveness."

She half-smiled. "Once again, you sound like my old Tactics lecturer."

He returned the smile, briefly. "Ultimately, though, Morgan, all the theory in the world will only get you so far. In the end you reach a point where you have to decide for yourself. When you have to *act*. War is as much about instinct as it is about higher thought. Indeed, one could argue that if we thought *enough*, there would be no war at all."

"Now what are you trying to say?"

"That it's your choice, and I don't feel qualified to advise you. If what I think you're saying is true, and you do somehow have this capability, then I don't envy your position. I don't think I could make a decision like that. I'm too narrowly defined."

She frowned. "I don't know what you mean."

"I mean that in some ways I'm like the enemy. I'm programmed to obey a small set of rules, inasmuch as a Human can be." His image shrugged. "I don't remember my previous life. Maybe I was no different from who I am now, the person I became after the experiment. But all that I am, now, is here within this hull. All I really care about is the ship and the people who travel within it."

"Well," she said, "it's nice to know we're in good hands."

He disregarded the compliment, his image staring over at her with a sober expression. "Morgan, I would be just as happy to leave this system and never come back, since we would all be safer that way. But I know we can't do that, and never will be able to until the business with the enemy is sorted out. I wouldn't be surprised if fighting has already started escalating outside Sol System. Soon, perhaps, if we don't do anything about it here and now—nowhere will be safe."

"If I could only be certain that it did in fact boil down to a 'them or us' decision," she said. "That would make it simpler. Or if there was some way we could negotiate, find some other solution, or . . ."

She ran her hand across her face. Her skin was clammy, and she felt tired, but she didn't want to rest anymore. She wanted to push this through to the finish.

"Have you told anyone about the Box?" she asked.

"No, of course not."

"Don't, then. Not that it matters anymore, I suppose."

She rested her head back on the bed, and the autosurgeon misinterpreted it as a request to lie flat. She didn't stop it lowering the bed, though. She just closed her eyes for a moment and put her forearm over them, to block out the glare from the ceiling light. Her mind felt full, heavy. There was too much to think about, too much to *do*, and simply not enough of her to go around. . . .

When she woke an hour later, it was on the crest of a soothing dream. She was a plant, absorbing nutrients and turning them into cells one by one, growing and stretching at a patient, steady rate. She existed; she was. Stripped of all fears, all concerns, she delighted in the simplicity of just *being*. . . .

Then the memory of the decision she had to make came rushing back, and she realized at once what was going on.

<Maii?>

<Yes, Morgan. It's me,> replied the girl, without the smallest trace of guilt. <You needed it.>

<Did I?> she said, stretching her one free arm and raising her head. She could at least feel her other limbs now, under the cast. <Actually, I *do* feel better.>

<That's the idea. Epsense therapy assists the biofeedback process better than any other known technique.>

<Did you have anything to do with my healing before?>

<No. This was the first time. It must have been the Box, as Uri said.>

Roche rested her head back on the bed's cushioned support. <Can I ask you something, Maii?>

<Of course, Morgan.>

<When I was kidnapped, why couldn't you find me?>

<I don't know.> The girl's reply was instantaneous and frank. <Even when I knew where to look, all I could pick up was a faint shadow. It was like you had retreated inward, hidden yourself somehow. I couldn't try too hard or else Lemmas would have noticed me, but I still should have detected *something*.>

Roche thought of the white sphere that had enclosed her from the torturer-reave. <How's my image now?>

<Rock-solid. More so than ever, in fact.>

<I thought it might be. The Box told me that it was complex enough for you to read, if you'd known how to look. Maybe it was making my n-space signature a little odd. Interfering with it.>

<Probably, I'd say, given the fact that you're almost back to normal now.>

<Then that could be what the *irikeii* meant when he referred to me as an 'enigma.'>

<It's hard to say,> Maii responded. <I never understood what he meant by that. But I do find it hard to believe that an AI could ever have an n-space image. . . .>

Roche was too tired to explain—not that she was entirely sure about it herself. Part of her wished she could return to the peace of mind her dream had offered, even though she knew it had been false.

<Seduced at last, eh?> Maii asked with a smile in her voice.

<Don't get too cocky,> Roche returned. <It's not every day I need it that bad.>

<True. But the first time is always the hardest . . .>

Roche resisted the girl's soothing touch. <Sorry, Maii, but I need some time on my own to think right now. I'll call if I need you, okay?>

<I'll be here, Morgan.>

Her mind felt cold when the reave had gone, but she was glad for the privacy. There were things she needed to consider that the girl had probably already read from her mind but which she didn't want to dwell on with an audience watching. The Box had left her in a difficult situation which, if everything it had said was true, required a clarity of thought she found difficult to achieve even at the best of times.

She went to fold her hands across her chest but was stopped by the white plastic shell of the surgical cocoon enclosing her left arm. She rested her right hand on her neck instead, finding comfort and reassurance in the beating of her own pulse. She was still on the board.

You must decide, Morgan . . .

The Box's words turned idly in her thoughts. It had said that the High Humans were reluctant to act against an inferior enemy, even if there was a possibility that the enemy might actually win against the mundanes they chose to attack. It had said that the Crescend, a noted Interventionist, was concerned about mundane affairs and would act against the enemy if allowed to by the rest of the High Caste. It had concluded by saying that the High Humans had agreed to abide by the decision of one mundane Human, thereby taking the moral dilemma out of their own hands. How they would do that, exactly, it hadn't said. Maybe the Crescend would modify others as he had modified her, to enable mundanes to locate the enemy within; or maybe he would act directly, using weapons more superior than she could imagine.

However they did it, she felt safe in assuming that the enemy would be destroyed. The High Caste rarely acted, but when it did, it always got what it wanted.

So the decision was hers: to wipe out the enemy or not.

She was amazed by how difficult it was. On the one hand, she could end all the squabbling in Sol System and throughout the galaxy, at the cost of a Caste which might have a genuine grievance. On the other hand, she could let the conflict run its course. If the enemy won, so be it. She had no idea just how great a cost that would be to the trillions of other mundane Humans inhabiting the galaxy.

In terms of lives, it was relatively easy to judge. She didn't know exactly how many clone warriors there were, but they seemed to seed one or two per organization they were trying to infect. On the *Phlegethon* there had been only five. There might be millions scattered across the galaxy—but even those sorts of figures paled if the chaos they had caused in Sol System could be extrapolated everywhere. Millions of lives versus trillions: on any scale, the test was simple.

But of course it *wasn't* that simple. If it was, she wouldn't have been Human.

Restless, she tried to roll over, but of course she couldn't. The autosurgeon simply rolled the bed onto a disconcerting angle, then swung it back when she clutched at it in alarm.

"Uri! How long do I have to stay in this damned thing?"

"An hour or two," came Kajic's voice. A second later, his form appeared in the holographic tank. "Nerve reconstruction and bone marrow grafts have yet to be finalized in your injured pelvis. I'm told complete immobility is advisable."

She grunted. "I'm not hungry or thirsty, either. Is that normal?"

"Completely. The autosurgeon is taking all your bodily needs into account. Except for boredom, I suppose."

"I'm not bored." She sighed. "I do need some input, though. It's hard to keep up without my implants. Can you give me a screen or something down here? I'd like to see what's happening in the system."

"Of course." Kajic's image dissolved, leaving a complicated display in its wake. "I'll leave you with full access to the data we have on the current state of play. Some of it is coming from the IEPC drones; the rest I'm extrapolating as we go. I think it'll be enough to give you an overview, anyway. It is voice-activated."

"Thanks, Uri."

She settled back to browse through the charts. The system was a mess of conflicts, the largest concentrated around the blue triangle of the *Phlegethon*. As far as she could tell, five whole fleets had declared war against the massive vessel; it looked as if it was holding its own, but she couldn't tell how much longer that would last.

Elsewhere the situation was more difficult to analyze. Red patches, indicating conflict in one form or another, had spread to cover entire sections in the system. Most were concentrated around the plane of the ecliptic, but there were some hot spots farther out. One concentration of fire was high above the sun's north pole, where two swarms of comet-chasers appeared to be fighting over a third party's observation complex. Another was very close to the sun, whipping up strange currents in the chromosphere.

Mines were marked with yellow stars and tended to form drifting sheets like two-dimensional shoals around protected fleets. Regions of weakened space were marked with purple cross-hatching and avoided by all. Areas suspected to be under enemy control were delineated by sharp black lines. There were odd white patches in the rings that Roche couldn't identify but guessed were installations of some sort designed to interfere with passing ships. The gray crosses indicating delelict vessels were everywhere—whether largely intact, smashed to fragments, or completely gaseous.

She could discern no pattern to the conflict, and the Box wasn't around to tell whether any one Caste was being consistently spared the fighting. All she could do was go by its earlier statement that no such bias was being shown. If the enemy did have an agenda, then she didn't know what it was.

That didn't *necessarily* mean that the enemy's goal was to wipe every other mundane from the face of the galaxy. It was possible that the events in Sol System did not represent how things would go elsewhere. Yes, she had heard of civilizations that had fallen under the influence of the enemy—Rey Nemeth's and Hue Vischilglin's were two—but they were only a handful out of millions. It was barely conceivable that all would fall. Once the element of surprise was lost, as it surely would be after Sol System, the enemy would face a stiffer, more organized resistance.

Unless that resistance was undermined from within. She had to assume that there was nowhere the enemy couldn't penetrate if it wanted to. The only way to keep them out was to conduct rigorous genetic testing—which would never be rigorous enough, as the *Phlegethon* had demonstrated—or to rely on others like her to find the clone warriors before they could do more damage.

If that was what the Crescend had in mind, she might agree to support it. But she had no way of knowing until she actually spoke to him.

"Uri?"

"Yes, Morgan?"

"This is going to seem a little strange, but I need you to give me an open communications channel."

"Communicating with whom?"

"I want to broadcast a message aimed at the sun. I don't want

you to wait for any reply protocol or anything. If the only way
you can do that is by radio or laser, that'll have to do."

"I can arrange that for you at any time, Morgan." Kajic
didn't ask why she would want to, but the question was present in his tone. "A tightbeam would be less likely to give away
our location."

"Okay. Give me the open line; audio only. And . . ." She paused
slightly. "I'd appreciate it if you didn't let anyone listen in."

"Of course, Morgan. Opening the line now."

Roche didn't say anything at first. If the Crescend responded,
that reinforced everything the Box had said; she still wasn't sure
she wanted that. But if he didn't respond, that was just as bad.
She would have no idea at all what was going on, then.

There was only one way to find out.

"Dawn comes," she said.

A familiar voice responded immediately from behind her right
ear:

"—to bring an end to the dark imbalance."

The table spun beneath her as she twisted by reflex. "*Box*? If
that's really you, I'm going to—"

"I am not the Box, Morgan," interrupted the voice, this time
coming from the other side of the room. "You know who I am."

Her skin goose-bumped. Who else could it be? For a few moments she didn't know what to say. "But your voice . . ." was all
she could manage.

"The Box was a part of me in the same way that your eye is
a part of you—or your finger, or your anterior cingulate cortex.
It was not me, and I am not it."

Roche looked around her. The voice changed position constantly. She couldn't tell if that was an effect of the way it was
being broadcast into the room, or whether it was something more
significant. Maybe it was just trying to keep her off balance.

He, she corrected herself. The Crescend wasn't an *it*.

"Where are you?" she asked.

"It has been a long time since last we met," he said with some
amusement, deliberately avoiding her question.

"It hasn't been that long since Trinity."

"I'm not talking about Trinity."

She frowned. "Then I don't know what you're talking about."

"Don't you? I thought you might have guessed by now."

"Guessed *what*?"

The Crescend was silent for a long time, long enough for her to wonder if the line had been broken.

"Uri," she called, "is this line still open?"

"He can't hear you," said the Box's voice, this time coming from somewhere behind the autosurgeon. "No one can hear us talk. It's just you and me. And your decision."

She shifted nervously in the cocoon. "You're not seriously going to leave it up to me, are you?"

"Why not?"

"Because it's crazy, that's why not! I'm just one person. I'm not in any position to judge—"

"You're better qualified than you realize."

"Well, I don't *feel* qualified."

"You can locate the enemy, for a start."

"How does that help my decision?"

"It's proof that I can back up my offer to assist you. Without such proof, my offer could seem empty."

"And that's all you're offering? A way to find the enemy so we can finish them off?"

"Is that the help you would like the High Caste to provide?"

She opened her mouth, then shut it. "You're not going to trick me into a decision like that."

"It's no trick. I'm genuinely interested in your answer: what do you want us to do, Morgan?"

"I don't know," she said, feeling trapped. "I don't feel I have enough information to decide."

"You have as much as you need."

"But I don't know why the enemy are here. I don't know where they come from, even. I don't know if they mean to kill everyone or just some of us. I don't know why the war began in the first place. I just don't *know*!"

"Some of these questions have no answers," said the Crescend. "At least for the moment. But I can answer that last one for you."

"Then please do," she said, annoyed that he had made her ask.

"The original war was fought over territory, as all wars are."

She waited, but nothing more was forthcoming. "What territory?"

The Crescend chuckled. "Now you are trying to trick *me*. You are hoping that I will specify a location which will help you identify the enemy's original Caste. Unfortunately, I cannot do that,

Morgan. And it's not because I won't, but because I *can't*. I don't know where the enemy originated—not for certain. All I know is that the original war engulfed the entire inhabited galaxy."

"Ending when the enemy were ultimately defeated."

"They weren't just defeated," he said. "They were completely erased. All trace of them vanished until forty years ago, when the first confirmed capsule sighting was made."

"Do you know the enemy's original name?"

"Unfortunately, that information has also been lost."

She shook her head. "You're not giving me much to go on. I mean, how can I judge what's right now when I don't even know if the enemy are justified in what they're doing? Maybe they're in the right, and I shouldn't interfere."

"Have you spoken to Adoni Cane about this?"

"More or less." She had given him the *chance* to speak, anyway.

"And hasn't the enemy had many chances in the past to reveal the truth behind their motives?"

"Yes, I suppose—"

"So why should it fall on me to justify their actions when they themselves feel no need to do so?"

She accepted his point. "But *do* you know why they're doing this?"

"Facts are hard to come by in this matter. We suspect, that is all. If it were more clear-cut, the High Caste would find it easier to reach consensus. There was guilt on both sides, perhaps."

"So why are you so keen for me to let you destroy them?"

The Crescend's voice was shocked. "Do you really think that this is what I want, Morgan?"

"Isn't it?"

"Nothing could be further from the truth. I am not asking you to do anything but decide. I am an advocate of neither position."

"But you're an Interventionist," she said. "That means you want to help us defeat the enemy."

"No. It means that I am *willing* to help you, should you decide that way. There is a great difference. Should you decide not to accept my help, I will retire into the background once again. My role will be complete, and future events will play themselves out without my interference."

"Even if the enemy destroys us completely?"

"Even so."

"That's a little harsh."

"Unfortunately, it is the nature of things. The nature of *nature*, if you like. I cannot say if your annihilation at the hands of the enemy will or will not come to pass, or will necessarily be a bad thing if it does happen. Not because I am reluctant to tell you, or because it is too close to call, but because it is not my role to judge such issues. I am a facilitator, not an instigator. The people of my Caste who *do* instigate have decided to pass their role to you. Perhaps, if the projected outcome *was* more clear-cut, the High Caste would have divined its role differently. Perhaps there would be no situation such as this at all: the enemy would have been eradicated before they even left their capsules. You might take hope, if you like, in the fact that this didn't happen—for it may mean that you have a chance. You might not. I am in no position to argue or suggest either way. All I want is for you to make a decision."

He paused now at length, then asked: "Do you have one for me, Morgan Roche?"

Roche didn't know what to say. "I'm not sure. I want to be *certain*—"

"As do we all. There is no certainty to be had here, except on one thing: that if you decide to accept my help, you will prevail over the enemy, and they *will* be destroyed."

"All of them?" she asked.

"*All* of them."

"Including the Cane I know?"

"He is one of them, isn't he?" the Crescend's voice chided her.

"Yes, but—"

"Would I be true to my word if I spared him?" he said. "One spared here might mean another elsewhere—and another, and another. This compact must be sealed in the sure knowledge that your victory will be total, and the enemy's defeat complete."

She grimaced.

"You don't like that?" he asked.

She was flustered for a moment by the fact that he could obviously see her. "It disturbs me."

"Then turn down my offer and end this phase of the war," was all he said. "I will abide by your decision."

"That's my only other option?"

"Would you care to suggest another?"

She took a deep breath. He was trying to trick her again. She wanted to scream that it wasn't fair, that she didn't deserve this, that she hadn't asked for it, that she didn't want it—but all she said was:

"Why me? You still haven't explained that to me. Why not the council?"

"The Interim Emergency Pristine Council is too large and unwieldy, and too exposed, for this purpose. It will play a role in organizing resistance or mopping up the damage—depending on which way you decide, of course—but it is not suited to the task before you. Like me, it is a facilitator, not an instigator."

"But why *me* and not someone else?"

"Because you alone are the one who must decide."

"But *why* am I the one?"

"Because that is your purpose."

"Stop avoiding the question! Tell me *why* it has to be *me*!"

He paused again. "It is not something you will want to hear, Morgan."

The Crescend's voice was full of sympathy but she didn't accept it for a second. She didn't believe a creature that advanced would use language to communicate; any emotion that appeared in his voice therefore had to be artificially generated. Either way, she wasn't going to give him any leeway.

"How can you know that?"

"I know you well enough to be certain of your feelings on this matter," he said. "Besides, it would undoubtedly influence your decision. Since I have gone to great lengths to ensure your freedom, strange as that may seem, and to keep you as impartial as possible, I would not have those efforts wasted. Page De Bruyn came close enough to doing that already."

Roche froze. "What do you know about her?"

"I know that she resented the fact that I was in cahoots with your Eupatrid regarding your mission with the Box, and your subsequent freedom. When she got in the way, she was dismissed and told to keep her nose out of the affair. I would not have anyone interfering in the process of your education. She misinterpreted what happened, believing that you were part of a conspiracy to undermine her power base, and embarked upon a personal campaign of revenge."

Roche absorbed the news in silence for a moment; the Crescend *had* been behind everything, after all. "So that's why she was after me, then."

"She unwittingly put the entire project at risk. Your purpose was to learn about the enemy and about your own abilities in your own time. The Box was to guide you until you were informed enough to decide. That was its prime directive, beside studying Adoni Cane. Losing the Box has forced us to move sooner than many had anticipated—but perhaps we would have reached this point now, anyway. Either way, we are here."

She nodded slowly, feeling oddly sorry for her old boss. De Bruyn had betrayed her, but had herself been the victim of forces beyond her control. She had been caught in the middle of the High Caste's convoluted plot. Like Roche herself.

"You know all you need to know," the Crescend said. "Does it truly matter who created the enemy? The fact that they are here is all that should concern you. Does it matter if they plan to kill all of you or just half? All death is tragic. Does it matter if you are the only who can find them or one of millions? *This* decision is yours alone. Decide, Morgan, and be done with it. I have waited forty years for this moment."

Roche didn't say anything. Why the war had started, half a million years ago, *did* indeed seem irrelevant. The same with who had made the enemy in the first place. It was too long ago. She had to concentrate on the situation before her. On the problem as she saw it.

That was what they wanted, she supposed.

"You're going to have to wait a little longer, I'm afraid," she said. "I need to think on it some more."

The voice chuckled. "You mean that you need to talk to Adoni Cane."

"He has a right to know what's going on," she said.

"And will you believe him, no matter what he says?"

"I think I owe it to him to listen."

There was a sound much like a sigh. "Very well, Morgan. I will continue to wait. Just remember one thing, though: your will is paramount in this instance. You must not let yourself be coerced by anyone—not even me. *Especially* me. You must decide as objectively as you can. That is all we ask of you."

She couldn't help a bitter laugh.

"Understand what I am trying to say, Morgan. Adoni Cane is one of the enemy. I would not lose all now to false sympathy or wishful thinking."

"You won't," she said. "Because that's what this is all about, really."

"Yes, it is." The Crescend's voice softened slightly. "Listen and think well, Morgan Roche."

The Crescend said nothing more, and she knew she was alone.

19

Roche settled back onto the bed and ran her hand across her face.

"Uri?" she called. "Can you hear me?"

"Of course, Morgan."

She was relieved to hear his voice. "That's good," she said. "I was afraid you wouldn't be able to."

"Why not?" he said. "I've been monitoring your room since your awakening."

Roche frowned. "But he said no one would hear us talk."

"Who said this?"

She hesitated for a moment, confused. "Didn't you hear me transmit my message?"

"Yes, but there was no reply. I closed the line when it became apparent that you weren't going to say anything else."

No reply. Part of her wasn't surprised. This was the Crescend she was dealing with, after all. Interfering with mundane technology—and mundane minds—probably came as easily as toying with an insect.

"Is everything all right, Morgan?"

"Everything's fine, Uri," she said. "Just a little tired, I guess. Listen, get hold of Cane for me, can you? I need to see him."

"Yes, Morgan."

"And make sure you monitor *this* conversation," she added hastily. "I want you to be ready if anything goes wrong."

"Understood."

Roche went back to watching the display of Sol System while she waited. Nothing much had changed, except the patterns of white on the ring. Now that the ship was closer, she could see them in more detail. They shifted like oil on water, sweeping in swirls with ponderous grace across vast sections of dust and gas. Indicating them, Roche asked Kajic what they meant.

"Electrical activity," he said. "Source unknown. This data comes direct from the Heresiarch's general navigation service. He believes them to be a hazard to shipping."

"A trap of some sort?"

"Conceivably."

She wondered if it had anything to do with the convergence on the system. The clone warriors might have rigged some sort of trap involving the ring, although she couldn't imagine what kind of trap it could possibly be. A solar-system-sized laser would be better based in the sun itself, and there was no sign of the exotic types of matter usually associated with hyperspace weapons. It *might* have been a natural phenomenon, but she couldn't afford to make such assumptions at this stage. It was too risky, and could end up being costly. . . .

"Cane is on his way," Kajic announced.

"Okay, Uri." She breathed deeply and slowly for a full minute, composing herself for what was to come. She had no idea what she would say, and even less of an idea how he would respond to what she had to say. *I have the power to kill you and all of your people unless you give me a reason not to.* If she was lucky, he would think she was crazy.

If she was unlucky . . .

"Hello, Morgan." Cane stepped into the room.

"Thanks for coming, Cane." Her voice was edgy; she hadn't heard the door open. "I wanted to—"

She stopped.

He stood before her with his arms folded, to all appearances completely at ease, and waited for her to continue.

"I wanted to thank you for rescuing me," she said, realizing only as she said it that it was the truth. "You took a great risk, and it paid off. Thank you."

"I did what I had to do," he said. His eyes revealed nothing about his thoughts.

"How *did* you know what to do, by the way?" she asked.

"I didn't. I just took a chance," he said. "The ship that took you passed through the blockade of the *Phlegethon* without resistance, so it seemed likely that it had an allegiance with the clone warriors. Using fragments of the command language we detected in Palasian System, I was able to convince the leaders of the blockade to let us through too. Once they believed that I was in fact one of the enemy, the rest was simple."

He seemed to be telling the truth, but she still couldn't read him. "What about the camouflage you ordered around the *Ana Vereine*?"

He shrugged. "You were taken by Hurns, so I assumed that they would respect the authority of a superior Hurn vessel. It wasn't difficult to retrieve the design of such a ship from the datapool."

"And the name of the ship? You called it the *Apostle*."

"I overheard the name when I arrived."

"What else did you overhear? Anything useful—like who they were, for instance?"

"They call themselves the Disciples of the Evergence," he said. He didn't wait for her to ask: "I don't know what it means."

"But they are in league with the enemy."

"It seems so. They accepted me readily enough."

She nodded. His explanations made sense, even if they were a little glib. She suspected that no matter what she threw at him he would be able to explain it away.

"I'd wondered," she said, "whether this might be proof that an epsense link of some sort does exist between you and your siblings. That way it would have been easy to know just what to say and who to imitate in order for my captors to be convinced."

"I'm sorry to disappoint you, Morgan," he said. "But that wasn't the case."

She studied him closely for a few seconds "Are you lying to me?" she asked, as she had when they had first reached Sol System.

"Why would I lie?"

"Why does anyone lie?" she said. "To conceal the truth, obviously."

"And if I were trying to conceal the truth, what would it gain me to admit that *now*?"

"*Are* you lying to me?" she pressed him.

"What do you want to hear, Morgan? That I'm in communication with my siblings? That I'm in league with them?"

"I just want you to answer the question! Why is this so difficult for everyone?"

"If I am lying now, then I must have been lying all along!"

The passion in his voice surprised her, but it didn't sway her from her own anger.

"Just answer the damned question, Cane!" she snapped. "*Are* you lying to me?"

There was a long pause in which he breathed deeply a few times, almost as if trying to calm himself. Seeing him so agitated was not a common experience; it was only the second time she had really seen him angry. It was a side of himself he kept carefully hidden.

"I'm not lying, Morgan," he said eventually, his even voice cutting across her thoughts. "Everything I have told you is the truth."

She sighed wearily. She wanted his assurances to take away her doubts, but they were still there, lingering, continuing to eat away at her.

"I want to believe you," she said. "But it's hard—"

"Why, Morgan?" he broke in. "Why is it so hard? How many times have I saved your life now? How many times more must I do it before you will believe me? How many more of my own must I kill?"

Roche was speechless for a second. For an instant, she remembered how he looked when he had rescued her—cold and dangerous—but that wasn't what she saw on his face now. He looked . . . *hurt*.

I can't afford to trust you, she wanted to say, *because I don't have the courage to risk so much. Because if I'm wrong there's no limit to what I might lose.*

But she didn't say that. She couldn't. It exposed her vulnerability, it cut too deeply to the core of her uncertainty. That's what it all boiled down to, after all: balancing the uncertainty of his trustworthiness against the damage he could do. If he was lying, if he was leading her into some sort of trap, if he was really one of the enemy and had been faking it all along—and if she alone could destroy the enemy . . .

Instead she said: "You told me once that we shouldn't trust you completely because you yourself don't know what you might do. Without knowing who made you, and why, we can't guess how you will respond to every situation. There's a chance you might be compelled, some day, to act in a way that goes against or subverts your conscious intentions. Do you still feel that way?"

His tension eased slightly. "That is a fair point," he said. "I guess I would still consider it were I in your shoes."

She decided to take a chance and ask him the question she really wanted an answer to: "Tell me, Cane. If you *were* in my shoes and you had the means to destroy the enemy at no cost to any other Human Caste, would you do it?"

He looked thoughtful for a moment. "It would be an attractive option."

"Even at the cost of millions of lives—of the lives of the enemy?"

"Yes, of course," he said. "Because so many more would stand to be saved."

"Is that how you justify genocide?"

"I'm not justifying anything, Morgan. I am merely answering your question."

Was he? she wondered. "But what if *one* of the enemy overcame its makers' wishes and demonstrated that it could achieve redemption? Would you kill that one, too, to make absolutely certain that there would be no recurrence of war?"

Again he hesitated. "For total victory?" he asked.

"For total victory."

This time he didn't hesitate: "I would let that one fall with the others, yes."

The answer chilled her. Not because of its ruthlessness—for she had guessed that this would be his answer—but because of what it said about him and how he regarded himself.

He knew what she was hinting at. He wasn't stupid. He was one of the most frightening individuals she had ever met, simply because he was so much better at everything than she. He could outrun, outfight, and probably outthink her to degrees she didn't dare imagine—and he had been watching her and the Box the whole time they had known each other. If he hadn't already guessed at the Box's connection to the Crescend, then she had surely given him enough clues to work it out.

He knew that she was talking about him, and he was telling her that if she had the power to do so, that she should use it and eliminate them all, including himself.

Or was he outthinking her even now? Was he gambling that this display of selflessness would in fact convince her *not* to wipe out the enemy?

His eyes stared calmly into hers, as if they were discussing ordinary politics rather than genocide. But what *would* he do were she to choose to destroy him with the others?

She couldn't allow that question to influence her. The decision had to be made on its own merits. What happened afterward was an entirely different matter.

If he could turn against his programming, maybe others could too. She couldn't justify the extermination of an entire Caste if that possibility existed. No matter how superior they seemed to her, they wouldn't stand a chance against the High Humans. And if they *were* superior to her, maybe they deserved a chance to prove it.

The galaxy had never been a peaceful place, and it probably never would be. If she sanctioned the destruction of the enemy, would that guarantee any sort of peace? Maybe for a while, as long as alliances lasted. But the enemy's influence would still be felt. Old grudges wouldn't go away, even if they had been inflamed to further a third party's ends. There would still be conflict and injustice.

And letting the enemy survive didn't necessarily mean that everyone else would die. She clutched at that thought, even as she made her decision. It wasn't a case of millions versus trillions. It was a case of an end to the present hostilities versus its continuation. Who would be victor was not clear. The enemy was too greatly outnumbered to take its success for granted.

Or so she hoped. She didn't like to think what it would mean if she was wrong.

"Morgan?" Cane was still standing in front of her, waiting patiently for her to say something.

"I'm sorry," she said. "I was distracted."

He nodded stiffly. "Is there anything else you want to ask me?"

"No, that's all," she said. "Thanks."

He looked as though he was about to say something, then turned and left the room.

When he had gone, she said: "Uri? Open that communications channel again."

"Opening now, Morgan."

"Dawn comes," she said.

"Does this mean you've decided?" asked the Crescend, his voice emanating instantly from somewhere near the door.

"Yes." But she was reluctant to say the words.

"And what *is* your decision, Morgan?"

She paused, not for effect, but to give herself one last chance to change her mind. She didn't.

"I can't allow you to destroy them," she said slowly, carefully. "So I guess I decide to let them live. We'll fight them ourselves, and either win or lose on our own merits."

"You know what this means?"

"Yes." She hoped so. "War—at best."

He seemed to pause a long while before speaking again. "May I ask why you have chosen this?"

"Because Cane doesn't deserve to die," she said. "He's helped me too much. He's proven—to me, at least—that the clone warriors *can* rise above their programming."

"And what if I said that Cane could be spared?"

"That's not the point. Who's to say there isn't another like him out there who doesn't deserve to be killed? You?"

"I could not make such assurances."

"Exactly. It wouldn't be right to take that chance."

"So you make this decision by weighing the certain harm to an individual against potential harm to the masses?"

"I guess so." She took a deep breath. "*Would* you spare Cane if I asked you to?"

"No, of course not," he said. "Nor do I believe Cane would wish it."

She thought about this and nodded to herself. "What happens now, then? Is there anything else I need to do?"

"Your role is played out," he said. "For the time being, anyway. I will leave you to communicate your decision to the rest of my Caste. All the information at our disposal will be disseminated simultaneously to concerned parties throughout the galaxy, including the IEPC. We will no longer try to hide this knowledge from the enemy. It will be crucial in the times to come."

"And what happens if I need to talk to you again?"

"Why? Do you feel you might change your mind?"

"No, I don't think so," she said, even though, now that she had made her decision, she was filled with a terrible sense of doubt.

"If you did, there is no guarantee that the High Caste would accept your change of heart," he said, his voice almost scolding.

"I understand." She wasn't sure if that option would have made her feel better, anyway. If things went badly with the enemy, she didn't want that decision hanging over her, to be made again and again.

She had given the enemy the freedom to fight; she had given her own kind the freedom to lose. When gods interfered in the affairs of mundane Humans, she doubted any decisions were easy. But that didn't make her feel any better.

The Crescend waited for a moment, as though to see if she would speak, then said: "Perhaps we will talk again some day."

The thought didn't fill her with pleasure. "Perhaps."

"Goodbye, Morgan Roche."

How much time passed after the Crescend left, she didn't know. She wasn't really thinking at all. Making the decision had drained her, leaving her feeling strangely empty.

"You have a visitor, Morgan."

Roche turned to see Kajic's hologram coalescing in the wall display.

"Who is it?" she said wearily.

"Defender-of-Harmony Vri."

"What does he want?"

"He hasn't said."

<Can't you guess?> asked Maii.

Roche sighed. <Can't you stall him?>

<I—> The girl stopped in mid-thought. <I'm sorry, Morgan. I didn't realize you were this tired. Is everything all right?>

<I'm not sure.> Maii didn't seem to know what had happened. She too must have been unable to read what had happened with the Crescend.

<*What* happened?> asked the girl. <Did I miss something?>

<I'll tell you later, Maii.>

Roche tilted the bed closer to upright and braced herself. She wasn't doing anyone much good moping around.

"It's all right," she said aloud to Kajic. "I'll have to deal with him eventually, I guess. Send him in, Uri."

The doors to the medical center opened and the tall soldier stepped through. His armor shone as always, golden and feathered like some Humanoid phoenix. He took four precise paces to the end of Roche's bed, where he stopped and bowed slightly from the neck.

"Thank you for seeing me," he said.

The bed tilted farther so they were closer to eye level. "How can I help you, Vri?"

"I wish to suggest another compromise."

She suppressed a sigh. "What now?"

"First, I want to say that I understand why it was not possible for negotiations to take place between you and the Agora on the *Phlegethon*. The circumstances at the time were not conducive to such discussions. So I do not blame you for this additional delay."

She was relieved about that. She'd half expected him to storm in, making demands and claiming she was deliberately stalling.

"Secondly?" she prompted.

"I have become aware that your work here may ultimately benefit the Surin Caste as a whole," he went on. "While I do not feel that Maii should play any role in this, I accept that she has made her decision—and since that decision can be interpreted as one serving the interests of the Agora, I also accept that it is not my role to intervene."

Roche watched him as he spoke. His broad, furred features were composed and thoughtful. He had obviously considered these words in great depth before coming to her with them.

"I'm glad about that, Vri," she said, a touch cautiously, wary of the sting in the tail. "But what's your point?"

"It is my hope," he said, "that you will also see my superiors' point of view, which is that Maii has been separated from the culture that might arguably be best for her development. Before her childhood is over, it may be beneficial to expose her to aspects of our Caste that give us pride. There is no denying that she has been hurt by members of our Caste, but all the Agora desires is the opportunity to right that wrong.

"I ask, therefore, that when the matter of the enemy is resolved you will see fit to return with me to Essai, to discuss the matter of Maii's custodianship with the Agora, and that I might be allowed to serve formally as her bodyguard until then."

He bowed again, and stepped back a pace.

For a moment, Roche didn't quite know what to say. It looked like he was handing her a simple way to put the problem aside for the time being, but she couldn't help but wonder if there was more to it.

<He means it,> said Maii. <He's trying to find a balance between his orders, which he must obey, and the situation he finds himself in. Although he knows our work is dangerous, he also knows, now, that I am an essential part of that work. Without access to a reave, you cannot find the enemy, and at the moment I'm the only reave you have. Although the Agora might prefer him to take me home by force, he feels that doing so might actually cause more harm. If you agree to this proposal, all his needs will be satisfied.>

<What about you, though, Maii? How do you feel about it?>

<That's kind of irrelevant at the moment, Morgan. I don't know if we'll *ever* make it to Essai. But if the chance does arise, I might take it. I suppose I should at least see what the Agora has to offer. Maybe they really do have my best interests at heart.>

Roche could accept that. <Naturally, I wouldn't try to stop you.>

<I know you wouldn't, Morgan. And I'm glad that you would be coming with me—if you agree, of course. I'd feel uncomfortable facing them alone.>

Vri shifted his feet. Roche snapped out of the mental conversation.

"I'm sorry," she said. "I was just talking to Maii about it. We think the compromise is fair, so I'll agree to meet the Agora when the time is right. Until then, you can travel with us and help keep Maii safe. After all, that is something we are *both* concerned about."

The Surin soldier bowed a third time, this time more formally. "Thank you," he said. "I believed that this was the decision you would reach. You have not disappointed me."

He turned and strode heavily out of the room. Roche smiled as he went. *You have not disappointed me.* That was probably as close to a compliment as she would ever get from him.

<I think you're right,> said Maii. <He's as stiff as they come.>

<May he never unbend,> said Roche.

<Are you going to tell me now what happened before?>

<I'm not sure I fully understand it myself, Maii.>

<The fragments I detect in your mind paint a strange picture. The events themselves are hidden, but I can read where you have thought about them—as though the knowledge is leaking out from behind a shield of some kind. But I've never seen one quite like this before. You were actually talking to the Crescend?>

<Yes.>

<I guess it shouldn't be a surprise that High Humans have access to epsense as well as everything else.>

<Maybe what they have makes epsense look primitive.>

<Maybe. It's something to think about, anyway. . . .>

Roche felt the reave withdraw slightly, and she tilted the bed back. Under the cocoon, she wriggled the fingers of her left hand and felt them clench. Whatever the autosurgeon had done to her in the last few hours, it had left her feeling almost Human again. Almost.

"How much longer now, Uri?"

"Three hours or so, Morgan."

"Can I at least have my other hand back now? I can feel it moving under this thing, so I know it's working."

"I'll check." Kajic conversed silently with the autosurgeon, then said: "On the condition that you don't exert yourself, it will allow free movement to be restored to that limb."

Even before he had finished speaking, the cocoon slid back down her left side, retracting like a fluid to reveal her left shoulder, arm and upper chest. She appeared to be wrapped in close-sticking bandages made from a white, tissue-thin material she didn't recognize. Through it, she could make out the healing red wounds through which her implants had been removed. Her left palm and wrist were still stiff.

At some point, she would have to be refitted. Like Haid, she had grown accustomed to working intimately with machines. *Too* intimately at times—an issue she still hoped to take up with the Crescend, one day. When the war eased enough for her to take some time off—the sooner the better—she would commit herself to the care of the medical center again and get the upgrade she had once hoped to obtain from COE Intelligence.

Exactly when that would be, she didn't know. First she had to get back in touch with the council and work out strategies for the coming war; they also had to find out if her talent could be replicated, naturally or otherwise. That was assuming, of course, that the *Phlegethon* survived its assault by the fleets of enemy-infected nations. Then there was working out what to do about Sol System itself: did the enemy actually have a reason for gathering here, or was it safe to go back home? If the latter, could the council coordinate the battle across the galaxy as a whole, or would its efforts need to be restricted to those areas considered the most important to save? And how would the governments of the Far Reaches—often overlooked by core-based interests, and the source of an ages-old resentment—react to that decision?

The future was full of uncertainties, as the Crescend had promised it would be if she chose this particular path. Roche didn't regret her decision, but she did wish it could have been otherwise.

Your role is played out, the Crescend had said.

As far as she could tell, her job was only just beginning.

20

IND *Ana Vereine*
955.2.16
0290

"Morgan?"

She snapped out of her thoughts. "What is it, Uri?"

"I'm picking up a ship on an approach vector," he said. "Its configuration matches that of the Hurn ship we impersonated to rescue you."

"Is it hailing us?"

"No."

"And we're still camouflaged?"

"Yes."

"Then how does it know who we are?"

"Maybe it doesn't," Kajic said. "Maybe its similarity to the other ship is only a coincidence. We may have just blundered into Hurn territory."

"And you believe that?"

"Not for a moment," he said.

She vacillated briefly. "Okay, broadcast an anonymous query for ID. Ask Cane and Ameidio to be on the bridge, if they aren't already there. And give me that screen again. I want to see what's going on."

Her bed turned back to the holographic display. In it, she saw the relatively empty space around the *Ana Vereine*, plus the colorful overviews of the system. The approaching ship appeared as a red triangle, swooping closer along a gently curving trajectory.

"I have broadcast the query," said Kajic. "If they're going to reply, the earliest we'd hear is in a minute or two."

Roche rubbed her chin with the fingers of her newly healed left hand. "If we had to fight, how long could we last?"

"Without the Box? Not long at all," he said. "I'd prefer to avoid conflict entirely."

"I agree, but if we *don't* have a choice, I'd like to know what our options are."

"It depends if they have independent fighters or not. Against more than three or four, I will be hard-pressed to maintain much of a defense."

"A minute?"

"Maybe two," he said. "At most."

"They may not even use fighters," Roche mused. "Depends what they want, I guess."

"True." Kajic's voice was cautious. "No response as yet."

"How long until they're within combat range?"

"One hour."

"Give them ten minutes to respond, then put us on alert. At fifteen we'll broadcast a warning. If we still haven't heard back by thirty minutes, we'll assume they're hostile and change course. If they follow, we'll take further evasive action. And if *that* doesn't deter them . . ." She shrugged. "Then we fight, I guess."

She watched the screen. The ship didn't seem to be changing course of its own accord, no matter how much she might wish it would.

"Where's Vri?" she asked.

"Back in his fighter. I've advised him of the situation. He's battle-ready, should we require him."

"And Maii?"

<I'm in my quarters, Morgan.>

"Perhaps you'd better head to the bridge too." Not that it made a great deal of difference where the reave actually was, Roche reminded herself; just as long as their minds were in contact. Still, she felt better knowing where the girl was. "Is everyone else on deck?"

"Cane has arrived," said Kajic, "but Haid is—"

"Right here," said the ex-mercenary as the doors hissed open. He was dressed in a mirror-finished Dato combat suit and trailing another that echoed his movements perfectly. "I figured you'd probably prefer being where the action was."

Roche smiled. "You figured right."

Returning the smile, he tapped a series of codes into the autosurgeon's manual console. It protested with a series of alarms and warnings, but capitulated under the weight of Haid's overrides. The cocoon enclosing Roche's half-healed body clicked, then hissed, then began to recede back into the bed.

Roche looked down in amazement as the rest of her body appeared, blotched red in places and wrapped in white like a barely formed chrysalis. Various sensors and drips retracted into the bed like worms diving away from sunlight. Her legs still felt numb. She moved one tentatively. It responded, but she wasn't confident of its holding her weight.

"Are you sure this will be okay?" she asked.

"Uri assures me you'll manage well enough, once you're in the suit."

"But I don't have any implants."

"We've thought of that. What the suit can't work out, I'll do for you." Haid swung her legs off the bed, then manually walked the spare armor into position with its back facing her. The ceramic shell split and cracked open at the touch of a pressure pad. Its interior was black and moist-looking.

She couldn't stand on her own. A twinge of pain shot up her left side as soon as she tried to take her full weight. Haid instructed the suit to go down on its knees; then he picked her up and put her inside. The suit's padding cradled her, allowing her to rest as though she were sitting, with the merest twitch of her legs magnified to become steps.

She paced the room, enjoying the newly found freedom of movement. Control was limited to a primitive electrode net draped across her shoulders. Luckily the autosurgeon's repairs of her damaged nervous system had progressed far enough for the device to work. It was years since she had trained to use one, and manual control wasn't an option.

"Ameidio, you're a genius!"

"Realize that I'm only doing this out of self-interest," he said lightly. "Trying to coordinate things with you stuck down here would have been just too damned awkward. So, if you will . . ."

He indicated the door.

She didn't move. "Since when are you giving the orders around here?"

Again, he smiled. "It's good to have you back, Morgan."

Together they clanked heavily from the room and headed for the bridge.

The ship's complement was complete by the time they arrived. As the ten-minute deadline came and went, a siren echoed through the ship, announcing full alert.

"What was that for?" asked Haid, assuming his position by Cane at the weapons board.

"Don't forget our passenger," Kajic chided him. "Alta's still down below."

Roche settled into the spot where Kajic's second-in-command had once sat. "Any change in the situation?"

"The ship is proceeding as per its expected course, decelerating with a constant delta-v. It has neither responded to my hail nor issued one of its own."

"Does it look like it's going to attack?"

"Apart from heading our way, it doesn't seem to be doing anything at all."

"Maii?"

<I'm getting nothing, Morgan. Their shields are tight.>

She turned. "Any thoughts, Cane?"

"If what we suspect is true," he said, "then I think we can expect at least one of my siblings to be aboard this ship. And they will be much more difficult to deceive than the Disciples who captured you."

"Do you think they'd respond if we hailed them in your command language?"

"They might, but that would only confirm their suspicions that we are the people they seek," he said. "We may yet be able to bluff our way out of this, though."

"I'd just like to know how they found us," said Haid. "Something's not right about all of this. I can feel it."

"I agree." Roche looked at the main screen, glad to have access to its greater area and clarity. The one in the medical center had been barely adequate. "Any idea where this ship came from, Uri?"

"It appears to have altered its course from this orbit here." A red ellipse circled the sun. "How long it followed that orbit, however, I can't tell."

The orbit didn't seem to intersect any hot-spots or suspicious-looking regions.

"The Disciples must have contacted them somehow," said Roche. "They must have traced our course."

"Sounds reasonable," said Cane.

"So what do we do?" asked Haid.

"We wait them out," said Roche. "They might be bluffing. If they intended to destroy us, they would've come in faster or slow-jumped right on top of us. They must want something else." She studied the creeping dot on the screen. "How long now, Uri?"

"Forty minutes until we change course."

"That gives us a little breathing space, anyway. In the meantime, I want to get in touch with the council, if we can. Uri, is that drone still following us?"

"Yes."

"Good. Send a tightbeam message requesting a conference with whoever's in charge at the moment. Tell them I have something they need to know."

"I'll try." Kajic's hologram faded into static.

"Why are we wasting our time talking to them?" Haid asked. "How many times do they have to knock us back before you take the hint, Morgan?"

"They still need us," she said, adding: "And unfortunately we still need them. Besides, unless they've found someone else who can locate the enemy like I can, I'm pretty sure they'll be prepared to talk."

"Yes," said Haid, "but will they listen?"

She didn't have long to wait. Barely five minutes passed before Kajic announced the receipt of a reply from the council.

"That was fast," she said. "Do we have a live feed?"

"Connecting as we speak. The signal is heavily encrypted and therefore low on detail but at least delay-free."

"Put it through."

A window opened on the main screen, revealing a grainy black-and-white image.

"Well, if it isn't Morgan Roche," said Salton Trezise. "How nice of you to get in touch. Rumor had it you were dead."

"As much as I'd love to exchange pleasantries with you, Trezise, I don't have the time. I need to speak with Murnane."

"He's no longer on the council, I'm afraid." Trezise's expression was smug. "Both he and Nemeth have been censured, along with their Exotic friends. The council doesn't take kindly—"

She cut him short. "So who's in charge?"

"Me, for the time being." He smiled broadly.

Her first instinct was to defend Murnane. Nemeth, she was sure, had been involved in all manner of underhand deals, but she doubted the older councilor had ever acted improperly. He had the change-resistant, inflexible air of someone who was not easily diverted from the straight and narrow.

But this wasn't the time or the place to get involved with petty politics. There was too much else at stake right now.

"If you're really in charge," she said, "then there's something you need to know."

"I hope it involves the imminent arrival of reinforcements," he said. "I've just been told that another fleet is jockeying for firing rights—"

"I'm sorry, Trezise, but there won't be *any* reinforcements." She didn't like to say it. He looked genuinely harried under the self-satisfied exterior. "I've been in contact with the Crescend. You can forget about the High Caste. They're not going to get involved."

His face dropped. "Why not?"

She hesitated momentarily, not wanting to tell Trezise that the reason the Crescend wasn't getting involved was because she had specifically asked him not to.

"Because it's not their fight. Would we intervene in a squabble between two Low Caste tribes on a mud planet somewhere? That's how this looks to them. Yes, one tribe might get wiped out, and things will certainly be messy for a while afterward, but that's just the way it goes. It's no big deal."

"Tell *that* to the tribe being wiped out," he said.

She was trying to defend the Crescend, but found it difficult to keep the bitterness out of her voice. "They will provide us with all the data they've collected over the years, but that's all you can rely on."

"Well, it's something, I guess." He looked thoughtful for a moment. "Tell me, how exactly did you get in contact with the Crescend?"

"I haven't got time for explanations right now," she said, certain the Crescend wouldn't talk to Trezise even if she told him how. "I have a situation here I need to deal with. When things have settled down at both your end and mine, I'll be in touch again to work out what to do next."

"This situation—it wouldn't have anything to do with the ring, would it?"

"No. Why?"

"The drone receiving your broadcast is on its outer fringes, and activity is rising in that area. I just thought there might be a connection."

"Not that I'm aware of," she said. She was about to close the line when she added on impulse: "Oh, and by the way, Trezise. I ran into one of our former colleagues the other day."

"Really?"

Roche nodded. "Page De Bruyn."

He raised both eyebrows. "What's she doing here?"

"Not much anymore," said Roche. "She's dead."

Something passed behind the man's eyes, but otherwise he didn't react. "That is unfortunate," he said. "Did she happen to—?"

The screen went black.

Roche waited a moment, but the image didn't return.

"Uri, what happened?"

There was no reply.

"Uri?"

Haid looked up from his station. "I'm getting a damage report from section gold-two."

"Which is what?"

"Uri's maintenance support and information management," he said. "Seems a cable has malfunctioned."

"What sort of cable?"

"One linking his higher functions to the rest of the ship, from what I can tell."

"He's cut off?"

"For the moment. Repair agents are moving in now."

She forced herself to quell a twinge of alarm. "Good, because we're going to need him soon to coordinate the course change."

Haid was about to respond when the floor shook slightly and a low rumble passed through the bulkheads. The lights flickered.

Roche was instantly on her feet. "*Now* what's going on?"

"I have red lights all through sections gold-one and gold-two," Haid said, tapping frantically at his board. "Security is down across that level." He looked over to Roche, the concern evident in his expression. "I think there's been an explosion, Morgan."

Roche met his gaze silently for a few seconds until she was able to ask the question: "What about Uri?"

"I can't tell."

She checked with the reave "Maii?"

<I'm not picking him up at all,> the girl replied.

Roche's sense of alarm became one of rising dread. "I'm going down there."

Haid also rose to his feet. "I'm coming with you."

"If anything's happened to him . . ." She hurried for the exit to the bridge. "You have the bridge, Cane."

Haid followed with heavy, urgent footsteps. "It *can't* be an attack," he said. "Our disrupters haven't registered the use of hyperspace weapons. There's no way they could've got something in here without us knowing."

"That's as may be," she said. "But I have a gut feeling that this was no accident."

She forced herself to hurry, ignoring the pain in her hip every time her left leg took a loping stride. Section gold-one lay midway between the officers' decks and the warren, in the middle of the ship's main inhabited nacelle. It wasn't far from the bridge, but it seemed to take forever.

"You don't think it might have been Vri?" Haid asked.

She was trying not to think at all, so she didn't answer him.

Pressure-doors had come down around sections gold-one and gold-two. Roche and Haid sealed their suits and keyed in the appropriate overrides. The heavy door before them slid aside, setting free a cloud of smoke.

Roche stepped cautiously through it. The walls bulged inward in places, reminding her that this area was close to the ship's main life-support vats. For a moment, she wondered if the attack might have been directed there, and not directly at Kajic.

But then they rounded a corner and found what remained of the four rooms that had contained his body and the equipment required to support it.

The external door was off its hinges. The walls were blackened and twisted. Roche passed through the outer chambers, crunching over piles of twisted wreckage to the control room. Nothing had survived intact. The window over the main console had shattered into a million pieces. Through the hole in the wall where it had once hung, Roche saw the smashed air-conditioning units, the melted fiber-optic cables, the cracked tank . . .

The tank itself was empty of anything but ash. Its organic contents had either boiled or burned away.

"Look at this," said Haid from behind her.

She turned mutely.

He was at the entrance to the rooms, holding up a section of the outer door. One gloved finger traced the smooth, curved edge of the fragment.

"It's been cut through," he said.

Roche had seen enough. Not trusting her voice, she called Maii by epsense.

<Maii? Is Cane still with you?>

<Why? What's happening, Morgan?>

<Uri's dead,> she replied bluntly. <Murdered.>

She felt the Surin girl's grief immediately but didn't indulge it.

<Maii, *is* Cane still with you?>

<Yes,> she said. <He's trying to patch into the security system.>

"It wasn't him," said Haid, overhearing their thoughts. "Someone had to cut through the door while Uri's defenses were down, when the cable was severed."

<Where's Vri?> Roche asked Maii.

<He's still in his ship.>

Roche shook her head in frustration. Then, like an energy bolt, realization hit her.

"Alta!" she exclaimed.

"What? That's not possible," said Haid. "She doesn't know the ship well enough."

"Who else *could* it be?" snapped Roche.

<I've got her, Morgan,> said Maii. <She's heading for the bridge.>

"We're on our way," said Roche, turning to run back the way she had come. "Can you find out for sure if it *was* her?"

<I'm trying now,> said Maii. <Her shields are tight—>

"Don't be gentle." Roche turned grief and apprehension into powerful nervous impulses that sent the suit hurrying through the ship. "Tell Cane!"

<He knows,> said Maii. <She's close; he can hear her.>

Roche urged her suit faster, even though at full stretch she knew they wouldn't arrive in time. "Just be careful!"

<I'm going to try to knock her out.> A wave of secondhand mental force rolled through Roche. <Her shields are—no, *wait!*>

A terrifying flash of fear caught Roche in mid-step, making her stumble. The suit fell heavily as a second explosion tore through the ship. This time it was much closer. The floor bucked as she landed on it, sending her flying into the air. For a giddy moment she was in free-fall; then she hit a wall with a solid crunch and skidded to a halt.

Her vision grayed for a moment.

"Ameidio . . . ?"

A silver-gray figure loomed out of the suddenly billowing smoke, hand extended. Haid helped her upright. "That came from up ahead," he said.

"This can't be happening!" She was moving even as she spoke.

Blast doors had come down across the entrance to the bridge. Roche keyed an override and stepped back as a wave of oily, black smoke exploded out of the entrance.

<Maii?>

The reave was silent. She had said nothing at all since that last, terrible thought. As Roche stepped cautiously into the slowly fading smoke, all she could think of was the fear she had felt in the girl's mind.

The air around them, as measured by the suit's sensors, was hot—much too hot to sustain life, even if the oxygen in the room hadn't been consumed by the fire. The crew stations were half-melted and spattered with fire-retardant foam. The walls had buckled, the main screen imploded.

"Pressure-mine," said Haid dully. "The same used on Kajic, but not as effective in an open space."

"Effective enough," Roche muttered numbly.

Haid stared helplessly at the blackened wreckage.

"Help me look," Roche said, refusing to give up hope.

"Morgan, they couldn't have survived . . ."

Roche ignored him, using the powerful limbs of the suit to sweep debris aside. The explosion had blown piles into corners or burned the tougher fixtures where they stood. Haid stepped over to her as she attempted to wrench a large sheet away from where it had stuck to the wall.

"I just want to make sure," she said distractedly. "She might have been taken hostage—or Cane got her out in time—or—"

She fell silent with a large piece of wreckage raised in one hand, staring at what she'd uncovered—at the evidence that dashed her last, desperate hope.

Haid stepped up beside her. "Is that . . . *her*?"

"Yes." The face and head of the body was scorched down to the bone where it showed above the neck of the blackened suit, but there could be no doubt. The body was so small, curled in a fetal position with one arm outstretched.

Blackness rose up in Roche like bile. She thought she could smell burning, even though she knew that was impossible through the suit. Her gaze fixed upon the open hand of Maii's outstretched arm, as if it were reaching for help.

An overwhelming guilt washed over Roche for not having been there . . .

"She's going to pay for this," Roche whispered.

"Maybe Cane's here too—" Haid began.

"I don't care." Roche heard her own voice as though listening to another person from a great distance. "I just want Alta Ansourian."

"Morgan . . ." Haid's hand had come to rest on her shoulder.

"We have to find her," said Roche without looking up, resisting his efforts to turn her away from the sight of Maii's body.

"But how? With Uri down and the bridge wrecked we've no way of tracing her."

She looked up and faced him. "The suit beacons."

"You think she might be wearing one?"

"If she's using Dato mines, why not a suit as well?"

The shoulders of his own suit jerked. "It's possible, I guess."

She clenched her left fist so tight, she imagined the ceramic finger joints buckling. "I don't have any implants," she said, keeping her anger in check. "So I can't operate my suit properly. You'll have to do it for me."

He slaved her instruments to his and searched for beacons anywhere in the ship. There was one, and it was moving toward the scutter docks.

"She could be trying to escape," said Haid.

Roche nodded. "But we can catch her if we hurry." She reached for a weapon, and realized only then that she was unarmed. Haid was in a similar position.

He raised his arms in a helpless gesture. "I wasn't anticipating combat within the ship," he explained.

"And we don't have time to go to the armory," Roche said. "We'll just have to manage without."

"Maybe we should split up," Haid suggested. "Tackle her from two directions at once—"

"No," Roche said. "We stay together. But we won't use the suit intercoms; otherwise she'll be able to hear us. Just stick to the suit speakers."

Haid nodded in agreement.

"What about Cane?" he said, the audio system of his suit clearly audible through hers. "Do you think he's dead also?"

"Not a chance," said Roche. Turning her back completely on Maii's body, she stepped past Haid.

"Morgan?" he called after her. "What happens when we find her?"

"She dies," she said, leading the way from the bridge. "Beyond that, I don't really care."

The internal transit tubes were inactive, killed along with Kajic, so they were forced to run again. The light brown corridors seemed too bright as they headed in a different direction this time, down through connecting corridors and access tubes toward the ship's fat central drive section. There the scutters and other smaller support vehicles were docked or stored between outings.

Halfway there, a growing suspicion about what the woman had in mind became a certainty as the first of a new wave of explosions rocked the ship.

"What the hell is she doing?" Haid gasped. The data available through his instruments confirmed that at least one of the five remaining scutters had been damaged.

Roche watched—beyond horror, beyond surprise—as a chain of detonations ripped the docks to pieces. "This didn't just happen overnight," she said. "Those mines must have been placed and armed in advance."

"We gave her the freedom to roam anywhere in the ship," Haid said. "We let her do whatever she wanted. I didn't *suspect*—"

"You had no reason to," Roche said. "How could we have known she'd do something like this?"

The explosions continued, damaging more of the scutters. Roche couldn't tell how many craft had been crippled or destroyed, but she knew the docks were ruined. The chain reaction would have left the place a raging inferno. If Alta herself hadn't got out in time, she wouldn't last a minute.

Roche found it difficult to muster any sympathy for the woman—especially given that Vri had been down there, too.

But the transponder kept moving. Roche tried to think one step ahead of the woman. No matter how hard they ran, the suits were identical; they would never catch her by dogging her heels. They had to try to cut her off.

The docks were in an outer layer of the drive section. The next obvious place to hit was two levels down.

"She's headed for the drive chamber," Roche said. "She's probably going to try and blow that, too."

"Can she do that?" asked Haid.

"She obviously thinks she can, otherwise she wouldn't be heading there." Roche considered her options while trying to maintain a steady pace, but the sheer size of the *Ana Vereine*—previously an asset—was now proving to be a disadvantage. "I doubt we'll arrive in time to stop her," she said, "so there's no point trying. But somehow I don't think she's going to be willing to blow herself up along with the ship."

"She'll be looking to escape," said Haid.

"And fast."

"But how? She's blown up all the EVA—" He stopped, realizing the only real option that Alta had. "The Hurn ship!"

"It's the only possibility I can think of."

"You think she's a clone warrior?"

"Maybe not," Roche said, "but certainly on their side. It's the only explanation I can think of for why she's doing this."

"So she'll rig the drive to blow, then jump ship?"

"That would be the simplest solution."

"Then she's going to need access to the hull."

"Exactly," Roche said. "See if you can pull up any plans on airlocks close to the central drive chamber."

Within seconds, Haid had the plans before them, via their suit's displays.

"Which do you think she'll go for?" Roche asked, studying the map.

"There's one likely candidate, and a couple of close seconds."

"Take us to the most likely, and we'll just have to wait for her there."

"Listen, Morgan," said Haid, "I know you want to keep us

together, but wouldn't it make sense to split up now? If we risk all on one airlock, and she picks another, that puts us in a bad situation. After all, we've only got one shot at this."

Roche pondered this. As much as she didn't want to let Haid out of her sight right now, his suggestion *did* make sense. If Alta had worked out how to locate them via her own suit, they could end up walking into a trap.

"Okay," she relented. "Ameidio, you take a secondary airlock and I'll wait for her at the main one." Haid was about to protest. "I have just as much chance against her as you, Ameidio. And besides," she added, "I'd like to be the one that takes her down."

"Okay, Morgan," he said. "But just take care, all right?"

She nodded. "Keep an eye on my beacon so you know where I am, but *don't* communicate unless you have to. The less she knows about us, the better."

"Okay. And if all goes well, I'll meet you out on the hull."

At the next intersection, he turned left while Roche kept going. She watched the dot of his suit angle away from hers with a feeling of apprehension. The pain in her side was a constant ache punctuated by spikes of agony. A rumble of distressed machinery came to her through her feet rather than her eardrums. She ignored everything, and concentrated instead on the task ahead.

Each stride was like the tick of a clock, taking her ever closer to some unknown fate. She hurried through the *Ana Vereine*'s extensive warren, through tunnels she hadn't visited since first occupying the ship. It was here that Cane, Haid, and Maii had hidden while Kajic left Sciacca's World and the Hutton-Luu System with the intention of handing Roche and the Box over to his superiors in the Ethnarch's Military Presidium.

On the tracking screen, Alta had reached the main drive chamber. Within minutes, a siren began to sound.

"That'll be the drives," Roche mumbled to herself. The lack of response from either Maii or the Box only intensified her sense of isolation and the ever-growing emptiness inside her.

She had hoped it would take the woman longer, but a warning through her suit only confirmed her worst suspicions: the drives were going to overload in about fifty minutes. She didn't know exactly what Alta had done, but it had to be something slow-acting, something she had prepared in advance. Had she freed the antimatter reserve, they would already be dead. But whatever it was, it was unlikely it could be stopped. It could take them hours just to figure out what she had done, let alone begin reversing whatever process Alta had set in motion. . . .

Roche studied the tracking screen. According to the display, Alta was on the move again. She was heading for the airlock that Haid suspected she would go for, but Roche wasn't going to be able to beat her there.

She considered calling Haid, but then thought better of it. Hopefully he would see what was going on. He was making good time toward his airlock; even if they didn't make it in time, there was a chance he would be able to intercept Alta out on the hull.

Fifty minutes, Roche thought to herself. In half an hour, the entire ship would be gone. Unless they could find a way off the ship, or someone to rescue them, they would die with it.

Part of her didn't mind that at all. The Crescend himself had stated it quite bluntly the last time they spoke: *Your role is played out.* As long as she took Alta Ansourian with her, she might be happy with that. . . .

The woman was also making good time, unfortunately. Hoping to distract her, Roche activated the open channel connecting the suits.

"Alta? Can you hear me?"

"I hear you." The reply was immediate. "And I can see you, too, Roche! But you can't stop me! You're too late! There's no turning back now."

The woman's voice was feverish, breathless. There was a raw edge to it. Roche couldn't tell if it was fear or determination—or perhaps both.

"What have you done to the engines, Alta?"

"The matter/antimatter mix is in disequilibrium," the woman replied. "The mix will become more and more unstable until it spirals out of control, and then the ship will blow. Trust me—you can't stop it; there isn't enough time."

"But there is enough time to get away?"

"You can get out of the ship, Roche, but you'll never escape!" The mockery in her voice angered Roche, and the image of Maii's helpless form with its outstretched arm returned.

"*Why* did you kill them, Alta?"

"To stop them from interfering, of course."

"But Maii was just a *child*. She never did you any harm!"

There was a pause before Alta spoke again, and when she did her voice was steeped in uncertainty.

"Those were my orders," she said. "I couldn't disobey."

"*Whose* orders, Alta?" Roche pressed, anger giving way to curiosity. "Why are you doing this?"

More assured now, Alta replied: "Because if it hadn't been for you, he wouldn't be dead now!"

"Who? Your *father*?"

"You killed him, Roche!" The hatred in her voice was intense and frightening. "You took him away from me!"

"What are you talking about! You *saw* Jans kill your father! You were there—"

"Lies that you planted!" Alta's voice was raised to a shout now. "But I know the truth! He showed me. He showed me your *lies*. Justice will prevail!"

The edge to her words unsettled Roche. There was a sense of desperation to them that suggested Alta was beyond reasoning with. She believed what she was saying; she was convinced Roche was responsible for her father's death. Why, though, Roche didn't know. Maybe it was simply because she was the nearest available target for reprisal . . .

Alta was much closer now. The air in the warren became thick with smoke as Roche neared the airlock. She passed emergency doors that had failed to shut. Some hung loose, half open, as though they had changed their mind in the act of closing. Without Kajic to run the ship, even the most basic systems were gradually running down. The rumble of complaining engines became steadily louder as she ran.

"Who showed you, Alta?" said Roche.

The woman said nothing.

"Alta?"

A loud explosion knocked Roche off her feet and sent air whipping along the corridor.

"The airlock," she gasped in the sudden hurricane, thinking: *We're open to vacuum*!

She scrambled to her feet, hurried along the corridor and around a corner to find the source of the hurricane: a blackened breach where the outer door of an emergency airlock opened onto space. The inner door hung invitingly open. Roche approached it cautiously, wary of a trap.

Then, she glimpsed a movement: a suit much like hers had just stepped out onto the hull.

Roche didn't hesitate. Using every joule at her suit's disposal, she jumped through the gap and after the fleeing woman. Even if Alta was armed, Roche could take a direct hit or two before her suit failed. And if she could catch her and somehow overpower her before she jumped ship. . . .

Upon exiting the hatch, Alta dropped and rolled, bringing her rifle up to cover anyone following her. Roche burst out of the airlock, only a thin veil of artificial gravity preventing her from rebounding off into space. Alta's first shot missed. Her second caught Roche full on the chest as she threw herself forward. The recoil of the shot knocked her to one side with her ears ringing, but she didn't hesitate. She surged forward again.

Alta kicked back to avoid the charge and scrambled to her feet, her gun coming up again. The third shot took Roche in the shoulder, spinning her around. Alarms in her suit flashed red, and the acrid smell of smoke burned at her nostrils.

"*Die!*" The voice came over the open line as Alta swung the rifle's sight up to her eye, training it on Roche.

Roche knew she had only one more chance. Ignoring the pain in her hip, she dropped to a crouch, forcing Alta to readjust her aim; then, taking advantage of the split second she had gained, she hurled herself forward—

She heard Alta's gasp at the same instant the energy bolt grazed her helmet. Unable to stop herself, Roche lunged awkwardly forward, colliding with Haid as he took Alta from behind, swinging her around and down onto the hull. The impact cost him his grip on the woman.

As both he and Roche tumbled backward, Roche saw Alta regain her footing and collect the rifle that Haid had knocked from her hands.

"Quickly!" Roche called.

They were barely on their feet when the rifle discharged. She felt the edge of the energy bolt that took Haid in the back, forcing him forward into Roche and sending them sprawling across the hull again.

Haid came to a halt, totally inert, a meter or so away from where Roche had fallen, a massive smoking scar stretching across his suit's backplate.

"Ameidio!" She heard the panic in her voice. The lack of response from the ex-mercenary filled her with dread. The bolt had taken out the suit's servomotor control; she wasn't even sure whether his immobility resulted from death or a simple inability to move.

She looked over to Alta again, saw the woman lifting the rifle once more to aim at her.

"I'm going to kill you, Roche." There was no longer any hysteria in Alta's voice, just a quiet determination.

Roche wanted to feel angry, but everything seemed to have been knocked out of her. All she could feel as she sat there, her friend lying prostrate on the hull before her, was a terrible exhaustion. All the fight went out of her; only acceptance remained as she stared down the barrel of Alta's rifle, and waited. . . .

A single rifle shot flickered through the vacuum, taking Alta at the weakest point of her suit between chest and neck plates. The woman jerked upright and staggered backward, trying to stanch the flow of air out the broken seal. Roche caught a glimpse of her terrified expression before the water vapor sucked out of her lungs plastered ice across the inside of her faceplate. She kicked spasmodically, staggering backward.

Roche heard the woman's cries over the suit's intercom,

"*Master!*" The words were carried on molecules of freezing air. "I have failed you!"

Roche turned to look at the figure who had fired, just in time to see him fire again at Alta Ansourian. The woman's suit stiffened, then went limp. It fell to the hull with a thud.

The sudden silence in Roche's helmet was broken only by the sounds of her own breathing.

It was a few moments before Cane spoke. He seemed to be waiting to make sure Alta wasn't going to get up again.

"Morgan?"

She watched him striding over to where she still sat; then his hands were taking hers and helping her to her feet.

"Morgan?" he repeated. "Are you all right?"

"I thought . . ." she began, before realizing she didn't know *what* she had thought. She hadn't believed he was dead, but she had been so taken up with pursuing Alta that she hadn't stopped to consider just what *had* happened to him.

"The explosion threw me through the blast doors before they could close," he explained quickly. "I realized it must have been Alta and so went after her."

"But the suit," said Roche. "It didn't register on the tracking display."

"I disabled the beacon," he said. "It was the only way I could get the advantage of surprise over her."

Roche was still very much shaken by everything that had happened, but she saw a flaw in Cane's explanation. "That would have taken time. How—?"

"Time is something we *don't* have right now, Morgan. Look."

He pointed above her. Only then did Roche look up and see the Hurn ship. All spines and strange glassy towers, it looked like a nightmarish sea anemone magnified a thousand times. It was enormous, ominous. Behind it, a faint glow marked where the ring surrounding Sol System's primary obscured the stars. Strange, pale sheets of lightning flickered in slow motion through the glow, lending the ship a surreal backdrop.

"How . . . ?"

"It must have slow-jumped," he said. A rumble came through the *Ana Vereine*'s hull. "Quick, Morgan. Use your thrusters and jump over to D nacelle." He pointed. "That one."

She faced him, puzzled.

"Just *do* it," he insisted.

"I'm not leaving Ameidio." She nodded toward her friend's lifeless form. His suit was immobile, but she still didn't know whether or not he was dead.

"Understood," he said. "I'll slave his suit to mine and follow you over. Now *go!*"

His urgent tone overrode her confusion and she did as he asked, though minus the usual grace with which he might have piloted the suit. Limited by her lack of depth through just one eye, as well as the lack of implants, she took the suit awkwardly up and out of the drive section's artificial gravity well and to the one enclosing the nacelle Cane had indicated. She resisted the disorienting change in gravity at first, then relaxed and let it hold her.

When she had adjusted, she was standing on a patch of hull apparently slightly above where she had been before. From this new vantage point, she could see a reddish glow clinging to the drive ports, the sole visual sign of the ship's impending destruction.

She looked around, expecting Cane to be following, but saw

him land instead on another nacelle some distance away, Haid's suit following like a ball on a string.

"Cane?"

"I'm sorry, Morgan." There was something different in his tone—something of the Cane that had rescued her from the Disciples. "But this is where we part, I'm afraid."

Roche felt a wave of nausea wash over her.

"What are you talking about?"

"Really, Morgan—think."

She did, and it hurt. "It was you Alta was talking about," she said softly. "*You're* her master."

"You sound surprised," he said.

"No," she said. She was beyond surprise; she felt utterly dead inside. "Disappointed."

"I'm only doing as my nature dictates," he said.

She didn't say anything for a moment. She was remembering what Haid had said about Alta being unresponsive, and that Cane had spent a lot of time talking to her. That was when it must have happened. With a veil of suspicion still hanging over him, he would not have been able to move as she had. He had bent her will to his; he had made her his puppet.

The silence on the open link between them seemed to hum with repressed energy.

"It was all lies," she said, more to herself than to him. "Your amnesia, saving me on Sciacca's World—everything. It was all just lies."

"Not just lies, Morgan. But lies in a game—a game between the Box and myself, between my kind and the Crescend."

"What about Inderdeep Jans?" said Roche. "Why—?"

"All strategic games require sacrifices, Morgan," he said. "But don't think I didn't feel her pain. It touched me deeply, as did the deaths of the five you killed on the *Phlegethon*. For a group mind, the loss of even one component is painful. But you couldn't appreciate that, could you? Coming as you do from such a hapless and disparate race . . ."

"A group mind?"

"The *irikeii* glimpsed it in the black speck at the heart of me and Jelena Heidik. You saw it too, when you looked at us through a reave. There's more to us than meets the mental eye."

"So you *are* linked?" she said.

"Of course," he said. "Everything I have seen and experienced was shared with my siblings."

"Another lie."

"All of them were necessary," he said. "It was part of the game."

Roche felt herself reel. "But why didn't you just kill me? Why have you kept me alive? Why all of *this*?"

"Because we want you to know the reason for it all." She could almost feel the coldness in his voice. "We want you to be aware of the consequences of your *decision*." He emphasized the word deliberately, almost viciously. "We suspected from the beginning that the High Caste would become involved. Coming into contact with the Box when I awoke confirmed it. I watched it as closely as it watched me. I didn't guess that it was inside you, but I knew you were connected, that you were involved. You were the key, and the Crescend was the lock. When you asked me about killing me, and when you told Trezise that High Humans wouldn't help, I knew that the lock had been turned."

She wasn't entirely following him, but that didn't seem to matter at this time.

"I let you live," she said weakly. "I gave your race another chance."

He raised the assault rifle.

"That was a big mistake, I'm afraid, Morgan," he said, and fired.

She took a step back by reflex, but the bolt didn't come anywhere near her. Instead it struck the nacelle's support girders. She couldn't believe he had missed; it had to have been deliberate. He was tormenting her, perhaps, before finally killing her.

She took a step forward again and stood her ground. She would defy him, she decided; she would not give him the satisfaction of seeing her afraid to die.

"Do you really believe you can purge the galaxy?" she said.

Another shot, again striking the support girders. This time she didn't move at all.

"You're going to wipe out everything that's not a part of your precious group mind?" she continued, trying to control the tremor in her voice.

A third shot, and she felt the impact vibrate through her suit.

"It's called justice, Morgan," he said.

"It's called genocide, Cane!"

She felt the hull shift beneath her as a fourth, fifth and sixth shot struck the nacelle girders in rapid, angry succession.

"You dare stand there and talk to us about *genocide*!" he flung at her vehemently. "We're here to avenge a crime no worse!"

"But that was half a million years ago, Cane! You can't blame everyone alive today for something that happened so long ago!"

When next he spoke a few moments later, the icy calm had returned to his voice. "Don't impose your values on us, Morgan," he said.

"What does that mean?"

"That you shouldn't expect mercy from us simply for mercy's sake."

He fired another shot, this one causing her to momentarily lose her balance as the nacelle rocked under her.

"Charge is running low," he said. "But you should tear free in a moment or two and drift away."

"What good will that do?" she said, regaining her footing. "Why not just kill me now and be done with it?"

"Like I said, I want you to have time to think. I want you to think about everything that has happened. I want you to consider what your people have done, and I want you to know why it would have been utterly wrong for the Crescend to have intervened." He paused before adding, with almost a hint of amusement: "Besides, it seems only fitting, given that you spared me."

"I spared *all* of you!" she snapped angrily.

"Yes," he said. "And I want you to think about that, too, as you slowly die, Morgan."

The nacelle rocked again.

"It doesn't have to be like this, Cane," she said desperately, hoping to reach that part of his nature she was sure existed, the part she had come to know over the weeks since they had first met.

"Yes it does, Morgan. We are programmed to exact revenge and we shall do so to the best of our capabilities. And we *will* win."

"But this is crazy! There is no grudge left to pursue! Surely we can get along?"

"History would disagree with you."

"No—history *agrees* with me. Humanity has diversified so much since your creators were around. We come in all shapes and sizes now, and we live in all sorts of places. But underneath it all, we're still all Human. Some may think they're better, but in the end we're all the same. And regardless of what has happened in the past, or what might happen in the future, eventually you will fit in too. It's inevitable."

There was a mocking laugh which filled her helmet. "Assimilation? How typically arrogant of the victors."

"There *was* no victor," she stressed, feeling the need for urgency as the nacelle continued to shift uneasily beneath her. "That's what I'm trying to tell you, Cane. There's just *Humanity*."

"Exactly," he said. "Humanity . . . the victor."

His answer caught her with her mouth open to respond, but the words stuck in her throat.

Humanity . . . the victor.

"No," she said. "That can't be, Cane. You're Human. You *have* to be."

"You're wrong, Morgan," he said.

"But . . . it's not possible!"

"It's more than possible," he said. "It's the essence of this entire conflict. You deny our existence, so we repeal yours."

"But . . ." The concept was so difficult for her to grasp, she found the words almost impossible to say. "You're *aliens*?"

"We are the indigens," he said. "*You* are the invader."

"Now I know you're lying."

"No, this time I *am* telling the truth," he said. "It's simply a matter of perspective. My creators were exploring the galaxy before Humanity's ancestors had even reached its moon. We had created the beginnings of an anchor-point network before you learned how to use hyperspace. By the time our expanding empires came into contact, you were catching up fast but you were still our inferiors, and would have been for some time. You were hasty, impetuous, prone to sudden advances followed by long periods of decay—the brutal disequilibrium of individuality. We on the other hand were patient, persistent, and compassionate. Ours was the steady growth of unity.

"Neither of our civilizations had encountered alien life before, so we were unprepared to deal with such differences; we had no warning of what would come. We didn't expect you to learn from us as quickly as you did. We didn't expect your expansion to be so rapid, and so inconsiderate of our own. You stole our worlds, Morgan; you appropriated our anchor-point network and you encroached upon the society we had accreted so carefully over thousands of years. And you hurt us! Maybe you didn't mean to. Maybe you didn't even realize what you were doing. But you did it nonetheless. And we, like any injured organism, struck back."

She shook her head, dizzy with the concept of what she was hearing. "There's no evidence for any of this. How do I know you're telling me the truth?"

"What reason do I have to lie to you now?"

She didn't say anything; she couldn't. There didn't seem to be anything *to* say. The reality upon which her entire life was founded now seemed as shaky as the nacelle that rocked and moaned beneath her.

She thought of the anchor points supposedly older than Humanity itself, and found herself believing him. As incredible as it seemed, maybe she *had* finally learned the truth.

"You won't find evidence of our existence," he went on, "because it was either suppressed or destroyed in the process of your expansion. And in time, it was forgotten entirely. Even the war that engulfed our two species was forgotten. The origin of my makers was one of the first details to go—for although wiping out an entire losing Caste was not unheard of, destroying the only other intelligent life you had found in the universe *was*. Even those military leaders who sanctioned the genocide ultimately realized this. Perhaps we *could* have learned to live together. Perhaps you were hasty in assuming that, where more than one of my kind existed, the threat remains that the group mind can emerge again, as strong as before—or even stronger. Perhaps you had been wrong in pursuing the war to its ultimate, deadly conclusion."

"And *were* we wrong?" she asked. "Could we have lived together?"

"No," he said bluntly. "You had proven too many times that peaceful coexistence—in the long-term—simply wasn't a possibility. There had been too many broken treaties, smashed peace accords, violated cease-fires . . . We had grown tired of tolerating you, and resolved to rid our galaxy of you."

"But you lost."

"No, Morgan. We didn't," he said. "We are tenacious. I am proof of that."

"But what *are* you? You look like one of us; your anatomy

is at least based on ours; you could almost *be* one of us, if you tried. What's happened to your precious origins now?"

"It exists in our minds, and will exist again when the data encoded in our introns is released. We carry within us the knowledge to re-create our race in its original form. Given time, we can restore the galaxy to the way it should be—the way it was *meant* to be—and we will reclaim our planets and systems. We will travel *your* anchor-point network. We will take from you all those things that should have been ours, and *make* them ours. The balance of justice shall be restored."

The nacelle suddenly lurched beneath Roche, throwing her off balance. There was a crunching, tearing sound, and artificial gravity failed. She used her thrusters to keep her against the hull while the suit anchored itself firmly into place. When next she looked up, everything was silent—even the rumble of the main drive was gone—and the nacelle was drifting away from the *Ana Vereine*.

"I want to thank you, Morgan," he said. The growing distance between them and the unsteadiness of the nacelle made it difficult for her to focus on him. "You have enabled us to continue the work we were created to do. Without the High Caste to interfere, the battlefield will be even. We can fight openly, if we choose to. We will prevail if we can, or we will die. History does not allow us a third option."

"There are always options," she muttered, thinking of the many times she could have turned away from the path that had led her here. "We make our own destinies."

"But sometimes they are made for us."

"Then they can be unmade."

"If you truly believe that, Morgan Roche, then you're more of a fool than I thought."

Light flashed from his thrusters as he leapt off the *Ana Vereine* and arced toward the ship waiting for him. She was too far away to make out whether or not he had taken Haid with him. Not that it mattered anymore. In fact, she thought it would be better for Haid to be left behind. If he wasn't already dead, she felt it would be better for him to die there rather than at the hands of Cane and his siblings later. . . .

She clutched the hull and waited for Cane to say something more, but nothing came. The flare of his thrusters disappeared into a wide-mouthed airlock leading into the Hurn ship. A minute passed in silence, then space became crowded in the vicinity of the *Ana Vereine*. Temporal echoes converged on the slow-jumping *Apostle*, creating a halo of flickering, short-lived ghosts around the spiny craft. As the echoes converged, the warp in space reached peak flexure until, with a flash of light so bright it left Roche blind in her sole eye for almost thirty seconds, it disappeared.

21

Seventeen minutes later, the *Ana Vereine* exploded.

Roche didn't see it; she was inside the nacelle, trying to find anything that might be of use. But she felt the expanding wavefront as it hit. It shook her like a die in a cup. When it passed, she disentangled herself from the remains of a solar antenna and went back out onto the hull to see. There was nothing else for her to do.

Cane had chosen the nacelle well. It contained little but packed storerooms full of raw materials for repairs and hyperspace disrupters that were useless without power to run them. There was no communicator, no long-term life-support and no means of turning the nacelle into a powered vehicle of any kind. If she could plug the leaks, she could survive a day or two, but that was all. Had she found a way to contact the council drone that had shadowed the ship, she might have got away a distress call to Trezise; she might have had a chance of being rescued. But even if Cane's friends hadn't destroyed the drone to prevent anyone's overseeing their actions, she had no way of finding it, let alone sending a message. She was trapped.

So, when the *Ana Vereine* exploded, she went up on the hull to witness the pyre of her former friends and allies, and the place she had called home for the previous nine weeks.

And she saw something else, too—something completely unexpected.

An elongated star flew unsteadily out of the cloud of debris that was all that remained of the Dato Marauder. Bobbing and weaving like a drunken bird, it angled in the general direction of the tumbling nacelle. Where it wasn't burned black, its hull plating shone bright gold.

Perched on the truncated end of an access corridor that had once joined the nacelle to the main drive section of the ship, Roche watched it come. Despite the damage, she immediately recognized the ship. When it was closer, she moved out onto an exposed section and waved for attention. It changed course to rendezvous with her.

"Your suit beacon was moving," said Vri over the radio. "I followed it on the off chance you were still alive."

Her relief at hearing the Surin soldier's voice could not be measured. "I'm glad to see you, Vri."

"And I you," he said as he brought his fighter down.

What relief she had felt on finding the Surin alive was quickly tempered when she climbed aboard his ship and realized his condition.

His golden armor looked worse than the ship. He had taken two powerful shots: one to the right thigh and one in a line across the back of his head. The back of his skull was a mess of blood, bone, and fur. The tiny cockpit—with barely enough room for the two of them—stank of his blood.

Roche didn't say anything because there didn't seem to be anything to say.

"I was coming to assist you," he said, his eyes going in and out of focus as he talked. "I shouldn't have left Maii. She needed me, and I wasn't there. But I—" He coughed, winced, and tried again. "Alta took me by surprise," he said feebly. "Shot me and left me for dead." He smiled despite the pain. "When I woke up, the docks were in flames. *Esperance* was undamaged, though. It had sealed automatically and could weather worse than a mine or two, if it had to—and it did, when the drive went up. I couldn't move before then in case I was exposed. I wouldn't have stood a chance against that other ship. I *had* to wait . . ."

"You did the right thing," she reassured him.

"*Esperance* . . ." He stopped, breathing rapidly, and shut his eyes. He seemed to be running out of energy. "I give it to you, now."

Roche unsealed one of her suit gloves and touched his forehead. His skin was extremely cold, but she had no idea whether or not this was a bad sign for a Surin. The same ignorance struck her when she examined the instrument board in front of her. Although she had flown Surin vessels before, this was nothing like what she was used to. It had been designed to suit him, she suspected, with every screen and switch tailored for his needs, his mind. She suspected that she would be able to open the airlock if she ever had the need to, but she doubted she would be able to pilot the ship.

She wasn't about to tell him that, though.

"Thank you, Vri."

He opened his eyes briefly, but didn't see her.

"I fear," he said faintly, "that I have failed."

He died before she had a chance to say anything more.

The first thing she did was seal Vri's suit and get his body out of the pilot's seat. He had set *Esperance* on a course to nowhere; the engines were firing at a constant, gentle rate, with no apparent intention of stopping and no clear destination other than away from the nacelle. Maybe he had intended to change the settings before he died, or perhaps he had assumed that she would be able to do so herself.

Distantly, she felt embarrassed at being so helpless. With the Box she might have had a chance. Even without implants, it could have told her what to do. At the very least she would have had someone to talk to.

She played with the controls at random and managed to find the attitude jets. All that did was send the fighter into a slow tumble around its long axis and made its course even more chaotic. Fearing she would touch the wrong control completely and blow the drive core, she sat back and tried to think. The life-support seemed to be working fine, and there was no shortage of power. She could survive in the fighter longer than she would have on the nacelle, so that was an improvement. Given time, she could work out how to operate the drive or the communicator, which would improve her situation even more . . .

The one thing she *could* understand was the navigation display. The small fighter's projected course—as near as she could tell—took it through the outer edge of the ring system; she would strike the fringes of it within a day. The electrical anomalies Kajic had noted seemed to be fading, but she was still wary of them. When she wasn't puzzling over the controls, she kept her eye on the screen. What she would do if it *was* a trap, she didn't know..

Even as fatigue wore her down into a feverish creature talking to itself and weeping in fits and starts, she resisted sleeping. She was afraid of her dreams, of what she would see on closing her eyes. She didn't want to see Maii alive *or* dead: that wound was too fresh, the grief too keen. The same with Haid, and Kajic, and the Box—even Alta Ansourian and Cane. *Especially* Cane.

She had trusted him, and he had betrayed her. Put boldly, in black and white, she could accept it. As soon as she looked beneath that pronouncement, however, at the emotional consequences and potential ramifications, she saw the pain. She didn't want that. She would have the rest of her life to dwell upon it, however long that might be. If she could forget about it just for a moment, now, she would be grateful.

In the end she did sleep. Not even she could put it off forever. But there were no dreams—and for that she was grateful.

Fourteen hours after she left the nacelle, the glowing haze of the ring had expanded to fill most of her forward view. It looked like smoke: yellowish and acrid, with denser wisps almost blocking out the stars behind them. Strange, glowing sheets rippled through it at odd moments, but with little more definition than a predawn glow. She could no longer make out the plane of the ecliptic, or tell by sight alone at what angle she was approaching it. It was just there, before her, something she could neither avoid nor find any pleasure in viewing.

Once again, she regretted Sol System's lack of grandeur. If she had been about to crash into the Soul around Sciacca's World, or be electrocuted by the ion bridge snapping across the gap between Kukumat and Murukan, Palasian System's double-jovian, that would have at least been something to marvel at. But here, all she was heading for was a cloud of dust. She didn't even know what it would do to her. It might not do anything at all, if it was thin enough. Even if it was as dense as the average planetary ring, the most the *Esperance* would suffer as it passed through the cloud was some wear on its ablative shield.

That was exactly what it *was* suffering from when she began to hear voices.

At first she thought she was dreaming. A snatch of phrase caught her ear, apparently from somewhere behind her, followed quickly by another. Then another, and another, until the sounds came in a continuous, muddled stream. The whispers belonged to people of all ages and many different accents; most spoke galactic standard—although she could discern maybe one word in three—and some spoke in tongues she had never heard before. There were too many of them, too many fragments, for her to follow. All she could pick up were the individual flavors as they rushed by her, like ghosts in an echo park, or a half-remembered dream. They were happy, sad, angry, hurt, proud, joyous—all colors of the emotional spectrum.

When her suit's life-support kicked in, she knew she wasn't asleep. The temperature in the fighter had risen to an uncomfortable point without her noticing, so intrigued had she become with the whispering. She must have underestimated the velocity the fighter had accrued during its hours of constant thrust. Even as she studied the data, annoyed with herself for not paying attention, she could feel a slight vibration through the bulkheads. Having no knowledge of how to access the ship's diagnostic systems, she couldn't tell if the hull was being damaged by the high-speed rain of dust. All she could do was worry about it. Eventually, the ship would pass through the ring and out the other side. Or it wouldn't. The situation was as simple as that.

"Oh, for an axe . . ."

The whispered phrase caught her ear. There was a pause, filled with other whispers, then the fragment continued. The words were buried under others, but she could make them out. She knew them. She had heard them before.

"—nuclear strike from one hundred meters. I know, I know, but if it wasn't for you, I wouldn't be in this mess. Can you understand how frustrating it is to be cooped up in here with nothing to do?"

Roche listened, stunned. That was *her* voice. She remembered the conversation, but not the context.

"The sooner we're back in HQ, Box, the better . . ."

And with these words, she placed the memory: in her quarters on the *Midnight*. She had been bemoaning her lot—bored by her mission, resentful of her attachment to the Box and frustrated by Captain Klose's refusal to let her examine the mysterious life-capsule the ship had picked up in deep space. This was where it had all started.

But why was she hearing it now?

There was only one answer: *this wasn't just dust she was falling through* . . .

"Hello?" she called.

She didn't use her suit's radio. She simply spoke aloud.

"Hello, Morgan," replied a familiar voice. "I wondered when you would guess."

She wasn't as surprised as she thought she should be. "These are your voices?" she said. "Your memories?"

"The boundaries of this identity known as 'the Crescend' are difficult to define at the best of times," he said. "In my long life I have been many individuals, have spawned many components. Like the Box, for example: it came from me, and its memories now form part of me, but it was not *me*—at least not in the way you would understand the concept. All the voices you hear around you, they are memories to which I have access, and yet none of them are truly mine."

She imagined the Crescend as a spider sitting in the middle of an enormous web, reeling in experiences along silken threads, capturing and absorbing entire minds full of information. . . .

"A colorful analogy," he said. "And perhaps not totally inaccurate."

"You're reading my mind?"

"I am aware of what you are thinking," he said.

"Why can't you just give me a straight answer?"

"Because the questions you ask do not allow it."

The voice of the High Human came clearly over the babble, but the endless whispering—combined with the sound of the ship slowly being battered—was making it difficult to concentrate.

She glanced at the forward view screen, at the dust particles of the ring that were taking up the entire display now, as impenetrable as a dust storm.

"It's you, isn't it?" she said. "The ring is you. Or the other way around."

"Both, and neither. The ring is a physical construct upon which this identity is presently generated."

"A computer?" said Roche, lifting her voice unnecessarily to be heard above the growing noise.

"The term is grossly inadequate," he said with no hint of condescension. "It is composed of the mass of an entire solar system liberated and allowed to interact as computational components: every atom of an ever-changing matrix circling—and powered by—the system's sun. A sun which, half a million years ago, birthed the species from which we sprang."

It was hard not to be impressed by the sheer scale of what the Crescend was describing. As camouflage, it was perfect: of everyone she had met, only the Heresiarch had any serious idea that the ring might be more than it seemed. The unsuspected truth explained the odd electrical impulses, and the navigational hazard the ring occasionally posed: even something as nebulous and innocent-looking as a cloud of dust could be disturbed by passing ships and would possess the means to defend itself.

But this wasn't all he was telling her. *Birthed*, he had said.

"That's why we're here," she said. "You, and everyone. Sol System is where it all began."

"It may not be much to look at anymore," he said, "but yes, this is where it all began. For those who know, the system is something of a symbol. Not a shrine; one's origins are not to be worshipped. Sol System just *is*, and that is enough."

"But what happened to the planets?" One of them, she assumed, must have been Humanity's homeworld.

"That is a long story, Morgan," he said. "Too long for now."

"You won't tell me?"

"There isn't time," he said. "You haven't that much left."

"So I am going to die?"

"Do you *want* to die?"

Another evasive answer. Before she could respond, however, the ship lurched violently, tossing her from side to side in her seat.

When the ship settled again, she said: "Can you get me out of here? Can you fix the fighter so I can use it and get back to the *Phlegethon*? If it hasn't already been destroyed, that is."

"Far from it, Morgan. The council has experienced good fortune since the enemy became aware of your decision. No longer required to concentrate their efforts on one location—in order to draw you out, to force you to make a decision, and to influence what that decision would be—many of their number have retreated from the system and begun the long journey home. To their *hosts'* homes, I should say. As the war in Sol System winds down, preparations for the war throughout the galaxy are heating up. We sit on the brink of a new age, Morgan: today, the peaceful domination of Humanity, founded on near-genocide; tomorrow, the battlefield of justice, in whose days lives will be lost and civilizations will fall, and which might, ultimately, lead to a more balanced future."

"Is that what you want, then?" Roche felt the same confusion about his motives that she had the first time she and the High Human had talked. "I still don't know whether you believe I made the right decision or not."

"Does my opinion matter?"

"Of course it does!"

"If I tell you that you made the right decision, I will be accused of wanting war. If I tell you that you made the wrong decision, I will be accused of wanting to commit genocide upon the enemy."

Roche fell quiet for a while.

"I just wish there had been another alternative." Her words were soft and low, barely audible above the whispers that filled the space around her.

If the Crescend had heard, he didn't answer.

The temperature continued to rise, along with the turbulence, and the voices were louder, harder to think through. A golden haze tinged the air around her; the walls of the ship themselves seemed to glow.

"Tell me about your final conversation with Adoni Cane," the Crescend said.

"What? *Why?*" She was irritated that the Crescend seemed to be trying to distract her rather than doing anything to actually help her.

"Did he reveal anything to you that you didn't already know about him?"

"Like the fact that he's an alien, perhaps?"

There was a sound like a sigh. "He said this?"

"He said Humanity wiped out his creators and took over the galaxy. Did you know about this?"

"We suspected," the Crescend said. "Few records exist from

that time, and only the oldest memories of the most inward-seeking of my Caste speak of such events, but we have always known of another race that preceded ours—which may have even co-existed with us for a time. It seemed likely that it was destroyed in the war about which we had also heard rumors. The possibility also existed that these two suspicions were linked to the emergence of the enemy and their convergence on Sol System. Linking all three was the most elegant solution."

"That explains why we couldn't find his parent Caste," Roche said. "He never had one, did he? It was a waste of time looking."

"Absence of evidence is not evidence of absence, Morgan—as you yourself recently said. We needed confirmation before we could be sure."

She suspected he was still trying to distract her, but she didn't care. She needed the distraction to take her mind from the sounds of the ship being bombarded by the dust outside.

"So who were they?" she said loudly. "Where did they come from?"

"They are referred to only by euphemism." The Crescend's voice never seemed to rise in pitch despite the ever-increasing noise within the cockpit. "And then most frequently as 'the Concinnity.' Where they originated, however, remains a mystery."

"Cane said that they're a group mind, and that they plan to resurrect the species from the data in their introns."

"It was always thought unlikely that revenge was the only thing on their agenda," the Crescend said. "Resurrection of the species was always considered a possibility."

"What are you going to do about it if they do?"

"What we have always done: observe."

"You'll let it happen?"

"It is in accordance with your decision, Morgan."

"But my decision was made with the understanding that they were *Human*! That if they wiped us out, there would still be Humans left, even if it was *them*!"

"There will always be Humans left," the Crescend assured her. "They will never destroy the High Caste. At least not until they have themselves evolved to our level, in their own way. And numerous Low Castes will survive too. The worst-case scenario would be that the mundanes will be wiped out, and then only for a time. In the enemy's eyes, it would even the score; in our eyes, it changes little."

Roche pondered this as best she could through the racket. It was true. As important as it seemed to her, the activities of the mundanes didn't amount to much in the big scheme of things. The High Humans were doing the real work, whatever it was, on a galactic scale. The mundanes just filled in the gaps, gave their superiors something to watch in their spare time. . . .

The cockpit's life-support suddenly failed, sending a blast of hot air into her face. She made sure her suit was completely sealed, then shut her eyes. Clutching the arms of the crash-couch, she rode out the turbulence, not knowing how much longer it would last and, irrationally, afraid that it might never stop.

"*Would* you change your mind?" The Crescend's voice was clear and calm in her helmet. "Knowing what you now know, do you think you made the wrong decision?"

She kept her eyes closed and fought down the fear by focusing on his question. "I don't think so," she said. "Cane and his race deserved at least a fighting chance. I just wish I hadn't been so stupid."

"In what sense?"

"Cane told me he was Human, and I believed him!"

"He never said that, Morgan."

"Yes he did," she said. "After Palasian System, when we woke him from that coma Linegar Rufo put him in. He tapped out a message in code—!"

"Yes, but that's not what he said," said the Crescend. "His exact words were: 'I am as Human as you are.' "

Her eyes opened, as if upon a realization she had been blinded to.

"What are you saying?" she asked. "That I'm not Human?"

"You are as Human as I am, Morgan. As Human as Cane. Even as Human as the Box, if you like," he said. "That's the way you were made."

She wanted to recoil from what the Crescend was saying, but she was trapped in her suit, in a disintegrating fighter. She had nowhere to hide from the words, no way to avoid them. All she could do was listen to him.

"The High Caste needed someone to make a decision it was not capable of making—or was not prepared to make. But we could hardly trust such a judgment to someone lacking the nec-

essary attributes. Since mundanes are inherently unreliable, and
since the person we required simply did not exist, we decided
to make one. We made *you*, Morgan."

She shook her head. "*Why?*"

"You are determined and not easily swayed. You see all sides
of a dispute and try to be fair. You have a keen sense of duty,
on many levels. You are honorable, and will not shirk from the
truth. You may not see yourself as such, Morgan, for we also
gave you a sense of humility, but you are a good person. A good
Human. If the fate of the mundanes was to rest in your hands,
it was important for you to be so.

"On the other hand, you needed access to information and
capabilities beyond the access of a normal mundane—especially
once the time came to bring you face to face with the enemy,
in the form of Adoni Cane—so my relationship with the Commonwealth of Empires was exploited to allow the Box to fall
into your hands.

"The only thing that set you apart from the mundanes around
you was your ability to detect the enemy, and even that was limited. You were, to all intents and purposes, an ordinary person,
but one fashioned in such a way that you would not break under
extraordinary circumstances. That was our gift to you, Morgan—
one which has served you in good stead these last few weeks."

"How much of me . . . ?" She couldn't finish the sentence.
Her mind was full of conflicting images, thoughts, and feelings.
Everything seemed to be shaking, falling apart around her.

"I can assure you that you are as real as anyone."

"Ascensio—the orphanage—?"

"Real memories," he said. "Taken from someone else."

She closed her eyes. "Bodh Gaya?"

"Your own experiences. Everything from your arrival at the
Military College was you. But that makes those memories no
more 'real' to you than the others. They are all yours, Morgan.
They all contribute to who *you* are."

She thought of the parents she had hoped to find one day,
and whom she had forgotten upon joining COE Intelligence. She
remembered her friends in the orphanage, and the conditions that
had led her to flee her home planet. She saw again, as clearly
as though it happened only yesterday, the flash of the COEI
Gegenschein's engines as it broke orbit and headed for her new
home, her new future.

All hers.

All *faked*.

A shrieking of tortured metal rose around her, as though the ship were tearing up.

"I've never had any choice, have I?" She raised her voice to be heard over the noise, even though she knew the Crescend could read her mind just as easily as it ever had.

"Of course you have, Morgan. That was the whole point."

"But you made me in order to do something. There was no way I could avoid that. There's no way you would've let me!"

"Perhaps not, but—"

"And could I have avoided all of *this*?" She saw Maii's body, the *Ana Vereine*'s pyre, the golden glow of the cockpit around her. "Was I always intended to end up *here*?"

"That question is irrelevant," said the Crescend. "You are here now, and the 'now' is all that matters."

A siren wailed in her ears.

"Why are you bothering to talk to me at all?" she said angrily. "Why ask me about Cane? Why not just lift the information from my memories? What is it you are after? You want me to absolve you for what you've done? Is that it?"

"I have no need of absolution, Morgan. I have no ulterior motives, either. Your role in this phase of the war is truly finished."

"So now I am being thrown out with the trash?" she shouted. "Is that it?"

"You are not a robot, Morgan," the Crescend said.

"But I'm not *real*!"

"You may find it difficult to accept, but you are as genuine a being as anyone else you have met. You have mind, you have will, and you have character. Where your body actually came from is irrelevant."

"Do you expect me to accept that?"

"In time, I think you will."

"But I don't *have* time," she said. "The fighter's burning up!"

"Yes," the Crescend said with no suggestion of remorse. "It is. In fact, you have less than a minute before it disintegrates completely."

She fought down a surge of panic, resisted the tears pressing at the backs of her eyes.

"I'm frightened," she said, the words both a whisper and a sigh.

The Crescend said nothing.

She closed her eyes again, bracing herself as the fighter began to shake violently. The sound of voices was drowned out by the rattling and creaking of the ship. She thought she might be screaming, but she could hear nothing at all over the noise. She *was* sound: sound and movement: movement and pain: pain and—

With a burst of heat, everything went silent.

Epilogue

There was no pain; there was no grief. There was only the darkness drawing her in, consuming her. She didn't resist the warm sensation; she allowed herself to be taken.

<That's it, Morgan. Just accept.>

The familiar voice of the Crescend filled her with a strange relief. But he sounded different somehow. Closer—almost as though the words were emanating from herself.

<The fighter . . .> she said, as if remembering something from long ago. <It . . . burned up?>

<Yes, Morgan. It did.>

She hesitated for a moment. <I'm dead?> she said.

<How could that be possible if you are speaking to me now?>

<So I'm alive, then?>

The Crescend didn't respond, and an interminable silence followed. She felt something approximating panic wash over her, soaking the empty dark around her.

<Tell me!> Her voice resounded through the void. <Am I *alive*?>

Another silence followed before the Crescend spoke again.

<Define 'alive,' Morgan.>

APPENDIX

THE ORIGINS OF HUMANITY
AN OPEN-ENDED QUESTION.

(by Provost Rejuben Tade, extracted from his welcoming
address to the Guild of Xenoarchaeologists' 13,333rd
Decannual Intake Expo.)

It is said that unless you know where you started, it is difficult
to tell where you are heading. You can plot your course with as
much precision as you like; you can map vectors, measure velocity and distance to the nth degree, but without those vital initial coordinates, you might as well be flying blind.

The authors of this axiom were, of course, referring to navigation on land or sea, or even in space. But why should it not
be equally applicable to Humanity as a whole?

Anyone with an education would know that the origins of our
species are clouded in mystery, buried under the obfuscating
weight of five hundred millennia. Half a million years: that's an
awful lot of dust. And if we look closely at this dust, we can
make out lumps and bumps along the surface which suggest things
that *might* be buried there. But unless we actually brush away
these layers of dust, we would never know exactly what lies beneath. When we do, sometimes we find what we imagined we

would; other times we find nothing at all. Most of the time, though, we simply reveal new landscapes of dust which seem to bear little relation to the ones above and which might, too, reveal nothing about what remains hidden beneath.

The mystery of the origins of Humanity is one known to all, although appreciated by few. Any individual fortunate enough to resolve this mystery would not so much earn himself or herself a footnote in some dusty xenoarchaeological journal, as guarantee themselves a place among the greats of science. For that person will not only return to us the sense of place, of identity, that has been denied us these long centuries, but will also thereby enable us—to return to our original metaphor—to know where we, as a species, are going. Not in the sense that evolution, social or physical, has a "destination" or a "purpose" in "mind," but in the sense that changes we do see occurring could finally be measured against a single fixed reference point—the elusive "Alpha Point" (as some scholars refer to it). Without this point, it is inevitable that any observations we make will be corrupted by our own subjective viewpoints, and any objectives we aspire toward will be difficult to achieve.

Some argue that we aren't flying blind at all, that the question of Humanity's origins has already been answered. Such people usually, in my experience, possess barely enough knowledge on the subject to have formed an opinion but a profound insufficiency to prove that opinion to anyone's satisfaction but their own. Exponents of the Out-of-Sol theory spring immediately to mind, along with their archrivals, the Multiple-Genesis-ites. Where they all fall down is in the assumption that we *can* know such things, that the evidence exists and has been misinterpreted or deliberately suppressed. The truth is in fact that information, once set loose in the massive information flows of the galaxy, is very difficult to contain—especially if it is of such revolutionary nature, and even more especially if it is completely verifiable. Were such evidence to exist, more people would know about it in an hour than will ever hear this speech in my lifetime.

In short, conclusive evidence simply does not exist.

So let's look at what we *do* know . . .

Roughly five hundred thousand years ago, probably slightly longer, at least four Primordial Castes colonized a large number of systems in a migration we would today call an "outsweep." This region of space contains several hundred stars, including

Sol, and is commonly referred to in old records as the Exordium Worlds; we suspect all were visited around the same time, making it difficult to isolate one as a definite home system. Of course, this difficulty might reflect the limitations inherent in our only available method of dating this expansion. In the absence of actual ruins of any kind, only the remnants of the anchor-point network established at this time gives us any kind of date at all, and even that is uncertain after so long.

To explain why this is uncertain, I always fall back on an old fishing metaphor. I imagine myself casting a line into a pond. On the end of my line is a sinker. As the sinker falls into the water, it creates a disturbance. Ripples spread out from the disturbance with decreasing magnitude until all trace of the disturbance is gone. But the line remains, and it too may create disturbances. My hand may vibrate, or I might tug the rod to attract a fish.

Now, if the line is the crack in space that allows us to break through to hyperspace, and the sinker is the shock that created the hole in the first place, and the surface of the pond is space itself, then the ripples are the echoes not only of the anchor point's creation but of its continued use. Although these ripples in space do not propagate the same way as ripples in water—tending to radiate in the temporal dimensions rather than those of space, forming localized distortions often and misleadingly referred to as standing waves—they are frequently used as navigational aides, or to find an anchor that has disappeared from charts. Xenoarchaeologists can use these ripples too, since their amplitude decreases at a known rate. One can tell at a glance whether an anchor point is a thousand years old, or ten thousand, or if it was created yesterday. That much is very simple.

The difficulty arises when an anchor point is more than three hundred thousand years old, or has not been used regularly for half that time. The amplitude of the ripples may decrease to the point where they are indistinguishable from the background fluctuations of the universe. While we can still detect ripples from the ancient anchors among the Exordium Worlds, we are unable to tell whether the decrease has come about because of age or disuse. If the former, they might be eight hundred thousand years or more old; if the latter, they might be as young as four hundred and fifty thousand. All we can say with any certainty is that each and every one of the anchors in this area was created around the same time—suggesting that hyperspace technology was only developed *after* the region was colonized.

We do not know where this technology came from or who developed it, but we know roughly when it occurred. Four hundred and twenty thousand years ago, Humanity suddenly boiled out of the Exordium Worlds in an outsweep known as the Second Expansion. This surge is much easier to account for. Lines of datable anchor points expand radially from the region, riding on the back of faster-than-light technology and forming the skeletal remains of vast trade routes that literally spanned the galaxy. Humanity, initially in the form of the four known Primordial Castes, spread like ink through water from planet to planet, star to star, jumping across gulfs previously unimaginable and daring even to send probes out of the galaxy itself—probes that have not as yet reached any of their destinations. What they will see, you and I will probably never know. Only the High Caste—the first members of which Transcended during this time—have that possibility open to them.

Some records paint this Second Expansion as a time of great conflict for Humanity. Some researchers suggest that there might have been one single, mighty war, or there might have been innumerable smaller conflicts. Certainly it was a time of tremendous change, during which Humanity began the speciation that has led to such diversity and richness today. Legends were founded and, almost as quickly, forgotten. We will never know exactly what happened in those times, and for that very reason we will never tire of asking the questions.

Inevitably, as the Second Expansion slowed, the centers of power shifted away from the Exordium Worlds to the core. The ancient shipping routes shifted too, until they settled into the familiar pattern we now call the Great Lanes. This almost certainly happened around three hundred thousand years ago—although, oddly enough, we cannot independently verify precisely when. The Lanes have been used almost continuously since their creation, and have been frequently re-created, so their ripples show few signs of natural aging. That hasn't stopped people trying to date them, of course, but the results are inconsistent and anomalous. One research group actually dated a pivotal Middle Reach anchor point to be in excess of nine hundred thousand years old— a conclusion which is patently not tenable, inasmuch as it is far older than Humanity itself.

But this is a small mystery, usually raised to trigger the what-if instinct in all of us. The fact remains that the vast proportion of evidence is in favor of the story as I have told it: that Humanity expanded outward from a single system only slowly at first, then much more rapidly when it discovered anchor point technology—changing as it went. And so we continue to change today, even though expansion halted long ago, with the colonization of the entire galaxy. The only new territories we can dream about are those across the intergalactic gulfs or within our own minds. Many observers note that since the most advanced of Humans always seem to choose the latter path, perhaps that says something about the long-term possibilities for physical expansion. Others point out that High Humans may indeed have found a way to cross the gulfs, but have either not yet returned or choose simply to keep their discoveries a secret.

Whichever way one looks at it, the question remains: Humanity has most likely not reached the end-point of its evolution, and where that end-point *might* be depends very much on its beginning. Has Humanity always been so changeable, or so insular at its higher reaches? Is the present ratio of High Humans to mundanes, which has been constant for hundreds of thousands of years, one we can assume indefinitely? Or are we just going through a phase—one that might change with little or no warning, plunging the galaxy into chaos once more?

Certainly, attempting to plot trends in the behavior of Humans throughout the last four hundred thousand years has been a thankless task. Castes tend to develop in isolation, usually from a Low form that has itself devolved some time in the past, occasionally with the help of a benefactor's biotechnology. Newly vitalized, the Caste then undergoes a period of expansion, sometimes fragmenting as it goes, leaving pockets of itself behind that might in turn one day also expand, depending on the Caste's ambition or its Batelin Limit. At the same time, many other Castes are behaving similarly, and these expansive types may meet and overlap, or meet and clash, or meet and rebound, depending on their compatibility. The possibilities for trade and conflict are endless, as attested to by the prevalence of the Commerce Artel throughout all reaches of the galaxy.

Other Castes are no longer expansive, having reached the peak of their development, and preparing—whether they know it or not—to change into something new. Lots of Castes advance, devolve, then rise again thinking they're the first to do so; legends and ancient folk tales tell of angels and the like, all metaphors for former glory days that goad them on, upward again. Some Castes disappear, of course, destroyed by war or technological suicide or absorbed by neighbors. Others never devolve, just go on to greatness, Transcending at the peak of their rise to become immortals of a type we can barely comprehend—secretive and elusive, and capable of understanding beyond our wildest imaginings.

Those who don't devolve, disappear, or Transcend, achieve homeostasis in the mundane and remain that way indefinitely. Only the names of their empires change, rising and falling like the vibrations in a cosmic string. The Pristines are most notable among these types. The ancient remnants of Primordial Humanity are reluctant to change, but tolerate it in others—for perhaps that is the way it must be, since to grow, one must change. But to change is to risk devolution, and that risk is a great one.

Just one Caste in ten thousand Transcends. The rest devolve or disappear. One school of thought says that the handful of Castes that achieve homeostasis, apart from the Pristine, might only be delaying inevitable decline. But we cannot be certain of this without greater knowledge of our origins. Perhaps Humanity has always been like this, and will never change.

Here we return to our original question: how can we know where we will end up if we don't know where we began? For an example of how the answer to this might have very real ramifications for all of us, one has only to ask: why *has* the ratio of High to mundane Humans been so constant? It might very well be a natural state for our race, as most people assume—but it might *not* be just as easily. And if not, it can tip either way, in favor of either the High Caste or the mundanes. We know that the ratio changed from no High Humans at all to a relatively fixed proportion in the early days of the galaxy, suggesting that Human nature did favor the High Caste at one point. If that trend had continued, we would not exist today: the galaxy would be populated only by the members of the High Caste, everyone else having devolved or Transcended at a rate too great for mundane stocks to replenish themselves. Clearly this has not happened— but *why* not? What shifted the balance away from the High Caste?

The most obvious possibility is that there is a natural rate of accretion of which we were not previously aware. The effects of a High Caste death-rate would only become visible after the initial members began to age, and there are indeed High Caste deaths on record. But these are exceedingly rare, and it is generally doubted that they would even brake the initial expansion of the High Caste, let alone halt it entirely. So what else is going on? Perhaps High Humans don't need to die before they need to be replaced: perhaps being old and insular is enough. After all, we are only aware of *active* High Humans; there may be many more who choose not to communicate with anyone, or who have entered a state of prolonged hibernation, or have undergone transformation to another plane of being we cannot imagine.

Whatever the truth, this issue raises a disturbing possibility: that the High Caste maintains the ratio artificially, by either limiting its numbers somehow or maintaining an artificially high rate of mundane replenishment. The latter, of course, might simply be to restock its own numbers—for if High Caste expansion continued unchecked and there were no mundanes left, where would future members come from? Or it might be to give them something to watch, just as some mundane and Low Castes keep inferior species as pets.

Is this our ultimate fate, then, to amuse, or to act as breeding stock for new High Humans? We will never know until we learn the truth about our origins. And to do *that*, we need more data.

This is where you come in. As alumni from institutions all over the galaxy taking the bold leap of faith into the rarefied air of xenoarchaeology, your job is to probe deep into these questions and to expose the truth. Or if not the truth, then a fragment of it. Or if not even a fragment of the truth, then another question for someone else to answer. This process is ongoing, and will outlast me just as it has outlasted two hundred thirty-seven Provosts before me. It will probably outlast you, too, and the ones who follow you. Perhaps future xenoarchaeologists will look back on our work with an indulgent smile for our ignorance—or perhaps they will regard our work as cornerstones in the great edifice of understanding under constant construction. I cannot say which will be the case, just as my predecessors did not know. All I *can* say is that these questions are worth asking, even if we can never answer them. Not knowing where we came from does not stop us from moving on—and that is perhaps the most important thing about our race that has brought us to where we are today, wherever that is. We are not inclined to stay still.

Once, millions of years in the past, a small, barely bipedal creature rose up on its hind legs and squinted at the stars above. Well, we own those stars now, and we're still moving. Only time will tell where we will ultimately end up. . . .

GLOSSARY

A-14 Higher Collaboration Network: an amalgamation of core-based High Caste members whose intentions include attempting to establish an objective frame of reference with respect to Humanity's occupation of the galaxy. *The Objective Reference Calendar* is one result of this work.

A-P cannon: a weapon that fires accelerated particles of various types. Common on spacefaring warships.

Absenger, Burne: chief liaison officer, COE Armada.

adytum: Skehan Heterodox term for the control room of a consistory vessel.

Alpha Aurigae: an ancient system, the precise location of which is presently unknown.

Alpha Point: a name for the single point in time and space from which some xenoarchaeologists surmise Humanity evolved.

Ana Vereine, IND: the first of a new class of warships—the Marauder—manufactured by the Dato Bloc as part of the Andermahr Experiment. Its design incorporates a captain surgically interfaced with the ship. Once part of the Ethnarch's Military Presidium, it is now an independent vessel registered to Morgan Roche.

anchor drive: the usual means of crossing interstellar space, but by no means the only one (see **slow-jump**). Indeed, the anchor method has undergone several radical redesigns over time; current technology is rated at 49th-generation.

anchor points: regions of "weakened" space from which translation to and from hyperspace is both easier and less energy-expensive; jumps from anchor points are therefore of a greater range than from "normal" space and usually terminate in another anchor point. They are typically located near inhabited systems (but far enough away to avoid distortion by background gravitational effects) or in locations in deep space which are considered strategically important. There are approximately ten thousand million anchor points currently in existence—one for roughly every ten stars, scattered across the galaxy.

Andermahr Experiment: a covert project specializing in cybernetic interfaces designed to allow mind and machine to merge. Founded by Ataman Ana Vereine, who desired captains that were as much a part of their ships as was the anchor drive—an integral, reliable system rather than a flesh and blood afterthought. Continued in secret until the Ataman Theocracy emerged from the COE as the Dato Bloc. Culminated in the DBMP *Ana Vereine*, the first Marauder-class warship, with Uri Kajic its captain.

Ansourian, Alta: only child of Atul Ansourian.

Ansourian, Atul: adviser and self-styled *éminence grise* to the administer of Perdue Habitat, Inderdeep Jans.

Apostle: a Hurn vessel in the service of the Disciples of Evergence.

Aquareii: a High Human renowned for being the most powerful member of the Interventionist faction.

Armada: see **COE Armada**.

Ascensio: the homeworld of Morgan Roche.

Asha: the single, warlike deity of the main Kesh religion.

Ataman Theocracy: a tightly knit empire that existed as an independent entity until its absorption into the COE after the Second Ataman War in '442 EN. After several centuries, it eventually seceded as the Dato Bloc ('837 EN).

AVS-38 & AVS-44: two of the *Ana Vereine*'s large contingent of scutters.

Basigo: a Caste not native to the COE region.

Batelin Limit: the ceiling above which the complexity of a nation exceeds the biological capabilities of the individuals inhabiting it. In the case of the Pristine Caste, the value of the Batelin Limit is approximately three and half thousand systems.

Black Box: the generic term for an AI. Usually abbreviated to "Box."

Bodh Gaya: former capital system of the COE and the Dominion. Its second moon houses the Military College of the COE Armada.

Box, the: an AI commissioned by COE Intelligence. Its binary identification number (JW111101000) is one digit longer than normal, indicating its unique status. Created by the High Human known as the Crescend, the Box is designed to infiltrate and subvert all available systems, thereby increasing its own processing powers until, at its most powerful, it resembles its creator. Once thought to be contained within a small black valise, it is now known to inhabit the cells of Morgan Roche.

Buk, Enver: the COE Eupatrid prior to Felix Gastel.

Calendar: the galactic standard timekeeping method consists of: 100 seconds per minute, 100 minutes per hour, 20 hours per day, 10 days per week, 4 weeks (40 days) per month, 10 months (400 days) per year. All dates are expressed in the form of year (usually abbreviated to the last three digits, i.e. '397), month, and day from the *Ex Nihilo* reference point. See also **Objective Reference Calendar**.

Cane, Adoni: the occupant of an unidentified life-support capsule recovered by the COEA *Midnight* near Ivy Green Station anchor point while en route to Sciacca's World. A genetically modified combat clone designed to mimic a Pristine Human, his origins are known not to lie with the Sol Apotheosis Movement, although who did create him, and many others like him, remains a mystery.

Cane, Adoni: field admiral, Old Earth Advance Guard; received a military Star for extraordinary acts of valor against the enemy.

Castes: following the speciation of the Human race, numerous Castes have proliferated across the galaxy. These Castes are too numerous to list, but they can be classified into three broad groups: High, Low, and mundane (which includes Pristine and

Exotic). There are seven predominant Exotic Castes to be found in the region surrounding the COE: Eckandar, Hurn, Kesh, Mbata, Olmahoi, and Surin.

Catiph: a High Human.

Ceyle's Hub: former home of Advocate Janil Coriett.

Chase, Auberon: head of COE Intelligence.

Clarke Cylinder: an ancient habitat.

COE: see **Commonwealth of Empires.**

COE Armada, the: the combined armed forces of the COE, responsible for external security. Active soldiers are referred to as Marines.

COE Enforcement: the policing body responsible for security and information gathering within the COE. Field agents are referred to as Enforcers.

COE High Equity Court: the department responsible for inter-system justice within the COE. Its usual purpose is to settle territorial disputes.

COE Intelligence: the body responsible for information gathering outside the COE. Originally and still nominally a subdepartment of the Armada, but an independent body in practice.

COE Intelligence HQ: the command center of COE Intelligence, a large, independent station located in deep space near the heart of the Commonwealth.

COE Military College: the main training institution of COE Armada personnel; situated on the second moon of Bodh Gaya.

COEA: COE Armada vessel identification prefix.

COEI: COE Intelligence vessel identification prefix.

Commerce Artel: a galaxy-wide organization devoted to initiating and coordinating trade between Castes and governments that might otherwise have no contact. It prides itself on remaining aloof from political conflict yet has some strict behavioral standards to which it expects its customers to adhere (such as the Warfare Protocol). Structurally, it is divided into chapters managed by indigenous Caste-members with only loose control from above. It has strong links, locally, with the Eckandar Trade Axis.

Commonwealth of Empires: often abbreviated to COE or Commonwealth. A relatively ancient Pristine nation currently in its 40th millennium of nominal existence—"nominal" in that the membership of the COE is fluid by nature, with provinces joining and seceding on a regular basis. It has had many different capitals and its borders have changed radically over the centuries. Indeed, it has drifted with time, and now occupies territories quite remote from its original location. One thousand inhabited systems currently fall under its aegis, and another three thousand uninhabited systems have been annexed. It is ruled by a democratically elected Eupatrid and a council of representatives who, when united, wield supreme executive power. Its security departments include Intelligence, Armada, and Enforcement.

Coriett, Janil: an advocate formerly of Ceyle's Hub, currently employed in Environment Control of the SHCV *Phlegethon*.

Crescend, the: a High Human of some note and great history. His time of Transcendence is not recorded. Little is known about him, beyond the facts that he is the founder and overseer of Trinity, an ally of the COE, and a key supporter of the Interventionist movement. He is assumed to be a singular entity simply because the first person singular is his pronoun of choice.

crypt: the Skehan Heterodox term for the engineering rooms of a consistory vessel.

Dark Stressor, HHAB: a compact habitat of ill-repute, known to be a gathering-point for mercenaries.

Dato Bloc: an independent nation founded on the ruins of the Ataman Theocracy that recently broke free of the COE. Although not hierocratic in nature, the Ethnarch exerts a strict rule. Its security departments include the Ethnarch's Military Presidium and the Espionage Corps.

Daybreak, COEI: a courier vessel belonging to COE Intelligence.

DBMP: vessel identification prefix for the Ethnarch's Military Presidium.

De Bruyn, Page: former head of Strategy, COE Intelligence.

Disciples of Evergence: a covert organization with Hurn connections devoted to serving the enemy.

disrupters: see **hyperspace disrupters.**

Dreher, Ralf: a name from ancient records connected to the enemy.

Drys: a caste not indigenous to the COE region.

E-shield: an electromagnetic barrier designed to ward off particle and energy weapons. Used mainly by medium-to-large spacefaring vessels.

Eckandar: (**Eckandi**, adj & sing. n): a Caste flourishing in the regions surrounding the COE. Its members are typified by their slight size, gray skin, bald scalps, and unusual eyes. They are a gregarious Caste, preferring trade and communication over conquest. They are also well-advanced in genetic science. Their past stretches back beyond that of the COE, although they lack the continuity of history that strong nationhood often provides. Their sole uniting body is the Eckandar Trade Axis.

Eckandar Trade Axis: the main society of the Eckandi Caste, devoted, much like the Commerce Artel (with which it has close ties), to facilitating free and nondiscriminatory trade with and between the COE and its neighbors.

Egarr, Gurion: senior councilor to Inderdeep Jans.

EN: see *Ex Nihilo.*

enemy: Interim Emergency Pristine Council shorthand for the clone warriors.

Enforcement: see **COE Enforcement.**

Enforcer: see **COE Enforcement.**

epsense: an ability encompassing telepathy and empathy. The ritual training of epsense adepts generally takes decades and incorporates elements of sensory deprivation. Note: telekinesis and precognition are not covered by epsense and are assumed to be nonexistent. Skilled utilizers of epsense are referred to as **epsense adepts** or **reaves.**

Erojen: a town on an outpost far from the heart of the Surin domain.

Esperance, **SAS:** the fighter piloted by Defender-of-Harmony Vri.

Espionage Corps: see **Dato Bloc.**

Espire-Mavrodis Coalition: one of the IEPC's major allies.

Essai: home of the Surin Agora.

Ethnarch: the title of the leader of the Dato Bloc.

Ethnarch's Military Presidium: see **Dato Bloc.**

Eupatrid: the title of the chief executive officer of the COE.

Ex Nihilo: refers to the date upon which the COE is believed to have been founded. Evidence exists to cast doubt upon the accuracy or relevance of this date—notably the fact the Commonwealth as a single body did not exist at all between the 13th and 15th millennia—but the date remains as a reference point. Usually abbreviated to EN.

Exordium Worlds: the region first colonized by the Primordial Castes.

Exotic: any mundane Caste that differs physiologically from the Pristine. There are a vast number of Exotic Castes, and, although no one type of Exotic comes close to outnumbering Pristine Humans, the Exotics as a whole mass far greater than Pristines alone.

fane: the Skehan Heterodox term for a ship's bridge.
Far Reaches: the name of the outermost fringes of the Outer Arms.
Fathehi Consulate: a habitat sent to Sol System by a Caste originating on the far side of the galaxy.
flicker-bombs: devices used in space warfare to attack an enemy vessel. Employing the fact that small masses (under a few kilograms) can slow-jump a small distance within a gravity well, these missiles skip in and out of space on their way to their target, which, it is hoped, they will materialize within, causing massive amounts of damage. They are easily deflected by hypershields, however, which form a barrier in hyperspace that no such weapon can cross.
40th millennium: the current millennium in the history of the COE. See *Ex Nihilo*.

Gastel, Felix: the current Eupatrid of the COE.
Gegenschein, COEI: a cruiser owned by COE Intelligence.
God's Monkey, **HIC:** a small vessel operated by the Disciples of Evergence.
Great Lanes: the network of shipping routes delineated by anchor points across the galaxy.
grayboots: see **Olmahoi retribution squad.**
Ground Corps: a military body referred to in ancient records.
Guild of Xenoarchaeologists: (GOX) an ancient and highly regarded professional organization of xenoarchaeologists.
Guo Sodality: an organization from the Middle Reaches dedicated to the study and training of epsense adepts.
Guidon Habitat: sibling-habitat to Perdue Habitat.

H'si F'ta: a Caste known to the IEPC.
Haid, Ameidio: former transportee, Sciacca Penal Colony, and ex-mercenary.
Heidik, Jelena: the name by which the clone warrior responsible for the destruction of Palasian System identified herself.

Heidik, Jelena: in ancient times, a general and recipient of a Mars St. Selwyn Medal for valor against the enemy in Alpha Aurigae.

Hek'm: the Olmahoi Caste homeworld.

Heresiarch: Skehan Heterodox name for the commanding officer of a consistory vessel.

High Humans (or **High Castes**): Superior intelligences that have evolved (Transcended) from the mundane. Enormously long-lived and farseeing, they concentrate on issues quite removed from the rest of the galaxy; indeed, due to their enormous scale, they are the only beings capable of comprehending the galaxy in its entirety. They generally leave mundanes alone, to let them progress (and, ultimately, to Transcend) in their own time. See **Castes** and **Transcendence.**

High Equity Court: see **COE High Equity Court.**

Hurn: a Caste typified by ritual and complexity. In appearance they are lean and muscular, averaging greater than Pristine height. They are predisposed toward music and mathematics. Socially they prefer oligarchies with a baroque middle class.

Hutton-Luu System: a much-disputed system of the COE near its border with the Dato Bloc. See **Sciacca's World.**

hypershield: a barrier erected in hyperspace to deflect or inhibit the passage of anything traveling by that medium. Commonly used as a prophylactic against hyperspace weapons. Hypershields operate under a maximum volume constraint: i.e. they will only operate as intended under two thousand cubic kilometers.

hyperspace disrupters: a form of hypershield which actively combats incoming hyperspace weapons, such as flicker-bombs. Unlike anchor points, which "weaken" space, disrupters do the opposite, making it more difficult for anything nearby to emerge from hyperspace.

i-Hurn Uprising: a civil dispute which broke out between two rival factions of the Hurn Caste.

IEPC: see **Interim Emergency Pristine Council.**

imaret: a Surin single-passenger fighter.

Imi: a system in which Ameidio Haid once worked.

IND: independent vessel identification prefix.

Intelligence: see **COE Intelligence.**

Interim Emergency Pristine Council: (IEPC) an organization that exists only in times of greatest duress for the Pristine Caste. With no fewer than thirty nations required to call it into being, it exists only so long as the threat remains.

Interventionism: a movement among High Humans—and some mundanes—that advocates closer links between High and mundane Castes. See **The Crescend.**

irikeii: one of very few Olmahoi "sound-thoughts" which can be equated with audible words; often translated as *unnamed* or *unnameable*.

Jans, Ehud: Inderdeep Jans's father and the previous administer of Perdue Habitat.

Jans, Eir: biological daughter of Ehud Jans.

Jans, Inderdeep: administer of Perdue Habitat.

Ju Mandate, Second: a government represented by Assistant Vice Primate Rey Nemeth.

JW111101000: see **Box, the.**

Kajic, Uri: former captain, DBMP *Ana Vereine*, physically bonded to his ship.

Katajalin Serai: a loose collection of trade and security vessels.

Ken'an: a mercenary operating from the habitat *Dark Stressor*.

Kesh: the most primal of the local Castes. The Kesh are typically warlike and predisposed toward violence. In appearance, they tend to be larger than the Pristine average and have mottled, multicolored skin. Their social structure is heavily ritualized, with a strong tribal or family base. They are known for being highly racist.

Kindling, **IND:** the name given by Page De Bruyn to her stolen fighter, formerly registered as TBC-14 and owned by COE Intelligence.

Kukumat: one of a gas giant pair occupying the sixth planetary orbit around Palasian System; the pair shares a single moon.

LaGoc: a Caste that contributed a mobile barracks to the crisis in Sol System.

Lemmas: A Hurn reave employed by the Disciples of Evergence.

Lenz, Uyeno: a mercenary frequently to be found on *Dark Stressor*.

Lleshi, Sadoc: captain, Ground Corps; recognized for excellence in battle against the enemy in ancient times.

Low Castes: devolved mundane Humans. These animal-like creatures come in many forms and occupy many niches across the galaxy. Some evolve back up to mundane status, given time and isolation, while others become extinct as a result of the forces that led to their devolution in the first place.

Lucence-2, **COEA:** COE Armada Escort & Assault Craft.

M'taio System: a system notable for its Caste Wars in recent times.

Maii: Surin epsense adept.

Marauder: an experimental class of warship developed by the Dato Bloc. See **DBMP** *Ana Vereine*.

Marines: see **COE Armada**.

Mars St. Selwyn Medal: an honorific bestowed in ancient times.

Mbata: (**Mbatan**, adj & sing. n): a well-regarded Caste known for its peace-loving and familial ways. In appearance they resemble the ursine species, larger and stronger than the Pristine. Their culture is egalitarian and open to trade.

Middle Reaches: the region of medium stellar density between the Outer Arms and the galactic core.

Midnight, **COEA:** COE Retriever-class frigate.

Military Star: an honorific bestowed in ancient times.

Military Presidium: see **Dato Bloc**.

minaret: Skehan Heterodox term for the prow of a consistory vessel.

Multiple Genesis Theory: a theory that the various Castes of Humanity evolved—or at least emerged into the greater galaxy—from several systems simultaneously.

mundane Castes: Castes of Humanity that are essentially similar to the Pristine in terms of size, mental capacity, worldview, etc. Naturally there is a spectrum of types across the mundane Caste—from the highly evolved (some might say near-Transcendent) Olmahoi, through the socially complex Surin and Hurn Castes, to the Eckandar and Pristine Castes with their societies based on trade and empire-building, and beyond, via the earthy Mbata, to the relatively primal Kesh. Mundanes are typically short-lived (a century or so, when allowed to age naturally) and build empires up to four or five thousand systems in size. There is a ceiling of complexity above which mundanes rarely go without Transcending. See **High Humans** and **Batelin Limit**.

Murnane, Esko: plenipotentiary envoy sent by the citizens of Pompili to stand on the IEPC.

Murukan: one of a gas giant pair occupying the sixth planetary orbit around Palasian System (see **Kukumat**).

n-body: the epsense "counterpart" to the physical body.

n-space: a word used by epsense theorists to describe an environment completely empty of thought.

Nemeth, Rey: Assistant Vice Primate sent by the Second Ju Mandate to stand on the IEPC.

Noske: a Caste not normally found in the COE region.

Nyberg: the founder of school of epsense training regarded as second-rate by superior adepts.

Objective Reference Calendar: a system of date-keeping established by the A-14 Higher Collaboration Network.

Old Earth Advance Guard: a military body mentioned in ancient records.

Olmahoi: an exotic Caste that communicates entirely by epsense. Physically they are of similar size to Pristines, but are much stronger; their skin is black and they possess little in the way of distinguishing features, apart from the epsense organ which dangles like a tentacle from the back of the skull. Their social structure is too complex to explore in detail here. They are renowned fighters, capable of feats of great skill, yet also possess a capacity for peace far in excess of any other local Caste.

Olmahoi retribution squad: renowned fighters able to combine perfectly their physical and epsense abilities. Also known as "grayboots."

Outer Arms: the low stellar-density regions of the galaxy between the Middle and Far Reaches.

Out-of-Sol theory: a theory suggesting that all the Castes of Humanity originated on one world.

outrigger: a unique Caste of miner / explorer found in sparsely populated systems; living within all-suits that double as mobile homes, outriggers typically scout uncharted dark body halos and asteroid belts, looking for viable mineral sources, which they then either mine or report to a centralized authority (if any) for a modest fee. Outriggers are notoriously self-sufficient, avoiding even other outriggers as much as possible, and have been known to exist for years out of contact with another being. Spending much of their lives drifting in hibernation between dark and cometary bodies, some live longer than three centuries. Few outriggers have family names, coming as they do from such small communities that single given names usually suffice.

outsweep migrations: brief, outward surges by expansionist empires. These usually occur in the crowded environment of the core or Middle Reaches, in the direction of the Outer Arms.

Pacecca: an overseer of the docks of Perdue Habitat.

Palasian System: a system of the COE quarantined by the COE Armada as a result of an enemy outbreak, then destroyed by an ancient Kesh device (see **Solar Envelope**).

Paraselene, **COEA:** a COE cruiser stationed near Perdue Habitat.

Paz: an educative device once owned by Morgan Roche.

Perdue Habitat: a habitat populated by approximately 11,000 people, predominantly Vax Caste, stationed to Sol System during the crisis. Its administer, Inderdeep Jans, is known to have been reluctant to commit her resources to solving the crisis.

Phlegethon, **SHCV:** a Skehan Heterodox consistory vessel from the far side of the galaxy.

Pompili: a founding nation of the IEPC.

Primordial Castes: precede the earliest confirmed records, half a million years ago. Little is known about them, except that they exist; ruins of several unique types are to be found throughout the galaxy. They are called Castes A, B, C, and D, for even their names are unknown. (See Appendix.)

Pristine Caste: the form of Humanity which most closely resembles the original race that evolved an unknown time ago on an unknown planet somewhere in the galaxy. The Pristine Human Genome, handed down from antiquity and regarded with near-veneration, is stored in innumerable places among the civilized worlds. Pristines themselves, however, are accorded no special status.

Quare, Oren: assistant to Overseer Pacecca, Perdue Habitat.

Random Valence: a habitat stationed close to Perdue Habitat.
reave: see **epsense.**

Rebuli: a Caste antagonistic to the cause of the IEPC.

Rench: dockmaster of Perdue Habitat.

Reshima System: a system in which Ameidio Haid once worked.

Roche, Morgan: former commander, COE Intelligence.

Rond-Spellor Outlook: home of Hue Vischilglin.

Rufo, Linegar: renowned xenoarchaeologist; see **Galine Four.**

Saa-hurod: a Caste maintaining an outpost in Sol System during the crisis.

Sciacca's World: the only habitable world of the Hutton-Luu System; once an agricultural planet of the Dominion, now a desert penal colony of the COE (**Sciacca Penal Colony**). Its ring of moonlets—the Soul—is owned and mined by DAOC Inc.

scutter: a small, swift spacegoing vessel with many uses, both military and civilian; also known as a singleship.

Sebettu, **SRF:** Kesh destroyer.

Second Expansion: an ancient outsweep known to have led from the Exordium Worlds into the greater galaxy.

Siriote: a government antagonistic to the IEPC.

Skehan Heterodox: a tolerant theocracy on the far side of the galaxy, significantly more advanced than the COE.

slow-jump: a common alternative to the anchor drive that utilizes similar technology. Most ships with an anchor drive can slow-jump if necessary. It is essentially a jump through hyperspace from any point in real space. A certain degree of kinetic energy is required before translation can be achieved, so ships must accelerate for some time beforehand. Even then, the hyperspace jump is short-lived, and the vessel emerges soon after (typically less than a light-year away from its departure point) with significantly less kinetic energy. The process must be repeated from scratch if another slow-jump is required. As a means of crossing interstellar space, it is inefficient and time-consuming, hence its name. Slow-jumping becomes increasingly nonviable closer to a gravity-well, but more efficient as mass (of the traveling object) decreases.

Sol Apotheosis Movement: a quasi-religious organization devoted to the pursuit of Transcendence via genetic manipulation and biomodification that reached its peak and was destroyed in the 37th millennium. Its fanatical followers were a source of unrest for decades, until an alliance was formed among their neighbors dedicated to putting a stop to them. In '577 EN, at the climax of the Scion War, a flotilla of allied forces encircled their base, which the Movement destroyed in order to prevent its capture. The resulting explosion annihilated them as well, of course, but also decimated the flotilla. Of the four stations involved in the battle, only one survived, and that was severely damaged. So embarrassed was the alliance that the leaders of the day ordered the event stricken from history. They even closed the anchor point leading to the system to prevent anyone learning what occurred there. Nothing survived of the base, and the rest of the system is an unsalvageable ruin.

Sol System: an uninhabited system in a nonaligned region near the Dato Bloc, one known for its antiquity and a possible contender for birthplace of the Human race. Former home of the Sol Apotheosis Movement and many other such sects. (See Appendix.)

Sol Wunderkind: genetically modified clone warriors designed and bred by the Sol Apotheosis Movement.

Solar Envelope: a device intended to provide a jump shield large enough to enclose an entire solar system. Two prototypes were built by an early Kesh Government. "Asha's Gauntlet" was used on one system, with disastrous results: the system's primary sun, modified to power the Envelope, was exhausted within two months; the entire system collapsed shortly thereafter. Useless as a defensive weapon, and forbidden by the Convention on Extraordinary Weapons, the second Gauntlet remained in the hands of the Kesh until it was used in Palasian System.

Soul, the: the local name for the orbiting ring of mineral-rich moonlets girdling Sciacca's World.

spine: the collective noun used to describe a loosely linked group of outriggers; from their means of traveling between systems, on the back of a naked real-space drive known as "the spine."

squt: a Surin word for someone who is both foolish and closed-minded.

Stryki: an epsense adept from Taborca.

Surin: a relatively minor Caste found in the regions surrounding the COE. They exist in isolated clumps overseen by a governing body that guides rather than rules. They are social beings yet fond of isolation, giving them a reputation for occasional aloofness. They are technically accomplished, especially in the biological sciences. In stature, they tend to be slight and have hair covering much of their bodies. It is occasionally speculated that they have re-evolved from Low Caste status.

Surin Agora: the ruling body of the loosely knit Surin nation.

Taborca: a region in the Middle Reaches.

Tade, Rejuben: 238th Provost of the Guild of Xenoarchaeologists (see Appendix).

TBC-14: see *Kindling*.

Teh, Sylvester: transportee, Sciacca Penal Colony.

Tocharia 13: a habitat maintained by members of the **Zissis Caste.**

Transcend: to break free of the constraints of mundane Humanity. A being or Caste that has Transcended typically has an extremely long life span and spreads its consciousness across a number of primary containers—such as neural nets, quantum data vats, and the like. Transcended entities, singular or collective, are referred to as High Human and accorded the highest status.

Transcendence: the state of being Transcended. Usually achieved when consciousness research and computer technology overlap, allowing an organic mind to be downloaded into an electronic vessel, thereby gaining the potential for unlimited growth.

Trezise, Salton: senior aide to Auberon Chase and envoy to the IEPC.

Trinity: the world on which AIs are made in the region dominated by the COE. The AI factory was founded and is overseen by the High Human known as the Crescend.

turcite: a type of high explosive.

Ulterior: a covert organization operating within—but not without the official disapproval of—the IEPC.

Ustinik, Alwen: a representative of the Commerce Artel.

Vacishnou: homeworld of the Vax Caste.

Vax: a Caste renowned for its peculiar breeding customs.

Veden, Makil: an Eckandar Trade Axis citizen and Commerce Artel ex-delegate. Deceased.

Vischilglin, Hue: co-adjutant sent by the Rond-Spellor Outlook to assist the IEPC.

Vri: a Surin soldier, who has forgone his family name and taken the title "Defender-of-Harmony."

Wamel: a Hurn pilot employed by the Disciples of Evergence.

Warfare Protocol: the code by which war is conducted within and between those nations that trade with the Commerce Artel.

Wehr, Vani: earned an Honorable Mention in ancient times for quick thinking on the Clarke Cylinder.

Weryn: deity of the Skehan Heterodox.

Xarodine: an epsense-inhibiting drug.

Xumai, Jancin: a Surin soldier who has taken the title "Fighter-For-Peace."

Yemena: a Caste not native to the COE region.

Yugen, Frane: leader of Random Valence.

Zissis: a Caste not indigenous to the COE region.